FLIGHT RISK

FLIGHT RISK

A NOVEL

CHERIE PRIEST

ATRIA BOOKS

NEW YORK   LONDON   TORONTO   SYDNEY   NEW DELHI

ATRIA BOOKS

An Imprint of Simon & Schuster, Inc.
1230 Avenue of the Americas
New York, NY 10020

First Atria Books hardcover edition November 2022

ATRIA BOOKS and colophon are trademarks of Simon & Schuster, Inc.

For information about special discounts for bulk purchases, please contact Simon & Schuster Special Sales at 1-866-506-1949 or business@simonandschuster.com.

The Simon & Schuster Speakers Bureau can bring authors to your live event. For more information or to book an event, contact the Simon & Schuster Speakers Bureau at 1-866-248-3049 or visit our website at www.simonspeakers.com.

Interior design by Hope Herr-Cardillo

Manufactured in China

1   3   5   7   9   10   8   6   4   2

Library of Congress Cataloging-in-Publication Data

Names: Priest, Cherie, author.
Title: Flight risk : a novel / Cherie Priest.
Description: New York : Atria Books, [2022] | Series: Grave reservations
Identifiers: LCCN 2022008106 (print) | LCCN 2022008107 (ebook) |
ISBN 9781982168926 (hardback) | ISBN 9781982168940 (ebook)
Classification: LCC PS3616.R537 F55 2016 (print) | LCC PS3616.R537 (ebook) |
DDC 813/.6—dc23
LC record available at https://lccn.loc.gov/2022008106
LC ebook record available at https://lccn.loc.gov/2022008107

ISBN 978-1-9821-6892-6
ISBN 978-1-9821-6894-0 (ebook)

FLIGHT RISK

1. GRADY MERRITT

WEDNESDAY

The man in the red plaid shirt fought to get away. He ducked, bobbed, and weaved, but Molly Merritt caught him regardless. She thrust herself under his nose and held up a flyer printed on bright pink paper, rattling it for emphasis. "Excuse me, *sir*," she said loudly, firmly, with an emphasis on the *sir* that suggested he had no one to blame but himself—and now he was trapped. Now he was going to answer some freaking *questions*.

"Um? Hello?"

"*Sir*," she tried again, pink flyer still six inches from his face. "Have you seen this dog?"

He squinted at the portrait of a smiling Lab mix. "Um. No?"

"He's yellow in real life. Our printer wasn't working very well, so I had to do it in black-and-white." She flipped the flyer around to look at it herself. "Black-and-pink. You know what I mean."

"Um? Still no?"

Molly showed him the flyer again. "His name is Cairo. I named

1

him after a Beanie Baby, but in my defense I was only, like, twelve years old when we found him in the Target parking lot. Obviously, I'd pick something else if we'd found him today. God, I hope we find him today."

"Um? Beanie Baby? Do people still collect those, or . . . ?"

"Focus!" she barked, as if she were a champion focuser herself. "The dog's name is *Cairo*. Like the city in Egypt. We were out here hiking and he got spooked, and he took off down the trailhead over there." She cocked her head in the direction of the trailhead at Mount Rainier's Paradise area visitor center. "Somebody's car backfired, I guess, and he's scared to death of loud pops. Big noises. Fireworks, thunder. That kind of thing."

"We don't get much thunder around here . . . ?"

"No, we don't, so he's usually okay. But he got scared, and he ran. We stayed out here until the park rangers made us leave, and we had to drive all the way back home to Seattle without him, and I have been losing my mind ever since, okay? One more time, take a real good look and tell me: *Have you seen this dog?*"

He hesitated like he expected another outburst. When none occurred, he cleared his throat. "I was just . . . I didn't . . . I haven't seen any loose dogs, I'm really sorry. Does he have a collar on? Is he wearing tags?"

She rolled her eyes. "Of *course* he's wearing a collar and tags."

"Then maybe someone will call you when they find him."

"Well, they'll call my dad." She looked up, looked around, and spotted her father with his own fistful of pink flyers, talking to a short Black woman with a pug on a blue leash. His was the number on the tags.

An awkward pause ensued. Finally, the guy said, "Hey, I'm sorry about your dog, and I hope you find him, but I've gotta go."

"Sorry. I'm sorry." She pushed the flyer into his hand. "I didn't mean to bother you. I just want my dog back." Her eyes were red

2

as she walked away, and her hands were shaking. She'd hardly slept since Sunday, when the beloved dog had panicked and bolted.

Grady Merritt gave the pug lady a more formal and polite goodbye than his daughter had offered the plaid-shirt man as he watched Molly seeking another person to accost and interrogate. "Molly!" he called her over.

She trudged toward him.

"Any luck?" her father asked.

"No. One guy thought he heard a dog barking somewhere around the southeast edge of the Wonderland Trail, even though you're not supposed to have dogs down there. A lot of people ignore that rule, so I don't know."

Grady gave her half a hug and squeezed her shoulder. "Hang in there, kiddo. We'll find him."

"It's been *three days*. That's like three *weeks* in dog time. He's probably lost! He's probably hungry!"

"He probably has indigestion."

Cairo would eat anything that wasn't secured, and Grady often privately thought that if push came to shove, his dog could crap out car parts. Or barf them up. Probably in the only carpeted room of the house.

"He's caught a couple of birds. And the rabbit that one time."

Grady nodded. "Right. He's a hunter. He'll find something to eat, and there's a lot of water . . . all those creeks and streams. He's still out there somewhere. We'll find him."

She sniffled and wiped her nose on the back of her hand. "I thought you weren't supposed to make promises in your line of work."

"This isn't a murder investigation, and Cairo is only lost. He's probably having the time of his life out there—chasing squirrels, rolling in the mud, and doing all the stuff we won't let him do at home."

"Yeah," she agreed with a narrowing of her eyes. "I'm gonna bathe the hell out of him when we catch him."

"There you go, think positive." Then he redirected the subject. "How's your flyer stash?"

"I'm almost out. I stuck them on all those car windows, and I stuck one on the trail map—at the corner, not blocking anything, because one of the rangers fussed at me. And I put one on the front door of the visitor center, because the dude inside said it was okay."

"Okay, I've got a few more—let me reload you." He reached into a messenger bag and pulled out the last of their stack, maybe fifty pink sheets with a smiling dog and a desperate plea. "This is it, though. When we're done, we need to pack up and head home again. I've taken all the time off I can afford, honey—and I *have* to work tomorrow. It's a long drive."

"But it's only Wednesday," she whined. "Can't someone cover for you?"

"I'm afraid I don't have that kind of job."

Grady didn't want to have this fight again, the one where he tries to break it to her gently that maybe, when all was said and done, they *don't* find Cairo. Maybe someone else finds him, and his collar is lost, and they take him home and keep him forever. Maybe he gets eaten by a bear or a mountain lion. Maybe the poor dog had run too fast and wandered too far, and he slowly starves in the wilderness.

Grady didn't like that last thought, but he couldn't lie to himself—and he wouldn't lie to Molly—about the cold, hard fact that sometimes dogs just don't come home, and you never find out why.

The truth was, they couldn't keep driving from Seattle to Mount Rainier even if he could talk his bosses into another few days of PTO; it was a two-hour trip each way. He was burning a fortune in gas, and they were getting up at dawn to get ready for the drive, then coming home well after dark. It simply wasn't sustainable, even in the summer, when Molly was out of school. They were both exhausted, and the odds of a successful dog recovery were dwindling.

"Look over there." Molly pointed to a thin white woman emerging from the trailhead with a matching pair of grinning pit bulls. "She's got dogs."

They'd already discussed prioritizing dog people, since dog people are likely to keep an eye out for other dogs. Grady nodded. "Hang on, I'll go talk to her." He readied his flyers and approached with a friendly wave. "Excuse me, ma'am? Those are beautiful dogs. . . ."

"Thank you," she said, warily assessing this strange man with a handful of pink paper.

"I don't mean to bother you, but—"

She cut him off. "I know the dogs aren't allowed on the trails. We're staying on the paved areas, don't worry—I'm just walking them down to the picnic area."

"No, no. I'm sorry, I'm not a ranger." He stopped a few feet out of licking range, which did not keep the pitties from wagging and wiggling at the prospect of getting petted. "My daughter and I were out here on Sunday, and our dog got away from us. He took off down the trailhead, but he could be . . . Jesus, I mean. He could be anywhere." He leaned forward and handed her a flyer.

She checked it out, shook her head, and sighed. "I'm sorry you lost your dog, but I just got here. I haven't seen him."

"But if you *do*," he pressed. "If you even hear any rumors about a lost yellow Lab mix roaming, please call this number."

"All right, I'll do that."

Suddenly, her dogs froze. They stood side by side, one black and white, one brown and white. Their ears perked up. Their tails stilled. Their eyes pointed past the big A-frame visitor center toward the other end of the parking lot.

Grady followed their look. He didn't see anything unusual, but at the very edge of his hearing he caught some kind of commotion. He concentrated, trying to sort the signal from the noise.

Molly joined him. "Dad?" Then she looked at the dogs and said, "Aw, babies . . ." but the dogs weren't paying attention to the teenage girl. Their focus remained glued to something in the distance, something through the trees. Something screaming.

The screaming was coming closer.

The woman who held the leashes asked no one in particular, "The hell is going on?"

Grady answered her. "Don't know, but it's coming from the Skyline Trail."

Before he could speculate further, two college-aged guys wearing Huskies gear burst out of the trees, down the steps, and into the parking lot, yelling their heads off all the way. "Call the cops!" one commanded. "Get the rangers!" hollered the other. The rest was lost as they talked over each other. Right behind them, a middle-aged Asian woman with a walking stick came charging up to the parking lot. "There's a body! A dead body!" she added to the discourse.

"Dad, *you're* a cop. . . ." Molly hinted hard.

The dog lady gave him a squint. "Really? You're with the police?"

"I . . . I don't have any jurisdiction here, and I'm not on duty." Even so, he wandered away from her, toward the growing crowd that congealed around the college guys and the walking-stick lady.

Another white guy came tearing down the Skyline Trail, red-faced and panting. "There's a . . ." He bent forward and wheezed. "There's a . . ."

"A body, yeah, we heard," Grady told him. "Where's this body?

Someone call nine-one-one. Get the local cops out here. Nobody touch anything," he added, with enough ambient cop authority that people started looking at him like maybe he knew what he was doing. He held up a hand and said, "I'm Detective Grady Merritt from Seattle homicide."

"Oh my God," the Asian woman gasped. "How did you get here so quickly?"

"No, it's not like that. I didn't . . . I'm not. Ma'am," he tried again. "My presence here is strictly a coincidence. Has someone . . . has anyone called nine-one-one? If there's a body on the trail, we need to get somebody official out here, pronto."

Half a dozen people held up phones and started dialing.

The wheezing man stood up straight and caught enough of his breath to say, "It's not a body."

Several people looked at him, confused. The pit-bull lady asked from the edge of the crowd, "What do you mean, not a body?"

"Not a *whole* body," he coughed. "Part of a body. There's a . . . there's a dog. With part of a body."

Molly went on high alert. "A dog? A yellow dog? Did you see a yellow dog, sir?" She darted to his side and shoved a flyer against his cheek. "Was it *this* dog?"

He pulled the flyer off his face, leaving the paper spotted with sweat. "I don't know. Maybe?"

"Was the dog guarding the body part?" asked Grady, on the off chance the corpse belonged to a lost hiker with a faithful companion.

The college guys shook their heads. "No, not . . . not guarding it," one said carefully. "More like . . . playing with it," said the other.

Back at the trailhead, fresh screaming rang out, and more people came scrambling frantically into the parking lot. They arrived in clumps of three and four, one and two. They scattered for the visitor center or ran for their cars.

"It's Cairo," Molly declared. "It *has* to be."

Grady wasn't so sure. "He doesn't actually have any precedent for getting lost or playing with body parts, hon."

"That we know of." She slapped her remaining flyers against his chest.

By reflex, he grasped them. "What are you—?"

Too late. She was already jogging against the flow of frantic tourists, crossing the parking lot in a few swift seconds—squeezing between parked cars and leaping curbs.

Grady smacked the flyers into the pit-bull lady's free hand and took off after his daughter. He heard the woman yelp as her dogs lunged in an effort to give chase, but she pulled them back and scolded them, and then the detective couldn't hear her anymore, and he didn't care what she did with the pink sheets of lovingly, hopefully printed paper. He pushed past a ranger who was hustling toward the commotion with a sharp "Pardon me!" and reached the trailhead just in time to get plowed into by a heavyset dude who was just trying to get away from something that was still coming through the trees, bounding up the trail.

The dude said, "Sorry!" then bounced off Grady and kept running.

"Molly!" But the nimble teenager had a good twenty-yard lead on him. "Molly! If you find any body parts, don't touch them!"

She screeched something in response. Was it a happy screech? A frightened screech? He couldn't tell, and he couldn't see her, because now she'd gone around a bend and was lost in the trees.

"Molly!"

"Dad!" she called back. "Dad, I found him!"

It should've been a happy screech, so why didn't it sound

entirely happy? He heard walkie-talkies beeping somewhere behind him, so someone official was surely on the way. He mustered all his waning energy, forced himself into another hard sprint, and finally caught up to his daughter and, yes . . . his dog.

Molly was holding out her arms. "Cairo, buddy—you're okay!" she said with forced brightness. "I'm so happy to see you, but you've gotta drop that. Drop it. *Drop. It.*"

It was a command that the trainer had taught him a couple of years ago, after what they'd come to think of as the "Mugging Incident," when the dog had stolen a woman's purse off a coffee shop bistro table and then bolted off down the sidewalk. Everyone blamed the adorable robbery on a packet of beef jerky the purse's owner toted around for post-workout snacks.

Grady joined the command. "Cairo, drop it. Right now."

But Cairo was a dog with something awesome, stinky, and dead in his mouth, and he didn't see any good reason to walk away from such a sweet trifecta. He backed up and let out a muffled *woof*.

Grady changed his tone. "Cairo, buddy. Whatcha got there, huh?" He approached slowly, holding his hands low, palms up. "You wanna give it to me? You wanna give Dad the gross old leg you found?"

Molly gagged. "Oh my God, it *is* a leg, isn't it?"

"Well, there's a shoe hanging off one end, so it's probably a leg and a foot," he said quietly. "Come on, buddy. Drop the leg."

The walkie-talkie beeps were coming closer. Grady called over his shoulder, "Hey, folks? Stay back, would you? We don't want to chase him off."

It didn't stop two rangers in brown uniforms from appearing, but it did slow them down and make them more cautious. One was a round white woman, and one was a tall Black man. The woman said, "Whoo boy howdy," and the man said, "Sweet Jesus, what is it this time?"

In a calm, measured, authoritative voice, Grady told them, "This is our dog, his name is Cairo, he got lost Sunday, and now we've found him."

The woman said flatly, "And he brought you a present."

"In a nutshell, yes. Have you called the police?" he asked.

The other ranger nodded. "They're on the way. That's a leg, isn't it? I'm not crazy, am I? That's a leg?"

Molly said, "Wait! I have an idea!" and she disappeared along the trail, heading up toward the parking lot.

Instinctively and without discussing it, the remaining humans all fanned out, trying to catch Cairo in a circle. Each one of them made soothing, welcoming noises to the best of their individual ability.

The dog eyed them one at a time, trying to decide if this was the best game ever, or if he'd somehow miscalculated and maybe these monkeys were planning to steal his treasure. The yellow Lab mix of dubious provenance was filthy from head to toe, with burrs clumping up his ear fluff and mud caking his limbs up to his belly. He did not appear harmed; he mostly looked happy as he assessed, retreated, and juked back and forth—trying to keep his distance from anyone who might take away his toy.

Grady was seriously starting to fear that the dog would fly the coop again when Molly came charging back to the scene, waving something in her hands. "Cairo! Ro-ro, baby, I've got you a *treeeeat.*"

Now she had his attention. His ears popped up, and his eyes fixed on her.

"*Treatos* . . ." she singsonged to the freshly attentive pooch. "Good bacon-flavored treatos from the nice lady with the pretty pit bulls. I will trade you *this* handful of bacon treatos for *that* maggoty-looking leg." They'd learned when he was a puppy that he could sometimes be bartered with. "Treatos," she told him again. "Right here. In my hot little hand. Come and get 'em."

He visibly considered his options, eyes darting between Molly and Grady and the rangers while he held the disembodied leg clamped in his mouth. Finally, he came to a decision, dropped the disgusting chew toy, and ran up to Molly to claim his reward.

Grady and the rangers exhaled; Molly squealed and let the dog trample her as he went back and forth between snorfling for treats and licking her face.

"No, no, no! You've been chewing on corpse parts!" she shrieked, but that didn't stop the dog—who hadn't seen his people in days. Even though he'd had a grand adventure, he was overjoyed to be found. Even if it meant he couldn't keep his toy.

The stinking, bloody toy in question lay in the dirt, covered in dog drool and speckled with wriggling white maggots. Grady and the rangers came in close, then covered their noses.

"Would you look at that," marveled the guy.

"Can't look away, sir," noted the woman.

Grady began to catalog. "Jeans, socks that look like they were pretty nice. Shoe looks like a Bostonian, brown leather. Size eleven, give or take." He called back to Molly, "For Christ's sake, stop that—don't let him lick you. You'll need a shower before you get back into the car. Or a sink bath in the visitor center restroom."

She wailed, "I'm *trying*," with an audible smile that suggested even the stinkiest of corpse breath was welcome so long as she had her dog again.

"Dog'll need a bath, too," observed the ranger.

"Not yet. He might have evidence on him."

"You a cop or something?" the woman asked him.

"Not one of yours, but yeah. And I'm *definitely* getting too old for this shit."

Back at the parking lot, the familiar *woop-woop* of a police siren cut through Paradise, and then there was a crime scene, and then a mostly good boy was held at Animal Control for a few hours so he could be combed for clues before being released to his owners. On the final drive home late that evening, Grady did not do any swearing out loud, even though he badly wanted to.

Cairo slept the sleep of a righteous adventurer, mostly in Molly's lap.

2. LEDA FOLEY

WEDNESDAY

Leda was watching a video of two kittens trying to fit inside a single shoe when a polite knock on her office door suggested she might have better things to do with her time. The knocker cracked the door open and peered around it uncertainly, as people tended to do when they showed up at Foley's Far-Fetched Flights of Fancy—the one-woman travel agency that she operated out of a tiny hole-in-the-wall in a little neighborhood just south of downtown Seattle. It wasn't much of an office: a small room rented in a tiny mid-century strip mall between a brewery and an arcade, around the corner from the heart of the 'hood. It was furnished with secondhand IKEA chairs and a big desk, plus a smattering of travel posters . . . and a lone woman with a laptop that was old enough to start first grade.

"Hello!" she said brightly, smacking the laptop shut before the squeaks of very small internet cats could chase away a customer.

"Hello?" said the visitor in return. He was a white man in his fifties, wearing khakis and a hunter-green cardigan. "Is this . . . are you . . . ?" He cleared his throat. "Are you Ms. Foley?"

"Yes, sir, that's me. How can I help you? Cruise season is in full swing, and the Alaska slots are filling up fast—but river cruises are increasingly popular, both here and abroad. Or do you need a flight? Someplace warmer and brighter? Maybe . . . damper? I don't know, it's pretty dry around here in the summer."

"Um, no. Nothing like that." He stepped slowly around the door and closed it behind himself, then pulled up a seat in front of her desk. "My name is Dan Matarese, and I read about you online."

"Ah." She leaned back in her chair, folding her hands in her lap and making a very good guess. "Sir, first things first: I'm not a detective."

"I know that, I do."

"But you're not here for travel assistance." It was getting easier to tell the travel clients from the psychic help clients. She'd been seeing more and more of each, since her adventures with Grady the year before and the subsequent media attention. And probably Ben's flyers for her events at Castaways.

"No," he said slowly. "But I'm fully prepared to pay whatever the usual travel fees might be. I wouldn't ask you to work for free."

She sighed. She'd need to come up with a separate rate card one of these days. Then she launched into a spiel that she'd been refining over the past few weeks.

"Okay, if you want to buy a block of my time, then I must be very, very up-front with you: Once again, I am not a detective in any real, formal, or legal sense—and any psychic abilities I may or may not possess are *not* guaranteed in any regard. They are inconsistent, and I sometimes interpret them incorrectly, which is to say, sometimes I'm just plain wrong, and I can't make you any promises."

He frowned thoughtfully but nodded along. "Is there something I should sign? A disclaimer, a waiver, or . . . ?"

Holy crap, he's right. I need a waiver, too. Did she know any lawyers who could draw up such a document for the low, low price of zero dollars? She'd have to ask around. "That's an excellent suggestion. But, um. No. I don't have anything like that. I just want to make sure you hear it from me, out loud, in front of God and everybody. I can't make you any promises, but I'll help if I can. If that's not enough, then I can't take your money."

Dan held up his hands in surrender. "No, that's fine—I appreciate your forthrightness in this matter. I realize that it's possible this is all a wild-goose chase, but my sister has gone missing, and I don't care what anyone says: she's not a fugitive or a criminal. I think something terrible may have happened to her. At this point I'm willing to try anything."

"Yeah, so far that's the number one reason people come to see me. I'm generally the option of last resort."

"Does this happen often?"

She shook her head. "Not *often*, exactly. But it's happened several times since that case last fall when I helped the Seattle PD put away a serial killer." This was a bit of an exaggeration but not strictly untrue. The perp had been less a "serial killer" than a "sloppy opportunist," but the whole escapade had given her media attention and credibility.

"Were you successful? With any of those 'last resort' cases?"

"Three of them, yes. One of them, no. I helped a woman find a lost parrot, I helped a different woman find her dead husband's revised will, and there was this one guy whose dad buried a box of war bonds in the backyard a few years before he died. I helped him find those, but they were ruined by the time we got to them." Her voice crept higher in small steps as she continued. "Who the heck buries *paper* in a metal box with no lining, no plastic, no *nothing*? In the *Pacific Northwest*?" By the time she got to the end, she was talking in a register that could have summoned dolphins.

"Someone who doesn't care if anybody ever cashes them in?"

"I must assume," she said grouchily, and in her customary register. "I got rust and mud all over my favorite boots, but hey. Mystery solved, right?"

"Right. What about the one you couldn't solve?"

Ah yes. The firmly-in-denial Mrs. Grundleson. "I feel pretty bad about that one. It was an old lady whose elderly Persian cat had vanished from her backyard. The kitty was old enough to drink, bless it, and both deaf and blind. She would let it lie in the sun on the deck and warm its poor old bones, I guess, and then one day it vanished. The woman was heartbroken, and I went over to her place to see if I could help, but she didn't need me. I tried to give her money back, but she wouldn't have it—so I gave it to the Humane Society."

"I don't understand—why didn't she need you?"

"Same reason she didn't need the cops. She'd filed a police report, declaring that Mr. Pancakes had been stolen. I tried to tell her that there wasn't much of a resale market for deaf, blind, geriatric, toothless cats, even if they *did* have a fancy pedigree. But she didn't want to hear it."

"What do you think happened to it?"

"Well, her yard backed up to a Cooper's hawk reserve, so I've got a guess or two. According to the report, the kitty only weighed four pounds in his old age."

"Raptor snack?" he guessed.

"Yeah, not every unsolved mystery requires a psychic." She

leaned forward, putting her elbows on the desk and striving to look both highly professional and keenly interested. "But let's talk about you, why don't we? What brings you here to my office today, if not a quest for airline tickets or cruise recommendations?"

"Well," he said slowly, as if he wasn't quite sure how to begin. "To make a long story short, my sister vanished from a construction site with a bank pouch full of cash, and I know that sounds terrible, but I promise she didn't steal it. You have to believe me . . . or you have to hear me out, at least."

This might get interesting. "All right, I'm listening." She sat forward and put her elbows on the desk.

He sighed, deeply and heavily. "Like I said, I know it sounds bad on the surface. My sister is a landscaping designer for a company on the east side. She's worked there for twenty years and is fully trusted by everyone, from the grounds crews to the business owners. No one is formally accusing her of anything, though obviously there is . . . concern. If nothing else, the company needs the money back. They're not a big corporate entity; they're still owned by the family that started it all."

She asked, "How much money are we talking about?"

"About thirty grand, in large, unmarked bills. My sister was helping design and structure the outdoor spaces at a strip mall that's being built outside Southcenter. Three of the businesses going into the strip requested very specific trees and shrubs, for which they were prepared to pay a premium. When you want fully mature plants, it's not a cheap ask."

"So they gave her the cash, and she was supposed to take it to the bank, is that it? Deposit it into the company account? You said it was in a bank pouch."

"That's right. Once the landscaping company has the money in the bank, then Robin can go shopping around local nurseries and farms on the clients' behalf. Or that's how it's supposed to work.

But apparently that day she took the zip-up bag, got into her car, and vanished into thin air."

"When was this?" Leda asked.

"Sometime around the Fourth of July weekend. We aren't sure exactly when she went missing; she wasn't on the schedule for a few days after the holiday, but the work site is the last place anyone saw her."

"Taking a little personal time?" Leda asked.

"That's what her boss said, but the money never made it to the bank, and my sister never came back to work. Look, she's not the kind of woman who'd steal money or wander off without telling anyone, and I think something's happened to her. Her name is Robin Reddick, and she's married to an English professor at the University of Washington, a guy named Paul."

"So . . . Paul called the police and reported her missing?"

He shook his head. "Nope. Her son's the one who forced the issue—he learned that his father hadn't seen his mother in days, and he did a little asking around on his own. Jeff's the one who filed the police report."

Leda asked, "What did Paul have to say about his wife's absence?"

"He said she must be visiting our sister in Olympia. Apparently, they had a fight and she stormed out—I'm not sure if it was before or after the day she got the money, because Paul said he couldn't remember. And for what it's worth," he added quickly, "they'd been doing that a lot in the last few years."

"Fighting, or staying with your sister?"

"Both. But our sister Pam swears she hasn't seen Robin in person since Dad's eightieth birthday bash, and that was back in April."

"Is there anywhere else she might've gone?"

"Not that I can think of. Robin didn't go to Pam's this time, and none of her friends have heard from her, either. It's like she just . . . stopped the planet and got off. My nephew is frantic and angry at his father for waiting so long to take action. The landscaping people are struggling with an insurance claim for the missing cash, and they've been great, honestly—but I know they're worried. They'd be crazy not to be. Robin is a woman in an iffy marriage, with a tendency to walk out on her husband and sudden access to a lump of cash. I know she looks like a flight risk."

"And the police have no leads?"

Dan shrugged. "Not really. They were interested in that bag of money, but the landscaping company hasn't yet reported it stolen, and I appreciate that. I don't know how long their patience will hold, or how long the insurance company will let them put it off."

"Not forever, surely."

"No, they can't afford to let it go indefinitely. But until they file that report, no crime has been committed. Robin is an adult of sound mind and body as far as we know. She's free to come and go as she likes. It turns out, the police are more likely to chase missing property than missing people."

"A cynical observation, but perhaps not an unfair one. Can you tell me what your sister and her husband argued about?" Leda asked. Then she clarified, "This time."

"Paul was cagey, but if I had to guess, I'd say Robin caught him stepping out with a student again."

She raised an eyebrow. "Again? Has it happened before?"

"A couple times, I think? I don't honestly know, but I wish she'd just leave him and stay gone."

"You are not this man's biggest fan, are you?"

Dan shrugged guiltily. "I don't know Paul that well, and I don't like him much. He's pretentious and arrogant, unless he thinks you can help him with his publishing career—then he's your best friend. Publish or perish—that's what they say about liberal arts professors, right? Well, he did publish a book a handful of years back, and that's where the trouble began in the marriage. It's called *Dark Days, Bright Nights*."

"Sounds sexy."

He sneered. "It's about a self-loathing Gen-X college professor with a boring wife. He starts cheating on her with a series of students and eventually leaves her for one of them."

The prospect of juicy details prompted her to ask, "Yeah, but fiction is . . . fiction, right?"

"That's what he told everyone. Plausible deniability and all that. But the protagonist's name was Peter, and his wife was called Birdie. Let's just say that *Robin* didn't respond too kindly to the caricature, and she started taking a much closer look at his out-of-office hours. That's when the trips to our sister's place began."

"Gotcha."

Now he sighed. "She's had enough circumstantial evidence to pack a bag and bolt for years, but for some reason, she never stayed gone. That's why I thought, at first . . . maybe they'd had the final blowup we all saw coming."

He might've said more, but Leda interrupted him with a sudden question. "How do you know that Robin and Paul had a fight? Did Paul admit to it?"

"No, but Pam said she got a phone call from Robin at the end of June. Robin told her she was fed up with the philandering and she planned to take off for good this time. But that doesn't mean she was planning to steal her employer's money and disappear, for Christ's sake."

"How long have they been married?"

"Oh, twenty-odd years. They tied the knot when they were both fresh out of grad school. Robin's the youngest of us siblings, and I'm the oldest. She'll turn forty-six on Christmas Eve. If she's still out there," he added. "I'm trying not to be too dramatic or grim about the situation, but I'm only human, and I can't help but fear the worst. If nothing else, she wouldn't just drive off into the sunset and leave Jeff, or me, or Pam wondering what'd become of her. We've always been close." Then he changed the subject. "You sure do ask a lot of questions. This isn't very different from how it went with the police, and I'm a little surprised? I'm sorry, I've never talked to a psychic before. Never knowingly. Not like this."

Leda laughed in what she hoped was a disarming fashion. "Oh, that's a running joke I have with my cop friend. I always have at least half a dozen more questions for people than he does, and he's a homicide detective."

"Oh," he said, sounding impressed. "You work with the police?"

"I have a consulting contract with the Seattle PD," she said proudly. "I haven't used it yet—my introductory case with a cop was off the books, shall we say. But it's there now, and I'm here if they ever decide they need me. The thing is . . ." she said, trying to line up her words carefully. She didn't know how much he needed or wanted to hear, so she kept it short. "This is an imprecise art. When I get flashes, or impressions, or whatever you want to call them . . . they're usually out of context, just fragments of images. The more I know about the person I'm looking for, the better I'll be at making connections between what I feel and what I know. Does that make sense?"

He nodded slowly. "Yeah, it does. I get it."

Whether he did or not, Dan gave Leda his contact information as well as some particulars about Robin's routine and her friends. She also got the rundown on Jeff and Paul, then asked if Paul had any known hangouts or hobbies.

"None that I know of. He's one of those academics who spends his entire life on campus." He let out a small, grim chuckle. "Until you need him for something. I went over there . . . must've been the day before yesterday, and he wasn't around. His assistant wasn't very helpful, either, and she wouldn't tell me when she expected him to return or where else I might find him. She said he was 'on sabbatical.'"

"You think he was hiding from you?"

"Yes, I do, like the chickenshit he is. You should really talk to Jeff. They aren't estranged, exactly, but they're not close."

"Give me his contact info, and I'll try that," she promised. "Does Jeff know you're here? Does he know about me, and what I do? Because I've learned the hard way, not everybody is down with the woo-woo stuff."

He frowned uncertainly. "I didn't tell him, but I don't think he'd care. I'll tell you what: I'll call Jeff when we're finished here, and tell him about you and why I'm giving this a try, even if it's a little . . ." He used her expression. "Woo-woo."

"Sir, this is *highly* woo-woo, and it won't offend me if he isn't interested in participating." Thoughtfully, she tapped one fingernail on the edge of her phone case. "But *you*. You're not put off by the . . . let's not say 'woo-woo' again—it's silly. Paranormal? Supernatural? Whatever this is?"

He took a moment to consider his answer. "The world is filled with things I don't understand, and I'm at peace with that. I've never had anything weird happen to me, personally, but that doesn't mean it never happens to anyone else." He sagged in the chair. "I just want to find my sister. If you can help me do that, I don't care *how* you do what you do."

"I can work with that," she confirmed.

"Okay, then what do we do next?"

"I'll ask you to give me—just temporarily—some of Robin's personal effects. The more personal, the better. Doesn't have to be anything expensive; it could be her keys, a favorite set of earbuds, a novelty T-shirt, whatever. Anything she values, anything she's held close. I need to touch it. That's mostly how this works."

"Mostly?" he asked with what sounded like genuine curiosity.

She shrugged at him. "Sometimes I get random flashes of insight here and there, though they don't usually make sense at the time. Generally speaking, I get my best info from objects."

"That's what you do at that bar, right? I read about your psychic song-singing . . . What was it called?"

Leda sighed heavily. "The psychic psongstress routine. I do it a few nights a week at Castaways on Capitol Hill. It wasn't my idea to call it that. I'm sorry, I know it's kind of stupid."

"Why don't you change it?"

"Because it would break Ben the manager's heart, and I can't stand to see him cry," she muttered. Then, louder, she said, "Everybody already knows about it, ever since that article in *The Stranger*. If I change it now, I'll just confuse people."

"All right, then, when I talk to Jeff I'll see if he has anything special he'll let you borrow—and I'll check around my place and ask Pam, too. This might take me a day or two, though. It's not like when we were kids and we had all the same stuff in the same place. Do you have any siblings, Ms. Foley?"

"No, sir, I do not. I have a best friend who's pretty much my sister. But I know that's not what you're talking about."

"We used to have another sister. She died of cancer years ago, so now it's just me, Robin, and Pam. And Jeff. He's been joking for a while now that he should change his last name to Matarese. Hell, maybe he'll actually do it. It'd be fine with us." He sighed again, looking very tired and sad. "Anyway, I'll see what I can find. Will you be here tomorrow or the next day?"

She slid a business card across the desk. She'd had them made only a month before, and she was very proud of her design: something simple, but with a little pop of gold foil around the text. No emojis, no exclamation points. Nary a typo. "Absolutely, sir. Go ahead and text or call this number to be sure I haven't stepped out for lunch or anything, and swing by whenever it's convenient for you."

With that, they thanked each other awkwardly, and Dan left the way he'd come in.

Leda grabbed her phone as soon as the door shut behind him. She *had* to talk to Niki about this—literally right this moment.

She began to compose a text, then changed her mind and deleted it. She called instead.

Niki picked up within three seconds. "Any thrilling travel agency news?" she asked by way of greeting.

"Two more flights to the Caribbean—one for an elderly couple, one for a pair of guests headed for a destination wedding. Also did my third cruise booking this week, this time for one of those river jobbies in Europe. But to answer your question: no, not really. *However* . . ."

"However . . . ?"

"I got another detecting gig!" she said, bouncing in her seat.

"Oh boy. Another lost pet?"

"No! A lost *person!*" Leda gave Niki a quick rundown. "I don't know if I can help Dan or not, but I'll give it my best shot. Hey, he also gave me a great idea. If I'm going to keep taking these psychic detecting gigs, I need to come up with a rate card for those services. And maybe a waiver while I'm at it."

Niki groaned. "I told you that months ago. Ben offered to print you up a flyer or something, remember?"

"Ben and his flyers, yes. But I thought the hype would die down and I wouldn't need it. Now I'm graduating from lost critters to lost siblings, so I've *clearly* leveled up. I need to charge like it."

"I thought you were all about helping people out of the goodness of your heart?"

"I am!" she protested. "I am also about getting paid, out of the goodness of somebody else's bank account. What do you think, should I charge by the hour? Daily? By the case?"

"Oh my God, I don't know. Want to talk about it over sushi?"

A smile spread across Leda's face. "You know what? I do. Meet you at Wabi-Sabi in twenty minutes?"

"Make it thirty. I'm about to leave work, and you know how downtown traffic goes."

She agreed to half an hour. Why wouldn't she? She could order a drink and bring her phone and do a little internet research on Robin Reddick while she waited.

Holy shit. Leda was starting to feel like a Real Detective.

3. GRADY MERRITT

THURSDAY

Back at home, Cairo got an extra bath and some pampering, which he took in stride. He also took the opportunity to beg for a few extra treats with big, hungry eyes that surely had not seen a single snack in the whole entire time he'd been gone.

"You're going to make him fat," Grady warned, without any serious urgency.

His daughter smiled beatifically at the perky-eared dog, whose face was at full attention—his eyes darting back and forth between her and the treat bag. "*Fat* just means well loved," she assured him. "It's okay if you get a little fat. Fat dogs are less likely to run away, I bet."

"They probably can't run as fast as a thin one, at any rate. Regardless, those treats are basically junk food for canines, and they should be doled out sparingly. He's spoiled enough already."

She reached in for another small bone-shaped biscuit, held it up, and tossed it gently into Cairo's mouth. It landed neatly on his tongue and vanished down the hatch. "You're not spoiled," she assured him. "You're appropriately pampered, as every good boy should be."

Grady rolled his eyes. "Either way, stop feeding him. It's time to attend to his *other* end. You heard Rudy. Every poop, every time, for three days. Start collecting his lawn deposits."

"Ugh, *why* do we have to do this again?"

"Because a sergeant over at the Mountain Detachment did us a favor, that's why. Look, if we hadn't agreed to bag and tag Cairo's crap, we would've had to leave him down at the mountain for a few days. The Pierce County folks want to hear about every single thing he produces, so take a baggie, follow your dog, and keep your eyes peeled for anything that doesn't look like . . . well, poop." Grady held out a roll of dog waste bags, waggled it enticingly, and tossed it to his daughter. "Here. Happy late birthday."

Molly caught the roll and scowled. "This is wildly unfair. Your birthday's closer than mine."

"Then do this round of poop patrol for me and call it my early present."

"Ugh, no wonder you hate birthdays. You have no idea what a good one looks like."

Cairo sat on the deck stairs behind them, eyes bobbing back and forth between them. He did not care who picked up his poop. To a certain degree, he didn't care if anybody did, but he always enjoyed watching people argue. It was among his favorite pastimes, right up there with taking enormous dumps and eating enough garbage to produce them.

"It's your job to pick up after him anyway," he told her. "You promised, back when I said we could keep him—and I *still* do it most of the time. Reclaim your responsibility and make yourself useful. He might've left us a deposit when I let him out this morning, so if you see anything fresh, make sure to check extra close. Smush it up, squeeze it."

"Oh God . . ."

"I'm serious!" Cairo had been processed for evidence back in Eatonville near the park, but he'd suddenly gone too shy to drop a deuce in front of strangers. "We have no idea what else he ate, and any of it could be evidence."

"I suddenly feel a kinship with your forensic folks. I never see shit like this on TV. No pun intended."

He did not tell her to watch her language. He didn't see the point, and she didn't curse that much—or in front of important adults—so he let that one go. She'd be an adult soon enough, and she already knew the rules of polite society. Life was too short to get hung up on four-letter words. "Seriously, a bag of dog shit is probably the least terrible thing they'll handle all week."

"Do I even want to know what's worse than this?"

"No," he said firmly. "Now, go on, start checking piles, and bag up anything that looks like it landed since we got home last night."

"Or anything that shoots out of his butt while you're getting dressed for work. I know, I know. Fine. If that's what you really want." She sulked off into the yard, eyes fixated on the grass, legs lifting high and stepping carefully. Stopping to check the bottoms of her shoes.

He climbed the stairs back up to the small deck and went inside . . . pausing only to watch and make sure Molly followed through on her promise to inspect every fecal molecule for anything of importance.

He'd sworn to the Pierce County guys that if anything turned up, he'd inform them immediately and send it straight to Eatonville, either overnight or by courier. What "anything" might be was anybody's guess. Had Cairo actually eaten part of this dead person? Or merely gnawed on a stray part to pass the time?

While he shaved, Grady's cop brain ran through the known details: the leg belonged to a white man between the ages of twenty-five and sixty, because it's very hard to judge somebody's age by their lower extremities; nice semicasual shoes, dark-wash Levi's jeans; the owner of the leg hadn't been dead more than a week, probably; no preliminary indication of illness or injury other than the fact that the leg was alone—with no other body parts to match it. Local police had shut down the visitor center and established a two-mile perimeter around the park, but that was just a guess.

Nobody knew how far a fifty-pound dog in good health could roam in three days, much less where he'd gone or what he'd been up to during that time. Did Cairo know where the rest of the body was located? If so, could he find it again? Just in case, Grady had offered to bring Cairo back on the upcoming weekend so he could roam around on the off chance he'd go looking for more chewable body bits, but this time he'd be on a leash, and perhaps a harness, and maybe even a waist lead, and definitely have one of those tracker things on his collar. You never knew. He might lead them right to the rest of the guy.

"And who *is* the guy, anyway?" he asked the mirror as he toweled off his face.

DNA analysis wouldn't be back for a while, and Mr. Leg didn't meet any of the criteria for any known missing persons in Washington State or Oregon, either. Of course, if he'd been dead only a few days, his absence might not have been noticed yet, much less reported. If he lived alone, worked from home, traveled a lot, it might be weeks before someone wondered where he'd wandered off to.

"Mr. Leg probably wasn't homeless. He was wearing bougie silk-blend socks. Or . . . a single bougie silk-blend sock." He used the towel to wipe steam off the mirror, then stuck it back on the holder. "He was at least middle-class, his clothes were newer, and the coroner's preliminary suspicion was that he'd had a pedicure in the last few weeks. How many men get pedicures?" Some, sure. But they usually aren't itinerant. "Hm. Could be a trans guy. He might have family that's reported him missing under a dead name and the wrong gender. Might be worth checking." He made another mental note: any missing persons reports with suspiciously old photos might be a clue.

But realistically, he'd probably just have to wait for the DNA evidence to identify the dead man. This could happen in as little as a few days, if Mr. Leg had committed a crime or two, and if he happened to be in the database. Or it could take as long as a few months, if he had a squeaky-clean record and there was a backlog at the lab.

A few years back, there'd been a rash of random feet washing up on Pacific Northwest beaches, and for an instant he wondered if the cases could be related. But no, this wouldn't be one of *those* feet; after all, it was more of a whole-ass leg, including most of the knee—and Mount Rainier was quite a ways from the beach.

He shrugged at himself. "Maybe a bear got him?" Bears killed people every now and again, and the coroner said the leg looked like it'd been torn off rather than sawed or otherwise cut. It takes a lot of strength to tear off a guy's leg. But a bear could manage it.

Cairo had returned to them with a few small scratches on his face and front legs—small enough that they hadn't even noticed them until he'd been "processed" down in Pierce County. He could've tangled with another animal, bickering over the juicy, delicious find.

"But a bear would've killed him. So would a mountain lion, I bet."

Outside, Molly called, "Dad?"

He barely heard it and almost didn't register it. He was thinking about bears and wayward legs. "Wolves? Do we have wolves out there? I don't even know." He was warming up to the idea of an animal attack. Animal attacks were terrible, but they weren't homicide. "Nah, a pack of wolves would've turned that dog into scraps. More likely, Cairo fought off a raccoon or something."

"Dad!"

Startled, he remembered Molly's quest for buried treasure. "Molly? Sorry—I'm coming!" He checked his watch, figured he could be a little late today, and dashed outside. "What is it? Did you find something?"

She held up her hand. It was inside a crinkly green poo bag that allegedly smelled like lavender but mostly smelled like plastic and canine colon contents. Inside her bag-shielded grip she held something small. It glinted slightly in the morning light. "Hey, this isn't yours, is it?"

He squinted, gave up on staying a pleasant distance away from the excavated item, and approached with caution. "What is it?"

"Looks like a wedding ring to me. A man's wedding ring, but . . ." She peered at it closely, using another poop bag to swipe more grime away. "Okay, it's definitely not yours."

"No, I put mine in your mother's jewelry box. In your room, on your dresser." His wife had passed several years before, though he'd removed the ring for good only last year. It'd taken him a while to get used to the idea. Now he wore no jewelry at all, a fact his daughter occasionally lamented—but he'd put his foot down in no uncertain terms when she'd suggested an earring.

"That's what I thought, but once I was elbows-deep in Cairo compost, I didn't want to run inside and check."

"Cairo compost, very funny."

"Yeah, I'm a scream." She bent over and wiped the ring in the grass, which was still a little damp from the dew. The ring came up mostly clean, and she held it out to her father. When he hesitated, she handed over the roll of bags so he could tear one off and create a makeshift glove of his very own.

This accomplished, he took the ring and held it up to the light, turning it over and examining it from every angle. "There's something inscribed here, inside the band—hang on." But it was too dirty to read.

"Can we wash it off? Or do they want it in the bag of poo?"

Grady said, "I honestly don't know. And I want to see it for myself, so . . . hang on." He went to the backyard hose reel, turned on the water, and got a good grip on the ring—then set the nozzle to "jet." When it was relatively clean, if not exactly sanitized, he held it up to the light and spun it slowly as he read. " 'My heart, my life, my one and only thought.' "

Molly waited, like she expected more. When none came, she said, "What? That's it? No initials, no names?"

"Nope. Just a sweet sentiment."

"It's not sweet," she objected. "It's corny."

He stared at the gleaming ring, turning it over and hunting for any further hints it might offer regarding its owner.

"Whatcha looking for, Gollum?"

"Clues. Not finding any. I wonder if it was engraved around here, or if anyone would have records, or if we were to publicize the inscription, would somebody recognize it?" He tossed it into the air and caught it in his palm. "It might be worth a try, but that'll be up to Pierce County. Technically, I have no jurisdiction here. Or over there. You know what I mean."

Molly gave him another few seconds to squint for hints, then said, "Hey, weren't you going to work? Or at this point, won't you be late for work?"

"Yes!" he replied suddenly. "Yes, I need to . . . hm." He held on to the ring.

"You gonna bag it, or whatever?"

He reached a decision. "I'll hang on to it, just until this afternoon. Then I'll call up the station in Pierce County and let them know what we've got. It'll buy some time for Cairo to do another round of deposits, and you never know, he might surprise us with something else. Where's the rest of the poop pile this thing came from?"

She pointed at a mushy spot on the yard. "Looks like there's some lumps in there, too. Rocks?"

"Probably . . . not rocks," he said, but she already knew that much. "He didn't eat the ring; he ate whatever was wearing it. Get every scrap and leave it . . ." He almost said to put it on the table, but that was a terrible idea. "Put it in the garage, on my workbench."

"The one you never work at?"

"Not a lot of time for woodworking these days. Maybe once you're out of the house," he said, and immediately regretted it. He didn't like the thought of living in the house alone. Some days it was too empty without his wife, even with the teenager and the dog to keep him company. He backtracked. "*Not* that I'm eager to see you off. Just . . . get the shit sorted, and I'll be home this afternoon, okay?"

"Yes, sir," she said with a little salute.

He grabbed a sweater that his daughter said looked like it belonged to the old man from the movie *Up*, shouldered a messenger bag, picked up his keys from the table by the door, and headed out. What he had not said was that he planned to take a long lunch break and maybe visit a friend to see if she could hold the ring and tell him anything useful about the man who used to wear it. He thought of Cairo, snoozing happily under the deck, blissfully oblivious to the world's keen interest in his bodily waste . . . and he hoped that he wasn't about to give Leda an unwelcome flash of canine butthole.

4. LEDA FOLEY

THURSDAY

Leda was taking a lunch break when a heads-up knock on her door and a friendly "Hello" announced that Grady Merritt was doing the same. "Hey there!" she attempted to reply, but she was still working on a mouthful of pizza, so it came out garbled and a little bit gooey. "Hold on a sec," she added, and that didn't come out too much clearer. Grady pulled up a secondhand IKEA seat while she chewed and then swabbed her mouth with a napkin.

He crossed one leg over the other and grinned. "Don't choke. If you choke, I can't ask you for a real quick favor."

Her final swallow was too big by half, and it stuck in her throat. She seized her soda and chugged it. "Sorry," she belched. She gave her mouth one more napkin dab, then wadded it up with her paper plate and stuffed it all into the trash with the last of her crust. "Sorry," she said again, this time without the bass reverb. "A favor? You want a favor? Sure, I'm in. Wait, what kind of favor?"

"Just a small thing."

"Is it connected to a case?" she asked eagerly.

"No. Yes. Well, probably—but it's not my case, exactly."

With one eyebrow raised, she said, "So it's not *exactly* for your job?"

"No."

"You're just . . . what? Chasing murder leads for funsies?"

"No," he said again. "It might not be a murder, though we're pretty sure the guy is dead. It might've been an animal attack, or an accident. Here's the thing: the dead guy checked out somewhere near Mount Rainier, in the park, so this one belongs to the Pierce County guys. Technically, I'm not supposed to be doing this."

Knowing that the favor was illicit made it that much more interesting. "Then why are you poking it with a stick?"

"Because my stupid dog . . ." He sighed, and then, before Leda could ask, he launched into the sordid tale of a spooked and fleeing Cairo, three days of agony and day-tripping down to the mountain, and then the triumphant return of the dog—bearing gifts. Or one big gift. And some subsequent smaller gifts, deposited in coiled piles in his fenced backyard. "We promised the Pierce County officers that we'd save his shit for three days, bag it up individually and date each bag, and then send it back for analysis. I think we've got some finger bones in a bag in the garage."

Fascinated and disgusted in equal measure, Leda leaned forward on her elbows, her chin in her hands. "That's wild. Did they find any clues *on* the dog? Did you brush him and everything?"

He chuckled and waved one hand like this was all old news. "Yeah, yeah, we dusted him for prints and the whole nine yards." Then, in case she couldn't tell he was joking, he added, "I'm kidding. But they processed him like a piece of evidence, brushing him out and taking a bunch of hair samples. He loved that part. He didn't love the part where they swabbed his teeth and gums, nor the bit where they put a little antiseptic on his scratches. But that was nothing compared to when they cleaned out his ears or trimmed his nails. He acted like he was being beaten with a sock full of pennies."

"They even trimmed his *nails*? Oh, wow, just like a murder victim. In case he scratched somebody, or something?"

"Yeah, we can skip the groomer this month. The Pierce guys were looking for some clue as to where the hell our dead man might have wandered—in case they can find the rest of his corpse. We're bringing Cairo back down to Rainier on Saturday; I'm going to let him look around and see if he'll return to the source."

She shook her head sympathetically. "Well, I'm just glad you finally found him. I'd be worried sick if Brutus ever ran away."

Grady's eyes narrowed. "Isn't Brutus a fish?"

"Swam away, whatever." She waved her hand as if this were a mere technicality. "I'd be beside myself."

"Have you ever had a real pet? Something you could hold, rather than . . . I don't know, what do you do with a fish? Watch it?"

Aghast, she clutched her chest. "What do you *do* with him? I feed him. I sing to him. I talk to him. I confess to him, and I give him mushy peas with a toothpick when he gets sick and bloaty." She settled back into her seat, as if this question had been sufficiently answered. In fact, she'd never had so much as a hamster. Her father always claimed to be allergic to literally everything; privately, Leda assumed that he simply didn't like animals very much. "But to answer your other question, no. My parents aren't really 'animal people,' and I guess I'm not, either. Except for Brutus. He's pretty special."

"All right, fine. You're fish people."

She rolled her eyes. "Don't make it weird. Anyway, what's this favor? I assume you've got something you want me to hold? See if I get any vibes, or whatever?"

"That is correct." He reached into his pocket and pulled out a plastic ziplock bag with a shiny gold ring inside. "Behold, one of this morning's findings."

She did not immediately reach for it. "This morning's . . . findings. Dare I ask where you found this finding? Or can I safely guess?"

"If your safe guess is that I found it in a pile of dog shit, you got it in one. But look, I washed it off. See? It's nice and shiny."

"You washed off *evidence*?"

Defensively, he said, "It'd already passed through a dog's digestive tract. What harm would washing it do? Erase fingerprints? Come on. Here, I did the gross part for you already."

She eyed it warily. "You touch it first."

"Fine." He unzipped the bag, pulled out the ring as if it were perfectly sterile, and, hell, he might just pop it into his mouth for good measure. But he didn't. "Here you go."

Leda leaned forward and collected the ring with the tips of her finger and thumb. "Ew," she declared.

"Don't you have to hold it tighter than that? Closer or something? Come on, give it a good, hard squeeze."

"I don't go down to the station and tell you how to nab perps, now, do I? Don't tell me how to do my job." She brightened and almost forgot what she was holding or where it'd been a few hours before. "Oh, hey, speaking of—I have a new psychic detecting client!"

"A what now?"

"A client who wants me to psychically detect something. Or find some*one*, to be more precise."

Grady's ears almost visibly perked up. "A missing person?"

"Yeah, this guy's sister has been missing for a couple of weeks, and he's bringing me some of her stuff to fondle in hopes of helpful woo-woo."

He wilted. "Ah. Well, never mind."

At first, his disappointment confused her. Then she got it. "Oh, so the leg belonged to a man? Not a woman?"

"I'm afraid so. For a second there, I got my hopes up. Not that I honestly thought it'd be that easy—that *your* new client was looking for the owner of *our* disembodied leg. I believe in synchronicity, but that would really be a bridge too far. But it was worth asking."

"It's *always* worth asking," she agreed. Finally, she let the ring sit on her palm. "Sorry, but let's see if I can tell you anything helpful about this nasty-ass ring."

"The ring isn't nasty. It's just a ring. A nice, clean ring. Don't think about the dog."

"I'm trying—shut up." She closed her eyes, closed her fingers, and concentrated.

"Getting anything?"

She cracked one eye open. "You know this can take a minute, right? Be patient." Was she getting anything? Yes. Could she tell what it was? Not quite. She felt like she was moving, a passenger inside a machine. She sensed the rumble of an engine and swift progress toward something, somewhere. "I feel . . . motion. Like I'm riding inside a car."

"Like a dog? Coming back from Mount Rainier, for example?"

"Could be," she admitted. "No." She changed her mind. "I don't think so, but I can't explain why." The quarters simply felt more cramped than Grady's vehicle. "Anyway, there's a window."

He shifted in his seat, wiggling forward. "What do you see out the window?"

She frowned and thought and listened, and examined the odd sensation for any clues. "Nothing, just the light combined with blue sky, I think. Could be a car window, I guess. Yours or somebody else's. I don't see it very clearly."

"Is that all?"

"Look, I'm not a vending machine for clues, my good sir. You get what you get, and you don't pitch a fit." She took a deep breath and tried to dive back in, feel around, see if there was anything else. "Hm. I don't think it's your car. I don't think it's Cairo."

"No?" he asked eagerly.

"No, there's a hand. Not *your* hand, because it's wearing this ring."

"Is there anything distinctive about it?"

"Dude, no," she said grouchily. "It's just a guy's hand. It doesn't look especially old or young, no tattoos or scars that I can see. Just the ring." She opened her eyes. "There's something . . . sticky about it, though."

"I told you, I cleaned it off—"

"No, I mean there's something about it that . . . It's hard to explain, but it's digging in and won't let go. It's very demanding. It wants my attention."

"Not sure the ring really *wants* anything, per se," he protested.

"Maybe it's my woo-woo brain insisting on something that I'm just not hearing," she concluded, unfolding her palm and handing the ring back to Grady. "There's something going on, I can tell— but I didn't really get any scene, or voice, or anything."

"No bright flashing arrows from your subconscious, pointing at the clue?"

"Not so much flashing arrows as a single flag waving very insistently—somewhere in the distance," she added with a note of irritation. "That thing is . . ." She pointed at him, at the ring. "Peculiar. It belonged to whoever owned the leg, but I can't say if he was murdered or died by accident or misadventure. That's all I know for sure, yeah. The ring was his and not something Cairo snacked off a completely unrelated disembodied hand."

"Is that your gut or your keen psychic senses?"

"There's a lot of overlap, if I'm honest. I can't always tell them apart, so I lend them equal weight, and it usually works out. I don't suppose there's any chance I could hang on to this for a while?"

"Nope, sorry." He tucked it back into the baggie and returned it to his pocket. "Like I said, it belongs to Pierce County. Oh well. Thanks for your time, as always, but my lunch break's over, and I need to get back to work." With that, he left her office.

When he was gone, Leda sat there thinking about the ring and its unusual inscription. It rang a bell in the back of her head—or else that was her woo-woo energy trying to flag her down. She didn't like not being able to help, and, honestly, a disembodied leg and a crap-contaminated wedding ring added up to an interesting mystery. No wonder Grady had held on to the evidence. She would've done the same thing.

She picked up her phone to text Niki but thought better of it. She opened her laptop and pulled up a browser. "What was that inscription?" she asked the screen, and then she asked Google. "Something like 'My heart, my life, my one and only love.' Right?"

That was close enough to get a hit when she combined it with "romantic," "ring," and "wedding." Her Google-fu was always pretty good, and it didn't often fail her.

"Holy shit, it's from Sherlock Holmes." No, wait. The quote didn't come from a Sherlock Holmes story, but it was a lesser-known line from one of Doyle's other books, one she'd never heard of, called *The White Company*. The full and correct quote was 'You are my heart, my life, my one and only thought.' A pretty standard romantic sentiment, and conveniently short enough to engrave on jewelry. She wondered how common it was.

Leda drummed her nails on the wireless mouse, on the mouse pad, on the edge of the laptop.

It couldn't be *that* common, could it? Surely the inscription would stand out to anyone who'd done the work. Maybe someone would remember it.

She tried her luck with Google again and turned up a couple dozen jewelers in the greater King County area. Then she shook her head. No, the leg came from *south* of Seattle. But then again, that didn't mean that its owner lived there, did it? Visitors came to see the great, quiet volcano from all over the world. Still, she looked up Pierce County jewelers to cover all her bases. Alas, she found almost as many prospective candidates down there as she did in King County. "What if I narrowed it down a little. . . ."

If she kept it to just Seattle and Tacoma, there were only about two dozen likely suspects between them. She glanced at her phone to check the time. Well, what else was she doing right then and there? Jack squat, that's what. Might as well make herself useful.

Or satisfy her curiosity. Or both.

One by one, she called up the jewelers and sweetly, politely, asked about a man's wedding ring engraving—an old quote from an old book. She got through nine of them before she hit pay dirt with a family jeweler in Seattle's Wallingford neighborhood, a little north of Lake Union.

The woman on the other end of the phone sounded both ancient and knowledgeable, and Leda was effusive in her thanks.

"You remember the engraving? Do you remember who had it done?"

"Oh, those rings were engraved probably . . . I don't know, twenty years ago or more, at least. I remember the quote partly because it was so unusual, but mostly because the husband brought his back to the shop last year to be cleaned and enlarged."

"We get older and wiser and fatter, right?" Leda teased.

"Some of us," came the arch and vaguely amused reply. "It's a fiddly task, enlarging a ring without damaging the inscription. That's why it stands out in my mind; we had to charge a little extra. Now, you understand that I can't just hand out customer information, don't you?"

"Yes, yes, ma'am, I do. I absolutely do, and I appreciate you even telling me that yours is the shop that did the work. I'll, um . . . I'll pass the information along." She made note of the shop's name, Harrison Hughes Family Jewelers. Leda's Spidey-Sense was tingling, as Niki would say. She thanked the woman again and hung up.

Then she dialed Grady. Before he could say anything, Leda blurted out, "I found the shop that engraved the ring!"

Pause. "I'm sorry, you did what, now?"

"I followed my gut!" she declared proudly. "Made a few phone calls. Guess what, I think your victim is local to Seattle, not Tacoma or Puyallup or any other points south of here."

"Why do you think that?"

"Because the work was done in Wallingford, a place called Harrison Hughes Family Jewelers. The woman on the phone remembered it because the guy it belonged to brought it back to be cleaned and embiggened."

"Em . . . biggened?"

"Come on, you know what I'm talking about." She explained what the woman had told her, about the difficulty of enlarging a ring without destroying the inscription.

"Huh. And this was last year, you said?"

"Yup, so he's probably still living in the area. Or he was until fairly recently. Not because he moved, but—"

"Because he's dead, yes. I get it," he said drolly. Then he said, "Thanks for the tip—that's really great; I mean it. I hadn't planned to call around, since this isn't my case and I won't even have the ring much longer, but—"

"Don't get too excited yet; the woman on the phone wouldn't give me the guy's name or contact info. But I bet she'd give it to *you.* I bet the Pierce County guys would be tickled if they thought you'd saved them the trouble of that legwork, *and,*" she said with excited emphasis, "best of all, the corpse is local! If he was murdered, maybe he'll become your case after all!"

"That's not how it works, necessarily. But it *would* give me a good excuse to look a little closer," he added. "I'll call the jeweler and see if they'll give me any of the details they wouldn't pass along to a civilian."

Leda let him go, and as soon as she'd ended the call, she got a text alert. It was Niki. Niki was already thinking about knocking off from her job at the Smith Tower bar and retreating to the bar her boyfriend managed instead.

Meet me at Castaways?

She considered it. **What time?** During the summer, it opened early.

Not now, but soon. The bar's dead. Slow tourist day.

Leda replied, **I don't feel like karaoke tonight.**

So what? Niki responded. **Meet me there for drinks when they open. No work, just hang.**

Leda liked the sound of that, and 3:00 p.m. was just an hour away. She *did* have a little work she could've been doing, but none of it was time-sensitive. She could follow up with her cruise passengers tomorrow and make sure their return arrangements were solid and sorted. After all, she deserved a little relaxation and day drinking; she'd just helped solve a crime—or a mystery, at least. She probably even helped Grady figure out who the leg belonged to, and that was something.

Screw it. I'm in. See you there in an hour.

5. GRADY MERRITT

THURSDAY

Grady did a quick lookup for the jeweler's phone number. It only took a minute, and he caught the same woman on the phone whom Leda had spoken with perhaps fifteen minutes earlier. This was established when she said, "Oh, how funny, the girl I talked to didn't mention that this was police business!"

He admitted, "She wasn't supposed to, because the details of our investigation aren't public yet."

"Is she your assistant? Your secretary? Your—"

"She's a consultant, and she was doing me a favor by making phone calls. Could you possibly tell me who the ring belonged to—or at least who had the work done?"

"I'm looking it up right now," she told him, and in the background he heard the sound of a metal file cabinet drawer sliding open, then folders and papers being shuffled through. He'd expected to hear keyboard clicks, but this would do just fine. "Can you tell me what it's about? I'm *terribly* curious."

He gave her the quickest, broadest answer he could think of. "We're hoping the ring can help identify a John Doe."

"Ooh, that's too bad," she said, but she said it like it was quietly thrilling all the same. "The man who brought the ring in seemed quite nice. It's a shame if something awful has befallen him."

"We don't know if our mystery man in the morgue owned this ring or not. But whoever had the work done might be able to give us a clue or two—even if it turns out that he lost it in the woods in an entirely unrelated matter." The ring could've come from anyone, and as interesting as it was, it could always turn out to be a dead end. As one of the Pierce County guys had told him, a shocking number of people go missing each year in national parks.

"Of course, of course. And I'm sorry this is taking so long. We've been saying for years that we should upload all our records to a computer, but my husband doesn't like computers; he's such an old fogey."

She dropped the phone; it clattered around until she retrieved it and put it back up to her ear. "Here we are! Yes, one moment, let me . . ." More shuffling, more papers flipping around. "The man who brought us that ring to clean and enlarge it . . . Oh, here's the receipt copy and the work order. Good heavens, we're disorganized around here; this is ridiculous. His name was Paul M. Reddick. I have an address here, I suppose you'd like to have it?"

"Yes, please!" he jotted it down and thanked the woman before hanging up and pulling up a browser on his computer. He ran the address and found the house in question, in the Roosevelt neighborhood at the edge of the University District.

Did he have time to head over there? It wasn't that far from the precinct, but Seattle traffic would make it an hour round-trip at least.

"Everything okay there, man?" Sam Wilco, Grady's partner, was peering over his own monitor.

"What? Yes. It's all fine, why?"

Sam grinned and adjusted his glasses. He looked rather pleasantly like a superhero's secret identity, all tidy hair and basic clothes with a couple of youthful accents—and the kind of resting grin face that says he's up to something, even when he isn't. "You're making that *hmm* sound again. Does that mean something's wrong?"

"Nah, it means I'm thinking. You know that leg my dog picked up at Mount Rainier? I might have a name for its owner."

"Nice!" he declared, offering an air–high five over the computer monitors. Grady mimed a somewhat less enthusiastic return high five, and Sam sighed. "But it's not your case."

"But it's not my case," Grady agreed. "I have no jurisdiction, except it looks like Mr. Leg might be a Seattleite. We may end up dealing with him, regardless of where he ended up."

"And Leda's the one who found the shop?" Sam guessed. He rolled his chair around the side of his desk and used his toes to awkwardly scoot-drag it forward until he was in Grady's personal space. "I assume that's the 'consultant' you were referring to on the phone. Man, I've gotta meet this woman one of these days. Did you seriously share that shiny bit of evidence with your psychic travel agent?"

"She's useful sometimes. Let the record reflect. If she wasn't, Lieutenant Carter would've never agreed to set her up with the consulting paperwork. Not that we've used it yet, but it's nice to know that if Leda ever brings in a bad guy, I can pay her with something other than my undying thanks."

"I still can't believe Carter tolerates it, much less that the captain signed off on it. Will Leda invoice us for this one?"

Grady shook his head and scooted his own chair back a foot—just to get the breathing room, and perhaps to dispel the suggestion of conspiracy. "Not unless something changes pretty significantly. So far, she's not really involved. I just ran past her office when I went to lunch and let her hold the ring."

Sam slowly pushed his chair back into its usual position. "So? Did she get anything?"

"Not much, honestly. Something about a window, and blue sky, and maybe riding in a car. However, once I was gone, she started making phone calls. I didn't tell her to," he interjected before Sam could ask. "She got curious on her own time. The jeweler who did the work is out in Wallingford, as it turns out—and now I have an address for one Mr. Paul M. Reddick in Roosevelt."

"Ah. You're thinking about driving out there. You want to see if the rest of the guy is home and ask him what's up with the leg."

"Correct. Well, *first* . . ." He pulled up the missing persons database and checked to see if Mr. Reddick was missing in the formal sense. "Nope. He's not on the Washington list of active missing persons, but that doesn't necessarily mean anything. It would have given me a good excuse to run out there. Maybe I'll do a drive-by, just to see if anyone's around and wants to talk. Or maybe I should call Rudy first."

Sam asked, "Rudy?"

"Rudy Germaine, one of the Pierce County guys. He's the guy who gets the ring . . . as soon as I tell him I have it." Grady hemmed. He hawed. He came to a decision. "I definitely need to call him. I can't step out any further than I already have. This isn't my case," he said for the umpteenth time.

"This isn't your case," Sam echoed. "But Roosevelt isn't that far away. Just call Rudy whoever and ask him if he wants you to do it. He might even appreciate the offer."

"True." He picked up his phone again and called the Mountain Detachment, reached Rudy, made his proposal, and got the green light. He hung up and smiled. "He's game. All right, I'm going to do it. If Carter or anybody asks . . ."

Sam gave him a little salute. "I'll cover for you."

"Just tell them the truth. Everybody already knows about Mr. Leg anyway. My dog is the talk of the precinct."

"You gotta get that guy trained. He could come with you, do a cadaver search or something."

"You overestimate both my training skills and Cairo's attention span." With that, he picked up the messenger bag that Molly called his man-purse. "I'll be back in an hour or two, depending."

"Godspeed. Let me know how it shakes out, eh? I'm as curious as everybody else."

Grady promised, and he left. The traffic gods were with him, and he reached a pretty, mid-century bungalow in about twenty minutes. It was landscaped with the local nod to Japanese trees and a Zen garden flair, with sculpted shrubs and tidy mulch, plus a flagstone path leading to a small porch and a bright blue front door that contrasted nicely with the soft yellow siding.

"Cute," he observed as he pulled into the driveway. He turned off the directions app on his phone and paused to check a couple of messages that'd come in from work. Nothing too important. He could respond when he got back. He unbuckled his seat belt, reached for the door handle, and yelped, "Jesus Christ!"

A face had appeared very close to the driver's-side window. It did not belong to Jesus Christ.

It belonged to an older man with frown lines where someone happier might've had laugh lines. He raised a fist and—despite the solid, unpleasant eye contact with Grady—rapped loudly on the glass.

"Hello? Hello there, you a cop?" he yelled.

Grady nodded slowly. "Sir, if you'd just back away, I'll get out of the vehicle and we can talk. Can you do that for me?"

The man nodded and took half a step back.

With caution and mild irritation, Grady cracked open the door and squeezed out sideways—rather than whap the stranger into next Tuesday. The old guy barely weighed a hundred pounds; he was bald and suspiciously tanned and wearing a small wool cap that must've been a little warm in the summer sun. A bright sheen of sweat illuminated his forehead.

"Excuse me, sir," Grady tried. "Are you—"

"I asked if you were a cop!" he said loudly.

"Yes. Yes, I'm Detective Grady Merritt, with the Seattle PD. Can I help you?"

"I saw all the equipment in your car. I knew you were a cop. I see everything. Somebody's gotta look out for the neighborhood."

"Very good, sir," Grady said calmly. "That's a very fine goal. Are you . . . ?" He looked around for a sign and, failing to see one, asked, "Are you part of the neighborhood watch? Or something?"

"No, we don't have one of those. I just pay attention. I'm retired, I'm bored, and I have a porch that lets me see every damn thing that comes or goes from our street." He pointed at a nearby house with a large wraparound porch.

"That . . . certainly sounds useful. Hey, since you see everything, maybe you can help me with something," Grady tried. Most of the busybodies he met liked nothing better than to tattle to police. "Do you know the people who live here?"

"I do!" he said, but he didn't sound happy about it. Grady got the feeling that the man was never happy about anything.

"Okay, could you . . . could you tell me your name? Maybe?" he asked, in case it would get him somewhere.

"John!" Everything came with an exclamation point. Grady wondered if maybe the man was hard of hearing, but he didn't see any aids. Maybe he didn't like to wear them. Maybe he liked to shout. "John Kellerman! You one of the fellas looking for Robin?"

His forehead furrowed into a frown. "Robin? I . . . no. Do you mean Paul?"

He ignored the question. "Robin Reddick has been gone almost a month. Figured she would've turned up by now. Wondered if you had any word on the matter. I've been watching for her car just about every day. Haven't seen hide nor hair of her."

"I'm sorry, are you saying that Paul's wife is a missing person?" It hadn't occurred to him to check for any other Reddicks, missing or otherwise, who might be in the system. "I'm actually looking for Paul. Do you know if he's home?" he asked, knowing there was an excellent chance that Paul was somewhere in the national forest adjacent to Mount Rainier. No need to freak out the neighbors.

"Paul? Home? No. Haven't seen him in a few days. Loaned him my power washer, oh, must've been the beginning of last week, but it doesn't look like he used it." He scowled down at the driveway, which looked fine to Grady. "Any chance you could let me into his garage and get it back?"

"I . . . No. I can't do that. But can you tell me more about the missing wife? You said she's been gone a month?"

"Something like that. A few of the university kids have been helping Paul look for her. Cops haven't done anything so far," he sniffed. "Thought maybe you were here to do something. Guess not."

"Sir, I'm a homicide detective—that's not my beat." Immediately, he regretted this admission.

Mr. Kellerman's eyes widened. "You think she's *dead?*"

"No!" he said quickly. "I'm here on an unrelated matter," he added, with what he hoped was a firm note of finality. "What's Mrs. Reddick's name again?"

"Robin. Nice woman. Does landscaping design." He waved at the nicely manicured yard. "Did all this, you know."

"Really? It's lovely."

"She does nice work. Or she did, before she trotted off a few weeks ago. Just vanished. Like she caught a bus to the moon.

Absolute madness. But you know what? It's just as well you're here, because I bet she's dead," he wrapped up. "Either that, or she finally left her slimeball husband and didn't feel like telling anybody when she hit the road." Mr. Kellerman leaned up against the front left fender of the car. He pulled a pack of Marlboros out of his sweater-vest pocket, tapped one into his hand, and lit it with a lighter retrieved from the same pocket. As he puffed, he said, "Hope you don't mind."

Grady did not believe for a moment that John Kellerman cared if he minded. He chose to ignore it. "It's fine. But tell me, why do you think Robin might've left Paul?"

"He's a teacher, you know. Works at the university over there." He tilted his head east, toward the campus. "Teaches English literature and writing to a bunch of pretty young things. He likes to host parties here sometimes, with some of his favorites. I don't think Robin approves much, but if she ever tried to stop them, she didn't succeed."

"Bit of a cliché, isn't it? The professor who's always trying to sleep with his students?"

"Cliché for a reason. Neighborhood rumor has it she caught him once or twice a few years back but they patched it up. Not sure how thoroughly, since he kept up his playboy ways. But she stuck around, so . . ." He shrugged.

"Good to know," Grady said, flashing a look toward the house. There were no other cars in the driveway, and through the windows he didn't see any lights on. A casual glance would suggest that no one was home.

"My wife thinks Robin did a 'Gone Girl' on him. Like the movie, you know?"

"Haven't seen it," Grady admitted absently, still staring through the glass, past the sheer curtains that were pushed aside to show what looked like a living room.

"It's about this woman who frames her husband for a bunch of terrible stuff, terrible stuff," Mr. Kellerman said. "But he didn't do it, see? He was a bad husband, but not a murderer. Might be the same with Paul. But if you ask me, he killed her. It's *always* the spouse."

Grady returned his attention to the old man. "That's quite a theory."

He shrugged. "Stranger things happen." Pale smoke curled up from the cigarette, past his sickly yellow index fingernail, stained from years of nicotine.

"I suppose they do. But for the moment, let's assume there's some other, less sensational explanation for what's going on."

The old man shrugged again. "Go ahead and assume it's boring if you want to, but you mark my words," he said, punctuating the sentiment with a sharp jab of his cigarette. "It's going to get weird. The cops haven't had any luck finding the woman, and her car's gone, too. It's an old Volvo, and it doesn't have what-do-you-call-it. That satellite thing so people can find you."

"GPS."

"Right, GPS. Their son works on cars. I think he rebuilt it for her. He could've helped her hide it if she took off. He could've taken it apart and sold it to a chop shop. It's far too ugly to pass along to anyone else as is."

Grady wasn't sure where to begin unpacking all those assumptions, so he went for something easy. "What's ugly about it?"

"The color, mostly. Old Volvos aren't sexy cars anyway, but this one's orange. Like, *General Lee* orange," he emphasized, name-checking the *Dukes of Hazzard*. "Not a tasteful color."

"No, that's . . . an aggressive shade. Hey, do you mind if I go knock on the door real quick?"

John glanced at the house skeptically.

"Why would you bother? Nobody's home."

Grady said, "I drove all the way out here, so I really should check—if you don't mind." Not that he needed Mr. Kellerman's permission to knock on the door.

"Yeah, on an 'unrelated matter.' What *is* that matter, anyhow? You didn't say."

He considered how much to tell this man, understanding instinctively that any information would immediately be widely shared. "We found some valuable items that belong to Mr. Reddick, and I'm hoping to return them." It was true. It was easy. It was safe to say out loud in front of this man, who would surely broadcast every word to the whole neighborhood the moment Grady was out of sight.

"Ah. Robbery-gone-wrong situation? Is that why you're here? Oh no, you don't think she actually took that money, do you?"

Grady paused. He wasn't aware of any money angle to anyone's disappearance, but it wouldn't be useful to admit it. "I didn't say anything about money."

The old man pointed one finger at him and tapped the air in front of his face. "That nice lady didn't take that money. She always did those bank deposits for the landscaping folks. Ask her boss. She wouldn't have done something like that, not even to get away from Paul." He cocked a thumb toward the house, as if it personified Paul Reddick and everything that was wrong with him.

Grady made a mental note to follow up on this angle when he got back to the station. It wouldn't be too hard to find out what cop was running the missing persons case on Mrs. Reddick. "Well, like I said, I'm not here on *her* case. I'm here looking for Paul, and to return his personal items if I'm able."

"What kind of personal items?"

He went vague. "Personal ones. These things might have simply been lost, for all we know. Or even discarded," he added, thinking of Mr. Kellerman's fondness for marital intrigue. "So let me go knock, on the off chance we're both wrong. At least I'll be able to say that I did due diligence."

"Go for it; be my guest," he said, waving his cigarette toward the front door. "But if you want to return some lost items, try talking to Paul's son. He's been around a bit lately. Or maybe the brother-in-law?"

"Robin's brother? What's his name?"

"Dan something. Starts with an *M*, but I don't remember it. The kid's name is Jeff, Jeff Reddick. Try them. Or don't, if Robin's not dead and it's not your job to look for her. Maybe that psychic can point her family in the right direction."

Grady almost choked, started coughing, and then excused himself, blaming the cigarette smoke. "Allergies, I'm sorry. Could you say that again? Something about a psychic?"

"I only met Dan a couple of times. Seems like a nice fellow, very worried about his sister. Told me he was looking into a local psychic. Some woman who runs a travel agency. Said he'd read about her online."

"You can't be serious."

"Robin's been gone almost a month!" he said again, his exclamation marks back in play.

"Sir, I realize that you think we're falling down on the job here, but the truth is . . . adults 'disappear' all the time, on purpose, and they're allowed to do so—assuming they haven't committed some crime on the way out the door. The majority of them are not in peril. They do not want or require police assistance, and you're the first one to mention any missing money."

He sputtered indignantly, "Robin is no criminal; I don't care what anybody says. But if you people won't make yourselves useful, who knows?" He paused to stare thoughtfully into the middle distance, absently dropping ashes on the hood of the car. "All I can say is, I hope Robin comes home safe. I hope this travel agent woman can help."

"Sometimes she *does*," Grady mused, marveling at the circumstance. "Sometimes she does."

6. LEDA FOLEY
THURSDAY AFTERNOON/FRIDAY MORNING

Niki Nelson smacked her hand over her mouth. "You can*not* be serious," she exclaimed. She flopped back onto the battered love seat against the wall of Leda's tiny travel agency. "This is too crazy for me. I give up. I'm tapping out."

Leda quit beating her head up and down on her desk long enough to say, "No you aren't. You never tap out. You stay seated with your belt fastened for the whole damn ride, that's what you do." Then she dropped her forehead onto the desk and let it stay there. "Anyway, it's not *that* crazy. If anything, it's entirely predictable."

"Maybe for a psychic." Niki put both feet up on the edge of Leda's desk and folded her hands behind her head. "Nobody *else* could've predicted it."

"I could have," Grady grumbled. He was sulking in one of the IKEA chairs of dubious provenance. "Hell, when I made the connection, it barely even surprised me."

Leda popped back into an upright position again, her hair mussed around her forehead. She smoothed it back with one hand. "It's not fair, man. I had my *own* case. A paying psychic detective case, and I wouldn't even have to do all that paperwork for the Seattle PD."

"Everybody has to do the paperwork if they want to get paid," Grady told her. "And before you get too sulky about it . . . if this shakes out, you might get a paycheck from us, too."

Now Niki sat up, her attention snagged. "Double paid? By the client *and* by the cops?"

"It depends. You're looking for Paul's wife on behalf of her brother, and we have a portion of Paul sitting on ice down in Pierce County—if we're assuming that the ring and the leg belonged to the same guy."

"You mean there's a chance the ring came from someone else's disembodied hand? Which your dog ate? Shortly before bringing you the leg?" Leda asked. "Come *on*. What are the odds?"

"Slim to none—that's why I said we're assuming. But look, if you help me find the *rest* of Paul, I'll vouch for you and sign off on the invoice. If you want to get paid by your client, you have to find the sister. "

Leda considered this. "Twice the pay, but twice the job. You know what? That's fine, actually. If we find the rest of Paul, maybe we'll find his wife, too. Do you think he's a suspect?"

"No idea. Her neighbors think something happened to her, but they also think there's a chance she took off on her own, because he was running around on her."

Leda said, "Her brother says he has a tendency to chase his students like a creep."

Niki said, "Yikes."

She couldn't argue with her. "There's always at least one in every department."

"That's a . . . cynical attitude, isn't it?" Grady asked.

"Spoken like someone who's never been a college-aged girl." She clicked her nails against the side of the laptop, thinking. Her problem teacher had been the Intro to Art professor. A short man with a wide waistline and a balding head who somehow, nonetheless, had at least one teacher's pet. Usually a redhead. But some things just weren't worth trying to explain to a guy who'd never experienced it firsthand. "Their disappearances *must* be related, though, right? It's too much of a coincidence: the wife disappears and then the husband goes missing, too."

"It's a coincidence, yes. That's all we know for certain right now, and the fact is, coincidences *do* happen."

Niki stared up at the ceiling as she reclined on the love seat. "Maybe he killed her and stashed her body out in the park, and then something made him go back to it. Then he got eaten by a bear."

Grady didn't push back too hard. "Honestly? I've been thinking along the same lines, because sometimes a killer will do that. Return to the body, I mean—not get eaten by bears. Paul might've realized he'd left some evidence behind and gone back to collect it."

Leda tried, "He could've been looking for her. Maybe she sent him a message, luring him out there. Maybe *she* killed *him*."

Grady considered this.

"Also a possibility, if a little more far-fetched. Let's not overthink it. I'm taking Cairo back down there tomorrow to poke around before they reopen the park to visitors, so maybe we'll get lucky."

"You think he'll take you to the rest of the body?" Niki asked.

Grady sighed. "Not really, but dogs love dead stuff. Smart odds say that the rest of Paul is dead, too, and that he's out there in the general vicinity of wherever Cairo picked up the leg. Cairo's not a trained cadaver dog, or a trained . . . any kind of dog, really. But it's worth a shot."

Leda failed to contain an eager, sneaky smile. "Long-ass drive, though. Long-ass . . . lonely drive . . . through the middle of nowhere . . ."

"Through the greater Tacoma area—it's not exactly the outback. Why are you looking at me like that? Oh God."

"Like you haven't been thinking about it already. Fine. It's settled. I'll come with you. Niki will, too."

Niki's eyebrows shot up. "Wait, what?"

"The only thing I hate more than hiking is hiking alone. I mean, without a friend. I mean . . . without Niki. You know what I mean."

Grady sighed. "Slow your roll, Miss Cleo. My car isn't that big, and I don't know if I have room for you, me, Niki, Molly, *and* the dog. Don't take it personal, but the dog is the most important part."

"Molly's coming, too?" Leda brightened. "She seems like fun."

"She *is* fun, mostly. She's also terrified of losing her dog again, and she cried until I broke, so she's coming with me on this semi-official police business trip. Niki, listen—you know we're all friends here, but—"

She stopped him with a laugh and a dismissive wave that told him not to worry about it. "Man, I'm allergic to dogs; you couldn't pay me enough to be stuck in a car with one. You two go have fun without me this time. *But,*" she said with a firmly pointed finger aimed right between Grady's eyes, "I get to come on the next field trip. As long as there are no dogs involved. Nothing against dogs. Or your kid. Your kid is fine. I'm not allergic to kids."

Grady exhaled like this was the best news he'd heard all day. "Okay, good. Leda, are you in for tomorrow morning—even without your emotional support bartender? It'll be pretty early, but it's a couple hours down there and a couple hours back, and we need the middle of the day for hiking and dog-following."

"Sounds . . . rugged," Leda said, with only the faintest hint of regret hitting the words. "I'll see if I can find my boots."

Niki frowned. "You have boots?"

"I *do* have boots," she insisted defensively.

"The knee-high leather ones with jangly silver zippers—yeah, I remember those. Do you have any boots that you could walk around the wilderness in without wanting to die? I know you have rain boots."

"Obviously, yes, I have rain boots. Tall, bootie, and midi height. Don't be ridiculous."

"How about sneakers?" Grady suggested. "We'll be on or near the trails; it isn't an obstacle course. Or a goth bar, or whatever. Leave the jangling zippers at home. They'll distract the dog."

With wardrobe thereby sorted, Grady left, Niki stayed for dinner, and then Friday morning rolled around—bright and clear and pleasantly cool. Leda didn't really care to be awake early enough to enjoy it, but at least it was summer and the sun was already up. The only thing worse than being up before dawn was being up before dawn in the northwest summer, when dawn started before 5:00 a.m.

Seven a.m. wasn't much better, but it was the latest she could talk Grady into picking her up.

He arrived two minutes early. She made him wait while she filled a backpack with a thousand items that she'd surely need while out of the house—including a couple of candy bars, a water bottle, a phone charger, an extra pair of sunglasses, a fresh Sharpie in case they got lost and needed to mark a trail, a first aid kit in case anybody else lost a leg, a small guidebook of edible plants in the Pacific Northwest, a Swiss Army knife, half a roll of toilet paper, two packets of travel tissues, three travel-size bottles of hand sanitizer in an assortment of scents, and a shiny silver whistle on a lanyard.

Finally, she was as prepared as she could reasonably (or unreasonably) get.

She fed Brutus a couple of small, smelly pellets and checked his water temperature. All good. No algae. One swimming blue betta fish, present and accounted for. He'd be fine without her for a bit, even if she got lost in the woods and somebody found *her* leg in a dog's mouth, days later. She'd already texted Niki instructions regarding the fish's care, in the event of her own untimely demise on a trail or in case the volcano blew while she was down there.

Niki told her to shut up and that she'd see her later that night at Castaways. It was Friday. The festivities at the bar would run late and fun, and she wouldn't miss it even if the volcano *did* blow. She'd find a way.

"Okay," she said to herself. She took a deep breath. She locked her front door and climbed into the passenger seat of Grady's sedan—a late-model Toyota with a couple of scratches and a silver-gray paint job. "I'm sorry I'm late." She buckled herself in and leaned around to address Molly. "Are you sure you don't want shotgun?"

"It's all yours," the teenager assured her. "Cairo gets carsick sometimes, and I'm the one with the trash bags and paper towels. I mean, if you really want to go on puke duty, I'll swap you. . . ."

The puker in question bounced and smiled, flinging drool around the interior. He didn't look especially queasy, but he hadn't been on the road very long.

"No! No, that's fine, thank you. Grady, thanks for the pickup. Let's go. Let's do this."

"Are you all right? You sound a little . . . tense," he noted, but he simultaneously checked over his shoulder and put the car into reverse, backing out of the driveway and into the side street in front of her little rented bungalow.

"Fine. I'm fine. I'm nervous, but I'm fine."

Molly said, "I'm nervous about losing my dog again, but I figure we've taken all the logical precautions, and now I just need to keep an eye on him. Have *you* taken all the logical precautions?"

She thought about the hand sanitizers and the guidebook to edible wild plants. "Probably. I hope I haven't forgotten anything."

"Then you'll just have to trust yourself. Right, Dad?"

"Yes," he said confidently. Then, specifically to Leda, he added, "I told her that. I'll have you know, I'm an excellent parent."

"A sterling example indeed, yes, you are. I just don't leave the house by this much distance very often, and there's most of a dead body in the woods somewhere, and I know we're supposed to be looking for it, but by now it's probably really gross, and I'm not entirely sure I want to find it."

"Like you've never seen a body before," he scoffed.

"Thanks to you, yes. I've seen a body. I've even touched a body, in a non-normal-body-touching situation."

Molly leaned forward, and Cairo's head came with her. "You can't possibly mean that like it sounds."

"Stop trying to fluster me!" Leda said, hoping it came off as joking. She scratched behind Cairo's ears. "I touched a body at a crime scene because your dad wanted to know if it'd tell me anything. Ordinarily, I assume that corpse-touching is the kind of activity that's relegated to funeral homes and coroners' offices."

"One would hope," Grady said, then added, "I still feel a little bad about that. I won't ask you to touch any more bodies. But if we find any more stray parts, maybe you can touch a few of those. Work your way back up to the full stiff."

"You're awful," Leda informed him. Still, the prospect intrigued her, just a little. She wasn't sure if she'd do it or not, should they stumble upon a couple of toes or a hand or whatever. She'd play it by ear. Hell, maybe they'd *find* an ear. She was reasonably confident that she could touch an ear without freaking out. It'd probably feel like a cookie. The soft-baked kind, without any chocolate or raisins.

Shit, now she was hungry.

They pulled into the visitor center parking lot before 10:00 a.m., even though they'd stopped at McDonald's because Leda was confident that she would die if she didn't get some food—and Cairo backed her up. Several bags of breakfast goodies later, the pooch was half-stuffed with hash brown cakes and pieces of biscuits with bits of cheese and bacon. He almost got one of the wrappers, too, but Molly reached into his mouth and retrieved it before it could vanish.

All those bags, that half-chewed wrapper, and all the dirty napkins went into the first trash can they found on the way to the visitor center's entrance.

Rudy Germaine was just inside—wearing plain clothes, chewing gum, and fiddling with a ring of keys hanging off his jeans. He locked the door behind him when he came to join them. "There are signs in the parking lot, signs on the door, and signs on the website—but people still pull up and try to let themselves inside. This end of the park is closed, goddammit! People act like they can't read."

Introductions were made, and while the group plotted its course, two cars pulled into the lot. Rudy shooed them away. He waved, aimed finger-guns at the signs, and then blew them a kiss when they flipped him off and drove away.

"You see?" he asked them. "People are stupid. Come on, let's get started. Now, your boy here, he came up the Skyline Trail, isn't that right? With the leg in hand? Or in mouth, I suppose."

Grady nodded. "Yes, but there were rumors of a dog barking out by Wonderland. Might have been him, might not. If we have time, we should let him go there, too."

For his part, Cairo was just happy to be the center of attention. He sat and wagged his tail, grinning at each person individually and occasionally glancing toward the nearest trailhead. Molly kept a death grip on his lead. Leda scratched his head. When Grady whistled to get his attention, his head popped up with interest.

"You've got him trained!" Rudy said happily.

Molly laughed. "Trained to know that whistles mean treats, sometimes. He's not exactly a well-oiled obedience machine, so don't get too excited. He knows his name, he knows how to sit when he wants something, and he knows he likes food. That's about it."

Rudy ruffled Cairo's ears and told him he was a good boy. "A good *enough* boy," he clarified. Then, in the universal grown-man-talking-to-a-dog-like-it's-a-baby voice, he asked, "You're gonna take us to the rest of Mr. Leg, aren't you, buddy? That's right. Yes, you are."

The dog's tongue lolled out the side of his mouth, and he closed his eyes, leaning into the ear rubs.

"I wouldn't hold my breath," Grady told him. "But let's give it a shot and see how it goes. Please," he said to Cairo, in the same voice he most often used on his teenage daughter. "For the love of God, don't embarrass me."

7. GRADY MERRITT

FRIDAY

Where the trail was wide enough, they walked four abreast with the dog in the lead. Where it wasn't, they hung back two by two—with Grady and Molly side by side, then Leda and Rudy behind them. The day was warm and sunny, but the trees were tall and shady, and beneath the canopy a breeze kept everyone from sweating to death. Sometimes between those trees, the old volcano Mount Rainier loomed large, depending on the direction and the topography.

Mostly everyone kept their eyes on the jubilant dog, who was getting another long walk through a beautiful park full of fresh things to sniff and pee on, in the company of his favorite people in the world . . . so he was having the Best Day Ever.

"What kind of dog is he, anyway?" asked Rudy. "Some kind of Lab? Retriever?"

"He's a mutt," Grady said.

Molly begged to differ. "He's half yellow Lab, and the rest is pit bull, some kind of shepherd, and Jack Russell terrier."

Leda and Rudy both gave Molly the same quizzical frown. Leda asked the question on everyone's mind. "Jack Russell? I'll buy the rest, but . . ."

Molly shrugged. "That's what the doggie DNA said. He also has, like, two percent 'unknown working breed,' whatever that means."

Grady grinned as he watched Cairo piddle on a signpost that directed visitors to several alternative paths. "Like I said, he's a mutt."

"You didn't pay money for him like that, did you?" Rudy asked.

"No, we found him like that," Grady replied. "He's a pretty good dog, though. You could do a lot worse for free."

"He'll be a *great* dog if he brings us to the rest of Mr. Leg. Or Mr. Reddick, if the ring and the leg belong to the same person."

Leda asked, "Didn't you run DNA on the leg?"

"Well, we sent in a sample," Rudy told her. "We might hear back in a few days, and we might hear back in a few months. It depends on a lot of things." He turned to his fellow officer. "Any other sign of the guy back in Seattle?"

He leaned his head back and forth, making his signature *hmm* sound. "No sign of him or his wife. But I don't want to assume anything."

"But come on, right? The wife has been missing for ages, and then this guy drops off the map, too. It's gotta be connected."

"Okay, let's say that it is," Grady countered. "His missing wife might have had a lover, and Paul could've killed that guy. The ring fell off in the melee. It could be the lover's leg, for all we know. If I'm not going to be thorough, I don't deserve to have this job."

"My dad the paladin," Molly said with an eye roll.

Rudy looked confused, so Grady said, "She plays a lot of RPGs."

Cairo yipped, seizing everyone's attention. He ran to the base of a tree and started barking.

"Does he have a lead?" Rudy asked excitedly. "What you got there, boy?"

Molly shook her head. "That's his *I see you* bark. Bet you a dollar it's a raccoon."

She wasn't far off. It was a pair of baby squirrels playing chase around the trunk.

Their host was not impressed. "If he's going to bark at every squirrel in the woods, we'll be here all day."

"Let's give it a couple of hours, at least," Grady suggested. "He's pulling us in a steady direction. He might be headed for something specific."

Molly disagreed. "He's on a trail. He usually just stays on the trail, even if the trail is a sidewalk or stairs or whatever. He's going this way because the trail goes this way."

"There's a split up ahead. Maybe he'll pick a direction and get excited."

Leda was getting sweaty and pink-faced. "How far do these trails go, Mr. Germaine? Officer Germaine."

"You can call me Rudy, ma'am. And to answer your question, we have upward of two hundred sixty miles of trails for your hiking pleasure."

"Well, not for *my* hiking pleasure," she muttered.

"For the pleasure of people who enjoy hiking, then," he said with a wink.

The trailhead came to a three-way split, and everyone watched Cairo to see what he'd do at the junction. The dog sat down and looked up at the sign tree like he was reading each line and considering his next path, but he didn't show any particular preference for any of them.

"Hang on." Leda walked around him, stared at the sign, and then touched it—resting the palm of her hand on the individual plaques, one after another. Then she turned and shrugged at Grady. "Nothing."

"Nothing?"

"Zilch."

Rudy looked back and forth between them. "What? Nothing what? And if you don't mind my asking, because I didn't ask before . . . what kind of consultant are you, ma'am?"

Grady jumped on that grenade before Leda could reply. "She's been looking into Robin Reddick's disappearance—completely separate from any Seattle PD investigation. It's a long story. But she's the one who made the phone calls and found the jeweler who did the engraving, and I felt like it was only fair to bring her along."

One day, perhaps, he would learn that there was not really any stopping Leda when someone asked her a question, but this was not that day. As if she were vaguely annoyed by his preemptive answer, she said, "I'm psychic. I helped him solve a case, and I ended up in the newspapers, so now sometimes people ask me to look for things. Robin Reddick's brother hired me to look for her."

At least it was concise. All things considered, she could've said something worse. Grady cleared his throat and gave her a look that was hard enough to crack a walnut. "And she psychically intuited that our cases were connected."

She took the hint and didn't mention that he'd shown her the ring before he'd told Rudy about it.

"Yep! So don't worry if you see me randomly just . . . fondling woodsy stuff like this. It's my job."

"It's a signpost; it's not exactly . . . woodsy stuff," Rudy said. He was wearing an expression that said he found it all both funny and kind of interesting. "But go on, touch whatever you need to."

She asked, "Don't you people usually tell tourists *not* to touch things?"

"I'm not a park ranger, so I say go on and touch whatever you want. It's not a museum." Then he amended the sentiment. "I mean, don't tear anything up. You don't have to do that, do you? It's just . . . touching?"

"Just touching," she promised.

Since it was out there, now, Grady asked Leda, "But you're not getting anything?"

"Not yet. I'll try to reach out and grab more stuff."

"Oh boy," he murmured. To Rudy he said, "Don't worry. This will be fine."

"You sound very confident."

"I'm . . . largely confident."

Molly laughed at them both. "Guys! There's nothing to break in the woods! Stop worrying so much."

Cairo sniffed each new trailhead with cautious interest, but he did not boldly determine a course. For the most part, he looked confused and low-key hungry despite his people-food breakfast calories. He retreated to Molly, who was holding the end of his lead.

"What is it, boy?" she asked him.

"I don't know that much about dogs, but I don't think this is working," Leda said. "He doesn't seem to know where he is or what we want him to do. How smart is he?"

"It depends on how many French fries are involved," Molly told her.

Her father agreed. "He's very food-motivated, as the trainer put it—but I was hoping that the rest of Paul Reddick might count as food, and he'd want to go find it."

Leda proposed, "Maybe people don't taste very good."

"People can't possibly taste worse than the roadkill raccoon tail I pulled out of his mouth last week," Grady said wryly.

"Or the sun-baked frog that had split open on the sidewalk. Or the half a rat he found in a puddle of that other dog's puke. Or the—"

"*Please*," Leda interrupted. "Stop before my breakfast shows up again. I beg you."

Grady laughed and continued the thread. "Remember when he ate those greasy paper towels that fell out of the neighbor's garbage? We had to tug them out of his butthole in pieces, like pulling wipes out of a plastic tub."

Rudy laughed, too. "You're really selling me on this whole having-a-dog thing. My girlfriend's been after me to adopt one with her, and I keep saying maybe one of these days, but now? Now I'm not so sure."

"They aren't *all* this bad," Grady assured him.

"Some of them are much worse!" Molly declared.

In an effort to escape the conversation, Leda wandered off down one of the paths a few yards until she hit a bench. She touched it. Lifted her hand up and down. Turned it over. Tried touching it with different fingers. But it got her nowhere. She gave up and came back to the split, picked another path, and tried again—this time stopping to touch a tree, another signpost, and a plaque that warned of poison oak.

Grady called out, "Any luck?"

"Nope!" she hollered, and picked the third path.

Quietly, Rudy asked, "Does she always work like this?"

"Touching stuff? Yeah." Grady watched her until she went around a curve and he lost her. "She touches things, holds them. Sometimes she gets useful information, and sometimes she doesn't. There's a specific term for what she does, but I forget."

Molly piped up with, "Psychometry!" When the two men looked at her funny, she said, "I looked it up."

"Leda?" Grady yelled, since she'd been out of his line of sight for thirty seconds, and he didn't trust her not to get lost.

"Still nothing!" she said in return, from reassuringly close by. She came back to the group and threw her hands up. "I'm running out of things to touch, folks. I'm resorting to random sticks and leaves, and I think I accidentally touched some kind of wild animal poop, but that's what hand sanitizer is for."

"I don't have any on me. . . ." Rudy said, patting down his pockets like he might magically reveal some, now that he thought about it.

But Leda was already rummaging around in her bag. "Oh, I've got it covered. I fully anticipated bear poop."

"I doubt it was bear poop. Then again, we haven't had any park visitors to speak of for the last few days, thanks to this investigation. . . . Maybe a bear wandered through while the people weren't around. Wouldn't be the first time."

"Didn't get any vibes from the poop, so it kind of doesn't matter what animal produced it." She doused herself in something that smelled powerfully of lavender and vanilla and rubbing alcohol.

It almost made Grady's eyes water from ten feet away, so he groaned when Molly asked if she could have some, too. The whole car was going to stink like a Bath & Body Works all the way home. "Let's pick a direction. Hey, Rudy, which one of these trails takes us closest to the Wonderland Trail? Do any of them intersect with it?"

Deep down, he halfway believed that if they could just get Cairo to the right spot, the right intersection, the right set of trees—whatever—he might remember that he'd left a stash of long pig for later snacking.

Rudy pointed out the most likely trail and together they all set off, the dog accidentally in the lead and quite happy about it.

Three hours later they'd found tourist trash, a dead possum, and half a dozen hikers who damn well knew the park was closed—so Rudy chased them off with threats of trespassing citations. Then with Cairo's help they also located somebody's lost or discarded sack lunch and two-thirds of a bird, which was more like half of a bird by the time they were able to wrestle it out of his mouth.

Leda never found anything worth touching, and she remained unusually quiet on the trip back to Seattle.

8. LEDA FOLEY

FRIDAY NIGHT

Leda sulked all the way up Capitol Hill and finally found a parking spot for Jason, her Honda Accord, named for the Friday the thirteenth on which she'd bought it. She kicked the door shut behind herself and squinted in the late afternoon sun. Northwest summer days were terribly long, and it felt like it ought to be . . . dimmer outside . . . but the rays hit her hard in the face, warming the asphalt and sidewalks around her. She was dressed in too many layers, and now it was uncomfortable. Maybe it would cool off when the sun went down, and then she'd be glad for the extra sweater.

Until then, she ignored the warm dampness of sweaty armpits and damp underboobs, and she made a beeline for Castaways—the bar on the hill where she semiregularly sang for her supper. A musical fortune cookie, that's what Ben Kane had called her, and he was the guy who owned the place—so she'd let it ride.

She wasn't really in the mood to do her regular routine, but he'd already put up flyers around the Pike/Pine corridor, and she hated canceling things, so she was showing up like a goddamn professional.

Was she doing this psychic-singing thing professionally? Yes, she assured herself. She got a cut of the cover charges and also the drink tickets. And free booze. It was in her contract. Or it would've been if she'd had a contract. What she actually had was an agreement among friends, and she knew those things could go south, but she refused to entertain the possibility that Ben—or Matt, the club manager and Niki's boyfriend, or Steve, the bouncer—would do anything to screw her over. They were practically family.

And Tiffany, the bartender, was the one who promised and doled out the free drinks. She was *definitely* family.

Leda bellied up to the bar looking and feeling like she'd rather melt through the floor than talk to anyone, but Tiffany always knew better. And she always had the right medicinal offering to help put things right.

"One of those days, eh, girl?" The bartender wore a fluffy purple dress with black accents and black fingerless gloves. She was pretty and young and Black, and for some reason tonight she was rocking a 1980s throwback look. "You look like you've been ridden hard and put away wet. In, um, the horse sense. Like, a horse that . . . and there's a barn, and . . . anyway."

Leda gave her a tired grin. "You're not wrong. I'm so exhausted I can hardly breathe. I went down to Mount Rainier with Grady and his daughter, and I haven't had that much exercise in years, and, worst of all, it wasn't even worth the trouble."

She scrunched up her face in an expression that wasn't sure if it was curious, concerned, or otherwise confused. "You went hiking? On purpose?"

"Well, nobody held a gun to my head, but I didn't really want to do it. I talked myself into it because I thought I could be helpful."

"And . . . you weren't?" Tiffany guessed. Her face settled back down into motherly concern.

It amused Leda, who was almost old enough to be the mom in this conversational scenario. She ran the math in her head and concluded that Tiffany could've been her junior prom baby, but she did not say so out loud. Instead, she said, "I was not. I touched all kinds of random woodsy stuff—even some poop that I'm told did not actually belong to a bear."

"On purpose?" she asked again.

"I touched it on purpose, but that was before I knew what it was. I thought it was a pinecone or something. There were all these . . ." She waved her hands around, miming something scattered on the ground. "Leaves. Anyway, the poop didn't tell me anything. Not even what animal had produced it. Good thing I packed that hand sanitizer."

"Well played, indeed. Sounds like you need a drink."

"What's tonight's special?" Leda asked.

"Still working on it. I'm experimenting with a Mediterranean-inspired spritzer, but so far it mostly tastes like that grape medicine mom used to give you when you stayed home from school. So. It's a work in progress. Got any requests?"

"Something fruity, but maybe not . . . grapey. Other than that, surprise me."

Twenty seconds later, Tiffany slipped her something orangish in a highball glass. "Give it a sip. Tell me what it needs."

Leda obliged. She smacked her lips and licked them, then pretended to be a sommelier. She gave it a swirl and then waved vapors over to her nose, all the better to sniff them. "I'm getting hints of . . . orange Fanta . . . and some kind of rum . . . and maybe some bitters?"

"It's silver rum, no bitters, but you're not that far off. It shouldn't be too strong."

"What?" Leda exclaimed, appalled at the thought of a weak drink before a show. "You know I have to sing tonight. Load me up!"

Tiffany folded her arms and cocked her favorite eyebrow. "Yeah, and I know you like to have two or three to warm yourself up. A couple of these will get you buzzing but won't leave you too knackered to croon."

"I'll have to pee, though. Probably a lot."

"Pace yourself. Please don't take another bathroom break midset and make poor Matt get up there and tell jokes. That was brutal. For everyone."

Leda was already swigging the fizzy beverage, and now she wondered if there wasn't some hint of rosemary-infused liqueur, but she didn't care because it tasted pretty good. Tiffany's alchemy had done her a solid. She unfixed her lips from the red-and-white straw. "What are you calling this one?"

"Its working title is Florida Sunrise. Bright, summery, and a little trashy. Might be good frozen into a slushie, hmm . . ." Someone waved for her attention; she threw the guy a nod and asked Leda, "You good for now? Or should I go ahead and start your second round?"

"No, this is . . . this is fine," she said, picking up the drink along with its white cocktail napkin. "For now. Thank you! You are wonderful!"

"Back at you, songbird. Knock 'em dead!"

She saluted with the beverage and sat down at a tiny table with a top that wasn't any bigger than a dinner plate. Set right beside the stage, there was little room for anyone to join her. Sometimes it was best to sulk alone.

But sometimes you got company whether you expected it or not.

Ben Kane swanned over to the table, pulled up a seat, and squeezed in despite the cramped location. Their knees practically knocked together, but at least he didn't have a drink and wasn't taking up precious tiny-table space. "Hey, Ben, don't worry. I'll be ready in a few."

He patted her hand. "Oh, honey, you're early anyway. I was just checking in. I heard you got a big new case—but you look so god-damn *glum*! Is everything all right?"

Tonight, the late-forty-something Asian man was wearing a navy blue velvet smoking jacket that was almost light enough to call a blouse, but not quite. His shoes were sleek vintage Fluevogs, black and gold. His manicure was tidy and understated, with just a touch of shimmer. The silver streaks at his temples were dusted with glitter.

Leda deeply admired his commitment to Sparkle Motion.

She made an effort to brighten at his question, not just because Ben owned the club (though he left most of its management to Matt), but because she genuinely liked him and appreciated his interest in her side hustle. Or her *other* side hustle, as the case may be. "I'm fine! Totally fine, please don't worry about me—I'm only tired, all the way down to my bone marrow. And yes, I *do* have a new case, but that's not my problem. Not exactly."

"Sounds complicated . . ." he prompted. "Come on, unload. You know me—I'm always here for your tired, grouchy sounding board needs."

She smiled despite herself. "Thanks, Ben. You know I appreciate you and your skillful sounding board ways." By way of launching into her tale, she began, "Have you heard about that U-Dub professor's wife who went missing a few weeks ago?"

His face said he wasn't, but he was game to play along. "I don't think so. Fill me in."

"Well, this woman went missing, and her brother thinks the cops aren't doing enough to find her. He tracked me down in Columbia City, and he's paying me to look for her with my woo-

woo vibes. I got an email from him this afternoon; he's PayPal'ing me the fee tonight."

"Ooh, sounds juicy! What about her husband? It's usually the husband, right?"

"When somebody's murdered, sure. It's usually the spouse," she agreed. "But we don't know for a fact that this lady is dead. Got some ideas about her husband. . . ." she muttered under her breath, but when it looked like Ben might ask a follow-up question, she quickly amended the sentiment. "I mean, I *do* think maybe he killed her. Occam's razor and all that jazz. But we haven't had a chance to talk to him yet."

"'We'?" he asked innocently.

She sighed. She should've been more careful. On second thought, maybe it didn't matter. "Grady is involved in a case that has some overlap with this one, so we're . . . not exactly working *together*, but working *adjacently*."

"I follow you, and my lips are sealed. But a new case is good news, so why are you so full of woe? And don't give me that *everything's all right* nonsense; I know you too well for that, sitting over here by yourself. Niki will be here soon, and I refuse to believe that you two can't be apart for more than an hour without one of you toppling into a deep, thirsty depression," he proposed, giving the drink a cocked eyebrow. "What is that? Is that on our menu, or is it today's experimental Tiffany special?"

The last question was the easiest one to answer, so she started there. "It's the Tiffany special, tentatively called a Florida Sunrise. Orange soda and silver rum, and some other stuff."

"Smells strange."

"I agree, but I dig it. You want a sip?"

He scooted his chair closer to the stage in order to make room for the alcohol delivery guy and his dolly stacked with boxes.

"Thanks, dear, but no. I don't share drinks, not even with superstars like yourself . . . and you've dodged the bit about looking sad. Do we need to cancel? You can tell me if you do. Then *I'll* be the one with the sad face, but I'll get over it. I only want what's best for you, and I hope you know that."

His gentleness touched her, and she had a passing desire to burst into tears of gratitude—but she squished it down. "I know, and I love you for it. I'm just . . ." It took her a few seconds to find the words. "I'm so damn disappointed in myself. Me and Grady took a field trip down to Mount Rainier, and I was completely useless the whole time."

"Good God, why would you willingly go into the wilderness?" He glanced under the table and recoiled. "Did you do it in *those* shoes?"

"Of course not. I changed before I got here. You should've seen me, though. I packed like a crazy person. Could've lived for a week out there, all by myself, on granola bars, bottled water, and breath mints." Her mom had always done likewise, toting around a bag as big as a suitcase, full of every possible item, for every possible eventuality. Everyone made fun of her, right up until the moment they needed something.

Leda secretly fantasized about an emergency scenario where she saved the day with something pulled out of her own "plus-five bag of holding." To date, she'd mostly provided emergency dollops of hand lotion and gum.

Ben nodded, impressed regardless. "I am proud indeed that you could live so long in the wilderness if you had to. If you could call breath mints and granola bars *living*."

"Fair point. Lucky for me, I didn't need any of it except the breath mints." She thought about the probably-not-bear-poop. "And the hand sanitizer. But I swapped my sneakers for heeled booties when I got home. You like?"

"I *do* like."

She took another deep swallow of the cocktail. It tasted better with every drop. "Anyway, I am disappointed in myself because I wasted a whole day hiking around outside, getting sweaty and bug-bitten, and I have absolutely nothing to show for it. I didn't pick up a single clue. It was a waste of everyone's time, including the nice cop or whatever he was from Pierce County. He said he wasn't a park ranger, but I'm still kind of unclear on how that works, when you're a cop but it's a public park."

The liquor guy rolled the empty dolly past them again and was gone back out the front door. Ben dragged his chair with his feet, hauling it into its usual place. When he was situated again, he said, "You claim it was a waste of everyone's time. Does Grady feel that way, too? Or did he find what he was looking for? I know that you're not allowed to talk to me about cop cases—don't worry," he said, with a curious inflection that said he'd dearly love to be mistaken but that he'd never be so gauche as to press the matter.

He was not mistaken. She kept it vague. "It was a waste of his time, too. That's all I should probably say about that. Nobody learned anything useful at all, no good came of it, and no one enjoyed it. Except the dog, I guess. He got McDonald's in the car, and he didn't puke it up or anything. So at least one of us had a stellar day trip."

"The dog? What dog?"

"Random yellow mutt. I think they found him in a parking lot when he was a puppy."

"Grady's dog, got it," Ben said, suddenly understanding. "You should tell him to bring it here someday. We're dog-friendly, for the most part."

"I'm not sure Cairo is anybody's idea of a well-trained dog to bring out in public."

"I believe you, but I still wish to pet him. Just throwing that out there," he said, hands up in social surrender. "One of these days I'll bring my cat in, just to show him off. You'll see. I welcome all things fuzzy, feathered, scaled, or otherwise—as long as they'll let me pet them."

"You've never invited me to bring Brutus into the bar."

He frowned, momentarily confused, and subsequently unsure if she was serious about that. "How would you even . . . a ziplock baggie or something?"

She laughed and squeezed his hand. "I'm just messing with you. Brutus hates riding in the car."

Ben glanced up and leaned back away from the table. It was either that or get whapped with Tiffany's elbow as she swiped Leda's now-empty glass and replaced it with a full one.

Leda lifted the new drink and toasted it at Ben. "Christ, she's good."

"She's literally the *best*," he corrected her. "All right, so let's talk about the show, shall we?"

"Yes. Let's do. What do you need to know?" Talking about karaoke was always easier than talking about personal failures. She was actually pretty good at the karaoke, and she was steadily (in her own opinion) getting better with the psychic angle, too. Come to find out, you could exercise that like a muscle, too. Who knew?

Together they sorted out the particulars: how long the set would run, details about the new karaoke system and how it worked, and announcements to make before she got started. Niki arrived before they were finished, and she did a little squeal to learn that they had a whole new song repertoire to choose from.

"That's awesome!" she declared. "I was starting to worry that our selection was getting dated."

"It's not too many more songs, but it's a few of the newer hits. Leda was saying the other day that she needed a song and we didn't have it—and such failures will not be tolerated in my establishment!"

His phone rang. He excused himself.

"Love that guy," Niki said, helping herself to Leda's second drink. It was still half-full, and Leda protested the theft. "Hey!"

"I just want to taste it! It smells . . . interesting. . . ." she said, nose hovering over the ice. She stole a sip. "Not bad, but it's not for me."

"Keep drinking; it gets better."

Niki rolled her eyes. "You can say that about literally any alcohol."

"Not, like, rubbing alcohol," she retorted, mostly to be contrary. Then she stood up and gently whapped Niki on the arm. "All right, the place is filling up and your boyfriend's got the stage looking good. I'd better get ready to rock. Or torch song. Or disco, who knows."

"Break a leg, cutie. I'll keep your table and cheer real loud. If you start bombing, I'll wave my hands around and you can pick me out of the crowd. I'll give you a hair tie or something and then start crying real dramatic-like when you start singing; I'll tell everyone you're a genius and that you saw right through my soul."

"Oh God, please don't do that," Leda told her, but all the same she laughed and felt better as she carried the limited remains of the drink away.

When the doors were closed because the bar was as full as the twitchy fire marshal would permit, she took her place on the stage. It wasn't a big stage. Nothing in Castaways could really be described as *large*, except perhaps the bar and its liquor selection. Leda positioned herself behind the microphone and welcomed the crowd.

"Good evening, everyone! I'm Leda Foley, and I'll be your musical fortune cookie this evening," she began—to happy cheers and general applause. "How many of you have been to one of my little shindigs before?"

About two-thirds of the relevant hands in the room popped up.

"And how many of you are new folks? I know, you'd think I could figure it out via process of elimination, but the lights are on my face and it's a little hard to see you, so please—humor me."

The remaining hands shot skyward.

"Okay, looks like we have enough new people on board that I ought to start with a little explanation. First, and for legal reasons . . . this is for entertainment purposes only. I have to say that, even though the truth is I take this pretty seriously and I'm working hard to improve my skills. It *is* a skill, you know," she added. "The more I do this, the better I get. At least, here's hoping."

A few chuckles. Excited whispers.

"Right. So. This is *technically* for entertainment purposes only, and please don't ask me for lotto numbers. If I had any, I would use them myself, believe me. This isn't that kind of show. Okay, then, here's how it works: I will hang out on this stage, and you will raise your hand if you want me to sing you a song that tells your fortune or answers your question, whatever it may be—you don't have to tell me, and you probably shouldn't. Then you will give me some small item to concentrate on. Or you'll loan me one," she corrected herself. "Don't worry. You'll get it back. This isn't *that* kind of show, either, for I am neither magician nor thief. I just need to hold it, that's all. Speaking of, please don't give me anything sticky. I hate sticky, and I will return the item to you unread. No bodily fluids, no condiments, no food residue. If you give me anything gross—and *I* am the sole arbiter of what *gross* amounts to—you will be asked to leave, and never permitted to return. If you think I'm joking . . ."

She pointed at the bar. Or rather, she pointed at the big mirror behind the bar, where half a dozen Polaroids were taped. "You see that top one on the left? That guy handed me a cat turd. Do not be like that guy. His karma is garbage and he drinks alone."

Everyone laughed, which meant the room was suitably prepped for action.

"Anyway, we didn't used to have rules, but then Cat Turd Man happened. Now we have rules. We have rules so we can have nice things like klairvoyant karaoke," she said, using her own preferred term that never appeared on the posters because she couldn't stand to hurt Ben's feelings. "And I am your psychic psongstress," she declared, following up with Ben's phrase even though the *ps* bit kind of felt like nails on a chalkboard in the back of her head. "Start thinking of your questions and start holding up your hands."

Hands shot up all across the room, and the evening was underway.

Matt worked the crowd so Leda didn't have to keep climbing up and down off the stage, and she left the prioritizing to him. First he brought her, with a gallant kneel and a flourish, a vaccination card. It was worn around the edges. She took care to avoid reading the name, because it might only send her off in the wrong direction. Her abilities worked on the object, not its label.

"All right," she said thoughtfully. She tuned out the crowd, the lights, the rounded stage with the little portable steps pushed up against the side. Her feet felt strange. She wiggled her toes and thought of sand, warm sand, salty sand right up at the edge of the water. The water was clear and bright, and the beach was crowded around her. "Kokomo"? No. That wasn't right. Wrong sentiment. Something else. She felt longing, and embarrassment, and regret at something unsaid or untried. "Got it," she said out loud, almost without meaning to. She cleared her throat and said, "Here we go. Matt? Where are you?" She squinted over the lights.

"Right here, ma'am!" He waved from behind the karaoke rig.

"Oh, good, you're already there. Looks like we're starting with a torch song. Can you get me 'The Girl from Ipanema'?" It was not part of the fancy new rollout of hipper lyric offerings, but that's what she was getting.

Matt flashed a thumbs-up. "You're the boss!"

"Not something I hear every day," she murmured into the mic, to a few loose giggles.

The notes queued up, the song began, and the fellow who'd offered up the vaccination card smiled. Had he visited Rio lately? Had he been too shy to talk to a pretty girl? It might've been that simple, or it might have been more vastly complex. Leda didn't know and likely would never find out.

The next item was a set of dog tags, and she didn't like those. Too often, she felt too much loudness. Even if she never picked up any war imagery directly, she was always afraid that she might. This one was a little too close. Deserts and heat, a flat blue sky without any clouds. Beige and boots, and camouflage in shades of tan and army green. Deep, profound boredom. The click of metal, of weapons being checked and cleaned. And something else.

She squeezed the tags and breathed slowly, counting out her breaths. Three seconds in, three seconds out. Three repetitions. Occasionally, it helped her find her way past the obvious. "Here we go, let's see. Aw, shit, Matt, I'm sorry. It's another one that's a few years old. Get me 'Modern Crusaders' by Enigma."

An Altoids tin that had been covered in stickers. "Queer," by Garbage. An eruption of laughter and wild applause from a table by the door.

A glass doorknob from an old house. "Evermore," by Taylor Swift. A guy got up and left.

A diamond engagement ring. Not a wedding ring. Leda shouldn't have hesitated, considering. She got handed rings all the time. But the wedding ring from a dog's ass was still fresh in her head, and she didn't want to confuse the two. Three deep breaths. In and out, to the count of three.

But she confused them anyway. All she could detect was a blank expanse of whiteness, and a soft breeze, and a faint rustling that might've been trees swaying. The distant hum of a car or motorcycle engine. A snow-dusted mountain.

A dormant volcano.

A park.

9. GRADY MERRITT

SATURDAY

S am Wilco came skipping up to Grady's desk—his business Skechers squeaking across the concrete floor. Technically, there was a dress code. Technically, it was business casual in the event that he needed to speak to witnesses or suspects. Black Skechers loafers counted as business casual, but his purple Chucks did not, so they were stashed in his locker. Today, Sam's tie had cartoon sloths all over it, like he was trying to be the school's coolest math teacher.

Grady groaned preemptively. "Why? Why are you . . . happy?"

Sam slid into his chair with enough momentum to send it scooting back. "Well, I'll tell you. For one thing, the baby *almost* slept through the night. Another few weeks, and we might get a stretch of sleep that lasts longer than a commercial break."

"That's definitely worth celebrating, but that's not skipping about."

"Second," he continued as if he hadn't heard him, "that seriously great taco truck from Georgetown is out front, and the guy at the window said he'll be there until three."

Now he had Grady's attention. "Hot damn! That *is* good news."

"But that's not the best part!" Sam declared before Grady could leap from his seat in a quest for tacos and elotes. He produced a folder from inside his blazer and waved it around. He gently tossed it to Grady, who fumbled it. "The best part is, Mr. Leg has a name."

"We have long assumed as much." He flipped open the folder, scanned the paperwork within, and said, "Hot damn" again, this time more quietly. "It's him. It's Paul Reddick. Those DNA results sure came back fast. Especially with the weekend and everything." Murder did not work a nine-to-five shift, and it did not confine itself to the space between Monday mornings and Friday afternoons. Grady temporarily pushed the promise of tacos out of his mind and ran his eyes down the rest of the sheet. "Oh, that's why. *Yikes.*"

"Not really," Sam protested. "After all, he was excluded as a suspect."

Grady kept skimming for key words. A rape on the UW campus five years ago. A number of adult male faculty had voluntarily done a cheek swab. "Did they eventually catch the guy? It doesn't say here."

"Yeah, it was the brother of the girl's boyfriend or something. Bad situation all around. But it wasn't Mr. Reddick; that's the important part—and his info was still in the database, so we got it pretty fast."

"I can't complain. It's gonna mess with the jurisdiction, though."

"Maybe, maybe not. Sounds like you've already got a buddy down south. Maybe we can all play nice and share information and evidence; that's what the captain wants, and what the lieutenant has ordered. Don't assume the worst. You and me, we play well with others. I'm pretty sure it's on our personnel evaluations."

Grady sighed. "Rudy's a good guy, and I like him—but how well we play together might not be up to him. We'll have to see how it goes with his higher-ups. We might get lucky." As he spoke, an email alert popped on his computer. "Hang on, it's Rudy's boss."

"A guy with killer timing."

"You're telling me," he agreed. "And . . . what do you know, we should go buy lottery tickets!"

Sam did a preemptive fist pump. "The news is that good?"

"Good enough. According to the Pierce County guys, I've got the green light to start interviewing people here in Seattle. The Pierce County folks are starting in their own backyard, which makes sense; the crime scene is theirs, if we ever manage to find it."

"As far as we *know*, the crime scene is theirs. . . ." Sam said carefully. "The professor could've been killed somewhere else and dumped in the woods."

"Sure, but how likely is it that someone drove a couple of hours to drop off his corpse? Odds are good he was killed at the park—or someplace nearby. For that matter, since we don't know how his leg got separated from the rest of him . . . we might even be looking at more than one crime scene. But the clues to figuring out who did it and why . . . we might find *those* up here."

"I bet you already have some thoughts. I bet you've already looked up some suspects."

"Jesus, no. That's just crazy talk," Grady protested weakly. "All I have on my list is Paul's next of kin: an adult son. And all of his background and contact information."

"Then what are you doing sitting here, talking to me?"

"I was waiting for that email with the green light. I'm going to see if I can catch this guy at work and have a word with him." He stood up and pushed his chair under his desk, then shut his laptop out of habit. "Back in a bit."

"Godspeed!" Sam called with a small salute.

All the way to Columbia City, Grady swore to himself that he would *not* swing by Leda's office first. There was no question that she'd *want* to join him for a chat with Paul and Robin Reddick's son, and if he left her out of the process, he'd hear about it later; he could count on that much. Even so, it wasn't *strictly* aboveboard to bring her along. Not that it had stopped him before.

"And not that it'll stop me now," he admitted to himself.

If nothing else, he should at least see if she was in—and if she wasn't, then so much the better. He could claim that he'd tried to find her first. It wasn't as if she hadn't made herself useful in the past. Lightning could strike twice, couldn't it? They were practically working on the same case.

Again.

Fine, yes. He'd stop by her office. She'd probably be there. People travel on weekends, right? Besides, she seemed to use her office as a general hangout spot when she had nowhere else to be.

He cruised slowly from stoplight to stoplight on Rainier Avenue, checking addresses and getting the lay of the land. Most of his forays that far south were at Leda's behest. He didn't know the area well, and he used his phone to navigate when he found himself on this side of I-90. Even his usual caseload skewed farther north.

But Jeff Reddick was an apprentice mechanic at a shop that specialized in German and Japanese cars, and this shop was about three-quarters of a mile from Leda's office. If she didn't know that yet, she'd figure it out soon enough.

His gut trusted her gut more than he'd ever tell her. Or it trusted her innate nosiness, whichever. Just one more reason to pretend he'd meant to invite her all along.

Grady parked around the corner from the oddly angled strip off the main drag, because half the parking lot was blocked off for some kind of beer-tasting event—with a big tent and a radio station DJ contributing noise pollution to the proceedings. It looked like the local station KEXP running some kind of joint promotion.

He used to be a KEXP guy, but now he was older, and (if he could be persuaded to admit it) he was one of those guys who mostly listened to music he liked when he was young. He did not recognize what song was playing when he went by. He did not recognize much of the music his teenage daughter downloaded, either. He refused to be embarrassed by this. Much. Recently, the "classic rock" station had started playing Nirvana, and that really threw him for a loop.

By the time Molly moved out in a couple of years—either for college or for some gap year, however that played out—he would surely feel like an ancient mummy, unwrapped and brought to life in the twenty-first century.

The thought of Molly leaving home hit him in the feels, out of the blue. She was growing up. It was ordinary and fair, if difficult to swallow. Well, her mother wasn't here for any of it. That part wasn't fair. But what could he do about cancer? Not much. Cancer didn't know and didn't care that it was not fair. Might as well be mad about the sunrise.

He shook off the creeping ennui in favor of resignation at the thought of Leda joining him. He had work to do, and he didn't intend to do it alone.

Leda's office was at the far end of the strip, past the brewery and next to the old-fashioned arcade. On the other side of the arcade, a hookah shop. On the other side of the brewery, a nail salon. It was, as he'd remarked once or twice in the past, quite an assortment of retail offerings.

He knocked on her door, noting that she'd finally added a proper plaque that announced the office by name, and herself as proprietor. He opened it and peered around it.

"I like the new sign," he told her. "The font's a nice choice."

She was seated behind the big desk that she might've stolen out of a school, and she grinned widely at him. "Thank you, I agree! I bought the font package online for eight bucks, and I spent a week torturing Niki with each one individually. I think the winning look walks a nice line between professional and whimsical. But without the soul-wrecking ubiquity of Papyrus."

"It's the font of the damned," he agreed like he was an expert in the subject. In fact, he only knew about it because his daughter mocked it every time she saw it. Apparently, "everybody knows" it looks like a Boomer trying to dress up a MySpace page. As if Molly had ever seen a MySpace page.

"For real. Come on in, have a seat. What can I do for you? Any word on Mr. Leg?"

He did as she'd suggested, so far as coming in and taking a seat. Then he answered her question. "Mr. Leg belongs to Mr. Paul Reddick, as confirmed by DNA."

She fist-pumped at the sky. "Yes! Then it's your case after all?"

"Not exactly. The crime scene belongs to Pierce County as far as we know, but Rudy and his boss are being very laid-back about letting King County do a little legwork up here. It turns out, my otherwise missing leg-owner and your missing person have a son in common named Jeff, and he works at this end of town—in that specialty shop that does foreign cars."

"Parker Volkswagen and Subaru? I thought they just did . . . Volkswagens and Subarus."

"They'll work on just about anything, if its parent company is German or Asian. I called on the way over. Jeff is working today, and he should be back from an early lunch any minute. I'm sure I'll regret this later, but . . ."

Leda lit up. "You want me to come with you!"

"I'm *letting* you come with me. If you want to. And if you have the time." He looked around the tiny office, which was entirely unoccupied except for the two of them. "I'm guessing you have the time. I called over there, and he's working today, so . . ."

In the blink of an eye she was out of her seat and stuffing her phone into her oversize purse. She shut her laptop with a little slap and popped over her desk like a 1980s action hero sliding across the hood of a car. "Let's roll."

They rode to Parker's together in Grady's car, and in five minutes they pulled up to the shop. It had three garage doors that faced the street, and a pedestrian entrance around the corner. Inside, it smelled like old oil cans and wet rust, with a dash of damp paper for good measure. The counters were stacked with manuals for Volkswagens, BMWs, Subarus, and Toyotas. A seating area with half a dozen grease-stained faux-leather chairs boasted a coffee maker that was old enough to join AARP.

A tarnished dome bell waited beside a computer monitor. Leda walked up and smacked it gently, summoning a tall, middle-aged woman in a pair of overalls.

"Sorry to leave you waiting. What can I do for you?" she asked.

Grady showed her his badge and said, "Hello, ma'am, I'm Detective Merritt with the Seattle PD. I called earlier with regards to Jeff Reddick; is he back from lunch yet?"

"Right, I remember. Take a seat, why don't you."

Neither of them really wanted to try any of the suspicious-looking chairs, so they lurked around the lobby for a couple of minutes—until Jeff Reddick appeared in the doorway to the garage. He was on the taller side of average height, with a muscular build and light brown hair pulled back in a ponytail. His gray jumpsuit featured his name on a patch just below his left collarbone.

Grady extended his hand for a shake, and Jeff took it. "Mr. Reddick, it's good to meet you in person. I'm Grady Merritt, and this is one of our consultants, Leda Foley."

"Nice to meet you." His words were polite, but his eyes were worried. "Is this about my mom?"

"Is there . . ." The detective glanced around the lobby. ". . . someplace private we could talk?"

"Oh God. Oh no." His eyes large, Jeff retreated until his back hit the counter. He caught himself on his hands and looked back and forth between them, seeking some reassurance or hint.

Leda reached out to give his arm a friendly pat. She flinched and almost withdrew, but instead she patted him again. "Mr. Reddick? Please, let's just sit down. How about . . . Is that an office?" She pointed at a closed door beside the garage exit.

"No. It's storage. We can, um. We can go outside. There's an alley behind the garage; we smoke out there sometimes, but it's . . . it's private enough."

Grady said, "That'll work. Whatever makes you comfortable."

"It's around here, out back." Jeff led the way.

Grady whispered to Leda, "Did you get anything?"

"What?" she whispered back.

"When you touched him?"

"*Later*," she told him.

They walked around the side of the garage and found a little seating area with four plastic Adirondack chairs that faced a cold firepit. It was shady, covered by an awning that would've kept it mostly dry in the winter.

"Nice little break spot you've got here," Leda observed.

"Yeah, it's okay. Got a fan for when it's hot. Got a pit for when it's cold." He dropped himself into the nearest seat; he looked resigned, defeated, and ready to hear the worst. "I'm sorry, I don't mean to be rude, but can you please just spit it out?"

Grady and Leda took the two seats across from him. Leda didn't say anything else. It was as if she'd very suddenly realized she was quite thoroughly out of her depth.

The detective wasn't. "All right, Mr. Reddick. I'll make it quick. We don't have any news about your mother's disappearance, but we do have news of your father."

His entire demeanor shifted. Now he sat up, leaned forward. Interested, if not happy. "Good grief, what's he done now?"

Leda opened her mouth. Grady shot her a look. She shut it again and stayed immobile in her chair.

"I wish I had better news for you, but I'm afraid I don't. We found partial human remains in Mount Rainier National Park, and DNA has confirmed that they belong to your father. I'm very sorry for your loss."

Jeff Reddick slumped back into the plastic chair. His eyes went a little hard.

"Huh," he said. And nothing more.

"You don't sound surprised," Grady noted carefully. "I hate to jump right into the questions after delivering news like that—but we do have a lot of questions. Do you know what he might have been doing in the park? Did he have any business that would have taken him there? Was he an avid hiker or camper?"

"No, and I'm surprised as hell that you found him in a park," he said. Then he shook his head. "I can't imagine what he was doing there. Dad's an indoorsy kind of guy—never goes outside unless he has to. He's . . . he's really dead?"

"I'm afraid so. Despite the incomplete state of his remains, the coroner said his injuries were not survivable."

A quick, savvy flicker crossed his face. "Wait a minute. Why didn't someone call me to identify him? Isn't that how it's supposed to work? Someone has to ID him? Without Mom around, I'm his next of kin, right?"

"We were able to confirm by DNA. A few years ago, he voluntarily provided some. After an assault on the UW campus," he said, answering the last part first. "The remains were . . . not the kind you could easily attribute to an individual. Since he didn't have any tattoos or scars."

Jeff took a deep breath and followed it with a drawn-out "*Ohh.* He's the volcano foot, isn't he? That leg somebody found in the park. I saw it on the news. A dog found it, right?"

Before Grady could muster a suitable reply, Leda jumped in. "Yes, the leg belongs to your father. But you can understand why we wouldn't want to lead with that, can't you?"

Now he laughed, one low, sharp bark that sounded as bitter as cold coffee.

"Yeah, I get it. Holy shit, I'm sorry, I don't mean to be such an asshole." He leaned forward and rested his elbows on top of his knees, looking like maybe he'd throw up, or maybe he'd cry after all.

"You're not being an asshole," Grady reassured him. "And even if you were, we'd forgive you. It's a lot to absorb. When I lost my dad ten years ago—"

Jeff held up his hand and said, "No. Don't do that. You probably liked your dad, and you didn't think he was a total dick."

Grady's dad had been warm and funny, supportive, and kind to animals. Right up until the heart attack took him, six months before retirement.

"A . . . fair assessment, yes."

Jeff's face sank into a cynical frown. "How nice for you, but I don't like mine. I mean, I *didn't* like mine. And he *was* a total dick."

10. LEDA FOLEY

SATURDAY

Leda found it difficult to imagine someone handling the news of their father's death quite so easily, but here was Jeff Reddick, eyes cold and posture stiff, swearing that his father was a jerk whose permanent departure was no concern of his. Working manual labor on Saturdays must make a man hard.

"Surely your father wasn't *all* bad. . . ." she tried, hoping to steer the conversation toward useful details rather than unnecessary condolences.

"I don't know if anyone's *all* bad, but he really worked at it." Jeff crossed his arms and shook his head slowly as he spoke. "Such a selfish guy. One of those people who doesn't understand anything, and doesn't care about anything, unless it touches him personally and directly. He didn't understand and didn't care why my mother was upset and embarrassed after he got caught with a student sidepiece a few years back. He was happy to be getting what he wanted. Why should anyone else be mad?"

Leda gasped. "He did *not* tell your mother that . . . did he?"

"Directly? No. But his behavior said it loud enough. The girl from a few years ago transferred to Pacific Lutheran to get away from the drama, and he only quit driving down to Tacoma to see her when the academic dean found out about it—and threatened to have him fired. He took a year off after that. Then the next year, like clockwork, he picked one of the underclass girls, and he was off to the submarine races again."

Leda wrinkled her nose. "Gross."

"Oh yeah. The older he got, the grosser it got."

Grady's interest was piqued. He pulled out his little cop notebook and clicked a pen to ready it. "Who's this year's lucky girl—do you know?"

"Nah. I've barely spoken to him in almost a year. That's when I moved out."

"Do you live around here now?" she asked him.

"I have a place in the Angeline," he said, nodding toward the big apartment building that overlooked the core of the Columbia City neighborhood. "It's expensive, but so's everything. I'm getting paid all right. I can swing it. Just before payday I'm down to ramen noodles and Tang, but once I've finished all my certifications and joined the union, everything will be easier."

Grady followed up on his question. "So what changed a year ago? Did he kick you out of the house?"

"A big fight, yeah, but I left on my own rather than stay there under his roof. He's such a goddamn snob," he said, once again slipping from past tense to present—not yet accustomed to the fact that his father was gone. But she knew from firsthand experience that these things took time. How long had it been, after her fiancé's murder? At least six months before she consistently used the past tense to refer to him. "He told me that no son of his would work on cars and that I had to finish a four-year college degree at the bare minimum. He had this idea that I would be the next Dr. Reddick."

"Doctor of what, precisely?"

"Books of some kind," he told Grady with a snort. "Literature, English—shit, even poetry would do in a pinch. Dad kept calling it 'indoor work with no heavy lifting,' but not everybody wants that. I like working with my hands. I like cars. There's so much variety, and, and, you know what? The money's good. When all is said and done, in a few years I'll make more money than he ever did."

Grady didn't look up from his notebook when he replied, "Money isn't everything. For some people, it's not even the most important thing."

"Yes, and I'm one of those people. I only played the money angle to keep him from using it against me. After all, there's more than one kind of job prestige. You know, he brought it up the other day? When I was over at the house, trying to find out what happened to Mom. She's been missing for weeks, and all he wanted to talk about is what a loser I was going to be. News flash, Dad—having a job with my name on my shirt isn't a goddamn embarrassment, okay?"

Grady ignored that last part. "When was this recent conversation? Can you give me an exact day?"

Jeff thought about it for a minute. "It was the week before last, not this most recent one. I went over to see him in person because he was dodging my calls and emails. Mom was missing, nobody had any leads, and he acted like it was totally fine. He said he was working with the police and with local search and rescue groups, and thought that she'd turn up before long."

"Did he seem worried about her at all?" Leda asked, already guessing the answer.

"Not even a little. I figured he had another nineteen-year-old hanging around to comfort him."

"But you don't know that for sure, and if it *is* true, you don't know her name," she pressed.

"No, but I think he still had the same reader from last year. You could talk to her. She probably knows who it is."

Grady paused his scribbling. "The . . . reader? What's that?"

"Reader, TA, whatever. She has a little office beside his—it's basically a closet with a desk. She's halfway between a secretary and a personal assistant; she grades all the homework, manages his schedule, stuff like that. But I don't think she's his Flavor of the Semester. She's not his type. A little short, a little heavy. Very pale. Wears glasses. He goes for the leggy ones with tanning beds. Doesn't like tattoos or piercings. He requires a certain level of purity from the students he sleeps with."

"Ew," said Leda, since she'd already used *gross*.

"The reader's name is Helena something. I forget what. I only met her once or twice when I swung by his office . . . back when I still swung by."

"Thanks for that. We'll look her up soon." Grady slapped his notebook shut and stuffed it back into his pocket.

Leda thought that was the cue for them to pack it up and leave the poor kid to funeral arrangements, or whatever happened next when someone told you that one of your parents was dead and in pieces.

But Jeff still had questions. "While you're here, I have to ask: Have you found *any* sign of my mom yet?" Now Leda could see the real worry, the real pain, on his face. "Her car's missing, her phone is either dead or switched off, and no one has seen any trace of her in weeks. My uncle and I have been brainstorming . . . we've been asking around, calling around. Looking however we can, but we're running out of people to talk to."

"I'm sorry," Grady told him. "I checked this morning, and there's been no movement whatsoever. We've got a guy running the case, but it sounds like he's low on leads."

Jeff snorted. "The cops have been low on leads since the start. My uncle even hired a psychic. I think it's kind of stupid, but we're all pretty desperate. I doubt it'll work, but you never know."

Grady tried not to look at Leda. He really tried. But a sideways glance slipped forth regardless, and Jeff saw it.

"Wait." His eyes tightened into a squint. "What kind of consultant are you?"

No point in denying it now. "A psychic one," she confessed brightly, as if she hadn't heard the rest. Well, nobody said the professor's son was stupid. Except the professor, and apparently his opinion wasn't worth much.

Jeff sat with the information for a few seconds. "Have you talked to my uncle Dan already?"

"He came by my office, yes. He said he'd send over some of her personal belongings for me to examine, but I don't have them yet. I'm hoping he'll bring them today." Then she explained in brief how she worked, and concluded, "I really *will* do my best to help find your mom." *Especially now that your dad is dead,* she did not add out loud. Partly because it was rude. Mostly because Grady was present, and she had a feeling he'd glare a hole straight through her forehead if she tried it.

"Okay, then I will . . . choose to appreciate that and not freak out about it or call Uncle Dan an idiot. Since you seem pretty nice, actually."

"Thank you. I do what I can." Then she asked, "Do you think your mom might've finally had enough of your father's philandering? Is she the kind of woman who'd rip off the bandage and never look back?"

He struggled with an answer. "No. I don't think so. No," he said again. "She wouldn't do that to me. And before you bring it up, I already know about the landscaping money. Mom wasn't a thief, and thirty grand is barely enough to fill a gas tank with first and last month's rent left over these days."

Grady said, "That's—"

But Leda headed him off. "An exaggeration," she granted, "but I take your meaning. It's not enough to start a new life."

Jeff nodded and continued. "If my mom was finally going to take everyone's advice and pack it in, she would've said something. She might've even shown up on my doorstep to crash on the couch. That's . . . that's my final answer. She did not steal any money and hit the road alone," he concluded. "Absolutely not."

Grady offered his canned condolences once more, and they excused themselves to let Jeff get back to work, or take the day off, or whatever he felt like doing—now that he was halfway to being an orphan.

"Even if he didn't like his father, losing him is still a meaningful life experience," Leda insisted on the car ride back to her office. "Losing a parent, especially if it's someone you've known all your life—not some stranger who left when you were little or something like that—that's *hard*. Jeff really took that well, all things considered."

Grady was quiet for a few seconds, chewing on some thought of his own.

"Jeff obviously has a lot of anger to process, but I agree that it could've gone worse. I hate having to deliver that kind of news," he finished with a sigh.

"I think you did a great job. I would've screwed it up beyond measure, I am confident."

He pulled up to her office door and put the car in park to let her out. Then he said, "Hey, wait a minute. Did you flash on him back there? When you touched his arm, right after we first arrived. You flinched. What did you see?"

She'd been afraid he would ask. It wasn't that she didn't want to tell him; it was that there wasn't much to say. "Ugh, I don't even know. It wasn't so much a flash as a burp. Like a hiccup or something."

"That makes no sense at all."

"I never promised it would. It felt like, for a split second, every-thing went dark and quiet and close, and I was sitting inside a car, maybe going through a tunnel. And then it was gone. I don't have a better description than that. I'm sorry."

He frowned but shrugged. "They can't all be directions to a missing person's location."

"That's correct. I don't think it means she's dead, necessarily. Before you ask."

"I wasn't going to. . . . I guess I should have."

She opened the door and stepped out, then leaned back into the car. "All I'm saying is, the more I think about it, the more I think I was just flashing on Jeff personally—not his mom. He works on cars. In a dark garage. You know?"

"Well, let me know when you get any of Robin Reddick's ob-jects or if they tell you anything useful. If we find *her*, we might find the rest of *him*."

"Or not!" she said, cheerfully and helpfully.

"Or not," he agreed. "But I'd love to find at least one of them."

She shut the door, and he drove away.

Leda fished around in her bag, found her keys, and unlocked the office before she realized someone had left a small bag by the door. She nudged it with her foot. It didn't move and it didn't smell like dog turds. It also wasn't on fire.

"Probably not a problem. . . ." she assumed, picking it up and spotting a note that was stapled to it. She carried the little package inside and set it on her desk, then popped the staple and opened the note. It was from Dan Matarese. She read it out loud. "'Here are a few things I found. They belong to Robin, and I don't think she'd mind. She left the watch and sunglasses at my place on Memorial Day, and she found the painted rock on a sidewalk downtown.' Watches and rocks, right on. I can work with that."

She upended the bag and gently spread the contents across her desk. One delicate ladies' watch with a rose-gold band, one travel-size bottle of hand sanitizer in a green silicone holder, a pair of sunglasses in a plain black case, and a small rock that had been painted to look like a heart. "Now all I have to do is play psychic psongstress . . . without the jukebox. I can do this."

"Can you, though?"

Leda's head jerked up. "Christ on a cracker, you're quiet."

Niki stepped into the small office and flopped down onto the love seat against the wall. "Truly, I am a ninja. What you got there? Is that your client's stuff?"

"Dan Matarese, that's his name. He's a trusting soul. . . ." she said, gazing down at the assortment before her. "He left this outside by the door with a note, like a kitten in a basket."

"Cool. Is this stuff valuable?"

"I think the watch is Kate Spade, but that's not the same thing as 'valuable.'"

Niki put her feet up on the IKEA chair that faced the desk. "I'd steal it."

"No, you wouldn't."

"I'd think about it real hard," she insisted. "If nobody claimed it from the lost and found, I might pick it up and say it's mine. Have you touched any of this stuff yet? Felt it up, or whatever?"

"Not yet."

"Can I watch?"

"I don't care," Leda told her.

It wasn't perfectly true, and Niki probably knew it, but Niki was deeply curious and clearly prepared to impose on her bestie's good graces—so why fight it? She dropped her feet and slid her butt to the edge of the love seat so she could see the items better. "Okay, no, on second thought, I wouldn't steal *that* watch. I don't like rose gold."

"Good. I'm glad you're merely a potential thief and that you have exacting standards." She tried not to sound annoyed. After all, over the years Niki had watched her squeeze more random stuff than a fresh-fruit grocer. But this was one of her first *real* clients as a psychic investigator.

Is that what she was now? She supposed so. She needed a separate set of business cards, in addition to that separate rate card. What should they say? Would *psychic investigator* cover it, or should she—

"Where'd you go, Leda?"

Her attention snapped back into focus. "What?"

"You spaced out on me. What were you thinking about?"

"Rate cards," she admitted frankly. "Should they say *psychic investigating*, or *clairvoyant consulting*, or what?"

Niki said, "Ah. You're procrastinating."

"I'm doing no such thing."

"You are, just like you always do when you're confronted with a task that intimidates you."

Leda scowled. "Maybe you *shouldn't* stick around and watch."

Niki made a losing buzzer noise that turned into a fart sound. "Obviously, I *should* stick around before you invent some new and ridiculous task, one that lets you avoid your actual work. I'm here to support and assist. So I'm gonna support. And I'm gonna assist."

"Fine." Leda pushed her laptop to the side, pushed Robin Reddick's personal items forward, and glared at them each in turn. "What should I start with?"

"What looks good to you? Is there anything in particular, some material or shape that gives you a better read?"

"What? No. I don't . . . well. Maybe." He held her hand over the sunglasses, the watch, the hand sanitizer. The rock. "Sometimes crystals and rocks are a little louder."

"Louder?"

"You know what I mean."

"I don't, but I'm prepared to pretend."

With two fingers, Leda picked up the heart-shaped stone and dropped it into her left palm, where it sat heavy and cool. She closed her eyes, closed her fingers, and listened.

The coolness spread until it covered her body and made her wish for a sweater. The weight of the stone increased until her hand sank to the desktop and stopped. The stone was a black hole that wanted to drag her down to the center of the earth.

"What are you getting, Leda? Talk it out."

She did not open her eyes, but she obliged. "This will sound stupid, considering it's a cold little rock . . . but I'm getting coldness and heaviness. Much more than one heart-shaped rock ought to have."

"And it's not your imagination?"

She opened one eye and used it to glare. "No. It is *not* my imagination." She closed it again. "But I'm not sure that it's important. Still, it's . . . weird. So quiet. So heavy."

"So cold?"

"Well, cool. It's not actually cold. There's a dampness, too. And the smell of . . . something earthy. Like . . . earth."

"You're a poet, babe."

Leda sighed, opened her eyes, and put the rock down again. "It's not useful. It's just rock stuff. Heavy and dark and damp. This rock was probably under a hill or something, who knows."

"No hint of the woman who found it?"

"Nope. No hint of anything, living or dead. Just cool darkness."

Niki sat back in the love seat again. "Like a *grave*," she announced dramatically.

She couldn't rule it out. "Possibly? But I don't think so." She hesitated a few seconds and continued. "You remember a few weeks ago, that woman who gave me that brooch at klairvoyant karaoke night? It looked like an owl, had a bunch of rhinestones."

"Yeah, I remember that one. You sang 'Someday We'll Be Together' by the Supremes."

She nodded. "That one was a dud, and I knew it. The woman didn't say anything when I gave it back to her, and she left before the next song. That's because I lied to her. I lied with a song."

"What do you mean?"

"When I held the sparkly little owl, I got a real strong impression of lying very stiff, very still, in a very tight place that was very soft and comfortable. It was completely dark, and I heard music playing and smelled flowers. Carnations. I remember I smelled carnations, and I was trying to think of a song that had carnations in it, or even generic flowers. But I couldn't think of anything. I was too distracted, because here's the thing: the woman took that brooch off a dead person in a casket."

"Yikes."

"I know, right?" she mumbled. "I knew, in an instant, that the person who owned the brooch was dead. It threw me for a loop, but I'm glad I played it off okay. I must have, if you didn't notice."

"You're a pro, darling."

"Sometimes." She gave the other items a gentle push, a squeeze, and a soft bounce in her palm, one by one. "But I don't think Robin Reddick is lying in a shallow grave, or a casket, or anything else. I don't know what the rock is giving me, but it's not a confirmation of death. There's still a chance that poor Jeff isn't an orphan."

"Is that the son?"

"Uh-huh. Grady picked me up, and we went over to talk to him. Jeff lives at the Angeline and works over at the foreign auto place down the street. We broke the news to him about his father. Or Grady did. I would've only mucked it up. But next time, Nik. Next time, if I find his mom and she's no longer with us . . . What if I have to do it?"

Niki didn't have an answer for that, and Leda returned her attention to the stuff on her desk, to no avail. No sparks or visions ensued. "I'm not getting anything else right now. I need to find more stuff. Maybe I can go to her house? Find out where she worked, and go there? I don't want to turn around and immediately ask Dan for more touchable loot."

"It's worth a shot," Niki said with a shrug. "You already know that nobody else lives there. The husband is either dead or . . . or hopping around on one leg, and the son lives down the street. Ask Grady. Maybe he'll give you some personal details that Dan left out."

"He's probably not supposed to share that information." Leda collected all the things Dan had left her and put them back into their brown paper bag, along with the note. There was travel agent work to be done.

She could take an afternoon to play catch-up on emails and invoices, and try something new tomorrow.

11. GRADY MERRITT

MONDAY

Monday morning, Grady asked Sam if he wanted to ride along for a visit to Paul Reddick's office at UW, but Sam had other work to tackle—and anyway, it wasn't *his* dog who'd run off with the dead professor's leg.

"Godspeed," Sam said with a wave. "Let me know how it shakes out."

Grady gathered up his things and headed out to the northeast end of town, not terribly far away from the tightly packed neighborhood that held the Reddick home. The University of Washington was practically a city within a city, and living close to teaching and studying was a high priority for students and faculty, but it was a real estate Thunderdome out there, for renters and buyers alike.

The campus itself was a psychotic board game from a navigational standpoint, with too many cars and not enough parking, combined with too much ever-present road work and construction—

plus too many people, and not enough places to put them. Members of the homeless population camped in alleys between pizza places and boba tea shops; students and residents shopped and lunched and dodged traffic, hauled books and adjusted backpacks.

Summer sessions weren't as populous as the fall-through-spring grind, but the district was still plenty crowded, and the pedestrian lights flashed loose suggestions as people darted into the crosswalks willy-nilly.

It took Grady a few minutes to find Padelford Hall, and another minute to achieve great relief when he realized there was a parking garage immediately adjacent. He drove at a crawl through the chilly darkness inside.

Finally, he found a spot that would let his car squeeze in without a shoehorn, between a black Forester with a bike rack on top and a '90s-era VW bug painted sky blue. It still took a vertical limbo to get out without hitting the Subaru's door, and he had concerns about how he'd get his car free again—but he called it a temporary victory, hit the fob to lock the doors, and took his chances. Another ten minutes of wending through the garage, finding his way out, and successfully tracking down an entrance put him inside the big humanities center—an enormous brick fortress that looked less like an admin building than a mid-century monastery. Or a prison.

Behind him, a teacher was carrying a messenger bag and backpack overstuffed with papers up the stairs. He got the door and held it for her. "Hey, do you work here?" he asked as the door closed behind her.

"Sure do. Can I help you with something?"

"I'm looking for Paul Reddick's office. He's an English professor."

An irritated look darkened her face for the shortest of seconds. "I'm in the math department, but I know who he is." She paused to lean against the wall and let a couple of students leave past her. "His office is on the third floor. Take the elevator; you'll see signs when you get up there."

"Thanks," he told her, and she went on her way.

He followed her directions. As he exited the elevator, a board with a list of names and office numbers said he could find Paul Reddick's base of operations down the hall to the right, so he set off in that direction.

When he found Paul's door, he was somewhat surprised to find it open and the office lit up within.

He knocked gently beside the nameplate and said, "Hello?"

Someone inside sighed. "Julie, if you could just give me a minute, I swear to God . . ."

Grady gently pushed the door open and peered around it. "Not Julie. Sorry."

A petite young woman with dark curly hair and bright red glasses looked up. "Oh God, don't apologize for *not* being her. Never do that. Come in. But if you're looking for Dr. Reddick, he isn't here right now. He hasn't been here for more than a week."

"No, I'm not looking for Dr. Reddick. Well, not *here*," he clarified. "Is there any chance you're Helena?"

Her eyes went cautious, and she said, "Helena Smith. And you are?"

"Detective Grady Merritt, with the Seattle PD."

She retreated to Paul's seat, an overstuffed brown leather beast that nearly swallowed her whole. She looked very small and more than a little afraid. "What do you want with *me*?"

"Do you mind if I . . . ?" he asked, gesturing at a seat that was usually occupied by nervous students, he assumed. Or he remembered. Had it been so long since he was in college? Surely not. Then again, his daughter was a high school junior. They'd be looking at colleges for her next year. He tried not to think about it. It was relatively easy, despite the location; all he had to do was think about Paul Reddick's leg.

Helena gave him a nod, and he sat down and pulled out his notebook. "Great, thank you. As I'm sure you've noticed by now, Dr. Reddick has gone missing."

"Missing?" she exclaimed. "I thought he was just . . . taking a sabbatical or something." She was a small woman sitting in the large chair. She wore a plain black dress and gray tights, not quite corporate goth, but you could see it from there. There was a touch of Hermione about her, a sense of someone young and little and confident that she knows more than you do. About literally everything.

"Is that the kind of thing he does? Skips work for more than a week at a time without telling anyone?"

She put her hand up to her mouth. It lingered there thoughtfully for a moment, as though she'd gotten lost in thought so thoroughly that she'd missed the question. Then she caught it and said, "Not often, but once in a while. He knows I have things under control in his absence, and lately he's been so preoccupied."

"It sounds like you don't really mind being left in charge, all alone. The professor must rely on you pretty heavily."

"Sometimes," she admitted, but to which assertion Grady wasn't sure. Maybe both of them. "Like many tenured professors at his level, he doesn't do as much actual *teaching* as he used to. But honestly, I thought he was—well, I really did assume he was out looking for his wife. But you're telling me he's just . . . *gone*? Do you think they're together?"

"We have no evidence that their disappearances were related, but we haven't ruled it out, either. When's the last time you saw Dr. Reddick?"

Instantly, as if she'd been asked a dozen times already by a dozen different faculty and students, she said, "Wednesday before last, after class. He doesn't usually teach summer sessions, but this year he agreed to take one of the second-tier freshman comps as a favor to the dean. We're short on adjuncts at the moment."

"Wednesday," he muttered to himself as he scribbled it down, "before last. About what time was that?"

"Class ended at three p.m. He came back to the office and put his things away. I was next door." She pointed vaguely past the door and to the left. "My office is smaller, though, and since he's been gone, I've been teaching the class. I needed more room, so I've been working out of this one. I need access to his lesson plans, his office phone, and the syllabus notes. I already have the syllabus, obviously."

"Obviously."

"Dr. Reddick won't be mad when he gets back," she insisted, as though Grady had suggested otherwise. "He knows I need resources if I'm going to keep his classroom on track. I just wish he'd return my emails, or my calls, or . . . or anything. I've been trying to reach him ever since that Thursday morning, when he didn't show up and I had a class full of people looking at me like I should do something about it."

"What *did* you do?"

She laughed, but it was a grim and exhausted sound. "I told them that Dr. Reddick had a family emergency, and he would be missing class. Possibly for a few days. I didn't know how long he'd be gone, and I didn't want to upset anyone—and everybody knows that his wife is missing, so nobody asked too many questions."

"Nobody?"

"Everyone assumed he was taking some personal time, maybe joining the search efforts more directly. But I've been trying to reach him, for all the good it's done me. I thought about going by his house, but he . . ." A vaguely annoyed look crossed her face. "He doesn't like it when students do that."

Grady was still scrawling a note or two about a possible disappearance window over Wednesday night while she spoke. When he had those details nailed down, he said, "Hard to blame him, but you're not *just* a student, are you?"

"No, I'm not," she said, a little grouchily. She did not elaborate.

"All right, well. He must have, what? Dozens of students?"

"Something like that." He got the distinct impression that she did not like being lumped in with the rest of the academic hoi polloi. "But I teach for him all the time, and I *do* have enough credit hours to be an adjunct. Even though that's technically not my official position," she said defensively.

He started to ask her about her own class schedule, but something was pinging in the back of his head.

"If you have enough credits to be an adjunct . . . wouldn't it look better on an academic CV to have the regular teaching experience, instead of just the administrative experience?"

She stiffened. "Dr. Reddick's recommendation as a reference will *more* than make up the difference."

He looked her up and down, made a guess, and put it out there. "You've been his aide for a while now, haven't you?"

"This is my third year."

"Third? How long do you plan to stay in graduate school? Don't those programs usually run about two or three years?"

"I'm doing a guided study, and I'm taking it slowly. It's easier that way, since I'm also Dr. Reddick's assistant, and it's . . . more work than you'd think. At my present pace, I have at least another year, and yes—I'll stick with Dr. Reddick, if he'll have me. I've proven myself time and time again, and he's never had a better reader—he said so himself. He'll take care of me when graduation comes around. I'll probably stay for a postgraduate program, so I'll still be around campus."

"You must really enjoy the guy's company."

Her face blanched white, then flushed pink. "He's a brilliant man, and I respect him tremendously. But we don't actually spend that much time together; it's mostly working in adjacent offices, ships passing in the night, and all that. But he's an excellent boss. Gives me plenty of autonomy and direction, without being too controlling. He doesn't watch my every move, doesn't micromanage. That kind of thing."

"Uh-huh." In his notebook, he scrawled beneath her name, *Unhealthy fixation on the doc. Not one of his chosen girls, but wants to be.*

As if she could read his chicken-scratch handwriting upside down and through the notebook, she said, "I don't know what you've heard, but it's not like that. Whatever it is."

He looked up from the notebook. He tucked it a little closer to his chest, just in case. "Oh? Then what's it like?"

"I know what people say about him," she sulked. "It's unfair and very cruel."

"Is it untrue?"

The question flustered her, but only slightly. "Which part?"

"You tell me. I'm not even sure what we're talking about." He held eye contact with her, his pen hovering over the notebook he held in his other hand.

Now her face locked down hard. She asked, her question dripping with suspicion: "Has something happened to Dr. Reddick? Do you know where he is? Is he all right? Is that why you're here?"

He let her dodge his original query, for the moment. "Paul Reddick hasn't been seen by anyone since, well, roughly since last you saw him. We're trying to determine if his absence is related to his wife's disappearance. All I want to do is find everyone safe and sound. I'm not here to hassle you, you understand?"

She didn't soften so much as crack. For a moment, Grady thought she might start crying, but she didn't. "I'm sorry, I don't mean to be a pain—I'm just so *stressed* right now, you have no idea.

I can teach, but I'm not a teacher. Not a very good one, if you read the student evaluations," she confessed. More strongly, she added, "And that's *fine*. I don't want to teach. I want to go into research and theory, like Dr. Reddick. I'm not really very good with . . . people," she concluded.

He tried to reassure her. "You're doing great, under difficult circumstances. I'm not here to wreck your day; I'm trying to help."

"Everybody's trying to help, I know. It's just so strange. Mrs. Reddick has been gone for at least a couple of weeks now, and . . ."

When she paused, perhaps calculating a more precise estimate or deciding what to say next, he interjected, "More like a month."

"I'm sorry? What? That can't be right. They've only been doing the search and rescue flights for a couple of weeks."

"I hate to break it to you, but Dr. Reddick wasn't overly concerned about his wife, and she wasn't reported missing until her son and her brother started beating the bushes. She's been off the grid for more like a month."

"Huh," she said, eyes wide behind the thick lenses and chic frames. She was really quite cute—pretty and a little soft, with good skin and a skilled hand at makeup. But no, not the kind of girl a philandering professor would choose, if he liked leggy blondes. "That's . . . weird."

"While I'm here, when's the last time you saw Robin Reddick?"

"Her? Oh, I've only ever met her a handful of times. I think last time I saw her was the Christmas party last December. Have your people circled back around with Julie and Carson? They're trying to help—organizing search parties and the aerial sweeps."

"Julie and Carson?" he asked, making fast note of the names. "Who are they?"

"The Colemans. Julie is a student here, and Carson is her older brother. He's a firefighter, but he has a small Cessna and a pilot's license, so he and his sister have been running search and rescue scans for signs of Mrs. Reddick, trying to help out. Or they're looking for her car, to be more precise."

He flipped back in his notebook, scanned a page, and said, "Bright orange Volvo?"

"Bright orange Volvo from the late seventies. Hard to believe it still runs, but she likes it. Dr. Reddick says she drives it just to embarrass him, but on the upside it's pretty easy to pick out of a parking lot. I honestly can't believe nobody's found it yet. Have you checked her son's garage? He's a mechanic or something. Maybe he was working on it. Maybe Dr. Reddick didn't know and that's why he didn't tell us."

"That's a lot of maybes."

She flipped her hand dismissively. "All I have are maybes, sir. I'm just trying to . . . to make some connections here."

"You and me both. What about Julie?"

"What about her?" she asked, visibly peeved by the question.

"Is the search and rescue Julie the same one you mistook me for when I knocked?"

"Yeah," she confessed. "She's . . . a student. She's been swinging by fifty times a day, asking for Dr. Reddick. She's the one who badgered her brother into taking up the case of the missing professor's wife, expanding the search from land and sea to air."

"You make it sound like a Hardy Boys story, but that certainly does sound helpful. Are they a rich pair of siblings? If the guy has his own plane, maybe they have money?"

"I don't know, but little planes like his aren't as expensive as people think. You can buy one cheaper than a used car. He uses it to go smoke-spotting on the peninsula, or so I'm told."

"All right, well. You've been very helpful. Is there any chance you can get me contact information for these Coleman siblings?"

She pushed the big brown chair back from the desk and left it for a file cabinet beside a small personal refrigerator. "Give me a second. I've got Julie's info somewhere."

When Grady had gotten not only an email address but a phone number and an apartment listing, he thanked Helena for her time and assistance, gave her a card with his cell phone number, and headed back to the precinct. He'd burned too much of his day on the quest to follow up further.

King County had suspicious deaths, too, and Pierce County's would have to wait.

12. LEDA FOLEY

MONDAY

Leda sat at her favorite tiny table in Castaways, poring over the new karaoke catalog. It was only four in the afternoon—far too early for a psychic psongstress event—and the place was mostly dead. Leda was mostly glad. She had spent the day so far batting cleanup on her travel agent duties, and now a bachelorette party was on the way to Hawaii via upgraded airline seats, two old gentleman widowers were taking a cruise down the coast together on a tall ship with a great pool, and a convention in Bellingham had made arrangements for three guests coming in for "a weekend of praise and worship" at some megachurch conference.

All in all, a productive day.

Now it was chill time while she waited for Niki to get off work. Niki worked at the Smith Tower Observatory bar. She described it as "pricier drinks and a better view, but more annoying clientele." Sometimes Leda teased her about spending her days bouncing from one bar to the other, but Niki never cared. She went where she earned money, or where she found friends. Mostly, that meant she'd worn a groove between the tower bar and Castaways.

But today she didn't get off work until five. She'd taken a shift to help a coworker, and that meant that Leda was on her own, except for the usual suspects.

Tiffany was behind the bar, slinging drinks and soothing the handful of early birds while wearing a black-and-green Betsey Johnson dress and a glorious green fascinator pinned in her hair. Steve the bouncer was sitting just inside the door, playing games on his phone and texting with a woman he'd met online the week before. Matt was taking inventory with the liquor delivery guy, going down a checklist that started with absinthe and ended with whiskey.

Ben wasn't around yet. He'd probably roll up closer to 8:00 p.m., when the night crowd started to wander in.

The new catalog was a pleasant break, one that Leda appreciated for all its fiddly mundaneness. Now she had a whole world of newer Taylor Swift songs, more Lady Gaga, and nineties boy-band stuff that she hoped she'd never have any reason to use. She also noticed a healthier country music selection (less bro country, more angry-lady country, which Leda could get behind), as well as some hip-hop hits that she wasn't terribly familiar with. "Not for pasty white ladies with questionable diction," she said aloud as she flipped to the next section.

"What's not for pasty white ladies?"

She jumped, smacking the book shut out of reflex or confusion. "What?" she asked, a quick and meaningless snap.

Jeff Reddick stood beside the table, hands fiddling nervously with a cotton zip pouch.

"Oh my gosh, it's you. I'm sorry. You surprised me, that's all."

"It's okay. I didn't mean to sneak up on you. Or interrupt, either."

"No! It's fine, please. Pull up a chair. I know there's not much room, but you're welcome to join me."

He looked both relieved and anxious when he took her up on the offer, dragging a chair to the far side of the small round table-top with the big paper catalog dangling off the edges. "I hope you don't mind that I looked you up. I'm not trying to stalk you—you're just easy to find."

"Stalkers don't announce themselves so politely. It's fine, I promise. Welcome to Castaways," she said, hoping it sounded friendly. He looked like a kid who needed a hug or a drink. She didn't know him well enough to hug him, and he was eyeing Tiffany . . . but lots of guys eyed Tiffany, whether they were that kind of thirsty or not.

"Maybe I should . . ." he began to say.

"Tiff!" Leda hollered past him. "Have you sorted out the special yet?"

"Are you brave enough to be a test subject?" she yelled back.

Leda grinned at Jeff. "Are you an adventurous drinker?"

"Sure?"

"Because I need for you to understand that whatever she brings us, it might be the best thing you've ever tasted, or it might be . . . regrettable."

Slowly, he mirrored her smile. "Yeah, that sounds good." Louder, so Tiffany could hear him, he called, "Two test subjects, reporting for duty!"

Soon enough, Tiffany swept up to the table with a round tray and a wicked grin. "Here you go, you two. One for everybody's favorite psychic psongstress . . ." she said as she set Leda's drink down in front of her. "And . . . one for a random dude who feels like taking chances." She winked.

The drinks were served in lowball glasses. The liquid was tantalizingly rich and red, and it sloshed around on the rocks with a lemon peel garnish.

"It's Jeff. I'm Jeff."

Tiffany said, "Hello, Jeff. Don't give me any stink-eye, either one of you. They're not poisoned, and they're not gross. They're barely even experimental."

Jeff asked, "You gonna tell us what it is first?"

"Usually, I do not, because that's half the fun. But since you're new here, and you're taking chances, and your name is Jeff and all . . . I'll indulge you." She cleared her throat dramatically, stood up straight, and held the tray flat against her chest like a shield. "This is a deconstructed vodka cran. I've brightened it up with a little sweet seltzer, a spritz of lemon, and a little garnish. It's not complicated, and it's not gonna kill you."

Jeff took the glass and lifted it up. "It looks delicious!"

"*Suspiciously* delicious," Leda said warily, but she took her glass, too, and clinked it against Jeff's. "Here's to trying new things, eh?"

"To trying new things," he agreed.

They simultaneously sipped.

"You know what? It's nice," Leda declared. It's a good summer drink. Not very strong, though, is it? You've been making them a little more . . . gentle, lately."

A wicked smile spread across Tiffany's face. "Yeah. It's, um . . . not very strong. That's the ticket." She cackled all the way back to the bar.

When she was gone, Leda told Jeff, "Well, I've been wrong before. This drink's pretty good, though. No regrets!"

"She didn't check my ID. . . ." Jeff noted, and he took another sip.

"You showed it to Steve at the door, didn't you? Anyway, you're with me. She trusts me. I don't know why, since I have literally no idea how old you are."

"I'm twenty-two," he told her, but for all Leda knew he could've been lying. He was more baby-faced than any adult man she'd ever met in her life, and the ponytail didn't help him look any older.

But she didn't push it. "Free and clear, then. So why'd you come all this way to track me down?"

He blushed very slightly. She could hardly see it in the semidark bar space, despite the daylight pouring in from the front windows. "After you and that detective came by the shop, I called my uncle Dan to talk about what happened to Dad. Me and him are pretty close. Closer than me and my dad, for sure."

She didn't know why it startled her. "Oh, right. Dan must not have known about your father's passing."

"I figured he'd want to know, not that he was real broken up about it," he said with a feeble chuckle. "He didn't like my dad too much. I think they might've been friends a long time ago? But once Dad started running around on Mom, that was the end of it. Uncle Dan has always been real protective of his sisters. They used to have another one, but she died a long time ago—before I was born."

"Oh no, I'm sorry. But it makes sense that he'd really look out for his remaining siblings."

"Yeah. It was nice to talk to my uncle, even if it was a weird conversation—like, we shouldn't have done so much laughing, maybe? But it felt good all the same. I didn't *hate* my dad," he said, changing tracks. "I didn't *want* him to die. I feel bad about what I told you, at the shop. I was surprised and mad, that's why I said it. Now I'm kind of sad."

Leda put down her drink and placed her hand over his. "Sweetheart. That's totally normal. Complicated feelings will stick around for quite some time, and it's all right if some of them aren't good. We're all just humans here, mucking it up as we go along."

"Thanks. I appreciate that." He retrieved his hand, and at first Leda was afraid she'd been overly familiar—but he used it to reach down into his lap and retrieve the zippered pouch he'd been holding when he approached her.

She picked up the karaoke catalog and set it on the floor by her feet to free up valuable table space.

He set the pouch beside his glass. He unzipped it and dumped out its contents: a small square locket, a points card from an arcade downtown, a small pair of nail scissors, and a tiny plastic container that looked like it had once held an old roll of film. "I drove by my parents' place after me and Uncle Dan talked, and I let myself inside. It didn't look like anyone had been there for at least a week or two, so I did a little cleaning; there was food rotting in the kitchen sink and everything." He paused to make a face. "While I was there, I'm not saying I *ransacked* the place, but I did some digging around. Uncle Dan said that you weren't having much luck with the stuff he left at your office."

Careful not to touch any of the items—not yet—Leda leaned forward and hovered over the assortment. "I felt terrible about that. I sent him an email yesterday, asking a couple of questions and fishing around for more information, if I'm honest. I got virtually nothing from what he gave me, and what I got, I didn't understand. It was useless to me, and probably not relevant to your mom's disappearance."

"Probably?"

She nodded. "This is not an exact science."

"That's what Uncle Dan said."

"I wish I'd known you were coming," she mused. "I would've brought the stuff Dan sent me, so you could give it back to him. But we're already planning to meet again for a catch-up session, so. No big deal, I guess."

"It's fine. He's not in a rush." Jeff poked at the little things, shuffling them around on the table while he spoke. "So . . . the locket here belonged to my aunt Debbie, the one who died of cancer when she was a teenager. My mom always kept it hanging beside her dresser mirror on a little hook. The card is from when she used to do these video game tournaments for charity downtown. She hasn't played in years, but she always enjoyed those contests. The scissors here, they're . . . um . . ."

"They're baby scissors, aren't they?"

"Yeah!" he warmed up a bit. "That's why they're shaped like a stork. Mom used these on me when I was a newborn, fresh from the hospital. She decided that my fingernails were too long, and she was going to cut them, but she nicked my hand and had a meltdown because I bled everywhere." His smile looked genuine this time. "And this thing, this little capsule, these are my two front teeth."

"Oh no."

"They're not gross or anything!" he protested quickly. "They're really old, and they're clean. They got knocked out when I was learning how to ride a bike. Mom was pushing me along, helping me balance, and the neighbor's cat ran across the sidewalk. I wiped out. Hit my face on the curb, knocked out three teeth altogether."

"Three?"

"Yeah, I swallowed one. Or that's what they tell me, since we never found it. I realize," he said, his tone shifting to something more worried and serious, "that these things might say more about me and my uncle, or my dead aunt, than they do about my mom. But they were important to my mom, and I thought . . . I hoped . . . you could see something of her when you held them."

"It's worth a shot," she told him, then she used the back of her hand to slide the items closer. Usually, a simple tap wouldn't give her anything, so it didn't upset or confuse her that she was not zapped by any shocking revelations while she arranged the pieces before her.

"Do you want me to leave or anything?"

She gave him a small wave of *don't worry about it.*

"That's not necessary. I don't even need quiet. If it's going to work, it'll work no matter where we are or what's going on."

"That's pretty wild." He looked like he badly wanted to ask follow-up questions, but he was both too polite and too interested in watching to do so.

She started with the plastic container of teeth. She popped it open and spilled the teeth on the table, and Jeff was right: they weren't especially gross. They looked like two little pebbles. "Aw, they're kind of cute."

"Right? I didn't think so for a long time, but now I see why she kept them."

Leda picked up both tiny teeth and held them in her palm. She added the little canister for good measure, and held them, and let them sit on her skin, and she listened as hard as she could. A spark. A tiny one. Rough and distant. The texture of concrete. No great mystery there. What else? A birthday candle, blown out on top of a white cake with blue trim frosting. The taste of lip balm.

She put the teeth back into their carrying case and gave it back to Jeff. "I'm seeing a few things, but they're all pretty clearly about you, not her. And that's okay!" she reassured him.

"Right, right," he tried to agree. "It means your powers still work, if nothing else."

"Indeed, though if they didn't, then Psychic Psongstress Night would be dead in the water—and Ben would cry his eyes out. So let's try the scissors." More kid stuff. Baby stuff, even. A nursery with gray elephants and blue birds. But something else. A pang—something hard and awful. "Guilt," she concluded.

"Guilt?"

"Your mom, cutting your finger. It doesn't feel more complex than that, and the sensation is pretty old. Okay, last item, let's go." The locket was small—barely bigger than her thumbnail—and when she opened it, she found a tiny picture of a girl's face. It looked like it came from a photo booth at a mall, back when those things were still a thing.

This was different. Leda closed her fist around it, loosely but firmly.

"Here we go. . . ." she said slowly. She shut her eyes, since that sometimes helped, but she kept talking because this felt more important than the faint blips from the baby things. "This is definitely about your mom and your late aunt. The picture was taken in a photo booth, and your mother used to be in it—but the locket is too little for both of their faces, so she cut out hers and chose her sister's." That last part was a good guess, gleaned from a slight seam between the photo and the edge of the window, and a hint of someone else's shoulder just in frame. She sensed a moment over a casket, with a body that was barely recognizable, it'd been so withered by chemo and illness. A split-second decision not to toss the locket inside. "Your mother . . . wanted it," Leda said carefully. "This locket, this souvenir, however you want to think of it. At some point fairly recently, she wanted it very badly, and wished she could hold it."

"Recently?"

"For a relative value of these things. Within the last couple of months, I'd say, but that's a guess. There's a powerful pull to it— and I think the pull is your mother, wishing she'd carried it with her."

"Carried it *where*?" he desperately wanted to know.

That was a trickier question. "Someplace dark. But not tight," she specified quickly. "Not like a coffin or a grave. More like a small room with the lights out. Someplace quiet, but not silent." She could hear something in the distance. Was it running water? People talking? "There's a sound I can't place; I don't think she could hear it well, either."

"Is that where she is right now?" he asked eagerly. "Do you have any way of homing in on her? Should I call that guy with that plane?"

Leda opened her eyes. "What guy with what plane?"

"Carson Coleman. His sister Julie is one of Dad's students. They've been doing volunteer search and rescue flights around the Sound, looking for Mom's car. It's . . . well, it's more visible from the air than she is, I guess."

"A student, you say?" she asked, not bothering to hide the note of suspicion.

"I haven't met her," he said. "I met her brother, though—just once, when he first started doing the search flights. He's all right. He's a firefighter with his own plane. He uses it to scout for smoke in the Olympics, but sometimes he goes looking for people, too; his sister Julie roped him into looking for Mom in his downtime."

She made a mental note of the names. "Hm. That sound I hear when I hold the locket . . . it *could* be a plane engine, maybe. A small one. Maybe?"

His eyes lit up, but they lit up cautiously. "Does Mom know we're looking for her?"

"I have no idea." She listened some more but heard nothing else. "Jeff, can I hang on to this one? Just overnight. I'll give it back to your uncle tomorrow, when we talk. I want to spend some more time with it."

"You're definitely getting something, though, right?"

"Oh, definitely," she confirmed. "Maybe with a little extra time, I can refine the vision, or . . . I'm sorry, I don't really have any vocabulary for this kind of thing, even after all this time."

"No, I understand," he assured her. He gathered up the other little things, back into their zippered pouch that looked vaguely like a makeup bag.

They shook hands, exchanged contact information, and Jeff left Castaways.

Leda tucked the locket into her purse and pulled the karaoke catalog back onto the table—but it was no use. Her concentration for song-picking had gone out the window. She needed a break. Or maybe—she pulled her phone out of her bag—she needed *help*.

Hastily, and with her thumbs, she typed out an email to a woman she'd met the year before, in the wake of her first big case with Grady. Avalon Harris had offered her services as a friend and professional mentor in the field of all things paranormal.

Maybe it was time to take her up on it.

13. GRADY MERRITT

TUESDAY

Grady had planned to swing by Julie Coleman's University District apartment for a word about Robin Reddick first thing Tuesday morning, but a better opportunity presented itself.

Julie and Carson are holding a meetup at Renton Municipal, read Helena Smith's text. **Today at noon.**

He replied, **What kind of meetup?**

Going over search plans, expanding the scope. Also looking for Dr. Reddick now.

He ought to skip it. He ought to reach out to Rudy and give him an update. In truth, he was falling behind on his other work because the whole nothing-left-of-him-but-a-leg angle was so much more interesting than the rest of his casework.

Sam was taking a personal day. His kid was teething, and he hadn't slept worth a damn in months. The long weekend would do him good.

Grady tapped one foot against the leg of his desk while he considered his options. Well, Renton was only a bit farther south than Columbia City; he could always see if Leda was down to accompany him. Maybe she could be helpful to the Coleman siblings, or maybe they could be helpful to her.

It was worth a shot.

She picked up on the second ring. "Any exciting news for me?"

"Hello to you, too."

"Hello, Grady. Do you have any exciting news for me?"

He grinned and settled back into his chair. "Yes and no. More like an investigative opportunity, down close to your neck of the woods. You want to come along for the ride?"

"Yes!" she said brightly. "When?"

"Today. Noon in Renton. I'll pick you up on the way."

"Excellent. See you soon."

"Soon" was an hour later, and Leda wasn't alone when Grady got to her office. Niki Nelson was camped out on the love seat, where her butt had left an impression as distinctive as a fingerprint.

"Good morning, Detective," she greeted him. "I hear we're going on a field trip!"

He sighed.

"Yes, I suppose 'we' are. Leda, you didn't mention you had company."

"You didn't ask!" She swept her bag up onto her shoulder and shut her laptop. "Come on, let's saddle up! Give us all the details on the way."

They piled into Grady's Toyota. Leda took shotgun.

Niki treated the back seat like a chaise. "All right," she declared as they pulled out onto the main drag. "What's the scoop? Where are we going? Who are we talking to? What are the stakes?"

"We are going to Renton Municipal, where some of Dr. Reddick's students are coordinating a search party."

Leda frowned. "Why are they having this meetup at the airport? Does this have something to do with the firefighter Jeff told me about?"

"I assume so," he said. Then, for Niki's sake, he added, "Teacher's likely pet has a firefighter brother, and he's been using his smoke-spotting plane to help. They started out looking for Robin, but yesterday I told Paul Reddick's assistant that he might not be coming into work anytime soon."

"You told her he was dead?" Niki asked.

"No, but I admitted that he hadn't been seen since last week. I'm not sure why I held back, but she isn't immediate family—and for all we know, she's involved in this mess. Sometimes it's better to keep your mouth shut and watch to see what happens. Of course, there's always a chance she's lying. She might have other reasons for staying quiet about his absence."

Leda agreed that this was wise, even if shutting up was never her strongest skill set.

"But she's bound to find out eventually, isn't she?"

"Eventually, yes—the identity of the leg will become public information; I don't know when, because we try to inform all the next of kin first. Jeff knows, and Dan knows, but since this is only tangentially my case . . . let's keep Dr. Reddick's death to ourselves for the moment. Niki," he said, his eyes on the rearview mirror so he could see her in a glimpse. "You can pose as a volunteer wanting to help with the search effort."

"Noooo . . . I want to be a forensic consultant again, like last year. That was sexier."

"If you want to come along, I need you to blend in—not stand out. Volunteer, or stay home."

She sighed, then rallied. "All right, I'm a volunteer. It's simple, it's elegant, it's easy to remember. I'll fade into the background, as requested."

"Attagirl." Grady returned his attention to the road ahead. "Leda, I've already introduced you around as a consultant. Jeff and Dan obviously know what you're up to, so I'm just going to run with *consultant* again. Please, please, *please* let me take the lead with the questions. I'm begging you."

"Don't be ridiculous. You're the official investigator. I am merely present in a supporting role."

"An opportunistic role."

"*You* invited me." Leda stuffed her bag down by her feet and kicked it to the side.

"I'm mostly joking. Now tell me how you knew about Carson Coleman and his plane?"

Leda explained that Jeff had come by Castaways the afternoon before. When she'd finished with the high-level overview, she added, "I got the weirdest vibe off that locket. It gave me a dark, enclosed place—and Robin wishing with all her heart that she was holding it."

"Why wasn't she wearing it?" Niki asked from the back seat.

"Jeff said she always left it hanging on her vanity table mirror. Their sister died when she was a teenager, and it's just a tiny memorial—not something she carried every day."

Grady made his *hm* noise. "What kind of a dark, enclosed place? Can you be more precise?"

"Lordy, don't I wish," she grumbled. "All I can tell you is that it was bigger than a coffin, since that's the obvious question. It feels more like a small room. Like she's locked in a closet or something. All I got was darkness, coolness, and a burning desire for that little locket. I have no idea what it means."

Grady made another *hm* and kept driving.

Fifteen minutes later, they pulled up to Renton Municipal. King County had an assortment of airfields, both locally private and internationally public; this little landing spot occupied a space adjacent to the Boeing plant, but it was also used by small, private operators. Even so, there were a dozen mostly finished big planes parked along the edges, with sheets of green and blue film covering assorted exterior parts with a protective patch-work.

Grady also saw a few delivery planes, and a couple of smaller carriers opened up for maintenance. Then, on the southwest corner of the field, he spied an older Cessna and a small crowd of college-aged people.

He found a place to park, then he and the two women climbed out of his car and walked over to join the small crowd. A blonde he immediately clocked as Julie Coleman was midspeech when they arrived.

"According to the manager at the landscaping company, Mrs. Reddick was working on a corporate strip mall project—about halfway between here and the mall at Southcenter. There's a lot of woods, a lot of water, and a thousand grassy lots to comb through, and we don't know if she was abducted or if she simply got lost and wandered away," she declared to the assembled volunteers. Julie was tall, perhaps five foot ten, with shoulder-length wheat-colored hair and a cropped shirt that showed a bronzed strip of stomach just above her low-rise jeans. "Truly, the nineties are upon us," Grady muttered.

Niki snorted. "It wasn't the *worst* decade for clothes."

"You come on," he countered. "What were you, in kindergarten in the nineties?"

"Technically, yes. My memories are blurry, but I recall a time of big bangs and belly rings."

"Sounds about right. There were also a few mullets hanging around, left over from the eighties—but what can you do," he mused.

Leda shook her head. "Sometimes I forget you're an old."

"An old? Like, a singular old? I can't have more than a dozen years on you."

Now she cocked her head at him. "I don't know. How old are you, anyway? When's your birthday?"

Not the smartest time to play stupid, but he did it anyway. "Birthday? What? Who cares?"

"I don't care, but I'm curious. Just tell me."

"No. I hate birthdays."

"You're a sad, sad man," she concluded.

"A sad man who doesn't like birthdays. Let it go, Leda."

"I'll let it go when you tell me. Maybe I'll pick your pocket when you're not looking and get a glance at your driver's license."

"I'd like to see you try."

Her eyes narrowed. "You will never see me coming."

Niki elbowed her. "Shh, you two. Knock it off. I'm trying to listen."

Julie's brother joined the announcement. "Rich and Tashina, you two have planes, and you're going to pick spotters." Several hands shot up in the crowd. "Spotters, you'll need a camera with a good zoom lens and a map." He was an inch or two taller than his sister, with darker hair and the farmer's tan of a man who spends a lot of time outside.

"He looks like a romance novel hero," Leda said with a touch of awe.

Niki did not argue. "Something something firemen, something something dramatic rescue . . ."

"Yeah. Like *that*. The romance is called, like, *Burned by Love*."

"*Hot and Heavy*."

Without taking her eyes off him, Leda proposed, "*Let Me Show You My Enormous Hose*."

Grady rolled his eyes. "Ladies. Please. Focus on the issue at hand."

Now Carson was passing out paperwork, flight plans, and instructions for keeping a search grid coordinated between a handful of folks in planes and cars. "There's a construction site adjacent to the landscaping project, and we think there's a chance she might have gotten hurt or trapped. We have a separate team of six volunteers on the ground taking that lot, don't we? It's twenty thousand feet of space with waist-high grass across half of it. Who's got their search poles?" More hands went up.

"He's so authoritative," Leda said with entirely too much impressed delight.

Niki said, "*Smokin' Hot*. That's another good title."

"*Charbroiled by Desire*."

"Would you two knock it off? He's young enough to be your . . . your little brother," Grady settled for.

Niki said, "I bet he meets the minimum dating age coefficient." When he flashed her a look that said he wasn't sure what she meant, she said, "You know. Half your age plus seven. Keep it safe, keep it legal, that's what I say. I'm thirty-seven, so. Let's say eighteen plus seven. Twenty-five. If that spicy fire bro is twenty-five, then I'm not a pervert."

"He looks about twenty-five . . . ?" Leda guessed. "Close enough."

"You're both horrible people," he told them.

"And you're no fun at all," Leda said with a beaming smile. "You won't even tell us your birthday."

"No. I will not. And please stop with the romance novels."

Niki said, "Fine, I guess I'll go join the other volunteers. You two hang tight and I'll report back."

"That works for me," Grady said with a heavy note of relief. "Just remember, I'm counting on you two to act like *adults*." He was staring at the Colemans when he said it. "But okay, you're not wrong about those two; they definitely won the genetic lottery. Christ, I wonder what their parents look like."

Julie gave everyone a quick reminder about calling her directly if they spotted any clues or found Robin's distinctive orange Volvo. Then she offered a final word about her professor. "As some of you know," she began, her voice loud and melodious over the hum of small-engine planes coming and going, "Dr. Reddick has also gone missing. We aren't sure when he disappeared exactly, but no one has seen him since the Wednesday before last. I realize that the odds are low we'll find any sign of him, but if anyone sees any indication of Paul Reddick while you're out there looking for Robin Reddick, *please* reach out to the authorities as soon as possible. He drives a black Subaru Forester with a bike rack. There are probably a thousand of those in King County, but keep your eyes open anyway."

Her brother put an arm around her shoulder and squeezed it.

Grady delivered one of his patented *hm* sounds.

Leda elbowed him gently. "What?" she whispered.

"That rings a bell. Hang on." He pulled out his phone and fired off a text message to Sam. **Do we have Paul's car yet? Because I have an idea. Check the parking garage outside Padelford Hall, second level, northeast corner. Black Subaru Forester with a bike rack.**

Julie wiped at her eyes and said, "He's been so important to us all, and I think today's crowd of volunteers really makes that clear." She sniffled loudly, and her brother released her to dig in his pocket for a tissue.

Grady, Leda, and Niki all exchanged knowing looks.

He returned his eyes to Julie and leaned over to whisper at Leda. "Welp, I think it's safe to say we found Dr. Reddick's chosen girl."

14. LEDA FOLEY

TUESDAY

When the bright-eyed volunteers had scattered in their prescribed directions, only Julie and Carson remained beside the old Cessna, talking quietly. The plane had the kind of paint job that was probably white, once upon a time, and now was mostly gray—with the kind of scuffs that suggested it'd been knocked against the hangar doors a time or two, or ten. It looked like a grasshopper and a Smartcar had a baby, then someone pushed that baby down the stairs.

Grady was on the approach. Leda hustled to keep up with him.

"Excuse me," Grady said, by way of interrupting a quiet conversation between the siblings. "Hello, I beg your pardon. You two must be the Colemans." He pulled out his ID and flashed it long enough for them to get a good look at his name, rank, and occupation. "I was wondering if I could ask you a few questions."

Carson got ahead of him. "Whoa there, sir—our flight plans are fully approved, and your department signed off on letting us do some looking of our own."

"We have a lot of departments," he told them. "But that's not what this is about. I know you're aboveboard here—and I wouldn't stop you if I could. I hope you're reporting your search grids and covered territory with the SPD."

Julie nodded, her shiny hair swishing in the breeze. It was held away from her face by a pair of designer sunglasses that sat atop her head like a crown. "Of course we are. We've been in touch with Officer Garcia almost every day, keeping him abreast of what we're up to."

"Garcia? Jack Garcia's the one on Robin's case? That's good to hear. Anyway, I'm Grady Merritt, and this is Leda Foley—a consultant with the SPD. How did you find out that Dr. Reddick was missing?"

Julie rolled her eyes. "I was putting up flyers about the volunteer roundup yesterday afternoon, and his reader came over to fuss at me because I wasn't using painter's tape. God forbid they should actually use that stuff for its intended purpose and *paint* the damn place every now and again." She pulled her sunglasses down over her eyes, unleashing that lovely hair. "Helena said the cops came by and told her that Dr. Reddick is missing, too."

Her brother's phone rang. He pulled it out of his pocket and excused himself, stepping away a few feet and saying, "Hello?"

Grady asked Julie, "When's the last time you saw him?"

"The Wednesday before last, same as everybody else, I guess. He was still in his office when I went by that evening, around nine o'clock. I forgot to grab the homework assignment, but he leaves extras in a manila envelope hanging off the back of his door."

Leda jumped in with both feet. "Did he seem distressed? Upset? Scared?"

"God, no. He was completely fine. He was packing up to head home for the night, so we didn't talk long or anything."

"But you *did* talk," she pushed. "What did he say?"

She shrugged prettily, and Leda hated her just a little bit. Or possibly more than that, for no real reason whatsoever. "I don't remember exactly, but it couldn't have been more than a few words and a friendly wave. Something like 'Hello, did you forget something?' and I probably said, 'I spaced on the homework, sorry.' Then I took the sheet and left."

"I don't suppose you have any ideas about where he went, or why." Grady had his handy-dandy cop notebook at the ready.

"Who knows? I just hope he's all right, wherever he is. Whatever he's doing."

Her brother came back to the circle, tucking his phone into the back pocket of his jeans, into which he had been vacuum-sealed. "Sorry about that." A breeze kicked up, tousling his hair. He swept it away from his face. If it'd happened in slow motion, it would've looked like a cologne commercial.

"No problem," Leda told him, just a touch too warmly. "Your sister was just telling us about the last time she saw Dr. Reddick."

Grady said, "We're trying to nail down a precise window of time when he might have disappeared. At the moment, it looks like he went missing sometime between Wednesday night and Thursday morning, week before last."

"Gotcha," said the firefighter.

"How about you?" asked Leda. "Did you know him? And if so, when did you see him last?"

"No, I don't know the guy. Only ever saw him a couple of times. The most recent one was . . ." His lovely brow furrowed, somehow making him even *more* good-looking. "Maybe . . . a couple of Fridays ago?" He shot his sister a moment of eye contact, checking for confirmation. "Right? When I picked you up at the quad."

She frowned, then started with recognition. "Oh yeah! He was there. He was, um, he walked me there from Padelford. He was headed off for lunch, we were walking in the same direction . . . you know how it goes," she said with a flip of her hand.

"I sure *do.*"

With quickness and subtlety, Grady elbowed Leda.

With neither of those things, Leda elbowed him back.

Carson shifted back and forth, one foot to the other. The brow furrow was back in play. "Hey, Jules? Listen. Um. That phone call just now? It was Officer Garcia."

She turned to him like a sunflower when the clouds part. "Does he have any news?"

"Yeah . . ." he said slowly, stretching the word at the vowels. He met Grady's eyes and asked, "Did you know about what happened to the professor? Before you came here?"

Julie asked, "Know *what* about him?" before he could answer.

Leda got a twisty feeling in her stomach.

Grady went ahead and told the siblings the truth. "Yes, I knew. We didn't come here to mislead you, but you have to understand: we don't typically spread the news around until the next of kin have been notified."

"Next of . . . kin?" Julie was pretty, but she wasn't stupid. "Did something happen to Paul?"

Leda caught the slip in his name. Maybe the girl was a little stupid after all.

He nodded. "Yes, I'm afraid so. Dr. Reddick is deceased."

"What? How? What?" Julie asked again. Before he could answer, she concluded, "You don't know he's dead. You don't know *anything.*"

Leda didn't feel like being gentle. "We know that one of his legs turned up at Mount Rainier, and the odds of him living through something like that in the wilderness are pretty damn low."

She went pale beneath that tan. It was quite a trick.

Grady sighed in Leda's general direction. "Dr. Reddick's partial remains have been identified through DNA testing. We do not believe that the injury that cost him his leg was survivable."

"In . . . jury?" It was as if the drawbridge between her brain and her mouth had been pulled up and locked.

"We don't know if it was an accident or assault. We don't know where the rest of him might be, either; there's a nonzero chance that he was the victim of a wild animal attack. I wish I could tell you more, but I can't. That's all we've got."

Carson snorted and shook his head like he just couldn't believe this shit. To Grady, he said, "Officer Garcia thinks that what happened to Dr. Reddick and his wife's disappearance are connected. He wanted to talk to us about the last time we saw Dr. Reddick, but I told him another officer was already here. He said we could talk to you instead."

Julie wobbled. Her brother reached out to help her, but she shoved his hands away and sank onto the asphalt in the shadow of the plane's wing—where she sat cross-legged and slack-jawed. "This isn't happening."

Leda said, "From a certain standpoint, it's happened already."

This earned her a second Grady warning, after the elbowing. "Leda . . ."

"I'm sorry, I'm sorry. I don't mean to be . . . unkind." Was that true? But sleeping with married men was unkind, too. Her own parents had once nearly split over it, back before she was in middle school. They'd stayed together and worked through it—plenty of people did—but it'd been a stressful time for everyone. Maybe Leda needed to get out of her own head or work on her empathy. Or maybe Julie needed to work on finding more age-appropriate, non–authority figures to bonk on the weekends.

Leda idly wondered, somewhere in the back of her brain, if

she wasn't feeling extra defensive of Robin Reddick because she'd handled a few of the missing woman's belongings. Was this a halo effect of her psychic abilities? She'd never noticed it before, but it might be worth examining later. Something about Julie and Paul felt gross to her regardless. Maybe it was her parents' close brush with divorce. Maybe it was her own cringe when she thought of that Intro to Art professor.

Or, yes, maybe it was the psychometry.

Julie, shell-shocked in her sunglasses, stayed where she was on the ground. "He's gone. He's actually gone."

"Okay, maybe we should . . ." Grady looked at his notebook and closed it as if to put it away. Then he changed his mind. "Carson. Can you tell us where you were, over Wednesday evening?"

"Sure, that's easy. I was in California, working the Sonoma County fire. I was there for nine days. Didn't get home until Friday night. I can get you my captain's contact information if you want to follow up."

"That would be great, thank you. How about you, Julie? Where were you, over that Wednesday evening through Thursday morning?"

She looked up at him and Leda. "Um . . . wait, what *did* I do after I left with the homework?" She lowered her gaze, staring off into space for a few seconds. "That's right. I went to that sushi place on the Ave, across from the bookstore. Then I went back to my apartment. Next morning, I was up at . . . I was up early? Why was I up early . . . ?" she asked herself. She answered herself. "Oh yeah, I drove one of my roommates to the airport. After that, I was in class until two in the afternoon."

"And you have witnesses who can confirm this?" Leda asked. She almost demanded it but reined it in at the last second.

"Oodles of them," she whispered hoarsely.

Grady asked, "How many classes are you taking? Aren't summer classes typically more concentrated?"

"I'm only taking two. One is Dr. Reddick's second-tier comp class, because it never fit my schedule before this year, and I need it to graduate. One is this math class for dumb people—oh well. I have to take that one, too."

Fine, Leda could feel sorry for her. But only a bit. "I know that one. I had to take it, back when I was in school." To Grady, she added, "It's mostly for liberal arts majors and people who can't count."

Julie nodded vigorously. "That's it. That's the one."

Grady handed her his card and said, "All right, I think that's all we need for now. Do me a favor, though, would you two? Send those references to me sooner rather than later so I can cross you off my list."

Grady and Leda said their polite goodbyes and left.

Niki caught up to them as they were walking back to the car. She rushed behind them and squeezed in between them. "Okay, so," she began excitedly. "First of all, *everybody* knows that Julie's been banging the professor on the down low."

Grady gave her a hard frown. "A little louder, Nik. There might be someone in Canada who didn't quite catch that."

She laughed and lovingly slapped Leda on the back. "Like I said, man—*everybody* knows. Nobody even cares, really. It's just an excuse to gossip. The volunteer squad folks, they seem like nice kids, mostly."

"You didn't learn anything new, I take it?" he asked.

"Other than the thing everybody knows about? Nah. They were full up on spotters with binoculars and cameras, and I have no interest in wading through waist-high grass all afternoon with a sticky pole or whatever."

They reached the car. Grady unlocked it with a beep of the key fob. Everybody piled inside.

Leda leaned around to face the back seat, where Niki was making herself comfortable.

"What's a sticky pole?"

"You know . . ." She mimed something halfway between a spear and a walking stick, making stabby motions at both the front seat and the ground. "A sharp pole. Or stick. You poke it into the ground if the vegetation is too thick to see it. It's like spear-fishing, but for body parts."

Grady groaned. "Must you put it that way? Must you?"

"Oh, just drive," she told him. "You're really prissy sometimes, for a cop who deals with dead bodies all day."

He checked his mirrors and pulled up to a stop at the single light that let people come or go from the field. "I'm not a coroner, for chrissake. On a real busy week I might see one or two—and it's never exactly a treat, you know what I mean?"

"Maybe you should look into another line of work," Niki proposed. She folded her hands behind her head and leaned back happily. "Leda, babe? Did you get any good vibes?"

"Nary a promising zap. Not even a faint light bulb fizzling to life."

Niki sighed. "Then it was all a waste of time."

But Grady argued, "I wouldn't say that. We set eyes on the Coleman siblings, we learned their alibis, and we might have narrowed down the window of Reddick's disappearance by a few hours. Paul's, not Robin's. We're not really sure when she went missing, since Paul couldn't be bothered to report it for so long."

Leda leaned against the window, letting the summer sun warm her face through the glass. "He was *suspiciously* chill about her absence."

"I would agree." The light changed at long last, and he pulled out toward the main drag, away from Boeing. "But I still haven't decided what it means yet."

"I have," Niki and Leda said simultaneously.

When they were finished cracking up at themselves, Leda added, "You might as well assume it. It's *always* the husband."

"It's *often* the husband, but sometimes it isn't," Grady pointed out. "And even if he *did* do it . . . what happened to him afterward? The wife definitely disappeared first, and when Cairo showed up with the leg, it hadn't been on its own more than a few days. Coroner said maybe a week, depending on when it became, uh, disconnected from the whole."

Leda asked, "Why's that? I thought you could tell pretty clearly how long somebody's been dead. Don't you have science? Don't you have fancy equipment?"

"Yes, but we also had a cold snap that ran from Thursday afternoon to Friday night—it got down in the low fifties there in the park; the leg was basically refrigerated off and on."

"Where to next?" Leda changed the subject. "Have you had lunch yet? I want pizza. Or sandwiches. *Bread.* Bread is what I want."

"*Next,* I'm dropping you two back at your office. I've had lunch. You two have fun carb-loading without me." Grady was as good as his word, and twenty minutes later the ladies were back in Columbia City and he was headed back to work.

Upon settling back into her office, Leda popped open her laptop and checked her email. "Yes!" she exclaimed.

"What?!" exclaimed Niki in return.

She leaned around the screen and said, "I shot Avalon a message last night." Avalon Harris had offered her services in the wake of last year's big case. She'd read about it in *The Stranger* and reached out, sensing a young novice psychic who could perhaps use a mentor—or, failing that, the occasional piece of advice from a seasoned professional.

"Avalon? That big, weird woman out on Bainbridge Island?"

"Show some respect," she chided. "Ms. Harris is a *proper* psychic with decades of experience." Leda clicked the email to read it but added, "Well, I think technically she's a medium—at least mostly—but I reached out because I told Dan Matarese I would help him find his sister. Or I told him I'd try, and I haven't had much luck with my usual methods, so I thought I'd ask a pro."

"What did she say?"

"Starts out with *Hello, nice to hear from you*, that kind of thing." After that, she read aloud from the screen. "'It sounds like a complicated case, and really, two cases—if the dismembered leg's owner is involved.'" She looked up and said, "Holy shit, I didn't tell her about the leg. She's good. 'And he *is* involved, isn't he? The leg owner, that is. I saw it in the paper the other day and had a very strong feeling that you were connected to the case.'"

"Okay, she's just spooky."

"Good spooky, though," Leda agreed. She kept reading. "'I've done some meditation and reflection, and I ran a couple of card spreads for good measure. The thing I keep coming back to is the weather. The weather had something to do with what happened to that woman.' Huh. What was the weather like around the Fourth of July?"

Niki pulled out her phone. "But we don't know that's exactly when she disappeared. . . ."

"Yeah, but plus or minus a few days. Wait, do wildfires count as weather? Some of them make their own weather, I know that much. I've seen videos online. They've got clouds and everything."

"I don't see why not. Climate change is a bitch."

"Carson talked about working the Sonoma fire in California while you were off learning about stabby sticks—that's what got me thinking about it. But he didn't know Paul Reddick, and I don't think he knew Robin, either."

"He's too hot to be guilty. I'm sure of it."

Leda snorted. "Wait. If he *is* guilty, does that make him . . . a little hotter? Or is that just me?"

"Just you, and your unbecoming fixation with villains."

"It's not my fault you can't see the beauty in Adam Driver."

Niki shuddered. "It's my eyes' fault, you weirdo."

Leda went back to the email and kept reading. "'I want you to meditate on the weather. I realize you don't likely know the exact circumstances of her vanishing, but that might not matter, for all I know. The world is large and strange, and it has much to tell us. But I am confident the weather had something to do with what became of her. Also, and I do hate to add this, but I am absolutely certain that she's dead.'"

Niki said, "Oh no."

"*Oh no* is right. If she's correct, then Jeff Reddick is an orphan. He's a sweet kid. He doesn't deserve this much heartache in a single month."

"Nobody deserves it. Or not very many people do."

She sighed and shut the laptop again. "*Deserve* is a stupid word. We get what we get, and that's probably it. I hope Avalon's wrong, but if she's not . . . we're not looking to rescue this lady, we're looking to recover her body. They're both gone, but I don't see how they could've murdered each other. Maybe neither of them murdered anybody. Maybe she just died and her husband got eaten by bears. And maybe it's petty of me, but I *do* hope he got what was coming to him."

15. GRADY MERRITT

WEDNESDAY

The next day, Grady, Sam, and Jack Garcia took a lunch break together to sync up and share information about the Reddick cases. They sat outside in a quiet little square on precinct property, perched on concrete benches with unwrapped sandwiches and paper-cup sodas filling the spots between them. The summer sun was high and bright in a cloudless sky; it was almost too warm for this, but a couple of half-grown shade trees and a breeze off the Sound made it all tolerable, and even pleasant.

Jack took a gulp through his straw that concluded with a belch. "The whole thing's just crazy to me. The woman disappears with all this money, her husband knows she hasn't come home, and he doesn't even wonder about it? Or he doesn't do anything about it until his son and her brother browbeat him into speaking up? Either way, something stinks."

Today, Sam was wearing a short-sleeve button-up with a tropical Baby Yoda print. He finished chewing a bite of pastrami on

150

rye and tried, "He might've thought she'd left him and been too embarrassed to say anything."

But Jack didn't think so. "Nah, everyone I've talked to said he wasn't the type to be embarrassed by anything. The guy got caught several times skirt-chasing in the student population, and there are policies about that kind of thing—especially here, now, in the twenty-first century. But it never stopped him for long, and he never cared who knew about it. Tenure must be one hell of a drug."

Grady thought of the brief, sour look that had crossed the woman's face at Padelford Hall when he'd asked about Paul's office. "And his infidelity wasn't even a secret. When I asked around, I got the impression that Paul was a known quantity, and not exactly beloved among faculty. At least, not among female faculty members."

"Sure, but did the *wife* know about it?" Sam pressed. "I realize there's more than one kind of 'knowing'—like some people know things and choose not to believe them. You think she was one of those, or was she totally in the dark?"

Grady said, "Her son and brother said she'd left him a couple of times already, or she'd threatened to. She knew what he was up to."

Jack Garcia shrugged. He was an older detective, a handful of years from retirement, and he wore the silver streaks in his curly hair as a badge of honor. The spreading waistline he camouflaged with bowling shirts, and deflected with shiny, pointed shoes. "Yeah, I'd find it hard to believe she didn't know, but then again, she didn't work at the university. In my experience, places like that are something of a closed system."

"True. And," Grady added, raising a potato chip for emphasis, "she didn't spend much time on campus. When I asked Paul's reader, she hadn't seen Robin since the Christmas party."

"What if she didn't know for sure that he was cheating—and she only suspected it? Does that change anything about what we know?" Sam was the youngest of the trio, and he sometimes came at things from the logic-puzzle approach. It might have had something to do with the new training and coursework for recruits—or maybe it was just his personality.

Grady didn't love it, but he tried to overcome his knee-jerk *kids these days* mentality. "What does it change? Well, it changes the likelihood that she ran out on him without saying anything, unless he was a terrible husband in some way we haven't discovered yet. No one has mentioned physical abuse—or financial abuse, either—but if there was some element of that, it might explain why she made off with the landscaping money."

"Likewise," Jack added, "if she *did* know for sure that he was running around on her, it doesn't change anything. She still disappeared with an awful lot of cash. Even if her family's right and she didn't steal it . . . Paul could've taken it before he went . . . wherever the hell he went. I don't know, guys. This one has a lot of moving parts—and I can't get my mind off that missing bank bag."

Unwilling to abandon the exercise, Sam gave it another shot from another angle. "All right, then what about *her*? Was *she* cheating on *him*? If she was, and he knew, that's motive for murder right there. If she was, and he *didn't* know . . . she might've run off with a lover."

Jack shook his head. "If she had a lover, she kept him very tightly under wraps. I talked to *everybody*," he said, and began counting them off on his fingers. "The co-owner of the landscaping company, who moved to Boca Raton five years ago and wouldn't know, anyway; the manager who reported directly to her and who'd worked beside her for a decade; her best friend, a single mom who lives in Mount Baker; two of her other good friends, her college roommate and the roommate's sister . . . nobody could imagine that she'd ever take her boss's money, much less explain why. But it's always possible that nobody knew her as well as they thought they did. Cash is a powerful motivator."

"So's shame," Grady noted. "And jealousy. All the skirt-chasing must've embarrassed her."

"That's fair. But maybe there was some academic overlap between them? Highly educated people tend to marry other highly educated people, don't they? Where did she go to school? UW?" Sam asked.

"Evergreen State, and she graduated more than twenty years ago. There's no school connection that ties her back to UW. I looked into that, too. I've been doing this awhile, son."

"Yeah, yeah," Sam demurred. "But something isn't adding up. Both members of a couple disappear independently of each other, none of their friends or family have a clue what happened, and they disappear at different times, in presumably different ways."

Jack said, "It *has* to be connected. It *can't* be a coincidence."

But the younger cop pushed back. "Yes, it can. The law of averages implies outliers in every situation. We can't rule out that this might be one of them," he said stubbornly.

Grady threw him a bone. "It's possible," he granted. "But Occam's razor is at least half of day-to-day investigative work. If it looks like a duck, swims like a duck, and quacks like a duck, it's probably a duck. The cases are probably related."

"I know, I know. When you hear hoofbeats, look for horses, not zebras."

"Exactly," Jack said, as if the kid had finally gotten it. "We're looking for horses, not zebras."

"But zebras *do* exist," Sam concluded.

Garcia's phone chimed an alert from his back pocket. He wiggled around on his buns until he retrieved the phone and checked the screen. "Right on. Campus Safety finally got me the security footage from Padelford. A whole week's worth, Jesus Christ. I only asked for Wednesday night. Who the hell has time to watch a whole week?"

Grady proposed, "Maybe we can find some newbie who's pissed someone off. "

"Wait, the security guy included some notes." He took a pair of reading glasses from his shirt pocket and put them on. "Oh, thank God. He cut out everything except the night in question—and he even trimmed it up for us, though the full version is available in our archives. This short version has Paul's interactions as well as his departure, all time- and date-stamped. Shit, Grady. He should've just sent it to you."

He shrugged. "You're the one who asked for it. You were trying to track down Paul, I assume?"

"Yeah, I was running out of ideas and called in a Hail Mary. It's hard as hell to interview a husband for his wife's disappearance when the son of a bitch skips out on you—then up and dies eighty miles away." He put his reading glasses away, tucking them back into the shirt pocket. "We should check this out on a big screen, not on a phone."

Sam perked up. "That's another thought. He might've simply gone on the run out of guilt or fear. He could've killed her, taken the money, and bolted."

Grady had his doubts. "This doesn't feel like a guy covering his ass and skipping town. According to Leda, the son said no one had been inside the house in a week or more when he swung by the other day. It doesn't sound like Paul grabbed a few belongings and bolted. And there's been no activity on his checking or savings account; I put in a request for that info as soon as I got the green light from Rudy. No fat cash withdrawals, no nothing."

"Any credit card usage?" Sam asked hopefully.

"None of that, either. Wherever he went, however he went there . . . he went empty-handed and on foot. His car is still in the garage beside the hall—or it was until yesterday, when we got the impound guys to pick it up." Grady took the final bite of his vegetarian meatball sub. When he'd finished chewing, he licked a bit of marinara sauce off his thumb, then turned to the napkins he kept tucked under one leg so they didn't blow away. "Could you do me a favor, Jack? Send the footage my way. Shoot it via email so I can watch it at my desk."

"Done," he said, and a zippy little sound effect confirmed it. "Watch it at your leisure."

Everyone was finished, so everyone bagged up their trash and tossed it. Grady headed back inside with Sam in tow.

"I'm not crazy," Sam said to him, as if anyone had accused him of it.

"I know you're not nuts, you're just new. We were all new once, but some of us are old now, and we know all the shortcuts."

Curious, Sam asked, "How long *have* you been here?"

"Here at the precinct? Here at the detective level? Or just how long I've been a cop?"

"The last one."

He thought about it. "Almost seventeen years? I didn't hit the academy until I was nearly thirty. Bounced around for a while first. But I graduated with the summer class, back in . . . 2006? Yeah, that's right."

"Which makes you how old, exactly?"

Grady gave him a narrowed squint. "You fishing for something, Sam? Have you been talking to Leda or Niki?"

"What? No. I've never even met them—though I'm absolutely dying to. Why?"

He sighed and slumped grumpily. "They've been hassling me

for my birthday. I think they might be up to something, trying to plan a surprise, I don't know. But I don't like it."

Sam recoiled. "You don't like birthdays? What, were you raised a Jehovah's Witness or something?"

"Episcopalian," he said. "Long lapsed."

"Do Episcopalians have terrible birthdays as a matter of liturgical tradition?"

"I just don't like birthdays. I don't like everybody staring at me, or singing at me, or making me appreciate gifts. Besides, no one on this side of forty thinks birthdays are fun anymore. They're just mile markers on the way to the grave."

He did not add that his wife was way ahead of him and that, when he joined her, he'd be leaving Molly an orphan. He didn't like to think about that. He went out of his way not to think about it when he thought about Jeff—now a young adult with no parents left.

But he thought about it, anyway.

When they reached their adjacent desks once again, Sam asked if he could see the footage from Padelford Hall, too. "I know it's not my case, but now I'm caught up in it. And you could, um, use a second set of eyes on it."

Grady grinned. "A third set, you mean? Since Jack will definitely watch it."

"Even better!" He scooted his rolling chair around so he could see Grady's laptop screen and leaned forward with his elbows on the armrest. "Okay, go ahead. Start the show."

"Let's begin with the abridged version," Grady suggested. He pulled up his email, downloaded the video, and clicked the Play button.

The angle confused him at first, but then he oriented himself. The footage was taken from a hallway camera by the elevator banks, down perhaps fifty feet from Paul Reddick's office—though it was hard to tell which of the open or shut doors along the corridor was the right one until they saw Julie striding down the hall like she meant business.

"Ooh, she looks mad," Sam said eagerly, like he was watching *The Bachelor* or something.

Her posture, her walk, and then her flinging open of Paul's office door backed Sam up. Once she stepped inside, they couldn't see what she was doing, and there was no audio to go with the video feed. She stayed for only fifteen seconds before storming out and slamming the door shut behind herself.

"This is the night he went missing?"

Grady nodded, never taking his eyes off the screen. "That's the going theory. Looks like they had some kind of disagreement . . . ?"

"Lovers' spat," Sam said with a snort.

"Where's . . . ?" Grady began. Then he said, "Ah" when Helena appeared from the other direction. She started toward her little side office, just beside Paul's—then changed her mind and went to his door, which had bounced back open in the wake of Julie's wrath. Helena gave the door a cautious knock and was apparently given the go-ahead to enter, because she stepped inside.

"I wish there was a camera in the office."

Grady waited another twenty or thirty seconds. "I thought this footage was edited to remove all the downtime."

"Wait, there she goes. There *they* go," Sam specified. "Helena and Paul are leaving together."

He nodded. "They sure are. I don't believe Helena mentioned that."

"What *did* she tell you?"

Eyes still locked on the screen, Grady reached for his notebook and flipped it open. A couple of glances down gave him what he was looking for. "She said she last saw him around three p.m., after his final class of the day. But this footage is more like . . ."

He checked the time and date stamp in the bottom right corner. "Eight forty-seven p.m. What do you know, Julie was telling the truth. Sort of. She was right about the time, at least."

"She admitted she saw him that night?"

"Yes, but she didn't mention that it got a little heated. Also, she said she took a homework sheet from an envelope outside his office—that one, I guess." He pointed with the tip of his pen. "But I didn't see her touch it."

"Well, she got the main bit right."

Grady nodded. "She probably didn't want to admit they'd had an argument."

"Then Helena's lying. Maybe it's time for another word with her."

"You read my mind, Sam." He checked his watch. "What do you have on deck this afternoon?"

"The Henderson job. I'm wrapping up the paperwork now. Go without me."

Half an hour later, Grady was back at UW and seeking a parking spot in the dark, cramped garage adjacent to Padelford Hall. Fifteen minutes after that, he was standing in front of Paul Reddick's office, staring at a sign that someone had printed off and taped up with blue painter's tape. It read, "Dr. Paul Reddick has passed away, suddenly and unexpectedly. His summer class will be managed by graduate assistant Helena Smith until further notice."

"Short and concise," he observed aloud.

"I was shooting for efficient."

Grady spun around to find Helena. She was standing behind him with an armful of books and red-rimmed eyes topping off a stricken expression. "Word travels fast."

"Julie has a big mouth, and so do her volunteers. It's all the English department can talk about. I just wish you'd told me." She sounded both tired and disappointed. She begged his pardon, and he stood out of the way while she balanced the books on her thigh with one hand and opened the door with the other. She stepped inside and left the books on top of Paul's desk. "But I understand why you didn't. I'm not family. But neither is Julie."

"I didn't tell her anything. The guy handling Robin's case told Julie's brother."

"You still could have told me. Unless . . . ?" She turned around and sat on the edge of the desk, perching there delicately so as not to disturb a single photo, file, or calendar note. "Rumor has it, you only found part of him. There must be questions about how he died."

"We don't know if he was killed or if he simply had some kind of accident. We're looking for anyone who can tell us what he was doing at Mount Rainier National Park. At the moment, we're all questions—no accusations."

She relaxed very slightly at this. "I understand, I guess. I want to know what happened to him, too."

He followed her into Dr. Reddick's office. It wasn't enormous, but it was tastefully appointed—and artistically messy with books and artwork, in accordance with liberal arts tradition. She kept her position on the edge of his desk, in an almost defensive posture. She did not sink into the big brown chair this time.

Grady took his previous seat, letting her have the high ground.

"What are you *really* doing back here?" she asked.

"Jack Garcia pulled the school's security footage. It landed in our inboxes this afternoon."

Innocently, she asked, "Oh? Who's Jack Garcia? Should I know that name?"

Grady waved his hand like it wasn't that important. "He's the fellow who's handling Robin Reddick's disappearance at the official level. Since she and her husband are technically two separate cases, they have separate detectives assigned to them. But there's more than a little overlap."

"Did the security footage tell you anything important?" She seemed to be fishing for something.

He knew what it was, but he gave her a little rope to hang herself.

"Important?" He shrugged casually. "Hard to say, just yet. It certainly raised some extra questions. For example, didn't you say that you last saw Dr. Reddick that Wednesday afternoon, around three o'clock? Right after his last class."

"I'm not sure. Now that you mention it."

He kept his tone neutral when he replied, "I had a feeling you might want to rethink your story. You want to tell me what you were doing that night, leaving with Dr. Reddick? After Julie came by."

"Julie, yes, she . . . all right." She had come to a decision, something like a surrender. "Look, it's been a couple of weeks now, okay? I don't remember every little detail about every little thing. I have a lot on my plate."

He didn't believe her and didn't trust her, but even if she was lying she might tell him something useful. "Start wherever you like. Just tell me what really happened."

"I didn't know those cameras even worked anymore," she complained to herself. Then she collected her composure, sat up a little straighter, and took a deep breath. "I was here that Wednesday night, and Julie was, too. But not for very long. She came by, yelled a little, and stormed out."

She was telling the truth so far. Grady retrieved his notebook and pen. "What was she yelling about?"

She visibly struggled to find the right words, the ones that implied the right things and not the wrong things. Her hands fluttered, and her forehead furrowed. "You have to understand, Dr. Reddick had a bit of a . . . reputation."

"Can you be more explicit? The man is dead. You don't have to cover for him anymore."

"I'm not *covering* for him, I'm . . . Okay, fine. You're right. He's dead—and whatever happened to his wife, it doesn't look like she's coming back. There's nobody left to protect."

She stared into the middle distance until he prompted her. "Helena, why did Julie come here to yell at him? I'll ask around the hall, don't get me wrong; I will absolutely talk to the other folks who have offices in this building and find out what they overheard. But I want to get it from you first."

Her eyes snapped back to attention. "She was mad at him about something, and I'm not sure what. I know they had some kind of relationship. Outside of school, you know. I don't know if it was . . . if they were . . ."

"Yes, you do."

"Well, I don't like to think about it. He was such a brilliant man, and so generous with his time, and such a wonderful mentor. It's not unusual that girls sometimes got . . . overly attached to him. He's only human." She crossed her arms and sulked.

"He *was* only human."

She failed to hide a small grimace of irritation. "Fine. He *was*. Julie is beautiful; I'm not too petty to say that. I don't know if she's smart, or if she deserved the trouble or the attention, but he gave it to her anyway. I don't remember exactly what she said, but it was something along the lines of 'You bastard, you said you'd meet me at Ba Bar. What the hell is this supposed to mean?' Then she called him a bunch of names and stormed out."

"The . . . what was that? Babar?"

"The Ba Bar. It's in the University Village. It's a pho place."

"Okay." He made note of it. "Dark and quiet? Plenty of nooks and crannies for quiet meetings?"

"Not really, but they weren't exactly discreet."

He let the notebook settle on top of his thigh and gestured with the pen. "So Julie showed up, yelled, chucked something at him, and stormed out. Then a minute later, you strolled into the picture, and you left together. Tell me about that."

"It wasn't . . . Me and him, we weren't like that. Not like him and Julie. Obviously."

"Obviously," he agreed, with enough seriousness that she seemed to think he was mocking her. Even if he was, he didn't mean to.

"Don't say it like that. He was my boss and my friend, and that's *all*. I went in there after Julie left to ask if he was okay, and if he could give me a ride to the light rail station in the village. I hadn't meant to be here so late that night, and it's a hike over there through a dark campus . . . or a slow ride on a bus. So he took me to the station. I'm sorry that the surveillance footage didn't give you anything useful, but there you go. Perfectly innocent explanations for everything."

"Perfectly innocent indeed," he muttered as he scrawled. Except that she had lied about it. "Just an affair with a student, nothing to see here."

"Oh, stop it. He's not the first and won't be the last. We're all adults, for God's sake."

"Tell yourself whatever you like." He rose to his feet and put the notebook away. Then he paused. "In the video, you can see that she throws something into his office. Do you have any idea what it was?"

"No, but it wasn't very heavy. Maybe some wadded-up paper? A note or something? He took it with him when he left. I went looking the next morning. I was curious."

He jotted all this down and said, "All right. Thanks for your time."

She didn't say anything else, and he left the way he'd come in—making note of the nameplates beside offices and planning to make some phone calls later. Helena was lying about something, and he wasn't sure exactly what. Not yet.

But he was going to find out.

16. LEDA FOLEY
WEDNESDAY

Lunch with Dan Matarese went down at the sushi place around the corner from Leda's office in Columbia City. She'd spent nearly every waking moment before their meeting trying to decide how to spin what precious little information she had, and how to spin it gently.

Dan was early, but he struck her as the kind of guy who was always early, given the opportunity.

She joined him at a table by the window and opened with an apology. "Hello, Mr. Matarese. I hope I'm not late."

He smiled at her and set aside his phone. Its screen held a *Wall Street Journal* article, but Leda couldn't tell what it was about, and if she'd tried any harder to get a peek, it would've looked nosy. "No, you're right on time."

As if her arrival had immediately tripped a booby trap, a waitress swooped in to take their orders—buying Leda another few precious moments to consider how she'd deliver her message. She ordered some salmon and tuna nigiri and a bowl of miso soup. Dan asked for a California roll and a side of fried rice. Then they sat back with their water, served from a glass carafe that had been left on the table.

Leda was out of time.

"So! What have you got for me? Jeff said he went to see you at some bar on Capitol Hill."

"Castaways, yes. He came by while I was getting ready for a set. We have a new karaoke list, and I was . . . You know what?" She shook her head and started over. "That's not important. Yes, I saw Jeff, and he gave me a few more of your sister's things. I asked to hang on to the locket, and I brought it with me today so I could return it to the family. Or to you, to be more specific. I think it's told me everything it can."

Eagerly, he sat forward. "You actually got something?"

"Yes and no," she said carefully. "Most of the things Jeff brought were connected to him and his childhood. But the locket was connected to Robin by someone else, and it had a stronger pull for her—I assume because the person it reminds her of is gone." She removed the locket from her purse and handed it to Dan. "This is the only piece that gave me anything about Robin, and I need to tell you up front: I don't think it's entirely good."

He stiffened and swallowed hard. "It's all right. Give it to me straight. By now, I assume the worst."

"My dad always says that if you assume the worst, you'll never be disappointed—but he's wrong a lot. The locket told me that Robin was absolutely miserable for wanting it so badly, and the thought of holding it was a comfort to her."

Dan said, "Oh." Two dry little letters, side by side. He took a swig of water and held the glass tightly.

"She was somewhere dark and enclosed, and she was badly shaken, possibly hurt. I don't know why, I don't know where she was or how she got there, or what she was doing there."

"She's trapped somewhere? Is that what you think?"

Deep breath. Hard truths. Honesty, best policy, et cetera. "I think she might have been, at least initially. I'm not sure what happened, but she was . . . derailed, for lack of a better way to put it. Something threw her off unexpectedly, and she was unable to right her course. The truth is, Mr. Matarese . . . wherever she is, I think she died there."

He nodded very slowly. He exhaled. He took a series of long breaths. "She's been gone for more than a month now, and I know her too well to think she's still alive out there."

"Which doesn't make this conversation any easier, sir. Even though it's always possible that I'm wrong. It wouldn't be the first time, but . . ." She almost didn't say the rest, but it only felt fair to give him everything she had. "I called a friend and asked her to take a look at the situation. I thought maybe an extra pair of eyes would be useful and maybe she'd see something I didn't."

"By *see*, do you mean psychically?"

"Yes. My friend actually worked for the Seattle PD for many years before I came on board, though she's retired now. We have different specialties; mine is psychometry, and hers is . . . well, I think she's mostly a medium, though she's very intuitive as well."

"A medium?" What little color was left in his face drained away. "Did she tell you . . . did she say . . ."

"No, no. She didn't make contact with your sister. But she told me that—as a matter of professional opinion—Robin is no longer with us. Also," she continued quickly, "she said that it had something to do with the weather."

"The weather? I don't understand."

"Me either. But she *insisted* that Robin's disappearance had something to do with the weather. If only we knew precisely when she went missing, it might be a more useful clue. But I wonder if . . ." She drummed her fingers on the table.

"Yes?"

"What if we could reverse engineer a closer date and time for her disappearance by taking a look at the weather around a month ago? If there was something specifically dramatic in the forecast, we might be able to narrow it down more tightly than 'sometime around the Fourth'—at least for working theory purposes. Did you bring that map I asked you about?"

"The map?" He was down to single-syllable questions.

Leda understood. She'd been there before, herself. She determinedly shook off the memories of collecting a big yellow envelope with her fiancé's belongings in it. She refused to think about his keys, his fraternity ring, or his wallet. "When we emailed about this meetup, you said she'd been working on a commercial landscaping gig and that you could show me on a map. You said you'd bring one."

A spark of recognition cut through the rising fugue of his grief. "Oh yeah, hang on. It's right here." He reached into his back pocket and pulled out a folded sheet of paper. He passed it to Leda.

She unfolded it and realized that he'd printed it off the internet, probably just through Google Maps. "Okay, so this is the south end of Renton, yes?"

"A little past it, out near Southcenter. Right now, it's basically a big overgrown field with a few walls and foundations."

"How big?"

He shrugged. "I'm a bad judge of that kind of thing. Think maybe . . . a third the size of the mall, when all's said and done. It's—" He might've said more, but their food appeared on a pair of round trays, and it took a minute or two to sort out what went where and what order to eat it in. Once they were settled in with chopsticks and spoons, Dan continued. "It's out near the inter-state, at the edge of Tukwila."

Leda pulled a pen out of her messenger bag. She handed it to him and said, "Can you mark it on the map?"

"Sure." He took the pen and circled a patch not far from the road and not far from the big mall, with its accompanying retail sprawl.

"What's all this stuff around it?" she asked, jabbing a finger down at the selected bit of map.

"Woods, I think. They've only just gotten started; there aren't even any real paved roads out to the site. The last quarter mile, you drive on dirt and hope for the best. Robin was out there every other day for a couple of weeks with all the architectural plans, deciding what shrubs and trees would go in which places and col-lecting money from the store owners in order to buy them. The county makes them preserve a certain amount of space for green-ery; she's specialized in working within those regulations for years. Do you think this is where she . . . where whatever happened to her, happened?"

"I mean, it's the last place she was actually seen, right?" She frowned down at the map and stuffed a bite of sushi in her mouth. She chewed, swallowed, and said, "There's nothing over here that looks or feels like it might have a closet, or a cell, or . . . or wherever I felt from her when I held the locket. But she might have been coming or going from this place. I did warn you, this is imprecise."

When they were finished eating and the bill was paid, Leda asked, "Do you mind if I hang on to this map? I might head out there myself and see if I can feel my way around. I might stumble upon something that gives me a good flash of insight."

"It's all yours, but the college searchers have already been over the place. Those Coleman kids have been amazing—I can't thank them enough. Even if Julie had her own weird reasons for launching the search."

She pressed her lips together, trying not to open her mouth. It didn't work. "You know about Julie and Paul?"

He nodded.

"Jeff told me about it. We all knew Paul was a louse; I just didn't know the specifics of who he was seeing this semester until my nephew spelled it out. That takes balls, don't you think?"

"Jeff, or . . . ?"

He shook his head. "No, the girl. Telling the world that she's so secure in her relationship with a married man, she'll spearhead the hunt for his missing wife."

Leda borrowed one of Grady's *hm* sounds. Then she said, "Maybe, but it sounds to me like an alibi. Like she's telling the world she couldn't have *possibly* had anything to do with the woman's disappearance, since she's trying so hard to find her."

Now Dan nodded thoughtfully. "Especially if she thought Paul had something to do with it. She could be trying to protect him. Or that might have been her original motivation."

"Sure, it could be a smoke screen. They've been out there beating the bushes, looking for Robin. And Julie even roped in her poor brother and his plane. Her poor, ludicrously good-looking brother and his dinky little plane . . ." she mused. "It's been a huge waste of time and airplane fuel if she already knows what happened to Robin. Maybe Paul knew she was dead—and he told Julie. Maybe the two of them even worked together to make his wife vanish."

"It's one hell of a ruse."

"We're only speculating here."

"Right. Only speculating," he agreed, with a wariness in his eyes that said he had his suspicions. "And now that he's dead, it's not like we can ask him about it."

"Jeff told you?"

"Jeff told me."

They might have discussed Paul's gruesome demise further, but the meal was over, and it was time for them to part ways. Dan asked if Leda could invoice him for her time, and she agreed to do so. She picked up her bag, and he double-checked the tip. They shook hands.

And Leda saw stars. Paul and Dan in a shouting match, but only in flashes—in quick screen-caps without any sound. She couldn't hear them, but the topic was clear, and so were the threats.

She blinked the fractured scenes away and—she dearly hoped—successfully hid the fact that she was zapped and startled as she left the restaurant and walked back to her office, her brain reeling from what she'd seen. Or what she thought she'd seen. Or what it meant, if she had seen it correctly.

She stormed into her office, where Niki was lying on the love seat and doom-scrolling her way through Twitter.

"Hey, girl," she greeted.

"Dan knows something he's not telling me!" Leda blurted.

Niki sat up straight and dropped her phone into her lap. "Go on. Did you get vibes? You look like you got *vibes*."

"We shook hands, and I got a spark that told me Dan's been lying. Or he's hiding something that's closer to the truth, I think."

"Dan's the missing wife's brother, right?" Niki asked.

"Right. He's the brother. And he hates, hates, *hates* his sister's dead husband."

"Enough to disappear him?"

"I think so," she said, with a fresh burst of confidence. "When I shook Dan's hand, I got a flash of him yelling at Paul—screaming right in the guy's face. It *had* to be about Robin."

"You should've asked, to make sure."

"I was a little distracted, Nik. Vibes are distracting. It took me the whole walk back here to examine it enough to sort out what I saw. Dan believes that Paul killed her. He accused him of murder, point-blank, and they fought. They were in a hallway, and it looked like the inside of some office building."

"Did it come to blows?" Niki asked with more enthusiasm than might have been strictly tasteful.

"I can't tell if Dan started swinging at him or if he only wanted to hit him really, really bad."

Niki absorbed this information. The gears in her head were visibly spinning when she asked, "So what does this mean for the case, if anything?"

"Which case?"

"Either one," her friend proposed with a shift of her shoulders.

"For either one, it means that Grady should have a talk with that guy and ask him where he was when Paul Reddick disappeared—because between you and me? I wouldn't put it past him to have done it."

"That's a big accusation."

"I know. That's why I'm not making it yet," she insisted. "I'm just saying that Dan had motive, and probably the means, and maybe also the opportunity, to make Paul Reddick disappear." Some of the electric enthusiasm from the handshake had waned, and now she was both tired and antsy. "We may not know exactly when Robin went missing, but we have a pretty good idea about Paul; he was last seen a couple of Wednesdays ago. And all I'm saying is, Dan needs an alibi."

17. GRADY MERRITT
WEDNESDAY AFTERNOON/EVENING

Grady rolled up to Castaways around six. The voice mail he'd gotten from Leda had sounded positively unhinged, if broadly enthusiastic—undertones of outright glee mixed with curiosity. Something about Robin Reddick's brother. Something about seeking outside counsel, but don't worry, she wouldn't invoice anybody for it because her friend didn't take paying gigs anymore. He shuddered to consider what Leda might mean by "outside counsel," but as long as she wasn't divulging police information to randos, he wouldn't complain. Maybe they'd get some fresh eyes and fresh results.

Steve the bouncer was sitting on a stool out front, protected by the shade of an enormous golf umbrella. "Hello there, Officer!" he said by way of greeting. "No cover for you, just get on in there."

"Isn't it a little early for a cover charge? What time does Leda go on?"

"Not until eight." Steve was a Black ex-con with warm eyes and a friendly smile for just about everybody.

Grady didn't know what he'd done time for and felt like it wasn't his business, so he'd never asked. He was just glad that Steve didn't act terrified anymore every time they met in passing. "Oh, good, so there's time for a drink or two before shit gets weird."

Steve's grin went sneaky. "You *say* that, but . . ."

"Oh God. What is it?"

With an air of merry conspiracy, Steve leaned forward and whispered, "She's not alone in there. There's some other woman, and I've never seen her before, but she's got *weird* written all over her."

Grady scratched nervously at the back of his neck. "Well, she said she was looping in a friend. Maybe it'll be all right."

"Maybe." Steve shrugged and sat back against the wall, settling into the shade of the big black-and-white umbrella. "But it'll *definitely* be weird. Oh—one more thing: beware of Tiffany's special of the day. I love that girl with all my heart, but order something you already know. Not every experiment of hers deserves a day in court."

"Thanks for the heads-up, I appreciate it."

With that, he headed inside.

The sudden contrast between the bright outside and the dim indoors made the place seem darker than normal, but his eyes adjusted to the relative gloom, and he waved at Tiffany, who hollered a joking "Cop alert!" upon his entrance, then asked, at a normal volume, "Are you off duty or working?"

"I'm off duty, but—"

"Let me make you the special!"

"Wait . . ." He approached the bar, where a chalkboard sign advertised the drink of the day. He scanned for key words and saw *kiwi, gin, bitters,* and *hibiscus liqueur.* "Not the special—I, um, I'm allergic to kiwi."

She froze, arm outstretched as she reached for the gin. "What? Allergic to kiwi? I've never heard of that allergy."

He shrugged. "Let me just have a whiskey sour. Is that all right?"

She shrugged back. "It's boring—but for you? I'll do boring."

He sighed with relief and turned his back to the bar so he could lean against it while she worked.

The usuals were trickling in, picking good tables and taking their lives into their hands, considering the daily special. But the best table in the house—the one tucked between the stage and the emergency exit that actually led to the building offices—was already occupied by Leda, Niki, and a third woman he didn't recognize.

She was older than the other two, and older than Grady as well. He guessed her to be in her sixties; she was both very attractive and gloriously fat. Her makeup was dramatic but tidy, just like the tattoos that covered her soft, pale arms and the shiny black dress that fit her like a gown. A small black cane with a silver knob leaned against her seat.

When Tiffany provided his drink, he gave her his card to set up a tab (and insisted, though she tried to wave it away). He took his plain, boring whiskey sour and strolled up to the table where Leda, Niki, and the stranger were poring over a sheet of paper between them.

"Hello, ladies," he said by way of introduction. "Leda, Niki. And . . . ?"

The woman held out a hand with some of the shiniest bloodred fingernails he'd ever personally set eyes on. She also wore several rings, all of them silver, some of them vaguely frightening. He glimpsed two skulls and a dragon, as well as an assortment of crimson stones and a peace symbol, which felt a bit out of place. Or did it?

"Call me Avalon," she purred. A lovely voice, and silver hair with a hint of lavender. "I'm a friend of Leda and Nicole's. Please, won't you join us?"

He shook her hand and pulled up a chair. "By all means."

Niki told him, "Avalon used to work with your folks, down at the station."

"Really?" She didn't look familiar, and there was no chance in hell that he'd met her and forgotten about her.

"It was before your time," she said with a pleasant smile. "I retired years ago. Back when Loretta Mosby was still captain."

"Right, right," he said, putting two and two together. Mosby had retired the year before he'd made detective. "I barely knew her, and she was gone before I'd been there long. At any rate, it's good to meet you. Leda, what's the big emergency?"

"We have a map!" Leda announced.

"It looks like the same map from the search party in Renton . . . ?"

"Yeah, but nobody gave me one of those. Now I have one in my hot little hands, for personal and thorough investigation. Avalon is helping us narrow things down."

"Well, I'm *trying* to help," she said humbly.

Grady wanted to know, "What's your, um, specialty? If you don't mind my asking."

"Oh, a little of this. A little of that. I don't have Leda's skills, but sometimes I can make myself useful."

"She has plenty of skills I don't," Leda added politely. "Like, I can't talk to dead people, but Avalon is a hell of a medium."

"Among other things. I haven't heard from your victim," she said swiftly as Grady opened his mouth to ask. "Though, for what it's worth, I *do* believe she's passed on to the other side."

"Robin Reddick isn't *my* victim," Grady clarified. "Her case belongs to a detective named Jack Garcia. Right now, Paul's the guy I'm looking for—and that's not really my case, either. Or it's not exclusively mine; I'm working in tandem with the Pierce County folks, since that's where we found his leg."

"Yes, Leda and Nicole briefed me."

"But you think Robin's dead?" he asked.

"I'm confident of it, for reasons that are difficult to articulate. She's been gone long enough that she's not lost or confused. She's moved beyond my reach, and that takes time. I think she's been dead since very shortly after she went missing."

"Despite my lack of psychic powers, I've been thinking the same thing," Grady admitted. "I suspect you're right."

Niki added, "We have no evidence to the contrary, and her son is confident that she wouldn't leave without saying something. That's what Leda said."

"Yeah, about the son . . ." Grady took a slug of the drink and set it back down. "I have some concerns. Not that he would've hurt his mother, but I'm not convinced he didn't take a run at his father."

"Hey, babe." They all paused and looked up as Matt Cline approached. He put a hand on Niki's shoulder and gave it a squeeze. "I'm going to make a bank run. Nik, could you handle Jim? He's here for a delivery, and you're the last one who had the inventory sheet."

"Oh, shit, yes. Excuse me, folks."

When they were gone, Grady continued. "Jeff's been letting himself back inside the family home."

"I know, he brought me some stuff the other night."

"Did he tell you that he did some cleaning while he was there?"

The older woman asked, "The suspicious kind of cleaning, with bleach?"

"Something like that. We know it was him; his prints were everywhere."

Leda refused to assume the worst. "So what? Jeff said he did some cleaning while he was there because his dad left food out before he went missing and got dismembered. He was looking for something I could use. That doesn't mean he's up to any shenanigans."

"That's true," Grady admitted. "But it was very convenient of him to mention it to you. He could have been establishing an alibi, or precedent."

"Was the house closed up as a crime scene?" Avalon asked. "Do you think he tampered with evidence?"

Ah yes, she *had* done this before. "Without a body, without a crime scene . . . there was no reason to cordon the place off, so it was a low priority. Now I wish we'd done it sooner, but this whole case has been on an odd timetable since we've had to coordinate with the precinct to the south. I wish we had a list of what was in the house beforehand, but that's all pie in the sky, I know. Leda, could you give me some contact info for the brother, Dan?"

"Oh, I'm *planning* on it."

Something about the way she said it made him groan inside. "What happened, Leda? What did you do?"

"I didn't do anything!" she protested. "Except meet up with Dan to give him back the locket Jeff gave me, and also to tell him what Avalon told me, and furthermore to get a map of Robin's last known general location. But then I shook his hand, and now I think you need to ask him where he was and what he was doing when Paul Reddick disappeared."

"Go on."

"Go on how? Where? That's it," she told him. "That's all I've got. He was filled with an unholy rage toward his brother-in-law, and I think he's a better suspect than poor Jeff. That kid is just in mourning; he's not in guilt—and that's why I want you to look at Dan. Dan feels *guilty*."

"Huh. Do you know when this argument occurred? Or where? Or what it was about?"

"It was about Robin," she said with perfect confidence that Grady found a little suspicious. "And it was about what happened to her—so it couldn't have happened more than a few weeks ago, right? Nobody knew she was missing before then."

"You'll have to narrow it down some more. I'm sorry."

"Okay, the fight was in a corridor of some kind. Not like one of those single-shot hallway fights in a martial arts movie, but those are really cool."

Grady pulled out his cop notebook and pretended to take notes. "Not . . . a martial arts . . . fight. Got it."

"Oh, stop it already. It was an office or something. Or a hallway with offices, not, like, hospital rooms. No windows or anything."

"Hm. Do you think it was at the university? Near Paul's office?"

She pounced on the idea. "Yes. Definitely. It was there."

"Then maybe you're in luck. They have security cameras, and we already have a bunch of footage. I'll have to find an intern or something and make somebody watch the rest of it on the off chance you've got something."

Satisfied with this, Leda smiled and returned to the subject at hand. She pushed the map across the table until it was under his nose. "I would appreciate that, but first, look at this. This is where Robin was working."

"The commercial project out around Southcenter. I remember. But we don't actually know she disappeared over there; it's just a guess."

"It's not *just* a guess," Leda objected. "The cops and searchers have tackled everyplace else—her office at the landscaping company and its surrounding blocks, her home and the entire neighborhood, the length and breadth of her commute, her best friend's place and six blocks around it—"

"They've tackled the construction site, too."

Leda frowned ever so slightly, and he wondered what he'd said to irk her. "The volunteers did, but what do they know, anyway? They're not psychics. They're not professionals. They're college students with sticky poles."

"You're not a professional, either. Not a professional *searcher*," he corrected himself quickly.

"That's fair, but I'm vastly more capable than your average college student—*and* I am prone to paranormal flashes of insight. Here, look. The map Dan gave me has all the topographical information for the site." She tapped her finger on the sheet of paper that was lying on the table between her and the woman who'd introduced herself as Avalon. "And we've been examining it. There's a ridge over there, see? And a pond on the other side."

"We've already checked the pond. No sign of her. No sign of anything in the water, except some runoff sludge from that bad storm we had earlier this summer. . . . ." He paused. "About a month ago."

Avalon and Leda exchanged a look.

Avalon explained in brief. "The weather had something to do with what happened. I've been saying so all along."

Grady wanted to say that weather generally affected everything, not merely missing persons cases, but he didn't want to be rude to this woman, who seemed like she was trying to help.

"Well, I'll take that into consideration—but the pond isn't even deep enough to hide a car. If she'd washed down into the water, we'd be able to see it because the roof would be sticking out. At any rate, does Dan's map tell you anything new?" he asked, trying to sound optimistic despite his doubts.

"Me? Not really. All I've ever picked up on Robin was a sense of being closed in someplace small and dark, and being very afraid. It wouldn't be an exaggeration to say that she felt a sense of impending doom. As awful as that sounds."

Grady asked Avalon, "You're sure you haven't heard anything from . . . from the other side? Any confirmation or denial?"

Avalon shook her head. "Not a peep from any spirits, guides, or other assorted helpful souls. But all my instincts are shouting that she's been lost to the living for weeks."

Grady didn't want to argue with the two nice ladies, who knew things he didn't, so he was careful when he suggested, "You're saying we're looking at a recovery mission, not a rescue mission."

She sighed. "I'm afraid so. It's just as well for her that she's not hanging around. I wonder if she had a guide, someone who came to retrieve her when the end came."

"Her sister," Leda said with an upsetting degree of certainty. "She wanted the locket because she knew she was going to die and she was thinking about her dead sister, almost unconsciously trying to call her for help. It's tragic, really."

"If that turns out to be true, you're absolutely right: it's tragic. But we still haven't . . . I just . . ." He reached for the map and turned it around so it faced him. "It's one thing to hide a body, but it's another thing entirely to hide a bright orange 1970s Volvo. We've had a BOLO out on it for weeks, and we haven't gotten a single tip. There's literally not another car like it in King County."

"Really?" Leda looked like she simply didn't buy it. "Not a single one?"

"I found two other models from the same year, but one was turned into the world's strangest hot rod—someone painted it cherry red and added a bunch of chrome several years ago; there are pictures of it in car shows going back to 2018. The other one was bright lime green and tricked out to look like a frog, but Facebook photos suggest this happened about six months ago."

Grady leaned back in his chair and made his own staring-off-into-space face, he was sure of it. He was thinking about the weather again. He pulled out his notebook. "Hang on, here we go. The fifth of July. That's when she left the job site with the big bag of money."

"Technically, it's more of a zippered bank pouch." Leda pulled out her phone and did some digging. "But yes, okay. July second. That's when the storm hit. KOMO Four did a story on it, see?" She turned the phone around and showed them the headline: two inches of rain in four hours. "That's a lot of rain, right?"

"Yes, but on the wrong day. She wouldn't have been out there working in the storm, anyway," Grady pointed out. "Hm."

"Hm?" Leda echoed. To Avalon she said, "He always makes that sound when he's got an idea. Or when he's thinking about something. He's like the Witcher, I swear."

Grady pushed the map back into the center of the table. "All right, so it's still a shot in the dark, but I'll . . . I'll talk to the landscaping manager again, and I'll . . . well, I'll get somebody on that security footage from Padelford Hall. Other than that, I'm not sure what to do."

With great sympathy and kindness, Avalon asked, "You're really flying blind on this one, aren't you, Detective?"

Ruefully, he agreed. "This case has a lot of moving parts—but I'm happy to have any lead you can offer, whether or not it's something I can use to get a warrant. Right now, I'm willing to accept all hunches, hints, and suspicions as avenues of inquiry." He downed the last of his whiskey sour and said, "If you'll excuse me, I'll go see about putting another one of these on my tab. I'll be right back."

When he stood, his thigh bumped the table and Leda's drink toppled forward.

With a quick "Eep!" she seized it, but a puddle of something lightly green but mostly clear spilled toward the map.

Instinctively, Grady picked it up—but not in time to keep it dry. That was when he noticed that the back of the page was not blank. He flipped it over and held it up to the light. "Hm."

Leda was swabbing the mess with cocktail napkins and the back of her hand, shoving excess liquid to the floor. "Jeez, Grady. Be a little careful next time . . . Hey. What was that *hm* about?"

He cocked his head at the sheet of ordinary white copy paper, or printer paper, or whatever they called it when you could stick it almost anywhere and expect it to fit. "Dan Matarese printed this off at home."

"So what?"

"So he'd already printed something on this page. He must've been low on paper and just . . . flipped it over. There's something on the back."

Leda made grabby hands toward the slightly damp sheet. "What is it? Come on, share with the group!"

He turned it around. "It's Paul Reddick's office and classroom schedule." He pointed at the top left edge of the message, with the sender and receiver information. "Sent to Dan by Jeff Reddick."

18. LEDA FOLEY

WEDNESDAY EVENING

Leda was dumbfounded and displeased in equal measure at the accusation Jeff might have had something to do with his father's disappearance. "That doesn't mean anything," she insisted. "They've both been looking for Robin, and they've both admitted to being in touch with Paul, or trying to get in touch with him, over the last few weeks. You saw the kid when we delivered the news. He didn't get along with his father, but he wouldn't have murdered him."

"What makes you so sure?" he asked, flipping the moist sheet of paper over again to look at the map, and then the email, and then the map again.

Avalon agreed with Grady. "He might be a very good actor."

"But *I'm* a very good judge of character," she replied with more confidence than she had any business feeling. She'd been doing that a lot lately.

Grady wiped his hands on his dad jeans and gave the map

back to Avalon, who was sitting closer. "He could be an actor, he could be a sociopath, he could have deep-seated regrets about his actions. He could be a murderer. *Anyone* could, believe me. I wish I didn't know it as well as I do. We can't rule him out. He came and went from the house, he knew his father's class schedule—"

"Circumstantial at best." She wasn't ready to stop defending the young mechanic's honor just yet.

Avalon proposed, "It could have been some kind of pact with his uncle. Say, a little murdery teamwork." Then, to Leda, she added, "I'm sorry, dear—but I haven't met the young man in question, and I can't give him your benefit of a doubt."

"Keep it all in the family," Grady said under his breath. "You know what? That's better than possible; it might even be likely."

Leda wasn't having it. "You don't really think that."

"Why not?" he asked. He stood beside the table, thinking hard and holding the empty glass that once had held his whiskey sour. "It makes good sense. They both loved Robin Reddick and hated Paul Reddick. They've each admitted as much, either directly or by their behavioral choices. And if they *did* split up their dirty work, it would be tricky as hell to pin a single murder on either one of them. Hey, give me a second. Let me go have a word with Tiffany. I'll be right back."

He walked away, still wiping one damp hand on the side of his pants.

Leda leaned over to Avalon and said in a conspiratorial whisper, "He's full of it. There's no way. That kid wouldn't hurt anyone."

"Do you have anything to back that up? Apart from your instincts?"

"I have . . ." She struggled to remember. "No."

With a gentle sip on the cocktail straw that stuck out of her

Shirley Temple, Avalon said, "According to you, he hated his father."

"He *said* that he did, and then he changed his story next time. He loved his dad, he just didn't like him very much—and people say a lot of things when they're angry or scared. When I touched him there was no . . . relief," she said, settling on a word. "No sense of closure or finality. Only fierce sorrow."

"Fierce sorrow, I like that." She swirled the tiny red straw with her bright red fingertips. "It's a nice turn of phrase, and I hope it's true."

"You believe me, don't you?"

"I believe that people sometimes tell the truth without meaning to. Hold on, let me just . . ." She set her drink aside and reached for her purse—an embroidered velvet number that looked like it'd been assembled from fancy carpet and curtain scraps in a funeral home. "Let's try it from another angle, shall we?"

Leda's eyes went large. "Ooh, what's that?"

Avalon held up a small green stone cut in the shape of a pyramid, hanging from a silver chain. "A pendulum. If any useful spirits are hanging around, they can use it to point us in a good direction."

"That's a thing you can do?"

"It's a thing *you* could do, too, if you want to learn how. It's a little fiddly, I must warn you." She held it up by the end of its chain so the pyramid point aimed down at the table and the eight-by-ten rectangle of faintly squishy paper. It was lying there map side up.

"How does this work?" she asked in awe. "I've done that little trick where you hold something up over a yes or no and ask it questions—but I've never done anything with, like, a map."

"When it works . . ." Here, she paused to give Leda a very

deliberate warning stare. "And it *doesn't* always work . . . but when it does, I ask for guidance, and something on the other side replies. If we are very lucky, they'll be helpful. If we aren't, they'll mess around with us for fun."

"Sounds like a crapshoot."

"At best." She closed her eyes, displaying a knack for eyeliner that Leda would've murdered for—at least metaphorically. Avalon began to mutter softly as she held the pendulum aloft. Leda only caught a few words. It sounded like a gentle, long-winded request for patience and guidance, along with a strong hint that any and all spiritual bullshit would *not* be tolerated.

Grady picked that moment to roll back up to the table with a fresh drink. "What's all this? Should I, um, should I come back later? I don't want to interrupt anything."

Avalon shooed his concerns away with her free hand, pointing at his seat. "You're fine. Be quiet, that's all. I'm trying to listen, and too many voices are trying to push through."

If Leda looked very closely, she could see a faint gold spark in the older woman's eyes. Barely a glint, not even a full speck of color. Something bright and sudden and hot, and it startled her. If she wanted to be honest, it frightened her a tiny bit. But she was the newbie here, and Avalon was the old pro, and she was going to be cool with it if it killed her.

She hoped it wouldn't kill her.

Grady slid back into position, bringing a handful of larger napkins to the table. He took a couple and swabbed the area around the map. When he was finished, he sat back with his hands in his lap, holding a wad of wet napkins. He looked like he desperately wanted to ask, *Now what?* but he'd been told to hush, and he was much better than Leda at following directions.

Avalon's low talking shifted to a hum and then a clearer question—whispered through scarcely parted lips. "Good to know, my darling. But where? I can't see her. My friend can't see her. Where did she go? What happened to her? *Someone* must know." Then she returned to the humming.

The pendulum began to sway, very slightly, left to right. Not a circle but an arc that was small and slow and imprecise.

She murmured, "Yes, very good. It's a start." Then, to the others at the table, she added, "Someone is listening and willing to speak through the pendulum."

Back and forth, back and forth. A pivot, no longer east to west but north to south. The soft dip and delicate swing.

Avalon lifted her hand higher, to give the sweep more range. To Leda's eye, she wasn't manipulating the small dangling device— but it was admittedly difficult to tell, considering the low light.

"Spirits of usefulness, spirits of light. Clockwise for yes, widdershins for no. Is Robin Reddick's physical form located somewhere within the edges of this map?" The green pyramid rocked back and forth, and it spun slowly clockwise over the map.

Grady failed to restrain himself or his skepticism. "In all fairness, that's a big chunk of King County, and I think . . ." He peered a little closer. "Part of Pierce."

Avalon nodded. "Let's narrow it down or rule it out." To the pendulum, or whoever was operating it, she added, "Come closer, friends." She lowered the tip of the green pyramid until it hovered just an inch or two above the map. "Pull me wherever you need me. I'm open to your instruction."

"It's real close to the commercial site," he noted. "Right? Isn't it? Am I missing something?"

"No, you're not." Avalon gave it another ten seconds, then gave up—pulling the small stone up into her palm along with the chain. "Well, that was a bust."

"Was it?" Leda asked, unwilling to let go of the excitement. "It hung around over the site, didn't it?"

"Only loosely. It didn't do anything except point us at the place we're already looking. I'm sorry, but this was not terribly useful. Detective"—she turned her attention to Grady—"you might as well keep the map. It might be evidence, or it might be leverage."

"If this turns out to have been a tag-team murder after all, you could be right."

"I bet it's not, though." Leda folded her arms. She watched Grady pick up the map and fold it with enough care not to tear it. "It doesn't feel right. I know that my feelings aren't evidence, but it's not. It's just not."

Grady tucked the map into his shirt pocket, even though it was damp enough around the edges to leave a little spot there. "I need to have another word with Jeff, that's for sure—and his uncle, too. It'll be convenient if I can catch them together, but it might be more useful if I catch them apart." His phone picked that moment to start buzzing wildly. He pulled it out of his pants pocket and glanced down. "Excuse me, ladies. I have to take this."

He walked away, back toward the stage, where it was quieter for the moment.

Leda was straining to hear his half of the phone call when Avalon asked her a question that threw her for a loop. "Do you trust this detective fellow?"

"Grady? Yeah, I do trust him. He's a good guy."

"Sure, but he's rather stuck in his ways, isn't he? That's how he struck me, at any rate—when you told me about your adventures last year."

Defensively, she shrugged. "He's come a long way since we first met. When it comes to woo-woo stuff, some people need to dip their toes in slowly."

"True, but his dedication to procedure might be more of a hindrance than a help."

Leda countered, "And his access to police resources, combined with his willingness to share information when he probably shouldn't . . . makes him more helpful than a hindrance."

Avalon gave this a moment's consideration. "Very well. He's just so . . . skeptical." She tucked the pendulum away in her bag. "But don't worry. We'll work on him."

The skeptic in question returned to the table and dropped himself back into the seat with a triumphant energy. "That was Sam. My partner, Sam. Detective partner, not . . ." He began to clarify for Avalon's sake but then changed his mind. "Anyway. On a lark this afternoon, I had him talk to the building manager where Helena Smith lives."

"The reader? TA? Whatever she is?" Leda asked.

"Right. The one who wasn't sleeping with her boss, so far as we know. First, she told me she saw him for the last time around three o'clock Wednesday afternoon. Then, when we caught her on security video, she admitted she'd seen him later that night, around nine o'clock. She swore he gave her a ride to the light rail station and that's it. But I don't think she was telling the truth."

Leda was all ears. "Oh?"

"Depending on traffic to the station and the timing of the trains, the trip from Padelford Hall to her apartment shouldn't have taken more than half an hour."

"Where does she live?" Leda asked.

"A building on Harvard, just off Broadway. Siri says she's two-tenths of a mile from the Cap Hill station, so that means she's . . ." He guessed which direction was west and pointed that way. "A few blocks in that direction."

Avalon made a knowing nod. "But she *didn't* get home from the office in half an hour or less, did she?"

"That is correct," Grady told her. "Her door code wasn't used at her building for another two hours and change."

"Do you want to head over there now?" Leda asked.

He glanced at his watch. It was a smart watch with a fitness app, and it had a shiny animated background. "It's a little late for that now. I'd need a warrant to push my way inside, but not to knock on the door and ask a question or two. How long is it until your set?" Then he stopped himself. "No, wait. Stop. Never mind. I've already had one drink, and I'm a lightweight. Let's not push our luck, eh? I'll put her on the list for tomorrow."

"Ooh! Can I come with you if you go to talk to her?" Leda openly begged. "Please, please let me come with you? I haven't met this girl yet."

"And I haven't met Dan Matarese yet. Maybe we should swap out."

"I like the way you think, good sir." Leda held up her own drink, which was a bright green Midori sour, because she hadn't felt too confident about anything with kiwi and gin, but she liked green. "Let's play text tag tomorrow and sort it out then."

A round of toasts were made, to maps and progress and tag-team investigations.

Leda excused herself to get ready for her set. She had only an hour left before the show was supposed to start, and she needed to change clothes and touch up her makeup, so she left Grady and Avalon alone together and went to Ben's tiny closet of an office, where she used to keep a murder board—back when she and Grady had first collaborated on the case that had closed an old wound: her late and beloved Tod, gone almost five years now. But his killer was behind bars, and she had room in her heart at last to put it all behind her.

Still, she looked at the magnetic whiteboard that she'd used to map out murder suspects and alibis. Maybe she should take another run at it. She had plenty of index cards and magnets. Tonight, she was staging for a karaoke show, or a psychic psongstress outing, as the case might be. But tomorrow? Tomorrow she might sit around in her thinking hat, playing with Sharpies and sorting out her thoughts.

A knock on the door surprised her enough that she blurted out, "I don't actually have a thinking hat!"

It was Niki. "What about that shiny pink hat you like so much? The one you found on clearance at Nordstrom Rack? That's kind of thinky."

"That's for rain, and it's not thinky, it's adorable. Do me a favor, would you? Shut the door."

"Wardrobe change?"

"Wardrobe change," Leda confirmed.

Niki stepped inside and closed the door behind herself. "Sequins or fringes?"

"I'm thinking sequins. It's been a long day, and I could use some sparkle in my life."

While she and Niki primped and prepped, she tried to push the murder board out of her head, but she was already thinking about what color cards to use and which names to put where. The case of the two missing and presumed dead Reddicks was a hot mess of assorted actors and motives. It might be time to invest in some string and some more magnets.

"Tonight, I deserve some sparkle," she promised herself as she did her best with some liquid eyeliner and wished hard for Avalon's effortless makeup skills. "Tomorrow, we buckle down, and then? Then this shit gets *serious*."

19. GRADY MERRITT

WEDNESDAY NIGHT/WEE HOURS OF THURSDAY

It was almost midnight by the time Leda put down her microphone and the tightly packed bar began to empty. Grady had thoroughly sobered up by then, even though he'd had a total of three whiskey sours. He was off duty, and now it was time to head home, where Molly would go to bed literally the moment she heard his car pulling into the driveway—and pretend she'd been there snoozing happily since ten o'clock. He bid everyone a good evening, felt around in his pocket until he'd snagged his car keys.

His phone buzzed.

It was Sam Wilco, and, given the time of night, it probably wasn't a social call.

"What's going on, Sam?"

"You sound like you're still up and around. You said you were headed out to that bar on Cap Hill tonight. Is that where you are now?"

"Yeah, I'm just leaving."

"Text your kid and tell her you won't be home just yet. Helena Smith lives over there on the hill, too. You know, the girl who's—"

"Paul Reddick's reader, I know."

"Right, right. There's been a break-in at her place. You want to swing by and let her cry to a friendly face? It might be . . . let's say, outside your purview, but . . ."

"But yeah, I can head over there."

Sam gave him the address for an older building on Harvard Avenue and wished him luck. "It's my turn to sit up with the baby, but he's asleep now. Finally. I can turn off the police scanner and turn in myself."

"You two are still using it for white noise while you feed the kid?"

"White noise and gossip, damn straight. Just thought you'd like the heads-up."

Grady said, "I appreciate it. Now go get some sleep."

He hung up and dropped the phone back into his pocket, then headed for the door—but Niki stopped him. "We're getting pizza across the street. Or hot dogs. I think the cart's still there. You want in?"

For a split second, he considered telling her about Sam's call. But only a split second. "Thanks, but Molly's waiting up for me back home. I'll grab a Seattle dog next time."

"Suit yourself!"

He excused himself, said his goodbyes, and left—retrieving his phone long enough to double-check the location of Helena's apartment and decide that he should probably drive rather than walk. Fifteen minutes later he was second-guessing that decision, having parked too close to a corner stop sign because it was either there or no place—given police presence and neighborhood gawkers. The thoroughfares around the building were all narrow side streets, and the traffic went both ways, in theory, but each one offered only a single open lane between a row of parked cars on either side. Even a couple of additional cop cars and a handful of nosy spectators made the scene feel unduly claustrophobic.

Helena's apartment was inside one of the older residential buildings on the hill, built sometime around the turn of the previous century in a neoclassical style with columns and brick. It had seen better days, but it had plenty of good-enough days ahead of it.

The young woman in question was sitting on the steps with red eyes and a paper cup of coffee. She was talking to a uniformed officer Grady didn't recognize, a tall Asian woman with black wire-rimmed glasses. The officer looked bored and a little annoyed with the nervously chattering crime victim, so Grady took a chance. He approached the officer and showed her his badge.

"Excuse me, I'm Grady Merritt, with homicide. I know this isn't my show, but—"

"Detective?" Helena greeted him with less enthusiasm than surprise.

He put his badge away and explained to his fellow officer, "I've spoken to Ms. Smith a couple of times in connection to a case, and I caught the break-in on the police scanner while I was in the area. Do you mind if I have yet another word with her?"

"Knock yourself out," she told him, sounding delighted to have been relieved of the task. She said something quick into the radio on her chest and retreated down the steps to one of the squad cars.

He turned his attention to the reader. "Are you all right?"

"I'm fine for now, but my roommate is going to kill me when she gets back from Portland tomorrow." She caught herself. "Not *murder* me, murder me. She's a little high-strung. But nobody . . . nobody will *really* murder anyone. Don't worry."

Grady said, "Okay, I won't. Did you see what happened, or did you come home and find the burglary in progress?"

"My neighbor across the hall called me about half an hour ago, asking if everything was okay, because it sounded like something was happening in my apartment. I was at the goth bar. I got home as fast as I could, but I didn't have my car so I had to call an Uber. Can't exactly run eight blocks in *these* shoes." She waved one foot at him. The shoe was sharp and black, and it did not look especially practical for an eight-block sprint.

"What time did your friend call you?" he asked, trying to do the mental math.

She scrunched up her forehead, then sighed and remembered to pull out her phone. "Eleven seventeen," she said, showing him the screen with a list of recent calls. "That's when it was happening."

"How bad's the damage?"

She shook her head and sighed again. "Not much is broken, and I can't tell if anything was stolen. My stuff looks okay, for the most part. I can't vouch for Nancy's."

"Your roommate?" Maybe the break-in was a coincidence. Maybe it was about the roommate and had nothing to do with Paul Reddick. But he had a feeling.

"Yeah."

While she was on a roll, answering questions with precision and evidence to back up her answers, Grady took a chance and redirected the subject. "Hey, your apartment is a ground-floor unit, right? That one, over there?" Through the curtains, he could see a uniformed officer pacing back and forth, talking on his cell phone.

"Yeah. I know, I know. My mom told me I shouldn't live on the ground floor, because I'm more likely to get . . . to get burgled that way."

"But it's a good location, though. You're nice and close to the light rail station, aren't you?" He didn't give her time to answer, lest she figure out where he was going. "It shouldn't be more than a five-minute walk. Of course, it was only a five-minute drive from Padelford Hall to the U District station—which makes me wonder . . . why did it take you two hours to get home Wednesday night?"

She stared at him blankly. It occurred to him that she was probably still a little drunk. She was wearing vinyl black and matte black, patent leather black and lace black, and a careful deep purple lipstick job that had been chewed down to the edge of her lip line.

Confused, she replied, "I got here in, like, fifteen minutes."

He shook his head. "No, I mean the Wednesday night when your boss went missing. Where did you go, Helena? Did he take you somewhere? Did you talk? Did I completely misread the nature of the relationship you two had?"

Recognition seeped into her eyes. "Ooooh. *That.*"

"This is the third time I'm asking, and this time you need to tell me the truth—or I need to bring you in to the station for a more formal line of questioning."

"Ugh, all right, Jesus." She sagged mournfully and set the coffee cup down beside her leg. "Wednesday night, I went to Ba Bar with Dr. Reddick. Not like a date," she specified at lightning speed. "We were both . . . I don't know. We'd both had a bad day, and he'd had that fight with Julie, and he was so bummed out. I only did it to keep him company. Nothing happened." She said the last part with such a pure, honest note of disappointment that this time Grady thought she might well be telling the truth.

"You can't keep lying to police like that, Ms. Smith."

"Well, I'm not lying now. Are you happy?"

"Why would I be happy?" he asked. "You're obviously having a bad night, and I don't want to make more trouble for you. I just want you to be honest. That would make me happy."

She exhaled through her nose, a reverse snort that said she

didn't believe him any more than he believed her. "I bet you aren't even supposed to be here."

He shrugged. "Be where, outside your building? On the sidewalk? I have as much right to be here as anybody else, but I'll steer clear of whatever investigation is going on inside. I don't want to muddy any waters. I just came over to make sure you were all right."

"And to see if the break-in had anything to do with what happened to Paul."

All right, so she wasn't *that* drunk.

"Right now, everyone who had a personal connection to the man is a person of interest in his death. Do you think this break-in had anything to do with him?" he asked, just in case she had any bright ideas or accusations.

She didn't disappoint. "Yes, I do. I don't know how or why, but I've been living here for almost three years, and I never had any problems until Dr. Reddick left. Disappeared. Died, whatever. A couple of days after I saw him last . . . on Friday, I think, after that Wednesday . . . I came home and somebody had tried to jimmy the door. The inside door, you know. Not the front door with the call box."

"But they didn't get inside?"

She shook her head. "No, but I think they came back later to do this"—she waved toward her apartment—"and I don't know why they bothered. I don't have any money. My laptop is usually with me or at school. That's the only thing I can think of. . . ."

"Where's the laptop now?"

"On my desk, inside." She jerked a thumb toward the open unit just past the entrance. "The burglar didn't touch it."

"Interesting," he concluded. "Very . . . interesting."

Grady hung around another five or ten minutes to make sure that no one was hurt, nothing of importance was taken, and

Helena had finished lying to him and everyone else. Then he went back to his car and squeaked back out into the side street, off the hill, and back to his home.

The lights were off when he pulled up. He heard a soft *woof* when he put his key in the door. Cairo was waiting for him with a toy in his mouth and a wag in his tail. Molly was asleep on the couch, but she shot awake when Grady shut the door behind himself.

"Dad!"

"Sorry! I didn't mean to scare you."

She looked at her phone. It was lying on her chest. It'd fallen there when she conked out. "It's after one in the morning! Where have you been, young man?"

"Very funny." He crouched down to rub Cairo's head and give the rope toy a tug or two.

"Must've been one heck of a karaoke night. Did you sing anything this time?"

"What? No. Nobody but Leda did. They only have open karaoke mics on her off nights. That's not why I'm late. Right when I was getting ready to leave, I got a call from Sam."

"They're gonna traumatize that baby before he's old enough to walk."

Grady grinned and dropped himself onto the free end of the couch. "According to Sam, that'll be happening any day now. Seven months sounds young to me, but you were walking by nine months, so what do I know, anyway? It was Sam, sitting up with the little guy this time. He's the one who told me there was a break-in at a suspect's apartment nearby."

"You left a party at a cool bar to work? Dad. No birthday parties, no late-night karaoke . . . it's like you've completely forgotten how to have fun, and that's pitiful. I honestly feel sorry for you."

"No, don't do that. Like I said, everything had wrapped up for the night. I went over to the scene of the crime and had a chat with the college girl who used to be the assistant for Mr. Leg."

"Are we going to call him that forever?"

"I might. As for the assistant, I think she always wanted to call him Paul but never felt like she could get away with it."

Molly made a face and said, "Yikes."

He groaned like an old man and sank back deeper into the couch. Cairo followed him and climbed onto his lap, then curled up and acted like he'd been there all evening and could not *possibly* be expected to move now. "There's a lot of yikes in this case, yes. There's something else bugging me, too. Sometimes with murders and disappearances, we'll see a break-in or two while friends and family look for clues themselves or try to find and hide evidence. I wonder if this is one of those."

"Do you think the assistant trashed her own place to throw off suspicion?"

"I don't think that's it." Thoughtfully, he petted Cairo's head. "And the more I think about it, I wonder if this isn't Jeff's handiwork. He got inside Paul and Robin Reddick's house the other day; I'm not sure I'd say he left it trashed, but he did some ransacking—and CSI found a suspicious stash of cleaning products and residue. Leda said Jeff was looking for trinkets for her to touch."

"But you think she's wrong?"

"I'm not sure." *Occam's razor*, he told himself. *Horses, not zebras.* He turned the case over in his head again, and again, and once more. "We know Jeff tossed his parents' place, or we believe he did. Did he take a run at Helena's, too? And if he did, what was he looking for?"

"*And,*" Molly said insistently, never missing a chance to be Team Leda, "if it *wasn't* Jeff, who did it? What were they looking for?"

"Those are excellent questions, and I wish I had even a flimsy, half-assed answer for you, but I don't. And it's getting late. And you have work tomorrow, don't you?"

"Not until ten in the morning. I'm doing late brunch and lunch rush for the corporate ladies who live on wraps and espresso. I'll be fine," she vowed with a tremendous yawn. "I'm going to bed. Right now. Watch this." Molly hauled herself slowly off the couch, dropped her feet to the floor, and yawned again.

"I'll let Cairo out for Last Chance Potty. Take yourself to bed."

She gave him a thumbs-up and disappeared down the hall.

He looked down at Cairo, who was pretending to be asleep. "All right, buddy. You've got to move."

The dog gave him a shot of side-eye, then rolled dramatically off his lap.

While Cairo was in the yard doing his business, Grady sat in the dark living room with the television off, alone with the silence except for the occasional thrum of a car's engine or a distant dog barking. He couldn't stop thinking about stray legs and gold rings, and happy dogs with good noses, and volcanos and snow and very big storms with lots of lightning, when he realized he'd fallen asleep on the couch. Cairo was scratching at the back door, eager to come back inside and climb into Molly's bed.

Grady heaved himself up and rubbed at his eyes. He was missing something, and he knew it.

He just couldn't figure out what it was. Not to save his life.

20. LEDA FOLEY

THURSDAY

"I missed a break-in?" Leda moaned and grumbled. "Dammit, I miss all the good stuff."

Grady threw up his hands. "I'm sorry! But you were still closing out your gig, shaking hands and taking your bows. I would never take that away from you. Not even for a break-in."

Niki laughed and put her feet up on Leda's desk. The remains of their breakfasts were scattered around the office, and the room smelled like hash browns and cheese. She used her ankle to nudge one to-go container out of the way. "I think he's starting to get you, Leda."

"But I could've gone along for the ride! The reader might have found the presence of another woman disarming, and I might've touched her and gotten some wild visions or vibes. You *have* to quit leaving me out of all the fun stuff."

"It wasn't exactly fun. The poor kid was beside herself, and if it makes you feel better, or . . . less like you missed out on something cool, the female agent who was taking her statement didn't do anything to set her at ease. Her mind was elsewhere."

Niki asked, "You didn't get anything good out of her, did you? I feel like you would've said so already if you had."

"Eh." He crossed one leg over the other thigh and put on his thinking face. "I think she finally told me the truth about the night Paul went missing."

"She told you where she was, in the missing two-hour gap?"

"Yes, and I think I believe her. She and the professor were both having a shitty day, so they went out to commiserate at some pho bar in the University Village. Then he took her to the light rail station, and she headed home afterward. She assured me nothing happened, and she sounded disappointed about it."

"Jesus, this guy was *not* especially hot!" Leda exclaimed with wonder and awe. "I don't get what college girls see in weird old men like that."

Grady protested, "He wasn't *that* old. He was about my age, for crying out loud."

Niki also protested, but on another wavelength. "It's a power thing. Happens all the time. Some girls just can't walk away from a kindly authority figure, even if he's trying to mentor his way into their pants. Daddy issues, baby."

Grady and Leda both looked at her in silence for a few seconds.

Then Leda said, "I mean, yeah—that happens. Saw it firsthand when I was in school, but I never did wrap my head around it."

"That Intro to Art professor?" Niki recalled.

"Short, fat, bald, old. And absolutely swimming in nineteen-year-old gingers. It blew my mind."

Grady shook his head at the world in general. "Liberal arts majors, man." He chose that moment to rise from the chair and stretch. "But this morning I don't want to hear any griping. Are you ready to leave, or do you need . . . maid service? I can't tell, and I won't do it, but I'll call somebody for you."

Leda smirked and shook her head. "It's just takeout from Geraldine's. It's not the leftovers from a kegger, come on."

"I'll get it. You two go on, and I'll lock up behind you," Niki offered.

"How come?" Grady asked.

"She's due at work in another hour. Thanks, Nik," she told her. "Do me a favor, though? Take everything all the way to the dumpster around back. We don't want ants."

Leda left with Grady and climbed into his sedan. "Are we going by the auto shop first?"

"No, Jeff's taking a few days off, in the wake of his father's death. His boss sounded very understanding about the whole thing."

"Maybe he hated his dad just a little less than he thought. Like he told me, and like I've been saying all along."

"*Or* maybe he's up to something else, considering he emailed Paul's schedule to his uncle just a few days before the man went missing. Let's swing by the Angeline." Grady drove them several blocks to the large new apartment building with a giant hippie grocery store occupying most of the ground level. He parked in front of a pet store on the corner. "He's on the third floor. Let's see if he's home."

But no one answered their knocks, and when Grady asked management to let him inside for a welfare check, there was no sign of the sole known surviving Reddick. The place was tidy and pet-free, if full of IKEA furniture, with Trader Joe's bags and milk crates serving as the primary forms of storage.

"Looks like a dorm room," Grady observed.

"Boy, dorm rooms must be sad, sad places."

"You're not wrong. Oh well, this is a bust." He thanked the manager for her time, and then he and Leda piled back into his car.

"I can't believe he wasn't home. This is bullshit."

"Happens all the time," he assured her. "Imagine how much harder this kind of work was before cell phones, internet, and GPS."

"I'd rather not. It sounds like a slog."

"I'm sure it could be. Let's move on to Dan's place. Maybe they're together." Grady made for the Central District and plugged an address into his car's GPS.

Dan lived in a duplex at the southern end of SODO—a pleasant and well-kept place that was a tad boring for Leda's tastes, but she appreciated a clean line of design as much as the next girl. It was gray with white trim and a small porch and a walkway shaded by a large alder tree.

But Dan was not home, either.

Leda was displeased.

She threw her hands up and said, "Fine! Maybe it's not a coincidence and they're in cahoots. But I say that's a stretch. I mean, think about it: Dan reached out to me for help finding his sister. Jeff is a big cinnamon roll of a young man. I just can't make it . . . make sense. You know what this calls for?"

The look on Grady's face said that he was afraid to ask. He asked anyway. "All right, surprise me. What does it call for?"

"Let's go back to my office. I have something to show you."

"That's . . . not an answer. Wait, did you do something ridiculous? Oh God."

"Give me an ounce of credit, please."

"Okay. But only an ounce."

"Hey, that's a full alcoholic beverage. Nothing to sneeze at, and I accept your confidence."

He did not rise to the bait but dutifully returned them to the office instead—where Leda let them both back inside to find that Niki was as good as her word and all the breakfast trash had been removed. Grady pulled the door shut. "All right, what do you want to show me?"

"It's right in front of your face, but you didn't notice it earlier," she hinted. Hard. And she waited for the detective to see the enormous whiteboard that lurked behind her desk. It was flipped over so the blank side faced the room.

He only took a few seconds. "I *did* notice it. I thought you were using it as a Zoom backdrop or something. But that's not what it is, is it? You actually hauled that thing all the way down here from Castaways, didn't you?" After a pause he added another question: "How did you get it into your car?"

She squeezed past her desk and flipped the board over so that the part that was covered with stuff now faced out into the room. "I didn't. Matt drove it over in his truck."

"How did he get it out of that office?"

"I didn't ask. Magic, I suspect. But he was kind enough to deliver it after the show last night. I was up late getting it ready, and then I was up early tweaking it."

Curiously, cautiously, he approached the freshly relocated murder board. "When did you sleep?"

"Sleep is for the weak." She stood beside him, staring at the board. Then she retreated half a step to sit on the edge of her desk. "Anyway, this is what I've got." What she had was chaos. Strings, magnets, strips of tape, and scraggly handwriting in several different colors combined to create a big rectangle with minimal white space and maximal confusion.

"You've been busy. Again. Oh, hey, new magnets. Nice."

"I found them at the florist down the street. Aren't they cute?"

"Aren't they . . ." He squinted at the round glass magnets. "Poisonous plants? Well, that one's a Venus flytrap."

"Plants to be wary of. I think that was the gist."

Together they stared at the board, divided into two sides: one for Paul Reddick and one for Robin Reddick. Beneath each column, a stack of index cards descended. In a few places, the cards were connected with red yarn.

"You finally got some string. *Now* it's a proper murder board," he said, with a faint note that could mean either general approval or gentle mockery—and she wasn't sure which.

Leda decided to take it as a compliment. "Niki's been teaching herself how to knit. I just stole some of her yarn, so it's not really *string*, per se. Still, it does the job."

"Yarn, string, whatever. All right, you've got my attention. And I think I know what's going on, but you should still walk me through it."

"I thought you'd never ask." She took up a position beside the board, facing Grady, and using a pencil as a pointer. "I know this isn't as dramatic as the reveal at Castaways last time . . . but I don't *have* a big reveal this time, so who cares, right?"

"Right. I mean, it would be great if you *did*, but we'll work with what we've got."

She cleared her throat and tapped the first card. "Let's start with Robin, because she disappeared first. Robin went missing about a month ago, give or take, sometime around the Fourth of July."

"Because of the rain. Based on your hunch, or Avalon's hunch."

"Based on that, and the fact that no one has seen her since then. We think—but we do not *know*—that she might have vanished somewhere around the big work-site gig she took this summer, out near Southcenter in Tukwila. But that's just a guess. That's why this card is pink. I used white ones for facts, pink ones for hunches."

"I can dig it."

"Thank you." She'd lost her place. She paused and found it again. "We also know that she was in possession of a big bag of money when she vanished into the ether. It's technically possible—no matter what her loved ones believe—that she took the money and ran. It's also possible that she was robbed for that money by some unknown . . . I don't know. Carjacker, or whatever. Though I don't know how, exactly, you'd get rid of that bright orange car."

"Me either," Grady agreed. "You'd have to throw it into the Sound to hide your crime, so let's leave carjacking off the table for now. Except . . . and I don't think you'll like this idea, but—"

"But Jeff, yeah, I already thought of that. I just didn't write it down."

"He has the skills, the tools, and the access to space necessary to break down the car and sell it for parts, or dump it, or paint it. I'm not saying that's what happened; I'm just saying we'd be stupid to leave it out of the possibilities pool. You should put it on a card and stick it on your board."

"Feels like you're peeing in my possibilities pool, but okay," she granted grumpily. "Jeff could have disappeared the car. I'll add another card later. But for now, here—these are the official suspects. The ones in the family go on this card, so that's Dan and Jeff. The nonrelatives are on this one: Helena and Julie. And here, on this one, the main suspect for my money."

"Paul. Just his name. All by itself," he observed.

She nodded. "That's also why the red yarn connects it to his column. He's gone, too, but that doesn't mean he didn't do something to Robin before he died."

"Fair."

"On the bottom pink card is all I've gotten so far from my flashes with regards to Robin. That sense of being enclosed and doomed. Also, a footnote with regards to the locket," she mumbled, scribbling that on as she spoke.

Grady eyed it all while drumming his fingers on the edge of the table. He did it so gently that Leda could barely hear it, and it was hardly annoying at all. "Okay, it's looking a little naked, but it's a good start. Now walk me through Paul."

"Paul's side is a little busier, because we have more info on him. For starters"—she tapped the top card and worked her way down— "we have his leg. We know it was found at Mount Rainier, and that he and his wife had problems for years. We know that . . ." She tugged the string connecting the next card to the bit about Dan and Jeff. "His son and brother-in-law both thought he was a true piece of shit. But we *also* know that he had both a girlfriend and an assistant with sketchy personal boundaries."

She pointed to cards for Helena and Julie.

She stopped talking and took a step back, sitting on the edge of the desk again. "Shit," she said. "You're right. This felt like a lot of work at two a.m., but now that I'm looking at it, it's pretty naked."

"That's okay; it's still a good start. Here, give me your cards." She did, so he pulled a pen out of her I'D RATHER BE ZIPLINING IN HAWAII mug and started to write. "The break-in. Let's put that up there. I won't know if they got any fingerprints from Helena's apartment for another day or two, but if there aren't any . . . it's circumstantial, but it starts to look like a pattern. Someone tried to get into her place once before, too. That tells me someone is looking for something, but what?"

"You should put this on a pink card."

"Why?" he asked.

"Because it's speculation. We don't even know if the break-in had anything to do with the Reddicks being AWOL. We just suspect that it might."

"Okay, give me a pink card."

Ten minutes later, the board looked busier but not clearer.

With a tremendous sigh, Leda said, "This is a big waste of time, isn't it?"

"Nobody said that." Grady spoke slowly as he thought out loud. "If someone got inside Helena's apartment by force, who was it? And what were they looking for? If we could figure that out, we might be onto something." Then he said, "Hm. Helena didn't know Robin, or at least she didn't know her well. By all reports, Robin stayed away from campus. If we assume that Helena's ground-floor corner unit was not merely burgled by a random opportunist . . . it was more likely to be about Paul. Let's put that pink card under his name instead of in the middle."

"Is your gut telling you that?" she asked. "Because you won't fully trust *my* gut, remember?"

"I've known my gut longer than I've known your gut—and I already told you, I give your gut plenty of weight. More than I should, maybe." If you'd asked him three years ago if he'd ever work a case with a psychic, he would've asked if you needed a psychiatrist. He drummed his fingers harder still on the side of the desk. If he was aware that it was driving Leda nuts, he didn't show it. Did her own fidgeting bug people this much? Surely not.

Leda caught a flicker. Not a vibe. Not a bolt of lightning. Just a flicker, like the beginning of an ocular migraine—a fancy white light tickling the edge of her vision. No, not a white light. A cloud, vivid and pale against a wide, bright blue. Like she was looking straight up on a Seattle summer day.

"Leda? You okay?"

She must have zoned out. "I'm good!" she declared without explaining, except to say, "I'm just really, really tired. I was up way too late last night." What good would explaining do? It wouldn't tell him anything, and it might only convince him that all she had left in her psychic tank was fits and starts, or images that would make nice desktop backgrounds. She stared at the board as hard as she could, willing it to tell her something new and useful that she could contribute to the case—because a very faint vision of a cloud just wasn't going to cut it.

Nothing new came to her.

But Grady's phone started ringing.

21. GRADY MERRITT
THURSDAY

Sam was on the other end of the line, and he sounded excited. "Got some news for you, man. Impound's finished with Paul Reddick's car."

Grady's ears perked sky-high. "Hit me." He shot one eye at the murder board.

Leda mouthed, *What?*

He waved to tell her to be quiet and wait a minute.

Sam said, "They're finished going over it, and everything's bagged and tagged. You'll need to give Rudy a call, send him a report, whatever."

"Anything interesting in there?"

"It's not my case, remember? But the impound guys were grinning when they dropped it off," Sam told him. "It's all yours, waiting for you here at your desk. I'm calling it now, though: the ungraded papers and takeout trash are probably *not* clues."

Grady picked up a white card from the little stack Leda had

sitting on the desk beside her butt. "Okay, I'll be back in half an hour. Don't let anything walk off without me." He hung up and clicked his pen open again.

"Who was that? What's going on?"

Upon the card, he scrawled, *Paul's car, and everything in it.* Then he picked up a stray magnet and stuck the card to the whiteboard on Paul's side of the evidence list. "Impound is finished with Mr. Leg's ride, and the evidence is waiting for me back at the office."

"Does that mean you're leaving now?"

"Yes," he confirmed. "I'll let you know if anything important shows up, all right? But it might be later this afternoon. I haven't heard from Rudy in a few days, so I need to give him a call. Maybe he's scared up some extra information in Pierce County."

Leda stopped.

"Wait, where was Paul's car?"

He tucked his notebook and pen back into his usual pocket. "In the garage next to Padelford Hall. I'll go check it out, but in the meantime, have a lovely afternoon."

"You too," she said with a wave as he left, but he wasn't sure she meant it. He was fairly confident that she wanted to come with him and go picking through the loot herself, in case of touch-zap vibes, but it was one thing to bring her cataloged evidence, and another for her to get first crack at it in the station . . . where he had to explain himself to other people. Like his boss, for example.

He still had a job to do, and that job still had rules. At bare minimum, he should pretend to follow most of them.

When Grady got back to the precinct and was once again safely ensconced at his desk, Sam was absent—but a box full of the Reddick vehicular contents was waiting right where he had promised. Grady popped the lid and started shuffling through the offerings.

He was just pulling out the first evidence bags when Sam returned. "You made good time getting back."

"Sometimes traffic will surprise you," he agreed. He scanned the items once again. "Is this all they found?"

"Apparently, the dead professor kept a clean chariot. Or . . . mostly clean. He stopped at Dick's a day or two before he left his car for good, and his leftovers had really started to stink, but other than that, the impound guy said it was fairly straightforward. CSI's finished with it, so all prints are secured and out for processing, as well as some, uh . . ." He reached into the box and pulled out an inventory sheet. "Assorted hair fibers and a few weird sticky spots that were sampled for the lab."

"Nothing screamingly suspicious?"

Sam grinned. "Well, the impound guys hinted very strongly about some paperwork that might be case-relevant. Keep digging."

Grady did so, setting aside a couple of folders filled with carefully stapled term papers that hadn't been touched, and now likely wouldn't be. Then he retrieved a bag with several crumpled pages inside.

"That must be what the guy was talking about. Open it up and give it a read. I'm told that it's rather, and I quote, 'juicy.'"

Grady slit the seal and removed the bag's contents, spreading them on his desk. "Oh boy. Looks like a Dear Jane letter."

Sam put his chin in his hands and pretended to make heart eyes. "Is it dramatic? Tragic? Thrilling?"

Grady didn't rise to the bait. "It's overwritten and tacky, considering he's dumping a student, but oh ho *ho* . . ." He changed his tone. He read slowly because the handwriting was as terrible as any medical doctor's signature. Maybe it was something that came by default with every postgraduate degree.

"What? Spill the tea, or however the kids put it."

"The first part's just . . . 'darling, dear, in these troubled times, some things aren't meant to be,' et cetera. He's mostly whining about how difficult it is to lead two lives. Here, it says . . . hang on." He squinted down at the pages, shuffled them, and put them in the correct order. "'I can't change the choices I made before you were born, and we both knew that this would take an outstanding degree of work from us both, if we wanted to create something strong and lasting. But I can't do this with so many external forces working against us.'"

"External forces?" Sam asked in a deliberately leading and eager fashion.

"Hm, yes. 'It's bad enough that my own family retreats to shallow assessments and snap moral judgments. But when yours joins the fray, it simply becomes too dangerous for us both. You are nearly finished with school, and to paraphrase Churchill, this is not the end. It's not the beginning of the end. It's the end of the beginning.'"

"Is the man seriously . . . is he dropping World War Two quotes in a breakup letter?" He sounded as if he was trying not to laugh.

"In addition to everything else, he's pompous as hell," Grady concluded. "But here's the good part: 'If you can't keep your brother away from me and my family with your sisterly pleas, I'll be forced to contact the authorities. Neither one of us wants that. We have had such wonderful lives together, these last eight months; now it's time for us to have wonderful lives apart. It's time for us to heal and recover and proceed into the future without each other's hand to hold.' Good God, this is cheesy."

"Cheesy, yes. But what was that about the brother . . . ?" Sam asked with exaggerated innocent curiosity.

"Carson Coleman said that he'd never met Paul, that he'd only seen him in passing. Even if his threats came via voice mail or email," he said, waving the sheet, "threats are threats. This needs to go on the murder board. I didn't have this guy on my radar as a likely suspect, but . . ."

Grady trailed off and was quiet for a few moments.

"But what? And what murder board? We don't have one handy, but we could probably requisition one from downstairs. . . ."

Grady was thinking. "I'm doing math in my head, give me a second. All right. So here's the timeline," he said, pushing the box to the side and sitting down in his chair. "Julie and Paul start hooking up roughly eight or nine months ago. It goes swell at first, but his wife and son don't like it—even if they don't know the exact identity of this semester's fling—and apparently the fling's brother doesn't care for it, either. At some point, Carson threatens Paul. Maybe he goes to the Reddick home and raises a stink. Maybe he goes to the office; we might need to hunt for more security cam footage, or I can try Helena again. She might know, and she might even tell me the truth, if I'm lucky. She knows Julie came by Paul's office and that they fought about something. I have to assume it was this letter, which Julie read and probably threw in Paul's face. Then Paul . . . Paul kept it, and he stashed it in his car."

"Why would he do that?"

Grady snorted. "Any number of reasons, not least of all to keep anyone else from finding it and reading it. Janitors, random students seeking guidance . . . His office was a high-traffic area. Hell, Helena told me up front that she'd gone looking for it but couldn't find it. He wouldn't leave evidence of an affair with a student just lying around."

"Fine, okay. But hear me out," Sam tried. "Carson Coleman is what, college-aged like his sister? Give or take?"

"He's a couple of years older than her, I think."

"Yeah, but he and Jeff Reddick are about the same age, right? And one works on planes, one works on cars. . . . They have some interests in common. They could be working together."

Grady hadn't thought about it that way. "That's not a bad angle, but I don't know if it holds water."

"I'm just saying, we've got two young guys with an enemy in common. If they ever met, they'd have a lot to talk about. They could almost pull off a *Strangers on a Train*."

"We don't know that they're acquainted, but that's definitely worth looking into. I wonder if either of them has any Pierce County connections they've failed to mention."

"I checked Carson's alibi, and he was squeaky clean. He was down in California fighting the Sonoma fire when Paul disappeared. *Although* . . ." Now he was bouncing in his seat and drumming his fingers at the same time. "There's a gap between Paul's Wednesday night or early Thursday disappearance and the time we found his leg, and we aren't sure how wide that gap is. We just know that he didn't show up for class on Thursday morning."

"Two guys working together can really muddle a scene," Sam added.

"That's true, but . . ." He went to his laptop and pulled up his email, then scrolled around until he found what he was looking for. "I like the way you think; however, if we're talking about two guys working together, we're more likely to be talking about Jeff and Dan."

"Why's that?"

Grady started ticking off reasons as he clicked the email and opened it. "They were close—closer than Jeff and his dad, by far. They were both deeply worried about Robin when they realized she'd vanished. They both confronted Paul about it."

Sam sat forward. "Wait, they both did? You said the son's the one who chewed Paul out and filed the missing persons report, but you didn't say anything about the brother taking a run at him."

"No, but Leda did. She said they'd had some kind of fight in a hallway. Not a martial arts fight," he muttered as he skimmed the email. There was an attachment. He clicked it. "More like a screaming match. And now we know she was right."

He turned the laptop around so its screen faced Sam, and he hit Play on a short, soundless video clip.

Sam leaned in. "I can't really tell what's happening here. One guy has his back to the camera . . ."

"That's Paul. The pissed-off guy facing the camera, looking like his head's about to explode like a cartoon atom bomb with rage . . . that's Dan Matarese."

"How did you find this?" he asked with wonder.

Grady grinned. "Jack said he got a tech to take a look through the unedited security footage."

Transfixed, Sam squinted at the grainy black-and-white scene. "Looks like it's all shouting, no swinging, and . . . yup. There he goes. Dan left without throwing a punch, but that doesn't mean he didn't kill him later."

"Correct. Look, Paul just goes back into his office like it was nothing."

"That assistant of his is still holding out on you, man. She didn't say anything about this fight, did she?"

"No, but right there, see? Her office door is shut—it wasn't like when Julie came by. Christ, a lot of people swung by to yell at this man. . . ."

"You think she wasn't in the office?"

"Yeah, Helena was someplace else. She watched Paul like a hawk and was always eager to console him. If she were present, she would've appeared." He turned his laptop around and sat back in his chair, drumming his nails against the desk yet again. "Maybe we bring in Jeff and Dan for questioning, separately. We don't have much pretext, but we don't need much to ask a few questions." He picked up a pencil and started using it like a drumstick on his knee. Then he stopped and went back to the box of items from Paul's car. "Let me see if there's anything else in here that might be useful."

But the rest of the box held an assortment of uninteresting objects, including a travel mug for coffee, a suction-cup window holder for a cell phone, the car manual and insurance cards, two ballpoint pens, and pair of sunglasses in a holder.

"Ordinary personal effects," Sam declared with disappointment.

"We'll return them to Jeff. He's next of kin, since there's still no sign of Robin." He shrugged to himself. "But when I went looking for him this morning, I struck out."

"Really?"

He nodded. "I called his cell, left a message. Called his work, went by his apartment. Ditto Dan Matarese. I hesitate to say that these two are in the wind, since it *could* be perfectly innocent, and I didn't peg either one of them for a flight risk. Goddammit," he swore. He loaded everything except for the letter back into the box. "I'd better call Rudy and catch him up on the latest. Maybe he'll have good news for me. That would be nice for once, wouldn't it?"

"Tell you what, I'll hold my breath."

Grady pulled out his phone and called up the Pierce County officer. Rudy picked up on the third ring, and he must have had Grady's contact info added to his phone, because he said, "Hello there, Detective. Got any good news for me?"

"Hey, Rudy. I was going to ask you the same thing," he said with a smile.

Rudy was smiling back on the other end of the line. Grady could hear it in his voice. "You want to hear my report first? Don't worry, it's short."

"Go for it."

"We don't know what Mr. Leg was doing here, we don't know how he got here, and we don't know where the rest of him is. That's it, in a nutshell. No one in or around the park will admit to having ever seen him before—around his disappearance or any other time."

Grady sighed. "No brilliant theories as to how it all happened, is what you're telling me."

"Right now I'm thinking . . . transporter accident. Like on *Star Trek*. That's why we only found his leg; the rest didn't make it through, due to some technical glitch. Maybe Scotty screwed up. It *had* to happen every now and again."

He laughed and said, "Sure, why not."

Rudy continued, a note of desperation bleeding through the line. "Now *please* say you have something for me. I've been out here doing all this stupid legwork for more than a week now—"

"Wocka wocka."

"Yeah, yeah. I heard it as soon as I said it. Anyway, it's starting to feel hopeless. Unless he disguised himself pretty thoroughly, or unless he clicked his heels together three times, I can't explain a damn thing about what he was doing in our park. Or what that one specific part of him was doing here."

"Still no hits from the cadaver dogs?" Grady asked.

"There are hits, and then there are *hits*. I think we might have narrowed the area somewhat, but that's the best I can say. We've had two teams of dogs searching daily, and none of them have found squat—but they've been clustering in the same general zone."

"How big is this new search area?"

"Maybe ten acres. I know it sounds like a lot to search on foot in the woods with nothing but a dog's nose to guide you, but in fact it's actually . . . okay, yeah, it's a lot. We're working for it. One of the dogs in particular has been real keen on a single acre, so I've been paying a little more attention over there. Mostly because it's my cousin's bloodhound, T-rex, and I've seen that dog find a single dead chipmunk in a waist-high field of grass the size of a football field."

"T-rex?"

Rudy nodded. "They supposedly had really great noses, just like a bloodhound. Haven't you ever seen *Jurassic Park*?"

"Not recently. But in case it makes your day a little brighter, I actually *do* have something that might be useful for you. If nothing else, it tells us what *didn't* happen."

"Oh yeah? What's that?"

"We found Paul Reddick's car right where he left it—in the parking garage beside the hall where his office is. Therefore, we know he didn't drive to Rainier. That's the only thing I'll say with close to one hundred percent confidence. As for the rest, I have a lot of speculation and rumor, and a crumpled-up breakup letter. This would be so much easier if this guy hadn't been so universally loathed."

"Better a loathsome turd gets whacked than someone perfectly nice."

"All right, you've got me there." Then Grady gave him a light rundown on the suspects and the stories so far, since there were no suspects or stories to relate from a couple hours south. When he'd finished with his rundown, he wrapped up by saying, "Now we're looking at the idea of a murder partnership between the uncle and nephew. But honestly, I'm talking out of my ass to even tell you this much."

"Still no sign of the wife?"

"Still no sign of the wife," he confirmed. "No sign of her, her car, or any credit card and bank activity. Just like her dead husband."

Rudy asked, "Do you think she's dead, too?"

"Probably. It's always possible that she took that money and ran out on him, and it's even possible that she set him up to look guilty for her own death—and for that matter, if we really want to stretch our credibility, we could argue that she set the whole thing up and murdered him herself. Maybe she took the cash to Mexico and is having a margarita on a beach right now. Anything's possible, man. This whole case is a hot mess."

"You can say that again. While I'm thinking about it, do you want to come along on another corpse-hunting hike? We're making one more go of it this weekend, before they reopen the park to visitors for good. After that . . . if there's any evidence left on the ground, who knows. Maybe a camper will find it and save us a lot of taxpayer money."

"And accidentally tamper with it, and maybe destroy it without thinking—or even recognizing that it's important. Man, I really hate that," Grady mused. "I understand why you're reopening the park, but I wish we had more time."

"Are you in, or what?"

"Yeah, I'm in."

Everyone hung up, and Sam shook his head. "You're really driving all the way back down there again?"

"One more time, and then never again if I can possibly help it. But I'll kick myself if we don't give the search another shot. Maybe I'll even bring . . . No. I won't bring Cairo. He wasn't any help last time, and he won't be this time, either. Also, my daughter will murder me, and then that'll be a whole lot of tedious paperwork for *you*, and I wouldn't do that to you, Sam."

"I appreciate you, Grady. You're all right."

"I do what I can." And all he could do right then was pick up the box and haul it downstairs to the evidence locker—hoping he hadn't missed anything obvious.

This time.

22. LEDA FOLEY

SATURDAY

At first, Grady had pushed back—but Leda was better at badgering than Grady was at protesting, and that's why they were once again road-tripping together back down to Mount Rainier and the Paradise visitor center. This time, they had neither the dog nor the teenager present, and Niki had been stuck working a double shift the day before, so she'd bowed out at the last minute, citing general exhaustion and an aversion to cardio.

"I'm sure you're positively *crushed*," Leda said as she tossed her bag into the car and pulled the door shut behind herself. "I just know you wanted to spend several hours in the car with both of us, and I hate to break your heart."

Grady was still in the driver's seat, having only just pulled up at Leda's rental bungalow. He'd sent her a text message to tell her he'd arrived. "Actually, I was kind of looking forward to it. You two can be very entertaining. At times."

"You know what? Even with that qualifier at the end, I'll take it."

"Good, because it's the best you're getting from me today." He put the car into gear and squeezed back down the narrow street. "I'm tired, I'm confused, and I'm annoyed with this case. These cases. Whatever."

"I feel that in my *bones*," she told him. "But I'm doing this one more time or else I'll go insane. I'm missing something, I just know it."

"I definitely agree with you there, but I might've gotten a lead out of Paul's car that plugs a few holes."

Since he hadn't called to update her the day or two previously, she'd been wondering about the car—but she'd also been distracted by her travel agenting gig. It was almost becoming a proper day job; she was thrilled her clientele was growing, but it meant less time for things like collaboration with cops for crime-solving purposes.

"Don't leave me hanging; spill the beans."

With his eyes still firmly on the road, he pointed one finger at Leda and said, "Beans. Right. You're a millennial. I say the same thing—'spill the beans.' But Sam told me to spill the tea the other day, and I only halfway know what that means."

"What are you, Generation X?"

"Yeah, I'm almost forty-seven."

"Happy almost birthday. So . . . when's the actual day?" she tried yet again.

"Let it go," he said firmly.

His refusal only told Leda that she'd have to ask Molly, one of these days. "My interest is casual and passing," she lied. "But fine, I'll drop it." For now. "Just fill me in about Paul's car."

Grady seemed happy to do so, and they spent much of the subsequent trip south discussing what the Dear Jane, Your Professor Is Officially Tired of Shagging You letter really meant, so far as suspects and motives went.

They also stopped for gas once, and then for a bathroom break, because Leda had had no compunctions about getting a fountain Diet Coke the size of her head despite the long car ride. "Life is short," she'd told him—adjusting her sunglasses and touching up her lip gloss in the side mirror. "Never settle for caffeine-free."

"But you went with sugar-free, didn't you?" he'd asked.

"Sugar makes me jittery. Caffeine makes me sharp."

The trip to the mountain was closer to three hours than two, when all was said and done, but they collectively blamed it on I-5 traffic when Rudy started to tease them about it.

"You're late!" he said with a wide smile and a friendly wave.

"Tacoma!" Grady told him through the rolled-down window. "You know how it goes. Anyway, we're here now—that's the important thing. Sorry to, um, interrupt . . . ?" he concluded.

Rudy shook his head and returned his attention to a man who looked rather annoyed by the interruption. The guy had a backpack and a walking stick, along with two girls in tow. One looked like she was thirteen or fourteen, and one was younger—maybe four or five. Family resemblance suggested they were his daughters.

"Sir," said Rudy. "I apologize for the inconvenience, but a man is dead. We are trying to find out why, and how, and under what circumstances . . . and that means we have to shut down the park while we look for clues. Do you understand?"

"But that was ages ago! Come on, just let me and my kids take our hike. We drove all the way out here."

He didn't specify from where, but when Leda got out of Grady's vehicle, she saw that the car he was leaning against had a license plate frame from a Pierce County dealership—so he might've been lying.

"Sir, the park reopens Monday. Come back then."

The thwarted hiker scowled at Leda and Grady. "What about *them?* You going to kick them out, too?"

Grady flashed his badge. "I hope not, since he invited us."

A dog was barking somewhere. Leda looked toward the visitor center and saw a large, excited, slobbery dog woofing madly through the glass door.

While Rudy and the hiker argued, the two little girls entertained themselves—the older one doing a good job of keeping the younger one occupied with a series of jokes. The little one was learning how to tell them, and it was very cute, despite their father's aggravation at Rudy.

"Knock, knock."

"Who's there?"

"Pencil!"

"Pencil who?"

"Pencil fall down if you don't wear a belt!" And the punch line caused the littlest girl to explode into giggles.

Their dad's Karen-esque tirade continued. "You're making me disappoint my children. Does that make you happy? Does it make you proud of your job? This is a public park, and I pay taxes. *Public*—you know what that means?"

"Got a pretty good sense of it, yes, sir, and I won't ask you a third time. You need to pack up and head home so we can finish our investigation, and then the park's all yours again."

Grady looked like he kind of wanted to intervene, and kind of wanted to spectate. Leda didn't have any real authority in the situation, and she wasn't sure what she could usefully contribute anyway—so she kept her mouth shut for once, and she kept her eyes and ears on the cute kids.

The bigger one said, "Okay, let's try this: look up."

The little one looked up.

"Look down."

She looked down.

"Look all around."

She did that, too.

Her sister poked her in the belly and said, "Your pants are falling down!" and then tickled her mercilessly. Apparently, pants were a common punch line with the under-ten set.

The dad's griping and the girls' cackling laughter and Rudy's polite-but-firm apologies faded in Leda's ears. It was as if she'd activated a set of noise-canceling headphones; the world was bright and loud, and then it was suddenly soft and muted. Something was wrong. Or something was right? Something was *happening*.

"Look up," she breathed. The sky was vivid and clear, with a skirt of stretched-out clouds wrapped around the mountain's peak. It was so blue, it was nearly white at the edges, and so empty except for the tip of Rainier and those scattered clouds, and a chemtrail or two, and a couple of large raptors. Eagles? Hawks? Either/or. "Look up . . . look down."

Down was a paved parking lot with only a handful of cars, likely belonging to cops or K9 handlers or assorted park personnel who had to work despite the shutdown. Down did not make her feel anything at all except frustration and confusion. "Look . . . down. . . ."

Down should be something that squished between her toes, and down should be dark and cool, not bright and too warm—for the asphalt sent every stray sunray bouncing around, spreading pink sunburns to folks who lingered in the lot too long.

"Leda? Leda . . . ?" Grady patted her arm.

"What? Huh?"

"You all right?" he asked, with an inflection that demanded to be told if she was having some kind of psychic seizure, which Ben would probably put on a flyer as "psychic pseizures," and then she'd have one for real if she saw that on a telephone pole.

"Huh? Yes. Sorry. It's very bright out here, and I need my sunglasses, hold on." She made a show of digging in her bag, which she had not packed as thoroughly as she had on her first visit. Now the park visit felt like a long ride to a familiar place—not an epic quest for a ring and a wizard. She extracted the sunnies from her bag and stuck them on her face in time to watch Angry Dad and his two charming children pile back into their SUV.

"Sorry about that," Rudy said, cocking his thumb at their car. "I've chased off maybe two dozen people already today. You'd think people could read a sign, but *noooo*."

Grady shook his head. "They can read. They just think the rules apply to everybody but them." He returned his attention to Leda. "Seriously, are you okay? You zoned out pretty hard."

"I'm fine, I'm fine," she swore. "Just been in the car a long time, and then it's so bright and warm out here, I just . . . I don't know. Spaced out. Hey, is that T-rex over there, inside the center?"

The change of subject worked for everyone, even though Leda could tell by the look in Grady's eyes that he didn't really believe her.

Rudy either didn't see it or else he ignored it, because he answered happily, "Oh yeah, that's the guy in question. Best damn search dog you ever heard of, right there. I've borrowed him for the afternoon, and he's raring to go. Give me a minute and I'll get him ready. Would you two do me a favor while I take care of that?"

"Name it," Grady said.

"Move those cones and barrels to block the front entrance a little better, and then move the sign front and center. I don't want any more excuses from people who come here to test my patience."

They flashed him a thumbs-up and set to work adjusting the temporary barriers that announced, CLOSED FOR POLICE BUSINESS. WILL REOPEN MONDAY AT 7:00 A.M. WE APOLOGIZE FOR THE INCONVENIENCE.

Leda suggested that they move his car to block the exit, too, but he shook his head and declined. "Some of these people are parked here for work; they have to get out one way or another."

As soon as they were finished, a brown galumphing beast came tearing down the walkway into the parking lot on feet the size of salad plates. He beelined for Leda, who squealed with joy and immediately commenced baby talk and pettings on a big male bloodhound named for another big boy with a terrific nose. "Who's a good-good dinosaur? Who's a sweetie wiggle butt? *You're* a sweetie wiggle butt!"

"For Christ's sake, Leda . . ."

"Shut up, I'm getting dog kisses."

"You need a dog of your own. Something other than a fish, anyway."

She stood up straight, leaving one hand scratching T-rex's head. "You take Brutus's name out of your mouth."

"I didn't use it," he said dryly.

Rudy laughed at the both of them and said, "I've got water bottles and maps, and I trust you all have your phones. We do have cell service in the park these days, and in a few spots you can even pick up a little Wi-Fi. But it's pretty spotty, so let's not lose sight of one another if we can help it." He handed them each a bottle of chilled water and shrugged both of his shoulders into a backpack. "Got extra in here, and a bowl for my main man here, right, Tee?"

The dog barked happily in reply.

Together, they set off down one of the side trails they'd hit the first time around, but Leda didn't remember much about it. All the trails looked the same to her, with a few obvious exceptions where trail markers and assorted minor points of interest broke up the monotony. A wooden boardwalk here, a trash can there, a park bench somewhere else.

Leda didn't *hate* the Great Outdoors, but if pressed, she

might've called it the Sometimes Good Outdoors, or the Often Okay Outdoors. She didn't love bugs, didn't like being sweaty, and didn't like the lack of city noise, but the weather was nice, if a little warm. The trees were pretty and birdsong was pleasant. Most of the birds she heard around her home fell into a small handful of categories: crows, pigeons, starlings, and other. "Other" mostly meant "little brown jobbies of indeterminate species." Here, she could detect the high-altitude cries of raptors, the chattering of jays, and the adorable cheeping of small round things that hopped in the grass, pecking at the ground.

Look up.

She didn't know much about birds. She wasn't even thinking much about birds. She was thinking about the sky, but the sky was full of birds, right?

Look down.

Down at the ground. The ground had birds, too. Bouncing ones, half the size of tennis balls. Skittish, small things that leaped into the air if you looked at them sideways. They scattered as light and fast as popcorn ahead of the dog's approach.

T-rex darted from one side of the trail to the other with the bounding, snuffling joy of a Good Boy with a job; he stopped at trees and roots and random bits of leaf litter for a sniff or a pee. Back and forth he wandered. Up and down he sniffed. Up and down the trail. Up and down the occasional trunk, before abandoning it in favor of the next good smell.

Look up.

Up gave Leda that flat, bright sky, wide and clear blue. The edges of clouds. The occasional jetliner swerving to let the people on one side of the plane get good pictures of the volcano from high above it. The flat, bright sky. Wide. Clear blue.

Her vision wobbled around the edges, but it might only be that she was getting warm from the sun and the hiking. She shook her head, fought it off, and asked Rudy, "So how far out are we going?"

"Oh, another half mile or so. Then we'll hit the area T-rex has been chewing on. Every time we get in this one little zone, he goes into recovery mode. It's hard to explain, but his behavior shifts. He gets more alert and antsy, and I feel a little bad because I get the impression that he's as frustrated as we are. He's a hard worker with a heart of gold, and he's eager to please. The poor guy gets absolutely mournful when he can't solve a problem."

"I know the feeling," she said.

Grady asked, "What does he do, cry or bark? Hold up one paw and point? What's his signal?"

"The barking, yes. They train drug dogs to sit when they find something, so they don't take a bite out of a brick of coke or anything, but a lot of other dog jobs require them to signal with a bark. It's a distinctive bark—or it is if you know the dog."

"Oh yeah." He chuckled. "I can tell whether Cairo wants food, a walk, attention, a toy . . . you name it. Just by the tone of his voice."

Leda had nothing to contribute to this conversation, and she would've zoned right out if she hadn't been trying so hard to keep her head on straight. Several things were banging around in there at once, and she struggled to sort the signal from the noise; she was also keeping her eyes open for useful things to touch, in case she could actually be helpful.

While the two men talked about dogs and T-rex zigzagged happily in front of them, she asked herself how much of her confusion was related to her psychic senses. How much of it was simply too much information, and too much confusion between two cases with so much overlap?

She was still debating the situation when T-rex froze—his legs stiff, his tail erect and quivering.

Look up. Look down. Look all around.

Rudy said, "Aw, here we go. We're getting close. Look at him, see? *Now* he's paying attention."

With a yip and a hop, T-rex took off at a dead run.

Leda looked at Grady, and Grady looked at Leda—then they both looked at Rudy.

Grady asked, "Should we chase him, or . . . ?"

Rudy shook his head. "Naw, we won't have to. He'll stop if he finds something, and he'll come back if he doesn't—or if we don't join him fast enough. We can just trail him. He's been concentrating his energy in a smaller and smaller circle, and I keep hoping he'll actually pinpoint whatever it is he smells."

"He'd better do it fast," Leda said. "If this is your last weekend with the park closed." Her own voice sounded far away. Like she was listening to herself on a voice mail. It was very strange. The woods were very strange. The men, the dog, the park benches, the signs explaining the trails and points of interest.

All very strange.

"We can still do this with the park open, but we'll be fending off helpful hikers the whole time." To T-rex up ahead somewhere, Rudy called, "Good job, buddy! Follow that nose!"

"Is that a formal command?" Grady asked.

Rudy cackled. "We don't stand much on ceremony around here. Hell, T-rex isn't even formally trained; he's just got a knack for this business."

Leda's head spun, and her eyes watered. Her knees went wobbly. She teetered, leaned, and caught herself on the side of a sturdy tree trunk that loomed beside the trail. "Guys? Guys, I need a minute."

"You all right?" asked Grady. "Where's your water? Did you finish it?"

Rudy agreed. "Come on, crack it open and drink it down. Dehydration will make you woozy."

"Haven't been here long enough for that, surely," she complained. But even to her own ears, it sounded weak. It sounded drunk. *Look up. Look down.* "Where's my water? Oh, wait, here it is." Sitting on top in her messenger bag, the condensation dampening the interior. She pulled it out and popped the cap, then guzzled enough to make the guys happy. It did not help. Static was flickering across her vision. Was she passing out? Is that what this was? *Look up. Look down.*

Look up.

Look up.

Look up.

23. GRADY MERRITT

SATURDAY

"Leda, come on—maybe . . . come over here. Sit down a minute in the shade," Grady suggested. He took her by the elbow and led her to a bench he'd spotted just down the trail. "We can take a minute. T-rex will wait for us. Let's sit down."

"Don't wanna sit down."

But she was acting too weird for him to let her keep strolling through the trees until she passed out.

Rudy said quietly, "I've got smelling salts in my bag. Got a walkie-talkie in here, too. I can reach the station if I need to."

"Don't be ridiculous." Leda was squinting like there was something wrong with her eyes. She took off her sunglasses and rubbed at her face. "I'm fine. No smelling salts necessary. I'm just getting the strangest . . . thing."

Grady patted her on the shoulder and handed her his water bottle. She looked at it with confusion, like this was ridiculous—

she had her own. Then she looked down at the bottle in her hand. It was empty. She'd downed it all without even noticing.

"Well, hell, I guess I'll take another round." She accepted the second bottle and took a swig from that, too.

"Is being thirsty part of the usual process?" Rudy asked with curiosity.

"No. Sometimes? Maybe? I don't think so. I spent all morning in a car, and this is more exercise than I typically get in a week, so I think I'm overexerting. Don't overthink it, and don't worry about me," she said more strongly, in an attempt to rally.

In the distance, T-rex was barking. Not wildly, not excitedly.

Grady asked, "Hey, Rudy, what does *that* bark mean?"

Rudy shook his head. "I think that's him saying he thought he'd found something, but then he lost it. He's been doing that a lot lately, and he gets real frustrated when he doesn't score any good hits, no matter how many treats I give him."

Leda was looking in the direction of the barks. "He's not roaming anymore. Let's catch up to him. Guys, I'm fine. Stop hovering. It's sweet, but it's not necessary." She hauled herself to her feet and gave Grady his water back. Then she set off toward the barks, leaving the guys to catch up.

"Is she always like this?" Rudy asked.

"Oh yeah."

Without looking over her shoulder, she said, "I heard that!"

Grady whispered, "Don't worry, she never stays mad for very long."

"I heard that, too! You two are the loudest whisperers I've ever met in my *life*."

By the time they caught up to T-rex, he'd run another quarter mile down the trail and found a wide spot in the road where he was sniffing in circles. The dog looked annoyed and confused, but determined to find whatever these people were asking him to locate. He had one dog job, and goddammit, he was going to do it to the best of his ability.

He shoved his face against every blade of grass, scrap of bark, and random footprint, to no avail—then sat down and threw back his head for a good howl.

"Not helpful, Tee," Rudy told him. "Come on, buddy. Pick a direction."

T-rex obliged, stopping the mournful *awoo* and selecting southeast as his next target. He strolled off with less enthusiasm and more determination. His tail swung low and swift, sweeping back and forth as he trotted, his nose taking the lead.

His temporary handler sighed. "Man, we're just doing this same damn thing all over again. Sometimes I wish to God that dogs could talk."

Leda muttered something behind them.

Grady turned around. "What was that?"

It looked like he'd startled her. "What? Sorry. I was just thinking."

"Anything you want to share with the group?" he asked.

"No . . . not yet. This is weird, so weird," she said. Then, more quietly, "Look up, look down, look all around. . . ."

Rudy asked Grady, "Is that some kind of mantra?"

He shook his head. "I don't know what the hell she's doing."

"Neither do I, if it makes you feel better," she said, speeding up so she could join them. "It's just something I heard back at the parking lot, and it's stuck in my head. My brain is hung up on it, trying to use it to tell me something. It does that sometimes. Tries to show me patterns, I mean."

Now they all walked abreast in a wider stretch of the trail, with the dog disappearing around a bend, then doubling back to make sure they were coming up behind him, then disappearing again.

Leda said it louder, now that she'd explained it. "Look up. Look down. Look all around."

Grady mused, "You know what? That's every investigation, in a nutshell. Look here, look there, look everywhere—and hope you find something."

But Leda wasn't listening to anything he could hear. She'd put her sunglasses back on, but he suspected that behind those lenses, her eyes were red and wet again. She wasn't really paying attention to anything or anyone except for the dog, and she was pulling away from her other companions—almost jogging now. After a quick trip over a jutting tree root, she caught herself and kept going.

"Do we . . . Should we chase her?" asked Rudy.

Grady started jogging, too. "I trust the dog; the dog knows what it's doing. I think Leda's on autopilot, so let's go."

She started running, so the guys started running, too.

"She's faster than she looks," Rudy wheezed.

Grady wheezed back, "No one's more surprised than I am. . . ."

Her bag's strap was slung across her chest, and the bag itself bounced up and down on her hip as she ran at a full tilt—surprising the dog when she caught up to him, and surprising everyone else when she ran right past him.

"Leda!"

"Look up!" she shouted back. She didn't look up, and she didn't look over her shoulder, either. She didn't stay on the path. Her breathing was loud and hard, and her feet stumbled when she jumped a fallen log. She caught herself on her right hand, then paused for an instant to shove the bag around so that it smacked against her back when she continued running again.

Rudy asked, "Where's she going?"

Grady said, "God knows," but it came out in a series of squeaks. He wasn't in the worst shape of his life, but he was a good twenty years away from his best shape—and he'd fallen off his twice-weekly workout routine with Sam when the baby was born. He could not remember the last time he'd gone running for any reason whatsoever. To catch a bus? To chase a perp? He had a car, and he rarely had to chase anybody. This was not in his job description, he was sure of it, and he was miserable about it.

His lungs were starting to burn.

How far had he come? They had to be at least two miles away from the Paradise center by now, surely. The uneven terrain was slow going even in his sneakers. He'd worn them because he hadn't thought to grab his hiking boots, and now he was glad for it. The boots were much harder to run in.

Rudy was wearing hiking boots, and he was bringing up the rear. He called for T-rex, and the dog came running toward them, bobbing and weaving between the trees like the boxer he in no way resembled. "Stay with us, boy!"

T-rex was down with this suggestion, happy to be outside and doing his job, and thrilled to be running around with people through a place that was chock-full of awesome sights and smells.

"Do . . . you . . . know . . . where . . . we . . . are?" Grady asked between gasps for air.

"Sure," Rudy said, but that was all.

Grady hoped the man knew his way back to the trail, or that their cell signals would hold, or that the walkie-talkie in Rudy's bag would have battery and range enough to get help when they inevitably got lost because they'd chased a psychic through the park. He was running out of steam, and he would definitely have to stop before long. He didn't have another fifty yards left in him. Not another thirty.

Twenty.

Ten.

He stopped, doubled over, and let his head hang between his knees while he tried to catch his breath.

Rudy pulled up beside him and did the same thing. After fifteen seconds of panting, he said, "I gotta say, I did *not* have that woman pegged for a sprinter."

"Me . . . either." He reached for his water bottle, then cracked it and downed half of it before he stopped to take a breath. "She's young, though. Younger than us, anyway. That's how she . . . how she got away so fast."

"Yeah, that must be it."

They caught their breath, stretched, and then looked at the dog—who watched them with his tongue hanging out of his mouth, dangling down one side of his neck.

"Leda!" Grady called at the top of his lungs, such as they were at that moment. It sounded like a protest cry from an angry horse. "Where *are* you?"

"And what are you *doing*?" added Rudy, who capped his own bottle of water and returned it to his backpack.

She called something in return, but they couldn't quite make it out.

"She's not far off," Rudy concluded. "Hey, Tee, follow that lady's voice, huh?"

"Does he know that command?"

"No, but I think he likes her. Go find that nice lady who gave you ear scratches, T-rex!"

The dog cocked his head, looking vaguely puzzled . . . then he arrived at a basic understanding of the job. He snapped his wayward tongue back into his mouth and bounded off between the trees in the general direction that Leda had gone.

"Leda!" Grady hollered, thinking maybe she'd call back and maybe the dog would home in on her more easily.

She shouted something in return, but he didn't understand it this time, either. She sounded at least as sore and tired as he felt, and he felt like he'd been kicked by a moose.

"Hang in there, ma'am!" Rudy added to the hullaballoo.

T-rex crashed over a log and rolled through some underbrush, then scrambled over a gully that was blessedly dry, with the two men hot on his furry heels.

Grady wasn't really ready to run again, but he couldn't tell from Leda's responses if she was safe or well, and he very badly needed her to be both safe and well—for his own sanity, if not her personal comfort. What if she'd fallen and broken a leg? Good God, would they have to carry her all the way back to the visitor center? Could they even direct a rescue team to . . . to . . . wherever she'd gone? They were well off the trail, by as much as half a mile by Grady's loose and half-assed estimate. Did anyone have a GPS? Their phones, sure, but not if they didn't have a signal.

His head rattled, packed with possibilities that jostled around in there while he ran.

Somewhere not too far ahead, T-rex started yapping.

"Oh, good, that sounds . . . that sounds like he's found her. Those are . . . those are . . . happy barks," Rudy explained, his answer halting as his breath tried to catch up.

Thirty yards later, they successfully followed the barks to Leda.

It wasn't a clearing, exactly, but there was a wide space between half a dozen trees that were so tall and so lush that the ground below them was fully shaded. Moss grew in soft patches the color of spinach and mustard, coating trunks and softening the ground between ferns, saplings, and a patch of horsetails. Dappled sunlight filtered through only faintly, dotting the scene with gold. It was quiet there, even with the panting dog wiggling his butt and jingling the tags on his collar. No birds chirped or squirrels complained. No hikers swore and argued over being lost, and no kids laughed and threw pinecones at one another.

There was only Leda, sitting down at the base of one of the

grand old giants. She leaned back against it and breathed heavily while she petted the delighted dog—who had solved one problem today, so he was prepared to give himself a pass for that whole not-finding-any-dead-bodies thing.

Leda's sunglasses were pushed up past her forehead. Her face was perfectly red and sweaty, and her hands shook when she petted the dog, but her eyes were bright and she was smiling like she'd made it to her gate right before the boarding door was shut. Exhausted but elated.

"What the hell was that about?" Grady staggered over to her and gave the dog a head pat. "You could've gotten lost out here."

"Sure, but. I knew you'd catch up. I knew. You had. This guy." She rubbed the bloodhound's chest. "Sorry, I'm not quite. Finished. Catching my breath. I'm not a runner. I don't . . . I don't run. This was *entirely* too much running."

"Couldn't agree with you harder. What are you doing? Did you find something? I don't see anything."

Rudy joined the scene, watching the dog more than Leda. "He's doing it again. Real hard, this time."

"Doing what?" he asked.

"Signaling that there's something to recover nearby, but he can't find it."

Sure enough, the dog was now spiraling in larger, then smaller circles—led by his nose and whining all the way.

Grady said, "Aw. Poor guy sounds upset."

"He *is* upset," Leda told him. "He knows there's something here, but he can't see it. Hell, I can barely see it—and as soon as I got here, I knew exactly what I was looking for. Sorry for running off like that, but I got so excited, and it was like, it was like . . ." She sounded stronger now, but she was clearly worn-out. "Like *I* was the one following a scent. I think some of T-rex's enthusiasm rubbed off on me."

"What are we supposed to see? Is it something that only . . ." Rudy narrowed his eyes and gazed around the quiet little spot. "Only *psychics* can see?"

"No, no. It's not like that." She leaned her head back, letting it rest on the tree trunk. "Have you searched this area yet?"

"Yeah, at least once or twice. It was in the early maps, right after Grady's dog found the leg."

"And this is the zone T-rex has been exploring with such interest?"

"Correct."

Grady sat down beside her, drawing up his knees so he could rest his arms on them. "All right, Leda. Spit it out. Don't leave us hanging."

She rolled her head around to look at him. She waggled her eyebrows and craned her neck until she was looking straight up the trunk. "Look up, look down, look all around. We could've found the rest of Paul Reddick a long time ago, if we'd only started with *up*."

24. LEDA FOLEY

SATURDAY

Leda was on her third bottle of water by the time Rudy's fellow Pierce County police showed up. She was almost feeling like herself again when the new guys stood around discussing how, exactly, they were going to get a man's corpse out of the top of a Douglas fir. The fir in question was approximately two hundred and fifty feet tall. The corpse was not fully intact, having been buffeted by the branches on its journey into the tree and picked at by turkey vultures—but you could just make out a head and torso lodged someplace around the trunk's midpoint. The torso was wearing a bright yellow windbreaker, which helped.

"Maybe a fire ladder?" suggested a guy in a PIERCE COUNTY jacket.

"Not even with a twenty-four-foot extension. Even if the fire department *did* have a ladder big enough, there's no way to get a truck through all . . . *this* . . . in order to use it." An older guy in a similar jacket gestured broadly at the trees, the moss, the ferns, and the dog, who was trolling for attention from anyone who'd rub his head for five seconds.

"Well, how'd he get up there in the first place?"

Grady raised his hand. "Someone must've dropped him out of a plane, D. B. Cooper–style."

"Jesus Christ. Was he dead already, you think?" asked Rudy.

"No idea. Leda, any thoughts?"

Leda looked up at her name, as if she had not fully been paying attention.

"Oh, I have thoughts," she informed them. "More than a couple of them have to do with getting some food, and I should probably call Niki and tell her what happened, and I need to get her and Matt to tell Ben I'm never going to make it to Castaways tonight, and . . . oh. You meant thoughts about how he died. Or when he died."

"Right."

She shook her head. "Nope. No thoughts about that."

Rudy took this opportunity to make a round of introductions, revealing that the younger Pierce County guy was Hanson, a friend of his, and the older guy with him was Madden. Madden was about to retire. Hanson was new and working his way up through the department.

Once they were all acquainted, they started throwing out ideas.

Rudy stared up into the foliage. "Am I just crazy, or is that guy not so much . . . in one piece anymore?"

Grady said, "We already know he's missing a leg."

"It's hard to see up there," Madden complained.

From the depths of his backpack, Rudy retrieved his own set of binoculars. He pulled them up to his face and adjusted them before saying anything. "Much of Mr. Reddick is intact, I think— but he might be short an arm, in addition to the leg we already know about. If you're right about him having landed in the tree by plane, the fall really did a number on his body. Most of him is about halfway down from the canopy top."

Hanson gazed up in awe. "We'll have to process the whole tree! How do you even *do* that?"

"Son, I have no idea."

"Maybe you only process the tree parts that have body parts on them?" Leda suggested. Everyone shrugged at her. "Okay, what about . . . Do we still have loggers out here? With the sharp climbing shoes and the hooks and stuff? Maybe you could bribe a crew of those guys to bring down the bulk of him. Or what about a team of arborists?"

"They'd tear up the scene," Rudy complained.

Grady wasn't so sure. "I don't know if it matters *that* much, because a hundred feet up in a tree can't *possibly* be the actual murder site. And the more I think about it, the more I think he was dead before he got thrown overboard. Especially if I'm right about the guy whose plane dropped him off."

She sighed, preparing to have her heart broken. "You think it's the dreamboat firefighter?"

"I'm afraid so," Grady told her. "If it was Carson, his plane wouldn't have held more than two or three people, including the pilot."

She perked up. "What you're saying is, the dreamboat might not have actually *killed* him. He might've just been kind enough to ditch the body."

"He'd do it for his sister. I guess this knocks Dan and Jeff off the top of my list of suspects." He pulled out his phone and waved it around while frowning at it very, very hard, in case that would give him more than half a feeble, flickering bar of signal. He sighed and put it away. "No signal."

"Don't worry," Madden told him. "I'll call King County and report our, um, arboreal findings when we get back to the station."

"I was actually thinking about calling my daughter, but it'll have to wait."

Hanson asked, "You've got a kid at home? In Seattle, all by herself?"

"I've got a teenager at home, and she's working today, but she'll expect me home sooner than I can get back. I'll call her once we get back to the visitor center, or whenever I can find a decent signal."

Rudy added, "I met her. She seemed like a good kid. I wouldn't worry about her too much."

Grady sighed and changed the subject. "We'll all make our phone calls when we're back at the parking lot and we've got a couple of bars. I need to talk to my partner and Garcia, and then we can decide on a strategy for handling what comes next."

Out of the blue, Leda suggested, "Helicopter? At least for the, um, for the bulk of Mr. Leg. For the big pieces. If that's not too gross."

Madden laughed. "Too gross? Last year we found a guy who fell halfway down the mountain. He'd been missing for more than a year, and by the time we reached him he was nothing but a rag, a bone, and a hank of hair—surrounded by all the little bits the animals shit out when they were finished. *Nothing* is too gross for us."

Hanson didn't look like he strictly agreed, but he was too cool to argue. He chose to add to the conversation instead. "What about that lady who got eaten by the bear, remember her? That was pretty bad, too."

"God, yes. The bear only ate part of her. We think a mountain lion had a go at the leftovers." He shook his head, like this was all a terrible shame—if a predictable one. "For all the signs and all the warnings, I swear: some people are just stupid as hell when it comes to wild animals. The last pics on her phone said she'd tried to get a selfie with the bear."

Rudy gently countered, "Okay, but sometimes people just get unlucky."

"Sometimes, yes. But only sometimes."

Now Leda had a better idea, and she blurted it out. "What about a big fire hose? You could shoot him down with that, like you're washing toilet paper out of a tree after Halloween. Do kids still TP people's yards? I don't know things anymore."

Grady groaned. "Leda . . ."

"What? It'd be a little messy, but so would everything else. The dude is rotting in a treetop! I say you do whatever it takes."

Firmly, he said, "*Anyway*, a helicopter might do it. We could see if the rescue guys can lower a board down, strap him to it, and lift him out. I bet it's easier to rescue a dead guy than a living one, right? Less wiggling."

In the end, no one proposed any immediately useful solution. Everyone agreed that the corpse retrieval would have to be Pierce County's problem, and that it was generally fair, because most of the actual murder-solving work had happened in King County. Grady and Leda were led out of the woods by Rudy and T-rex, and once they'd reached the parking lot, Rudy said his goodbyes.

"It's been real and it's been fun," he told them, giving each a handshake. "But now I have to do the hard part."

"You get to do the *next* hard part," Grady corrected him. "The hard part after that will be chasing down these siblings with the plane and pulling together enough evidence to arrest them. And that'll be on me."

"Nah. If you're lucky, that'll be sorted out by the time you get home."

"Wouldn't that be nice?" he replied wistfully. "But we both know better than that. Well, I'd better get going, and you'd better call . . . the world's longest ladder company, or an arborist crew, or a helicopter. Have a good one, Rudy."

When Rudy was gone, Grady and Leda sat in the car with the doors open for another ten or fifteen minutes. Grady made phone calls explaining what he thought had happened, and he discussed strategies for bringing in the Coleman siblings and impounding Carson's plane.

Meanwhile, Leda texted the whole adventure to Niki, who had just gotten off work and was sitting at Castaways—allegedly doing a live dramatic reading of the texts to Ben, Tiffany, Steve, and Matt. It was nearly four o'clock, so the place was open, but quiet. Or it was, until the cheering started . . . if Niki could be believed.

Leda promised to give them all the whole sordid saga when she saw them next, and begged forgiveness for canceling that evening's festivities. **Srsly I am so sorry, but I am exhausted from all the running and hiking and screaming, and there's no way I can sing tonight.**

Niki replied, **Don't worry. Ben says we can slap a POSTPONED sticker on the posters. He also says you should tell this story at the mic, because everyone will love it, even if it isn't fortune-telling via karaoke.**

"I hope he's right," she said out loud.

"You hope who's right?" Grady asked, hanging up and stuffing his phone into his pocket.

"Ben. I canceled tonight's klairvoyant karaoke. I'm too hoarse, and by the time we get home I'm going to sleep for a week. After I feed Brutus. I hope he hasn't missed me too much."

"He's a fish. They have famously short memories. He'll forget you were ever gone, the moment you drop off his dinner."

"He loves me," she insisted. "He knows he can count on me. I've even made Niki promise to take care of him if I die. I could get hit by a bus tomorrow; you don't even know."

Grady shut the driver's-side car door. "Close your door, would you?"

"Oh yeah. Let's get out of here. I'm starving."

"You know what? I could eat, too."

They stopped at McDonald's and ate in the car with the windows down because the day was nice and the wind was refreshing. Tacoma traffic stopped them for more than an hour, but they were back in the city by dark. He was pulling up to Leda's place in order to drop her off when his phone rang. He answered it at the curb.

Leda waited, out of pure curiosity. He didn't shoo her out, so she assumed that this was fair play. She listened hard but couldn't understand the voice on the other end, and mostly Grady just said, "Hm," "Uh-huh," "Uh-uh," and "Okay, thanks." Then he ended the call. "That was Sam."

"I gathered that much, but nothing else. What happened? Did they pick up Julie and Carson?"

"Carson is back in California on a relief crew containing some fire or another, but apparently this one isn't as bad as the Sonoma one. He's supposed to be home tomorrow."

She asked, "Can't they just arrest him in California?"

"Jesus, you're trigger-happy. No, they can't just arrest him in California. Right now, we only want them for questioning, and I want to do that here in Seattle. We don't yet have any hard evidence tying either one of him to Paul's actual death—your gut doesn't count, remember? In this case, mine doesn't, either. But between us, I think we can probably conclude that Dan and Jeff are off the hook. Wherever they are. Tentatively," he added for the sake of caution.

"Then why don't you pick up Julie? Stick her in an interrogation room and let her sweat until her brother comes home. See if she'll give up anything useful."

"We've got eyes on her apartment, and we'll be all over her if she tries to go anywhere, but if we pick her up first, she might tip off Carson. If she does that, he might run. There are a lot of reasons not to play too fast and loose with this one."

"How frustrating."

"Welcome to my life. Please don't go chasing Julie down, and please sit tight until we can get everyone corralled and questioned. Can you do that for me? Please?" he begged.

She shrugged. "Sure, since I get paid either way."

"You get . . . wait, oh, that's right. Sure. You *did* technically find the body, and I'd say that's pretty useful. You still have those invoice sheets?"

"You know it." She reached into her bag and whipped one out, just to wave it around as she got out of the car. Before she shut the door she said, "I'll fill this out and give it to you tomorrow."

"Excellent. You fill it out, and I'll file it."

She headed inside to unload and decompress, and then delivered dinner to Brutus—who had definitely missed her while she was out. "Hey, little dude," she greeted him as she unscrewed the cap on a plastic capsule of foul-smelling fish pellets. "I hope your day was peaceful without me. And warm," she added, checking the sticker on the side of his tank. "Yup. Still eighty degrees. Stay toasty, my friend."

She gave him a couple of pellets and wished him well, then she went to the fridge and pulled out the whole box of pink wine she'd had sitting there for a couple of weeks. It wasn't her favorite, but Niki liked it for low-key nights with trashy Netflix binges with weed and takeout, and besides, she was out of everything else alcohol-related.

She pulled down a plastic tumbler from a stand-up comedy show she'd caught five years before. She filled it up, dropped herself onto the couch, and lit up the television.

She was just thinking about where her handy-dandy TV-and-wine-night marijuana vape pen might have run off to when the doorbell rang. It was a funny sound, not original to the 1930s bungalow, but a peculiar 1990s addition that always made her think of *Star Trek* for some reason.

She hopped up off the couch, spilling only a few drops of the cheap pink wine, and by the time she'd reached the front door, Niki was already letting herself inside.

"Oh my God. You went shopping," Leda said, sagging with relief. "All I had was your pink wine, and it's kind of awful."

Niki strolled inside with a big brown Safeway bag hanging from one hand and her keys in the other. "It's delicious, and you know it. But I didn't think you'd be home quite so fast. I was gonna surprise you. Sorry."

"Why on earth would you apologize for that?" Honestly, Leda thought she might cry. She was very, very tired. And thirsty. And desperate for someone to talk to.

"You're right. I won't. I've got . . ." She set the bag down on the tiny bistro table that served as a dining set and began rummaging around. "Rum, because that's always safe, and some of that Scandinavian vodka you keep mooning over. Also a couple of fresh weed cartridges." She whipped out a smaller brown bag she'd picked up at the head shop down the street. "We like 'sour diesel,' don't we?"

"Sure, why not? I mean it sounds awful, but they always do, unless they're named after cookies or pies. Even though they never taste like cookies or pies. What are you feeling tonight?"

Niki paused thoughtfully, holding the bottle of rum. "Something old, but not too old. Retro, not vintage. Did we finish *Remington Steele*? I feel like we watched about a thousand episodes."

"Yes, but not *Murder, She Wrote*. We're only halfway through season one. You want me to put it on?"

"That works."

They never watched as much of any given show as they planned to, and tonight was no exception. Leda gave Niki the tumbler of pink wine, since she didn't want it anyway, trading it for the rum and a stinky weed cartridge. They flopped onto the couch, turned the volume down halfway, and made themselves comfortable.

Niki slouched into the corner of Leda's couch, a secondhand find she'd nabbed off a Facebook group. It was plush and purple and velvety, and it didn't match everything—but it looked amazing in any room that held it, and it was very comfortable. "Tell me about your day, babe. You found a body in a tree, and then what?"

She took a swallow of rum that should've been half its size. It burned as it slid down her throat, but she didn't mind. "Then we waited around for the Pierce County guys, and then we all stood there and argued about how to get Paul Reddick down from a Douglas fir that's taller than the Tacoma Dome."

"Oh, wow, I can see how that would be . . . tricky."

Too tired to explain, she flopped her wrist in a tiny shrug. "I'm sure they'll figure it out. That's not my problem. My problem is that I only found *one* body. Most of one body. Grady's dog found the leg, and they think Paul might still be missing an arm, but God knows where it landed. Maybe it got carried off by an eagle, I don't know."

"Is Grady getting you paid for this corpse-hunting work?"

"He promised to, yes. But Dan Matarese has already paid me, and I've given him nothing in return. I feel like an asshole."

Niki wasn't having it. "Nope. You're not allowed to feel like an asshole. You were very clear about the odds of success when he hired you, and he knew the risks. He was well aware that he might be flushing his cash down the toilet."

"I wouldn't necessarily say *that*."

"You know what I mean." She took a long draw from the vape pen and passed it to Leda, who waved it away.

"I've already had enough. I'm so tired, I can barely keep my eyes open as it is."

"Suit yourself. But my point stands: if you can't find Robin Reddick, that's not your fault. Your hit rate is good, but we all have our off days. Don't beat yourself up about it."

"Tomorrow, maybe, I ought to go out to that construction site where she was doing the landscaping. Maybe if I poke around out there, I'll find something useful or get a good hit. Hey, it happened today, right? Maybe I need to be a psychic on-site for my powers to work at an optimum level."

"Your brain isn't a CPU, and this isn't a science. You've said so yourself, many times. Every time you get onstage, I think."

Leda nodded. "I'm still learning. Anyway, it's not like it matters right this moment; we don't even know where Dan is. Or Jeff, either."

"What? You didn't mention that."

"Grady and I couldn't find them yesterday, and he sent somebody to keep an eye on their respective homes, but no dice. Neither one of them came home last night, which is extra strange. I don't like it."

"Why not?" Niki asked.

Leda didn't have an answer on the tip of her tongue, so she took a few seconds before she said, "It looks like Julie and Carson *probably* killed Paul, and—"

"Wait, not the dreamboat? Oh no, I liked him."

"You liked to look at him, which is completely fair. He's gorgeous. And he might not have done it, but he has a plane—and that *has* to be how Paul got into the canopy out there at Mount Rainier. Unless someone has access to a circus cannon."

"It could've been any plane; you don't know."

"Technically true, but actually . . . well. I hope I'm wrong."

Niki downed the last of her pink wine from the yellow tumbler. "You're not usually wrong, though."

"True. Terribly, tragically true." She took the TV remote and pulled it into her lap, then adjusted the volume up. She was more tired than she'd been in ages, and she was disappointed in the world and in herself. Yes, they had the rest of Paul Reddick. Or most of the rest of him. But the case wasn't closed, and Robin was still out there somewhere, someplace cold and dark and dead.

Look down.

25. GRADY MERRITT

SUNDAY

Julie Coleman was still ensconced in her apartment when Grady came into work the next day, so the Powers That Be had decided that she could stay there until her brother returned from California. Sam Wilco gave his partner a rundown in checklist form.

"Julie is still at home, where she's been pacing around and yelling at someone on the phone, or else sitting around in her headphones watching videos on the internet. She called in to work today. She said she's taking some, uh, 'personal time.' Carson will be back from California any minute now, according to his supervisor—who is starting to wonder why the King County PD is so interested in that nice young man and his ratty little plane. In other news, Leda's suggestion that they use a fire hose to wash Paul Reddick out of the tree has been formally rejected. And while I'm at it, there's still no sign of either Dan Matarese or Jeff Reddick, neither of whom went home last night, either.

So they've been in the wind since yesterday morning at the very least, which isn't *not* suspicious, if you ask me. And now you're all caught up."

Grady simply and unhappily said, "Well, shit."

"Why? One body down, but still one to go?"

He shook his head. "I *really* like the Coleman siblings for this, but if Dan and Jeff have skipped town, there's a chance that I wrote them off too quickly. But thank God about the fire hose, huh? What a mess that would've been."

"That corpse would have been in even *more* pieces by the time they got it down. The guy's been dead for, what, a couple of weeks now?"

"At least. If he hadn't been so far up in that tree, he would've been found by the stink alone a whole lot sooner. You wouldn't have even needed the cadaver dogs," Grady speculated. "Oh, I forgot to ask: Did we get that warrant for Carson's plane?"

Sam reached for a stack of papers on his desk and pulled out a couple of packets—folded and paper-clipped. "Two. One for his plane, one for Julie's apartment." He tossed them across the expanse of their desks.

Grady failed to catch them, but they landed safely beside his laptop. "Thanks, man. I guess I'll start with . . . eenie meenie miney moe . . . Carson. I'll hit the airfield first, if he'll be landing any minute. You want to go pick up his sister?"

"On it." Sam flashed him a pair of finger-guns.

"Thanks, man. If you beat me back, tell them I'll need room three when I get back with her brother."

He collected the warrant for Carson's plane and left the other for Sam. He was halfway out to the parking garage when his phone rang. It was Leda. Did he dare answer it?

He dared. "Hello, Leda. What do you want? What did you hear?"

"Ooh, sounds like you've got something juicy! You hadn't called to fill me in yet, so . . ."

He sighed directly into the phone. "It's barely nine o'clock. I *just* got to work. There's nothing juicy to share."

"I don't believe you. Did you find Dan and Jeff?"

"No. We still don't know where they are."

"Shit."

"That was my sentiment exactly."

She changed her mind. "Actually, I'm gonna walk that back. If Dan and Jeff are still on the table, then the dreamboat is . . . only partway on the table. Right?"

"Everyone is still on the table, Leda, even the people you like a lot and would prefer not to consider murderers. No one is ruled out; no one is a confirmed killer. Or accessory after the fact, either—and unless I get a confession this afternoon, I'd still like a word with the son and his uncle. Everything remains up in the air."

She snorted. "Just like Paul. Did they get him down yet?"

"I have no idea."

"You're a fountain of helpful information this morning, and overly cautious, that's what I think. Dan and Jeff don't have a plane. They *couldn't* have done it, and you know it." She was silent for a few seconds. "Wait, where are you?"

Carefully, he said, "As I told you, I'm at work. The precinct downtown. Why would you ask?"

"No reason," she said, and he could almost hear her batting her eyelashes and pretending to be as innocent as a baby bird. "It just sounds like you're outside, maybe."

"I could be anywhere. We have lots of outside places around the precinct." It was his turn to be quiet and listen. A large rumbling passed by rather close to the woman on the other end of the line. "Leda?"

"Yes, Grady?"

"Where are *you?*"

That same perfectly innocent tone. "At work."

"You don't have any outside places at your work. It's a three-hundred-square-foot office in a strip mall."

"We have seating out front."

"The brewery down the strip has seating out front, and that's not where you are, is it?"

Another loud roar came and went. "No sir, it is not."

"Leda, are you at the airport?"

"Can't imagine why you'd ask that."

"Something about all the planes I hear in the background."

The call became muffled on her end; it sounded like she'd held the phone against her chest, or perhaps out of the wind. Then her voice came again. "Before you ask, I haven't *done* anything. I may have *gone* somewhere, on a perfectly ordinary mission to the Landing to get some office supplies."

"What, you're at Staples? Because I don't think planes take off and land from the parking lot."

"Those could be cars. You don't know. You can't see them."

"Yeah, but it's something about how the engine sounds start low and then goes up, up, and away." He reached his car and unlocked it with the fob. He opened the door and sat down inside, leaving the door open because the day was already warm—even in the shade of the garage. "Okay, seriously, though, if you're at the airfield, you need to leave it. Right now."

"Let's say hypothetically that I was headed to Target because they have much cuter office supplies in general, and *also* I heard a rumor that they were putting out their Halloween stuff—even though it's way too early for pumpkin spice season. It's not my fault that the route to the Landing takes me right . . . past . . . a certain . . . airfield."

He thought about it, chasing a mental map around in his head. "That can't possibly be your closest Target."

"It's either the Renton one at the Landing or the one out at Southcenter. They're about the same, time- and distance-wise. I like this one better, though."

"I bet you do."

"No, for real!" she protested. "I *do* always go to this one. But that's not the reason I'm calling."

"Here we go, yes. Please tell me why you actually called."

"I was driving past the little airfield on the way to the Landing, like you do . . . and I saw a familiar plane, with a familiar pilot. He just landed, literally not thirty seconds before I called you."

"You were sitting there waiting for him to arrive, got it."

"Sitting where? There's nowhere to sit," she declared dismissively. "I'm parked. It's totally different."

"Fine, you're parked. You're watching. And now the dreamboat Carson Coleman has returned from his heroics in California."

"Correct! Which begs the question: Why are you still downtown at the office?"

"That's not . . ." he began, then he changed his mind, because life was short and he had ample reason to believe that Leda did not care about logical fallacies. "Because I didn't know exactly when to expect him back, for one thing. For another, I needed a warrant. The warrant was here. At the precinct. Without it, there's only so much point in going out there to look at the plane. Or talking to him."

After a pause, she said, "That's boring, but it makes sense. Are you on your way over now, or what? It doesn't sound like you're driving."

"I'm coming, I'm coming. Give me . . ." He checked his watch. "Twenty minutes."

Entirely too eagerly, she asked, "You want me to stall him if he tries to leave before you get here?"

"I want you to leave him alone, and if he leaves, he leaves." He shut the door and started the engine, then headed toward the exit. "Unless he leaves in the plane, and I have to assume he won't—since he's just flown back from California. He probably needs to refuel."

"Right, got it. Stay here until you arrive."

"That's not what I said. You *know* that's not what I said."

In the background on Leda's end, Grady heard another voice. "Is he on his way, or what?"

Which compelled him to ask as he slipped his parking pass into the machine and escaped the garage, "Is that Niki? Did you bring her with you? Oh, for the love of . . . of *course* you did."

"It's fine! She's fine. We're fine. We will stay out of the way and not bother anyone and not, absolutely not, stall the man if he tries to leave before you get here. It sounds like you're driving now. Are you driving?"

"Yes, I'm driving," he told her, with a bitchier tone than intended. "I'll be there as soon as I can." With that, he hung up and tossed his phone onto the passenger seat. He hit the gas, then hit traffic, and then hit up a couple of side routes he'd memorized years ago.

He did not make it to the airfield in twenty minutes, but it hadn't been much longer than that when he pulled in past the big sign. As Grady fully expected, he'd already been disobeyed.

Niki stood beside the dirty little Cessna, chatting up the handsome firefighter—who was soot-free but rumpled, as if he'd freshly rolled out of bed to fly home. She leaned against the plane, touching it with admiration and asking flirty questions—he could tell even at a distance.

Leda was nowhere to be seen. He didn't even see her car.

He parked at the closest spot, still some ways from the plane and the shameless flirt. He climbed out of the car, adjusted his sunglasses, and made sure to tuck his phone and the warrant in his blazer pocket. "What will Matt say if he hears about this?" he asked no one in particular.

Leda answered him anyway. "He'll think it's hilarious. You know we're going to tell him, right?"

He jumped. He turned and almost smacked her without meaning to. "Jesus! Where did you come from? I've been looking for you. . . . Where's Jason? That's the car's name, right?"

"Yes! You remembered!"

"You've only told me a million times."

"I left him in the parking lot across the street, at the weird little shoe store for people with wide feet."

"The . . . what now?" He glanced at the place she'd indicated, outside the airfield and across the street. "Huh. How did I never notice that before?"

"Can't imagine."

"Look, you." He shut his car and pulled her aside so he could talk to her more quietly. "I said you weren't supposed to stall him."

"I'm not stalling him. *Niki* is stalling him."

"I see that. Letter of the law, if not the spirit."

"Attaboy."

He almost told her to go back over there and wait for him to do his job before she got everyone into trouble, but he couldn't find the energy. "All right, this is how we're doing this: you're keeping your mouth shut, and I'm doing the talking."

"Got it."

"But will you do it?"

She nodded. "Yes, I will."

He gave up and said, "Fine, come with me if you're coming. Let's go interrupt whatever honeypot she's trying to set for that guy and hope he plays along nicely."

"What if he doesn't? Shouldn't we plan for every eventuality?"

"We couldn't do that if we wanted to." With that, he launched into a quick, professional stride that Leda had to hustle to keep up with.

They passed several small planes on one side, most of which were in better shape than Carson's beater, but one looked like it needed to be towed to the lake and pushed right in. On the other side, they passed a larger model from the Boeing plant across the lake; it was still half-covered in green sheets of plastic to protect the exterior parts before they could be painted. A Ryanair plane was parked for maintenance, and a local transport company had another big one half-disassembled beside the tarmac. Then, up on the left, just past a matching set of Pipers with complementary paint jobs, they caught up to Niki and Carson—who was blushing down to the roots of his hair.

"Good morning," Grady opened the conversation before they could take notice of them. "Do you remember me? We spoke the other day, when your sister was here."

Carson's rugged pink face fully desaturated. "Detective . . . That's right. I remember."

A wide, pleased-with-herself grin spread across Niki's face. She took a step back toward the plane, removing herself from the field of whatever was about to happen. Either she wasn't taking any chances, or she was bracing for mayhem.

To weather it, or to cause it—Grady had no idea which.

He reached inside his blazer and pulled out the warrant paperwork.

"I have a warrant to search your plane." The last words were barely out of his mouth when the panic hit Carson's eyes—and

Grady knew, in that small flicker of an instant, that the kid was going to run.

Carson looked left, looked right, calculated the time and distance to get back into his plane, and went for it.

He spun around and grabbed the door, but it didn't open. Niki was in front of it, leaning against it with all her weight. He juked left; she juked right. He tried to shove her out of the way, but she grabbed his arm and levered him away from the plane in a move that looked suspiciously like karate.

Startled, scared, and closed off on two fronts, Carson gave up on the aerial escape and hit the tarmac on foot.

Grady groaned. "Not again . . ."

"Not what again?" asked Niki, who sidled away from the Cessna, oozing smugness all the way.

"More running," he said with a murmured curse, and he set off after the firefighter, who was at least twenty years his junior and in better physical shape than Grady had ever been at any point in his life. For a split second, he wondered what had become of Leda; she wasn't beside him anymore, and she wasn't running ahead of him, either. He didn't have time to worry about it, even as the back of his brain warned that he should probably worry a tiny bit. Considering.

But he was running, and Carson was escaping. There was no getting away from the fact that the younger guy was getting away, the distance between them growing wider by the second.

Sure, the firefighter may have been awake for several days, and of course, he'd just finished a long flight first thing in the morning. But a guilty conscience and a good pair of sneakers meant he had a hearty lead regardless, and he intended to keep it.

Grady was wearing loafers. The tasteful and professional kind that nobody wants to run in, even in an emergency.

This was not strictly an emergency.

Was he only chasing Carson because he'd run? Grady had a warrant to search the plane, but like he'd told Leda, there was no reason to stop him except that he was probably guilty of something, and if Carson kept running fast enough, he might get away with it.

That was good enough for Grady, even if it wasn't good enough for his feet, or his legs, or his lungs. His whole body ached from yesterday's dash through the woods, and his feet were beginning to blister; he could already feel it.

But he couldn't stop now. He could still see Carson, growing smaller and smaller in the distance. As long as he had him within his line of sight, he couldn't let it go.

A loud *pop* declared that his knees were no happier with this situation than the rest of him. This was not sustainable. How long was the damn tarmac, anyway?

They'd drawn attention from the mechanics and pilots and other assorted crew who came and went from the little airport, with its squat concrete control tower and bicycle-friendly paths that were frequently occupied by big-calved people with spandex clothes and aerodynamic helmets. If he'd had more time, Grady could've flagged down some of those cyclists for help, if he'd seen any. If he'd known sooner that Carson would bolt, he might have blocked the main exit with his car or summoned backup. But once he'd seen Niki out there by the plane, flirting against orders, his brain had short-circuited, and he'd lost his concentration. His whole plan, his whole process, had been upended.

This was definitely her fault.

And Leda's.

Except that it wasn't, and he knew it, and he was simply winded and still, somehow against all odds, running at top speed. And making virtually no progress closing the gap, because Carson had almost made it to the side road that would take him up to

Rainier Avenue and the civilization of some fast-food places, a couple of weed shops, a trailer park, and a run-down apartment building. If he made it that far, he'd be home free with a million and one hiding places.

Grady's lungs were just about to cry uncle when a strange noise came rumbling up behind him. Instinctively, he veered over to the left. Something was coming—was it a small plane, arriving for a landing?

No. That would be too easy.

It was Leda, driving Jason like her own personal bat out of hell. The car bounced when it hit some equipment that had rolled out onto the asphalt, dipping and bobbing so the front bumper scraped the ground—but the car recovered, straightened, and roared.

Grady flung himself as far out of the way as possible, into the blessed shade of a DHL plane wing. He stopped there and doubled over. Somewhere back from where he'd come, he heard a fast-slapping patter of running feet. A glance over his shoulder said it was Niki chasing after him or—who knew?—maybe even the firefighter. She was younger than Grady by a decade and in considerably better shape—but she was wearing flip-flops. That was the only reason he'd outpaced her for as long as he had.

Meanwhile, Leda was on the move. Jason the Accord blew past Niki, sending her hair blowing wildly in the backdraft. Then it blew past Grady, who flashed it a thumbs-up because it didn't matter—nothing mattered; Leda was going to do whatever Leda was going to do, and he was little more than a bystander.

A guy in a blue jumpsuit ran up and asked if he was all right. He said, "Yes," in a single bright wheeze and pulled out his phone. "Just calling . . . for . . . backup."

"Sir, do you know that woman? She can't drive on the runway. . . ."

"Go tell her, if you can catch her."

She was on Carson's heels in an instant—much sooner than it occurred to the firefighter that anyone might be homing in on him. When he glanced to the rear to check Grady's progress, Grady waved at him from the shade of the yellow plane.

Carson looked confused. He stumbled. He caught a glimpse of Leda incoming, and he dove off to the left between a couple of planes.

Or it *looked* like that had been his plan, when he made a hard turn and face-planted into a refueling truck. He went down like an anvil had fallen on his head, and he stayed down, right there on the too-warm asphalt beside a traffic helicopter that was getting some maintenance work.

Leda hit the brakes. Jason's tires squealed like outraged kittens, and the car fishtailed until it came to a stop. She leaped out so fast she almost fell over; she dashed to Carson's side—to help him, or keep him from going anywhere, or yell at him for being such a bastard.

But Carson was down for the count, out cold.

Grady was on the phone with Lucy from dispatch, explaining the situation as best he could without giving too much information about the involvement of unauthorized parties—and he added a request for an ambulance. He almost thought about asking for one purely for his own personal use, but he restrained himself.

Niki, who'd passed Grady thirty seconds before, approached the downed dreamboat with her slip-slapping jog. "Is he . . . ?"

Leda didn't answer that question, but she gave away her game and kicked Carson's leg for spite. "Son of a bitch! I was gonna hit him with my door."

26. LEDA FOLEY

SUNDAY

Leda watched through a two-way mirrored window, knowing that she couldn't be seen by the firefighter on the other side of the glass, but also knowing that *he* knew he was being watched. Everyone who's ever seen an episode of *Law & Order* knows somebody's watching when they're sitting in an interrogation room twiddling their thumbs, waiting for a cop to come ask them a bunch of questions or maybe slap some cuffs on them.

Carson Coleman looked miserable. He was clearly tired, he still hadn't been home to shower, and he'd been crying, too. Never mind the large bruise on his forehead that was swiftly swelling into a full and proper goose egg.

"Not so dreamy now, is he?" Grady asked.

She shot him a side-eye and said, "He's had a rough couple of days. Rough week, probably. I'm prepared to let it slide."

"Rough several weeks, if he was involved in what happened to

Paul—and at this point? It's pretty safe to say he had something to do with it. Innocent people don't run just because a cop shows up to talk to them."

"He didn't run the first time," she noted stubbornly.

Grady acknowledged this shallow fact. "Right, but the first time he had no reason to think we were onto him. Some people have hair-trigger guilty consciences and panic at the sound of a siren; some people are better under pressure and have less trouble locking it down. That man fights fires for a living. He knows how to handle himself under pressure."

Wickedly, she grinned. "I bet he does."

"Oh, knock it off. He's probably a murderer."

"You're just jealous," she told him. "He outran you fair and square."

"*You* outran me fair and square yesterday, and I'm not jealous of you, either. I just don't want to see you bring too much warm, fuzzy feeling to a guy who chucked a corpse out of a plane. Assuming Paul was a corpse when the chucking occurred."

"And we *are* assuming that?"

"Well, yes. You saw the plane. You really think there's room inside that tiny cockpit to physically murder someone without crashing into the side of a mountain?" Grady was checking through his little cop notebook while he talked. He always kept it in some pocket or another, and now he was reviewing his notes before settling in for a conversation that was unlikely to make Carson feel any better at all about his circumstances.

She shrugged. "Someone could've slipped him a Mickey."

"All right, yes. That's possible. And if it's true, he's a murderer, and I don't want you getting too attached. Not every guy in a uniform is a real American hero."

"You're thinking of *G.I. Joe*."

"Of course I am. I'm also old enough to have actually watched it on TV, thank you very much." He slapped the notebook shut.

"Are you ready to drag a confession out of him?"

"Ready as I'll ever be, and there won't be any dragging. You know the drill. Keep your mouth shut, don't knock on the window, don't make any unnecessary noise, and so forth. Where'd Niki go?"

"Bathroom, I think. Maybe coffee. She'll be back in a minute."

He sighed. "Fine. The rules go for both of you, okay? You're here as a professional courtesy to me, and if anyone higher than Lieutenant Carter finds out about it, you'll probably get kicked out. So be on your best behavior."

"Absolutely." She gave him a little salute as he left the room, letting the door swing shut behind him.

For once, she meant it. Police stations had always held a mild terror for Leda, ever since she'd been present for a robbery at a gas station when she was a kid. She and her parents had gone downtown to give a statement, but the whole time she'd been operating under the impression that the cops thought she'd done it. As a six-year-old. Why, God only knew, because Leda sure as hell didn't do it, and there was no way the cops believed otherwise. Rationally, she was aware that it was nonsense. They'd even given her a lollipop when they'd sent her home.

But something about the atmosphere in a station still gave her the willies, so yes. She would be on her best behavior.

Niki, on the other hand . . .

Niki had no such hang-ups about authority figures in uniforms or badges. She strolled into the observation room with a to-go carrier holding two iced coffee beverages from a joint down the street. "All hail the conquering hero!" she announced far more loudly than they were supposed to be talking in there.

"Shhh!" Leda commanded.

Niki swooped around Leda and set down the coffee. "Yes, ma'am, of course, ma'am. Whatever makes you happy, ma'am."

"Grady was very insistent," she whispered. "Look—he's going in."

Niki popped a couple of straws out of their wrappings and dunked one each into the clear plastic cups. She handed one to Leda, who took it and held it without tasting it. Niki gave her own a giant slurp. "Got it. Everybody shut up so we can eavesdrop."

Grady sat down facing Carson Coleman, with a metal table between them. On this table, he put his notebook, a clipboard with some other paperwork, and a couple of pens—along with a hand-held recorder. He spent an unreasonable amount of time getting settled, in Leda's opinion, but for all she knew it was some kind of psychological trick—intended to make Carson uncomfortable, and more likely to spill any beans he might be hiding on his person. Or tea? Or guts?

Finally, Grady pulled his notebook back into his hands and flipped it to the page he wanted. "Carson Coleman, you just got back from fire duty in Northern California, correct?"

He folded his hands together. Unfolded them. Put them on the table and watched the condensation from the warmth of his fingers spread across the steel. "That's right."

"You were in a different California location when Paul Reddick went missing."

He nodded.

Grady gave him a look like he would rather have a verbal answer, but he did not ask for one. "Pretty good alibi, all in all."

Carson was pale and getting sweaty. "I guess."

"I can think of maybe a dozen ways around it. It's not even that hard. First, Reddick goes missing, and a couple of days later, you come back from fighting fires down south . . . but for all we know, he'd taken a couple of personal days. Went on sabbatical. He might not have died until after you got back. Obviously, I'm just spitballing here. Why don't you correct my timeline, huh? Fill in some gaps for me."

The suspect stared down at his hands.

"For all I know, you could've stashed him somewhere before you left. Maybe he was dead. Maybe he was still alive, but you had him someplace he couldn't escape—and you weren't worried about it. Or maybe, and here's where I'd bet *my* money"—he tapped one pen against the notebook—"your sister did it, and you were mostly batting cleanup."

Now Carson looked up. Only halfway, so he was staring at a spot somewhere in the middle of Grady's chest. But he didn't say anything.

"That's the most obvious answer, frankly. No alibi is airtight; in fact, hers didn't shake out at all. Her roommate caught an Uber to the airport; Julie didn't drive her. Yours is better, but there's always a chance of a leak, and I *will* find the leaks in yours if I look hard enough. But I don't think I need to. I think she did it while you were out of town. You probably got a panicked phone call about it, but what could you do? Nothing. You were at work a few hundred miles away. If anything, that probably gave her the idea for what came next. Unless that part was *your* idea. Was she still sitting on his body when you got back? Did she stash it somewhere?"

Niki leaned over and whispered to Leda, "What's he doing? How does he know all this?"

Leda whispered back. "He doesn't, not for certain. He's baiting him, trying to get Carson to correct him when he speculates, or offer new information. He's playing mind games. Cops do it all the time."

Grady was still listing off hypotheticals about how Carson and Julie could have murdered the professor and disposed of him in such a dramatic fashion, when the firefighter interrupted.

"Stop."

Grady's pen hovered over the notebook, no longer tapping.

"Is there something you'd like to tell me?" He reached forward and checked the voice recorder. The red light was blinking away, telling the world that it was listening.

"Leave Julie out of this."

Niki and Leda slurped their iced coffees and leaned closer to the glass.

Grady had gotten a rise out of Carson when he'd brought up Julie, so he leaned into it, speculating out loud as he went.

"I'd love to, but we both know that's not an option. She's the only thing linking you to Paul Reddick, so far as we can tell. We checked your emails and your social calendar—such as it is—and nothing else ties you to a man who turned up dead in a tree eighty miles from here. What we *do* have is a body that fell out of a plane. *Your* plane." Now Grady pulled out one of the notes from CSI. "We've got preliminary evidence out of your Cessna. Didn't take any time at all. 'Visible dried blood residue between the passenger seat and the interior door,'" he read. "'Hair samples consistent with Paul Reddick tangled up in the door latch,' et cetera, et cetera. I'm sure once they're done with the plane, we'll have a whole book full of evidence to throw at you and your sister."

Now Carson lifted his eyes and glared directly at Grady. He'd come to some conclusion; that's what his face said.

"I want to confess."

Leda and Niki leaned forward so fast, so hard, that they bonked their foreheads on the glass. The sound reverberated around in the interrogation room, startling both of its occupants.

Carson asked, "What was that?"

Grady squeezed that spot between his eyebrows. "Someone in the observation room being an idiot."

The women took a step back. It wasn't like coming closer let them hear anything any better. The sound was all piped in via a speaker on the wall.

"I want to confess," Carson said again. "I did it. I killed him, the professor. He was a scumbag, and I'd wanted to kill him all year, so I finally did it. I couldn't take it anymore, the way he treated my sister."

"Yeah, we heard that you didn't care for him. He even used your contempt in the breakup letter he wrote your sister. Did you call him? Email him? How'd you threaten him?"

"I didn't . . ." He hesitated. "I just told him to leave her alone, stay away from her. His email address is on the university website. He wasn't very hard to contact."

"All right, that's fair." Grady made another quick note or two. "Now, I'm not saying he named you as the number one reason he was dumping her, but you *were* on the list. The guy was a real creep, I agree with you there."

Carson was blushing again, a vivid fuchsia that crept up from his shirt collar. It painted his neck, his chin, his cheeks. "You know he did this every year? To somebody? Taking advantage of students like that, and nobody cared. Nobody gave a damn at all, and then . . ." He stopped himself. "I did it, that's all. Just write that down and arrest me. I don't care. I'll . . . I'll give you the emails where I told him to get lost. I didn't trash everything."

Grady nodded. "Good to know, yes. We'll want those. But what happens when we find your sister's prints in the plane?"

He scoffed at the prospect. "She's flown with me before; that's not a secret. And it's not like that plane would hold three people anyway, so you know she didn't do it, all right? She can't fly, and my plane couldn't hold all of us. It's just like you said: I killed him, I put him in the plane, I flew him south, and I pushed him out over Rainier."

"That's a good start for a confession, even though you've left an awful lot of holes in your story."

He shook his bright pink head. "Nope. No, that's all you need. I did it. Leave Julie out of this. She's suffered enough. I did it to protect her."

Grady decided to indulge this line of conversation. "If that's how you want to play it. Tell me, how did you do it?"

"I hit him. Right in the head. He fell over dead."

"You're a good-size guy, and you're in a lot better shape than I am. But I don't quite believe you. Sell me on it. Come on. What did you hit him *with*?"

Carson visibly struggled with an answer, his eyes flashing around, hunting for inspiration. "I don't remember. It happened really fast."

"Go on, then, set the scene. Walk me through it. Where did it happen and when? Start there."

He nodded, leaning into Grady's words. "Right. Okay. We were . . . It was Wednesday night. I did it in the parking garage."

"Near his car? Is that why it was still parked there, after we found his body?"

His eyebrows twitched, like this was news to him but he was ready to run with it. "That's right. I caught him on the way to his car. The garage was empty; it was late at night. I hit him with . . . with . . ."

"No, I'm afraid you're already off the rails. Paul Reddick drove home that night—he didn't leave his car in the garage. He and his assistant went out for a drink-and-bitch session, then he drove her to the light rail station, and then he headed home. He must've come back the next day. There's a streetlight camera outside the garage. We got the footage."

The observation room door opened. Leda and Niki both jumped, sloshing their beverages.

Sam entered the room with Julie Coleman, who did not look happy to be there. Her hair was in a bun, and she was wearing a T-shirt-and-joggers combo that she might've slept in. No makeup. Not even a touch of cherry ChapStick.

"This is ridiculous," she told Sam, who ushered her inside regardless of her protests. "There's no reason for me to be here. I have nothing to say to you, or to . . ." She just then noticed Leda and Niki. "Anybody else. Who are these people?"

Leda and Niki each waved with one hand. They held their drinks with their other hands and did a simultaneous sip through the straw that would have done a team of synchronized swimmers proud. Then Leda said, "We're consultants. Actually, we met you at the airfield last week."

She eyed them warily, then came closer to stand beside them. "I guess you look kind of familiar."

Leda used her cup and straw to point at Grady through the glass.

"We were there with that guy."

Julie Coleman had the traditional Scandinavian blond northwesterner skin of alabaster, pure because it so rarely saw the sun apart from a few months in the summer. Now she had a faint pink cast to her cheeks, and it might've been sunburn, or it might've been the realization that Grady was not alone in the interrogation room.

Sam gave Leda and Niki a nod of hello. "Ladies? I'm Sam Wilco, Grady's partner. You must be Leda and Niki."

"That's us," Leda confirmed. "The show just got started. You haven't missed much."

To Julie, Sam said, "Settle in, unless you feel like interrupting."

Her mouth hung slightly open, and her eyes were very bright, very wet, as she watched the detective grill her brother. She swallowed hard and looked back at Sam—who didn't show her any sympathy. He reached over to a panel on the wall and turned up the volume so everyone could hear better.

Grady was talking. He was also shaking his head. "I don't buy it. You can't remember a weapon, you can't remember when you hit him, and you can't tell me how you got him into your plane."

"I don't have to tell you any of this."

"Eventually, you do—if you want to absorb all the blame for this and see your sister walk free, which is what I assume you're up to. But between you, me, and the flies on the wall . . ." He flashed a glance at the window. "Your story is so flimsy, there's not a chance in hell that the DA will leave your sister out of the criminal filings. You're a terrible liar, and she looks too good for it. One way or another, you're both going down. The only question is, will we charge you with murder or accessory after the fact? I don't want to think you threw him out of the plane while he was still alive; you don't strike me as a cruel guy. You strike me as a guy who loves his sister and would do just about anything to protect her."

Julie whispered, "You can't do this. *He* can't do this." She turned to Sam. "You leave my brother out of this; it's not his fault. None of it."

"Ma'am, nobody made your brother punt your boyfriend out of a plane and into a volcano."

Leda giggled. Niki took a long, deliberate swig from her straw. It ended in a burbling announcement that she'd finished the beverage.

"Nobody threw anybody into a volcano," Julie argued.

"How would you know that?" Sam asked with an eyebrow lifted, ready to drop like the fist of God.

"Because I saw it on the news: You already found Paul's leg. It wasn't *in* a volcano. It was *beside* a volcano," she countered.

"Ooh, quick on your feet. I like it. It won't save your brother, though."

"Stop this. You have to let him go—I'll . . . I'll tell you every-thing," she begged. "Cut him loose; he didn't hurt anybody. He's a hero firefighter; you can't arrest him for caring about his sister."

Sam shook his head. "People go to jail every day for trying to protect their loved ones. Many of them are misguided, like I think your brother probably is. He hated Paul Reddick, and you knew it. It was probably easy for you, getting him to help dispose of the body. He'd do anything you asked, wouldn't he?"

Leda reached the bottom of her iced coffee much faster than she expected, and the slurping, slushy bottom happened way too suddenly and far too loudly. When everyone turned to look at her, she said, "Sorry?" and set the drink down on a ledge, as if it were a fragile bomb and she dared not molest it further.

Julie returned her attention to Sam. "You *have* to let him out. Let me in. I'll take his place. Let me talk on the record, and I'll clear it all up. Just let him *go*."

"I can't do that yet, Ms. Coleman. And I think you know it."

Through the glass, she watched her brother struggle under Grady's keen eye and the flashing red light of the recorder. He was sweating and sniffing, eyes darting from corner to corner, from door to window, from floor to ceiling. Looking for a lifeline.

"I can't watch this," she said. She pushed past Sam—who let her go—and opened the observation room door to flee.

Niki set her drink down beside Leda's and started after Julie, but Sam waved her back.

He said, "She's not going far."

He was right.

She went around the corner and beat on the interrogation room door. "Let me in, for Christ's sake! Leave Carson alone, and I'll tell you whatever you want to hear." She was sobbing now, wrestling with the door's handle until she got it to swing free and she rushed inside. To Grady she said, "I'll tell you anything—everything. Leave my brother alone," she begged. "He didn't kill anyone. And anything else he might have done . . . he did for me."

27. GRADY MERRITT

SUNDAY

Julie Coleman's outburst—inburst?—took the interrogation room by surprise. Carson shot to his feet, confused and angry in equal measure. "What is she doing here? I told you I'd confess!"

Grady stayed seated, through conscious effort and sheer force of will, while the siblings stood over him and argued viciously about who had done what—each one insisting that they should shoulder all the blame. Most of his interrogations did not go this way.

It was almost refreshing, but not quite.

Sam came in ten seconds behind Julie. He stepped between the siblings and held them apart with outstretched arms. "Okay, everybody, take it down a notch. Everybody settle down; everybody shut up. You," he said to Carson. "Come with me, and let's give your sister a chance to talk. You weren't saying anything true or useful anyway. Come on."

Carson looked like he wanted to fight, but a steely glare from his little sister convinced him to let the cop take him by the arm and lead him out of the room.

When the door shut behind them, Grady—who still had not left his seat—gestured with his pen for Julie to take the chair her brother had freshly vacated. "I suppose this means it's your turn, Ms. Coleman." He pointed out the recorder, still recording.

"Am I under arrest?"

"Not yet. You want me to do that now and read you your rights? You got a lawyer you want to call, or do I need to chase down a public defender?" he asked, as if these were all trivial things, part of a tedious process and scarcely of any interest to him at all. It was a trick he'd learned early on in his career: sometimes apathy worked like a sponge to draw out other people's messy emotions.

She took the chair slowly, buying herself time and working out her story in her head. When she was seated, she began to speak. "My brother has never hurt a soul in his life, and that includes Paul Reddick."

"All right, then let's talk about who *did* hurt Paul Reddick." He turned the page in his trusty notebook and clicked his pen for dramatic emphasis.

Julie's eyes were red and overflowing, but the sobbing had stopped, and now she looked like she only needed some tissues. She didn't ask for any.

"It was me. You know that already, I can tell. I don't know why you've got to make such a show of it."

"You think this is a show, Ms. Coleman?"

"It is for *them*," she said, glancing hatefully at the two-way mirror.

Well, she probably wasn't wrong about that. "A man is dead, and that's something to be taken seriously. His killer will go to jail for years, and that's also not a matter of frivolity, wouldn't you say?" She didn't answer, except to wipe her nose on the back of her hand. "And yes, I think you're the one who did it, but I can't say for certain. After all, we've got two suspects trying to confess over here, and the first one has a seriously sketchy story. Will you give me a better one?"

"I'll give you the truth, but only if you agree to leave my brother out of it."

"No, that's not how this works. You're not in a position to make demands or bargains." He adjusted his position in the chair, leaning forward in the seat. "Now, here's what I can actually do for you: I can make a recommendation to the prosecutor and ask that your brother be treated with lenience . . . *if* it turns out you're the brains of the operation and he cooperates with the investigation going forward. He'll face some consequences, but he'll get off easy. I suspect that he's an accessory after the fact, and that's all. If he testifies against you, he might even walk."

"That's not good enough."

Grady said, "Too bad, because that's all you're getting. I no longer need your cooperation. My pal Sam back there"—he cocked his thumb at the door, where Sam had just left with Carson—"right now, he's having a word with our CSI team about the parking garage where Paul's car was found. Your brother said he killed him there, and we have to go see if that part of his story holds water."

"But he didn't!"

"I'm inclined to agree with you," he admitted. "However, somebody did—but not on Wednesday night. It took me a minute to put two and two together, even after we found his car. The last we knew, he'd driven Helena to the light rail station, and then he'd gone home. But his car wasn't at his house."

She swallowed again. It was dry enough that he heard it across the table. "Can I have some water?"

"Sure." He snapped his fingers toward the window. "Somebody back there want to give us a hand?" He had no idea which one of the people behind the mirror would make herself useful. It turned out to be Leda.

She strolled in with a pitcher and a couple of glasses. "In case you wanted some, too," she said when she set it down in front of him.

"Thanks," he muttered without looking at her. Julie had his full attention. He could deal with accusations of abruptness from Leda later on. To her credit, she left without making a scene.

Julie poured herself a glass of water with hands that shook only a little. She downed a few sips and put it on the table. "You have to understand," she began. In Grady's experience, people often got started that way. So desperate to be understood or heard. "Paul was the best of men, and the worst of men. Very easy to love but hard to like—does that make sense?"

"Explain it to me like I'm five."

"He . . . he had this way of making you feel like you were the only person in the world when he talked to you, when he looked at you. He made you feel like someone was listening, and that someone saw you for who you were, and who you wanted to be."

"He was your teacher. That was his job."

"Yes, but not everyone has the knack for it."

He was willing to grant that much. "I suppose that's true. How did you win his direct, specific attention?"

She shrugged her shoulder like she meant to flip her hair, but it was tied up in a bun, so nothing happened. "I'm just his type, I guess. He picks a new teacher's pet every year. He has a gift for choosing girls who are starved for that kind of recognition. Girls who haven't heard that they're good at something, that they're worth something. Not in the right ways, from the right people. Yeah, he has a gift. *Had* a gift," she corrected herself.

"Until you killed him."

"Until I killed him. You're right, I didn't do it that night. I was waiting for him when he came in to work the next morning. I knew he'd get an early start; he was behind on his work, what with the missing wife and all, and he'd told me plenty of times that he didn't need a lot of sleep. The great thing about the garage is that before classes get underway, it's pretty dead in there. Especially in the summer, and especially in the stairwells."

Grady had accidentally clicked his pen one time too many. He clicked it again and started writing. "What time was this?"

"Maybe around six in the morning? I got there at five thirty, and I was so pissed off about that stupid letter he gave me. I knew we weren't going to run off into the sunset and get married after graduation. I'm not stupid." The sniffles were coming faster and harder now, and Grady had a feeling she wasn't being entirely honest with him—or herself, either.

He was about to ask her another question when the door cracked open. This time it was Niki with a box of tissues. She tossed it to Grady and ducked back out. He caught it with one hand and pushed it across the table.

Julie took a couple in a single grab, swabbed down her face, and blew her nose. She crumpled the used tissue and squeezed it in her hand. "Sometimes we believe things temporarily because it's convenient, or because we want to, I don't know." Then she spoke more quickly, needing to get something into the open before she changed her mind or chickened out. "He got out of his car, and I followed him to the stairwell. It's all concrete in there; everything feels cool and damp even when it's not, and everything echoes. He heard me coming. I wasn't really trying to be quiet anyway. It's not like he was going to run away. He didn't know what I was going to do. *I* didn't even know what I was going to do."

She stopped long enough that Grady decided it was time for a prompt. "What *did* you do, Julie?"

"He was looking around, wondering who else was in there with him. I called his name right as he got to the stairwell entrance. He . . . he smiled. Like he was happy to see me, like everything was fine and normal, and he hadn't just dumped me because . . ."

Another prompt, to get her over whatever hump she was stuck on. "Why *did* he dump you, Julie? It sounds like the relationship was working pretty well for you."

"I'm not sure." Something about the wobble in her voice told him she might be telling the truth. "It was good, and then he was bored. Maybe it was that simple? At first I thought it was something about the search and rescue stuff we were doing, looking for his wife. But he thought that was great when we first got started. Eventually, I think it annoyed him."

"Eventually? You hadn't been running sweeps very long when we caught up to you at the airfield."

"He wasn't the world's most patient guy," she said, an unmistakable note of bitterness underpinning the words. "He thought it was a waste of everybody's time; he kept telling me that she'd left him—the money she took was proof of it—and it wasn't a big deal. He'd been expecting it any day for years. He said it was dumb to blow so much energy looking for her, and that we'd never find her."

"Huh. Did you believe him?"

"Not really? I know their relationship . . . wasn't much of one, if you know what I'm saying. But he was so casual about it, so callous. In the back of my head, I always thought he knew more than he was saying, but hell. Maybe he didn't."

"That leads me to an obvious question, though. Did *you* hurt Robin Reddick?"

"Me? What? No. I never even met her. I only know what she looked like from pictures."

"What about Paul? Do you think he hurt her? You've hinted as much."

She still had her doubts, but she also had her suspicions, that much was clear. "I . . . I think he *might* have, but I don't have anything to back that up. Just a feeling."

"Feelings can be useful. Was it the way he talked about her? The way he treated her? Or the way he reacted to your efforts to find her?"

"I told you, I never met her—so I never saw them together. I don't know how he treated her, but I have to assume it was with contempt. That's how he treated everybody when he was done with them. That's how he talked about her: like she was beneath him, with her stupid little landscaping job and her stupid little romance novels she liked to read—like he wouldn't have cut off his arm and waved it around in front of a publisher for a chance at romance novel money," she said with disgust.

Grady didn't have to ask what the disgust was aimed at. "He did write a book, though."

She rolled her eyes hard enough to see her own brain. "God, I know. He made me read it. Or he didn't *make* me, but I wanted to impress him, so I did. It was the worst wish-fulfilling fantasy garbage, about a teacher who keeps sleeping with students until he runs off with one of them for a happily ever after. From a certain angle, that's a romance, right?"

"Sounds right to me. My wife used to love them." The reference slipped out of his mouth so casually that it nearly surprised him. This was getting easier, in a way. He forced his brain to avoid that trap and forget about the upcoming anniversary of her death. "Still got a stack of them in a closet somewhere. My kid won't let me toss them out. At any rate, I take your point. One man's romance is another man's creepy id on full display."

"I know I'm young, and I know I've made stupid choices, but I still know a red flag when I see one—and I saw one when I read that book. But somehow, in the back of my head, I had this feeling that I might be the final girl, you know? The one who gets the happily ever after."

They were getting off track. Grady steered her back to the subject at hand. "Even though someone else already had that . . . well, the 'ever after' part. Sounds like it wasn't especially happy. So you swoop in and help the poor professor with his sad personal life, but it turns out you're just a well-worn detour, not the girl who gets the ring."

"Yes. But seriously, I didn't know Robin. I didn't hurt her, and neither did Carson. He only participated in the search and rescue efforts in the first place because I begged him to. I thought, with his plane and my people-organizing skills, we could cover a lot of ground, maybe actually find her and help her. Save her, I don't know. By the time we'd done a couple of searches, it was already clear that Paul was finished with me, and something about that realization made me want to find her even more."

"Seems like a weird hobby for you to take up in the first place."

She nodded. "Carson said the same thing. But word was getting around about me and Paul—even though we were basically over—and it felt like it would look good, or something. I don't know. Maybe I was still trying to . . . to . . . keep a foothold in his life and give him time to see that he was wrong, and I was good enough, and I should be the final girl after all. But then, the more I looked for his wife, the more I felt sorry for her, and the more I wanted to meet her and apologize, or whatever. I don't know what I wanted."

"Yeah, I'm getting that impression. Let's say I believe you about Robin, and that you didn't hurt her—though maybe Paul did, and you don't know any details. I'm willing to let you have that," he said, turning the page in his notebook.

"I'm literally sitting here confessing to murder. What's the difference if I killed her, too? I'd just tell you if I did it," she said almost flippantly.

Grady decided not to fill her in on the difference between manslaughter and first-degree murder twice over. "All right, so let's go back to the killing you're admitting to. You followed Paul into the stairwell at the parking garage. Then what?"

"The door shut behind us, and we were alone. I didn't have a weapon or anything. I didn't go there intending to hurt him physically. I mostly went there to swear at him and maybe cry, and threaten to tell his wife if I could ever find her, or go to the dean, or his boss, or . . . I didn't plan it. I only wanted to ruin him."

"Okay." He didn't really believe her, though if she hadn't brought a weapon she might successfully plead out to manslaughter. Nobody ever admitted to planning anything. Everything was always an accident, always spur-of-the-moment. Crimes of passion were sexy. Premeditated murder was evil, but not the sexy kind.

"So that's how it started. I tried to talk to him, and when he realized I was there to have a real conversation . . . he wouldn't even look at me. He was so rude about it, like we hadn't been hooking up for months and he barely knew who I was. He treated me like any stupid freshman who wants an extension on a deadline. It was just so goddamn insulting."

"And you wanted a little respect."

"Yes," she said eagerly. "Getting a little eye contact from the man wasn't asking so much, was it? Especially not when he gave me HPV. He owed me eye contact."

"Ouch."

She nodded. "Bastard. Anyway, it turned into a fight, and I didn't have anything to throw at him, so I shoved him."

"Down the stairs?"

"No. I just shoved him, there on the landing. He tried to catch himself on the handrail, but he slipped and fell. Cracked his head on the concrete stairs. He wasn't the world's most agile guy."

"Well, he was a lot older than you," Grady said, then wished he hadn't. He didn't care about coddling her feelings, necessarily, but it wouldn't do him any good to piss her off. "I say that as a fellow old person who poorly handles being shoved. Was there any blood?"

"Not a lot, and I got most of it. I was wearing this big sweater, because it was kind of cold first thing in the morning. I wrapped his head up real fast, thinking maybe he wasn't hurt that bad and I should call nine-one-one. But I can take a pulse. He was gone. I panicked."

That's how it went sometimes. Shorter and shorter replies as a perp got closer and closer to the crime. "What'd you do with his body? It was early in the morning, but there were people around."

"There's a maintenance closet down on the first level. Right by the stairwell exit. It wasn't locked. I chucked him inside. I used my Swiss Army knife to break the lock so no one else would open it. Tried to buy myself some time to think."

Grady looked up at the mirror, wondering if Sam was still back there and if he'd heard all that. A soft *tap-tap-tap* from the other side gave him the yes he was looking for. Good. Sam could pass the intel along, since they already had CSI en route to the parking garage anyway. He wanted to confirm as much of her story as possible.

She kept going. She was beyond the point of needing prompts. "I called Carson, and when he got back from California we waited until the garage was empty—or empty enough—in the middle of the night, and we went and got him. Carson did the heavy lifting. We put him in my car. Then we put him in Carson's plane, and you know the rest."

She sagged heavily in the chair. "Then it occurred to me that he'd written this letter, and that it mentioned Carson, like he was afraid of him, and I know that my brother is the world's worst liar. I shouldn't have thrown the letter back in Paul's face. I should've hung on to it; that would've been the smart thing to do."

"Angry people do careless things. It's normal."

"I decided that I had to find it. It wasn't in his office—I know that because I hassled Helena until she let me in. It wasn't there. It wasn't at Paul's place, either, because I let myself inside and looked. The son of a bitch didn't remember that he'd given me a key. To the *back* door," she added, like this made it extra insulting. Maybe it did. "But I couldn't find it. Then I tried Helena's place, thinking maybe she'd taken it. She's nosy, and obsessed with Dr. Reddick, and not above blackmail."

"How do you know that?" Grady asked. "Did she rat you out at any point?"

"No, but she wanted to; he probably asked her not to. She didn't even pretend to like me. And she didn't have the letter—or if she did, I couldn't find it."

Grady threw her a bone. "The letter was in his car. You wasted your time with all that burgling."

She sighed and slumped down lower in the chair. "It figures." Then she straightened herself up again. "But you know what? You can think whatever you want about me, and what I did, and what I chose, and how I handled it. I'm the bad guy here, I know that. I can accept that, and if you can get Carson out of this with just probation or the like, I won't even feel bad about it. I'll sit in jail and rot, feeling all right because that bastard won't do it again."

He shut the notebook and slipped it back into his pocket. "That's what a lot of people tell themselves."

She gave him a look somewhere between a sneer and a scowl. "You don't get it. You'll send me to jail, and I deserve that. But *he* was the one with all the power, the whole time, right up until I took it away from him for good. The whole semester he just used me and threw me away—like he did to at least nine other girls I found online. We have a Discord group where we hang out and talk, and then we feel less insane about what happened to us. That man jacked up our whole lives because he wanted to, and he thought he deserved to. He took and he took and he took, because he thought he *deserved* to, and no one made him stop until I came along."

Julie took another tissue. She didn't blow her nose with it; she stared at it like she hated it. "Well, he *did* deserve something; he was right about that. And I'm the one who gave it to him."

28. LEDA FOLEY

MONDAY

"**O**ne down, one to go," Leda complained. She packed up her messenger bag as if she were heading out on a weeklong camping trip, with a water bottle, first aid kit, multi-tool, sunscreen, hand sanitizer, lip balm, markers, and a pink plastic key chain vial of Mace. When Grady gave her a funny look, she said, "I don't have any bear spray. This will have to do."

"Bear spray? Who said anything about bears?" Niki asked, dropping a lipstick into her own tiny crossbody. Leda never understood that bag; it was hardly big enough to hold her phone. Why bother? Get a fanny pack and call it a day, that's what Leda thought (and often said).

Grady told her, "I'd be stunned if we encountered any bears. We aren't going back into the woods; we're going to poke around in a field down the road from a giant mall. You're more likely to encounter ticks."

289

"Bug spray!" Leda announced with a snap of her fingers. "I *knew* I was forgetting something."

"Oh, for the love of God, we aren't stopping for bug spray. This is ridiculous," he told her.

But Leda had no intention of asking for a quick pit stop, unless that pit stop involved getting a diet soda the size of a bucket. "I wouldn't dream of suggesting it." She pulled open a drawer in her desk and retrieved a travel-size bottle of something that smelled like Pine-Sol and DEET when she spritzed it into the air above her desk—just to make sure it still worked.

She tossed it into her bag and zipped it shut.

"Are you done now? Actually finished? Ready to go?" He sounded like *this* time he was ready to leave her in her office if she didn't say yes.

She said, "Yes. Nik?"

Niki shot her a thumbs-up. "Ready when you are. Shotgun!"

Grady shrugged. "Sorry, Leda, she beat you to it. You could always just . . . drive your own car," Grady proposed. "If you must have a front-row seat."

Leda shrugged back at him. "It's fine. Jason is in the shop. I did some damage to the oil pan when I launched him off the tool bag at the airport."

"Let that be a lesson to you about interfering in police business."

Leda ushered everyone out and locked the office behind her. "We both know it would've been awesome if it'd worked the way I planned. I was gonna open my door and sweep up behind him, and . . ." She dropped her keys into the bag's front pocket. "Alas."

Niki patted her shoulder. "It was fine, I promise. Very action-hero-y, even though he wiped himself out before you could whack him with the door."

"Let's all cross our fingers for no heroics today, please?" Grady beeped his key fob and opened the sedan. "Ladies?"

Leda spoke for both of them. "We promise."

"As long as no heroics are called for," Niki clarified. "But in the event that the day needs saving, all bets are off."

He shook his head as they all loaded into his car, and he was still shaking it when they hit the interstate. Then he perked up.

"I meant to tell you: Julie's been booked and she's headed into the system. Carson made bail, but he's staying close to home like a good boy."

"What if he needs to go fight more fires? It *is* fire season. . . ." Leda observed.

Niki added, "And wildfire smoke *is* California's chief export to the Pacific Northwest."

"If he wants to go fight fires out of state, he'll have to clear it with a judge. We still don't know for a fact that he and his sister weren't involved in Robin's disappearance, and even though I personally think the Colemans didn't have anything to do with it . . . the state of Washington isn't so sure."

"What will it take to *make* them sure?" asked Leda, still halfway thinking about a very sad dreamboat who once dropped a body out of a plane. At least the body was dead first. He could be forgiven for such a minor infraction.

"Finding Robin would do it, and figuring out exactly what happened to her. I mean, finding Dan and Jeff would also be helpful, since we don't have any other real suspects. Bluntly, I don't think they did it. I had fifty-fifty odds on them for Paul, but not her."

Niki held up a finger. "But we all know Paul's the one who probably offed her, right? Can we agree about that?"

Grady wasn't so confident. "I don't know."

From the back seat, Leda pondered. "But he tried to stop the search and rescue efforts. He acted like he wasn't surprised to see her go, and he didn't really care. That was my takeaway from watching you grill Julie."

"I don't disagree, but something about it isn't sitting right with me. Anyway, we got a hit on Dan's credit card out at a hotel in Tukwila, so let's see if we can kill two birds with one stone, so to speak. Maybe we'll find him and Jeff while we're out there."

"I don't know how you live with all this uncertainty." Niki put her head back against the seat and her feet up on the dash, her flip-flops leaving dust prints on the glove box.

"And I don't know how you grabbed Carson and pushed him away from the plane. What was that, some kind of martial arts defense?" he asked. "It was well done. Don't get me wrong, I just didn't know you had it in you."

She grinned and stretched her toes; her glittery peach nail polish sparkled in the sun. "You remember I work in a bar, right? Ask Tiffany, next time you see her. I bet she has a whole catalog of moves for evicting problem customers."

"Joint-locking," Leda chimed in. "That's what she did. We took a self-defense class together a couple of years ago."

His eyes hit the rearview mirror. "*You* can do that, too?"

"Oh no. Not really. Niki was the A student. I was more of a C minus."

"That's too bad. I was having fun picturing you tackling perps with something other than your car."

"I didn't actually *hit* him with my car."

Niki chuckled. "It was still pretty funny, though."

The drive to the cleared construction site where Robin Reddick worked didn't take half an hour, even though it was well off the beaten path and the road to the working zone was not exactly paved. They passed great swaths of cut trees, bulldozer-scraped rectangles, and early signs of an electrical grid going in with poured concrete posts for streetlamps curing in the sun.

Grady didn't so much park as pull over to the side of the dirt road and turn off the car.

Everyone piled out, blinking against the sun. The site was presently unoccupied by workers, due to a special request from the Seattle PD. They had the place to themselves.

Leda extracted her biggest, fullest-coverage sunglasses from her bag and stuck them on her face. "It's a wasteland out here. Seriously, you could film something apocalyptic, no problem." She gazed out across the flat, leveled expanse of building foundations, freshly poured sidewalks, and markers where parking lots would eventually go. Everything was covered with a coating of dry dust, or dried mud from the deluge more than a month ago, now. To the west of the scene, a high, tree-covered hill overlooked the spot where an exit ramp would one day go. The interstate was carved into its side. The sound of distant cars on I-5 was little more than a far-off hum.

"Looks like it'd be fun to drive around with a couple of ATVs. . . ." Niki proposed.

"Ooh, good point."

"Ladies," Grady said, and there was a note of alert in the word. "We're not alone."

Leda squinted around the scene, and sure enough, at the edge of the remaining trees, a pair of figures walked slowly, staring at the ground. "No, we're not. And if I'm not mistaken, we've found Dan and Jeff."

"I think you're right," Grady agreed.

Niki shielded her eyes, using her hand for a visor. Leda would've felt sorry for her if she hadn't brought such a tiny, useless bag that wouldn't hold a pair of sunnies. "What are they doing out here?"

Leda thought about lying low and following them, watching to see if they'd give away any good clues or lead the trio to something useful; then she came to her senses. "Dan Matarese! Jeff Reddick!" she hollered, jumping up and down and waving.

Niki asked, "What are you doing?"

But Grady only sighed. "There's no sense in hiding from them. They're probably out here doing the same thing we are, and if that's the case . . ."

She kept bouncing and waving. "Dan! Jeff! Over here!"

The two small figures in the distance stopped what they were doing, consulted between themselves, and waved back.

"Let's go compare notes," she suggested. In the back of her head, an insistent buzzing suggested, *Look down.* "Look up, look down," she mumbled as she began trudging across the dirt. Looking down, it was wavy in places, almost like the bottom of a dry creek bed or a gully. "Look down."

Niki asked, "What?" because she'd only barely heard it. She rushed to catch up. "You're talking to yourself."

"At the park the other day, when we were hiking around looking for the rest of Paul's remains . . . it's something I overheard in the parking lot. These two little girls . . ." Her voice trailed away. Dan and Jeff were stomping through the dirt piles and across the half-cleared acreage to meet them. "These two kids were playing a game. One of them said, 'Look up, look down, look all around.'"

"Okay . . . ? What's the punch line?"

"'Your pants are falling down.' These were kids. It was some kind of joke or game." Leda wasn't really paying attention to her answer; she was trying to pay attention to the ground, and to the inbound Dan and Jeff, who were taking their own sweet time about the whole thing.

Finally, everyone caught up to the same spot—a cement landing that looked like it was destined to be the entrance to a parking lot.

Dan and Jeff were sweaty and grim-faced, but they appeared roughly as prepared as Leda. Each wore a backpack, each had a camera and binoculars, and Dan was carrying a metal detector. "Hey, folks," Dan greeted them collectively. "Fancy running into you out here."

Introductions were made, since Niki hadn't met everybody yet. Then Grady said, "Yeah, I think we're probably on the same fool's errand, searching for Robin out here—but I wouldn't be doing my job if I didn't give it a shot."

Leda was almost offended. But only almost. "Um, more like *I* wouldn't be doing my job. I'm the one who asked you to come with us out here, and technically Robin isn't *your* case." To Dan she said, "I'm the one who told him the police should close the construction site for the day. Tell them, Grady."

Grady said, "It's true, Leda and Niki are the ones who talked me into doing a sweep. I tried to get Jack Garcia out here, too. He said he'd wait until tomorrow, when the job site was crawling with construction dudes, rather than psychics and weirdos."

Leda frowned. "I resemble that remark. But I'm glad we caught you both out here. Everyone's been wondering where you are!"

The two men frowned at each other. "Why?" asked Jeff. "We haven't done anything."

"You fell off the map," Grady noted. "The credit card hit out at the Hyatt was the first sign that either of you were still alive. I was starting to get worried."

Dan made a long *oh* sound. "Gotcha. Maybe we should've said something before getting the hotel, but we both called in to work. Nobody's trying to hide from you, Detective."

Jeff added, "Seriously, man. We're adults. We can leave the

house without raising our hands and asking the teacher for permission."

"I know, and you're right, absolutely. You were loose ends, that's all." Then, as if it only dawned on him in that very moment, he said, "I guess no one's told you: we found the rest of Paul's body, and the killer has confessed."

Jeff said, "Holy shit, seriously? Did he say anything about my mom?"

"She," he corrected. "It was Julie Coleman. Her brother helped her dispose of the body, right out of his plane over Mount Rainier."

Dan shook his head slowly. "It's about time one of those girls pushed back." He adjusted his grip on the metal detector, slinging it over his other shoulder.

This prompted Leda to ask, "What's with the heavy equipment? What kind of treasure are you hoping to find out here?"

"Eh, maybe Robin's phone or her bag of work gear—it's full of metal tools and soil meters. It's a stupid shot in the dark, I know, but this metal detector belongs to a buddy of mine who likes to use it at Alki Point. We're grasping at straws here."

"No, it's not stupid," she countered. To Niki, she said, "Like I said, I think we need to look down."

Dan asked what she meant, so she explained the story about the kids in the parking lot for the second time in twenty minutes. "And *that's* how I found Paul. The rest of Paul. You know what I mean. He was up in this enormous tree, stuck in the branches."

"Minus the leg and an arm," Grady added. "We found the missing arm in a coyote den a quarter mile away, sans the ring finger and pinky—but most of those probably wound up in a tightly coiled pile of dog shit in my backyard. The lab that's processing Cairo's, um, deposits won't be finished with their results for another few days, but I'd be stunned if they didn't turn up some finger bones."

Niki hadn't heard that part yet. "Oh, really? They found the arm? I should've known it'd get picked up by a coyote. Dogs can't resist dead stuff." Then she smacked his shoulder. "But no one knows that better than you, am I right?"

Jeff asked, "How did they get him down?"

Leda looked at Grady. "Yeah, how *did* they get him down? Since everyone dismissed my thoughtful and pragmatic recommendation."

Grady said to Dan and Jeff, "She wanted to wash him out of the tree with a fire hose."

Jeff barked a laugh. Dan said, "Like cleaning toilet paper off your porch after Halloween?"

Niki said, "You all live in much more violent neighborhoods than I do."

To which Leda said, "Literally just last week you told me about that heroin dealer who picked a fight with the drag queens who were smoking under your bedroom window."

"Those glitter-clad ladies beat him into the ground. I was very proud. The tall blonde had a brick in her purse, and she knew how to swing it."

Grady, attempting to return to the topic, said, "I think they used a helicopter and a rescue team to get Dr. Reddick down. The end result is that most of him is cooling in the morgue. Sorry again, Jeff. I know this can't be easy."

"It's not easy, no. But if we can just find my mom . . ." he said. He did not sound especially hopeful. He sounded tired and discouraged. "I don't want to be the next of kin. I don't want to have to . . . to . . . finish whatever unfinished business he left behind. Or any business Mom left behind, either."

The admission at the end made Leda want to hug him, but she held herself back.

"We will do our absolute best. That's what we're here for right now. Let's see what we can find."

Grady asked, "Can you point out where you've searched already, and the places you still haven't hit yet? We can divide and conquer what's left. And Leda, you keep talking about looking down. What exactly are we looking for?"

"I'm not sure," she said, but she still said it with confidence. "It'll come to me, you just watch. It always does, eventually."

"So we're not scanning the treetops this time," Niki concluded. "All right. Let's all focus on what's at our feet. Or at least don't ignore what's at your feet, if you'd rather not put your faith in a kids' game from a parking lot."

"Thanks for the vote of confidence, bestie." She wasn't honestly annoyed. She was already distracted by the mowed-over fields and paved-over strips. God, she hoped Robin wasn't buried out there under the concrete someplace.

On Grady's suggestion, they split up: Niki and Leda stayed in a pair; everyone else spread out on their own.

It was coming up on midmorning, and the sun was already too hot for northwestern blood, but Leda still had her water bottle and her hand sanitizer—which was very refreshing in a pinch, as she noted when she offered some to Niki.

"No, thanks. But you know what we should've brought?"

"What?" Leda asked, vaguely horrified that she'd forgotten anything at all that might be useful.

"Umbrellas. We could have used them like parasols, since there's no rain. Until all the trees and whatnot get planted out here, there's no damn shade. They cut everything down, and it's so naked out here. So miserable."

"Next time we have to stand around in a huge hot field—a series of fields? Are these connected? I can't even tell—in the summer sun when it hasn't rained in a month. Yes, I will bring an umbrella."

Something pinged in her brain. Something about the rain. *Look up, look down. Look all around.*

Look down.

Down was the pale brown earth, rippled and cracking from the direct sun. Down was her own shadow, its hard lines stretched out across the ground. Down was the edge of a concrete pad that could've been intended for any eventual use, God only knew. One corner of it was buried in the same sandy beige detritus that covered everything else.

Now that she saw it, she couldn't unsee it. She called out, "Grady?"

"Yeah?"

"Something's off about this. Look at the ground."

"I know, I'm looking down, okay? We're *all* looking down."

She shook her head. "That's not what I mean. Or maybe it is. What I'm trying to tell you, or ask you, is if you see this, too: It looks like there was some kind of flood through here, right? These patterns in the dirt, they're waves, from running water."

Jeff piped up from almost forty yards away. Leda thought he must have the hearing of a bat. "It's from the rain we had a few weeks ago, one of the foreman told me. Part of the development's preliminary drainage system was too preliminary, I guess, because it didn't hold. They had to scrap a bunch of work and start it over, because it messed up some of the new concrete. I think they also had to redo some of the electrical stuff. It really set them back."

An idea was forming in the back of her head, and she didn't like it, but her psychic tingles absolutely *loved* it.

Dan added from a bit closer, "It's not *all* the rain's fault. I talked to the lead contractor a couple of weeks ago, when we first started thinking maybe Robin had gone missing out here. He said there was a brushfire off the interstate over there, something about a homeless camp's cooking fire getting out of hand. That's what made the *real* problem."

"The real problem," she echoed thoughtfully.

Dan strolled up to her, the sky and clouds bouncing off his mirrored sunglasses. "The fire killed off a bunch of trees and brush, so when the big storm hit last month, everything washed out down the burn scar."

"The burn scar." She looked up at the nearby hill and could see for herself that, yes, a fire had come blazing over the ridge. The big seasonal infernos mostly hit the other side of the Cascades, out in western Washington. Either that or farther south, past Portland.

But Seattle had plenty of small fires to go around, every time the summer dry season hit.

Her eyes followed the scar down the side of the hill, and when she took a few steps back she could see it, yes, how the water had come rushing down into the conveniently level and low area where someone wanted to put a Bass Pro Shop and a CVS, among other random strip mall fillers. "Okay, so the fire came first—clearing the way for the rain to run down the ridge, right? But it wasn't just water, it was mud and trash and everything else. Look at this place. Look how filthy it is. Look at the corners where the curbs have collected all that debris. There was a landslide here. It might not have happened at the same time as the rain; sometimes it doesn't. Sometimes it catches people by surprise. Where did the rest of it go?"

Dan's eyes went wide. "Oh God," he breathed. "Oh God, you're right."

They both turned around and backed up, trying to take a wider view of the place.

Niki did the same. "The mud would have washed down this way, and there's not much of a grade over there on the other side of the road leading into the site. Look at the trees." She pointed. "They're buried, right? Their trunks are, at any rate—look at those lower branches; they're way too close to the ground, by a couple of feet at least. That's not normal, is it?"

Dan started jogging toward the last paved road before everything went to dirt, mud, ashes, and dead leaves.

Leda set out after him.

Grady, who'd been facing the other way at some distance from the others, noticed the sudden movement and called out, "Did you find something?"

"Not yet!" Niki yelled as she joined the chase.

"Not more running, please . . . I beg you." He'd already been left behind, but he did not start running after them. He walked. Semi-swiftly, and with a hitch in his step from where he'd strained a groin muscle chasing Carson at the airfield.

Leda saw him over her shoulder as she charged after Dan—who reached the other side of the single-lane paved strip, which was nearly white with dried mud and dirt, scraped away where tire tracks had come and gone since it'd been shoveled off weeks before.

"Hurry up!" she called.

He did not hurry up, so she did not wait for him.

She leaped over the dirt road and barreled down a very slight grade to the one-lane paved road, crossed it, and found herself in a small clearing that was suspiciously level. Conspicuously level, even, now that she had a chance to look at it.

"This is where the runoff collected," she said to Niki. "Everything that got washed away was washed down into those trees." She indicated a tree line at the edge of the clearing.

Dan had whipped out the metal detector and was swinging it left to right, back and forth. It made faint blips, beeps, and boops but offered nothing firm.

Niki was now up to speed. "A car couldn't have washed between those trees."

"Nope, it would've stopped over here," Leda agreed. Just as

Grady caught up to her, she commanded, "Everybody spread out! Look for signs that something bigger than a lawn mower got knocked off the road by the landslide!"

Testing the ground as she stepped, one careful foot in front of the other, she wiggled her shoes around. She shouldn't have worried: the mud was dried to the consistency of baked clay, preserving every wrinkle, ripple, and pebble that had come cascading down off the ridge on the other side of the development.

"I should've brought a shovel," Niki said.

"Shovels and umbrellas. Next time, Nik. I promise."

Together they peered at the ground under their feet, walking in tight circles or narrow rows. The sun was absolutely brutal, and Leda had already finished her water. No one wanted to find what they all now suspected they might find, but no one could quit looking, either. No one wanted to believe it, but no one could think about anything else.

Leda stumbled. She kept moving. She stopped.

She backed up.

A short, skinny strip of metal edging was sticking out of the dried mud. She rubbed it with her shoe, and it revealed a somewhat longer, shiny line, very narrow and thin, about the length of a hardback book. "Found something!" she called. She reached into her bag and pulled out her multi-tool. It had a fairly big blade, and she could use it to dig up something small in a pinch.

Dan ran to her side and aimed his metal detector at the shiny metal line, and the machine went wild. He got down on his knees and helped, using his fingers—and then a conveniently flat rock he found.

Between them, they soon revealed a license plate.

Jeff said, "Oh no," and Dan stood up straight to put an arm around him.

"Do you know your mother's tags?"

"No," he admitted. He half kicked, half scraped the plate out of the ground. "It's King County, though. This could be her. She could be . . ." He gazed across the patch of ground that once had been a depression at the edge of the trees. "Under here. Under all this. If she's down there, if she's . . ."

Dan now pulled his nephew into a full-body hug despite the heat. "Hang in there, kid. We don't know anything for certain yet."

"And if we *do* find her here," Grady tried to say gently, "it's better than wondering for the rest of your life."

Or knowing that someone built a T.J. Maxx over her final resting place, Leda thought, but had the good sense to keep to herself.

Niki wandered back and forth, taking in the sights and seeking some other sign of Robin Reddick. She found one. She cleared her throat loudly, to collect everyone's attention. "Everybody? Hey, I don't know how to say this, so I apologize if this comes out wrong, or if it hurts anyone, but Robin is definitely here."

Jeff clutched the filthy, battered license plate. "What do you mean?"

"Your mom drove an old car, right? A vintage Volvo?"

"Yeah . . . ?"

Niki reached down and touched something that glinted in the sun. It was long and skinny, thinner than a pencil. It swayed like a reed when she flicked it with her finger. "I honestly, truly, and deeply hate to be the bearer of bad news. But those old models have a metal antenna, right? To catch the radio signals?"

One by one, the remaining members of the search party joined her. They stood around the battered bit of jointed metal and stared in disbelief, trying to convince themselves that it was something else, belonging to someone else.

But it was bent at the top, and its busted tip pointed like a finger.

Look down.

29. GRADY MERRITT

FRIDAY

By Friday, Grady was already eager to fling himself into bed and sleep for a month. It had been a long week, even if he'd taken the afternoon off. The Colemans had been collared, arrests had been made, evidence had been collected. Robin Reddick's car had been excavated from the mud flow. Her body was found inside. It didn't help to know that she hadn't actually lived terribly long in there, after the accident. She'd hit her head on the steering wheel and had likely been unconscious when she'd run out of air. Small comfort, and he hadn't even known the woman. But after a considerable amount of paperwork, legwork, and just plain *work-work*, both cases were effectively off his plate for good. He hoped. He might have to testify with regard to the Colemans, but not for a while.

Then, as soon as he'd gotten home, he learned that Cairo had escaped the house by popping out a screen window. And it wasn't like Grady could simply leave the house closed up with the dog inside without ventilation; like the majority of Seattle residences, his mid-century bungalow didn't have AC, and the daily highs were in the mid-eighties. It'd taken half an hour to chase him back to safety; then the poor thing barfed up something that once had feathers all over the living room floor, and Molly had come home from work early due to a gas leak.

Of course, she had not come home in time to help with the dog-chasing or the puke-cleaning.

But now Grady was free. Molly had left almost as soon as she'd arrived, taking off with a friend for some unclear shenanigans elsewhere in the city. The dog's stomach eventually stopped making terrifying noises, and there were no more half-digested bird bits on the floor.

Except. He still had one more thing to do. He didn't really want to do it, but he'd promised Leda.

Now he regretted it. He was tired. It had been a long week.

"But a promise is a promise," he said out loud from the comfort and calm of the couch.

Still, he couldn't get happy about driving out to Castaways, even if it was supposed to be a big show with big psychic stunts and a general reveal that Leda had helped solve another case or two. Her regulars loved hearing about her exploits in legitimate investigations, and if Grady didn't hang out in the audience for fact-checking purposes, there was no telling what she'd say into the mic.

But if he was going to leave the house, he wanted to have some drinks and relax to the best of his ability—which meant that he didn't want to drive. He pulled out his phone and called up a car to pick him up. It was seven minutes away and closing in fast.

No time for a shower, but the show was supposed to start in another half hour. Early for a weekend evening show, considering it was—he checked his watch—only about four thirty. Why did these people have to run things at such odd hours? Didn't they understand that weekends were for relaxing?

He tidied himself up to a standard of "presentable" with a clean shirt and a freshly washed face. It was cooling off out there, not as hot as predicted. He closed some of the house's more easily accessible windows and left a swamp cooler running for the dog. "You'll be fine," he assured the dubious yellow mutt. "Don't eat anything appalling while I'm out, please?"

Cairo thumped his tail. Grady took it as confirmation that he'd been heard, and would likely be ignored.

The car arrived. Grady dropped himself into the back seat and stared into space all the way up to Cap Hill, where he told the driver to let him out at a crowded intersection that desperately needed a light, rather than a four-way stop. "I've got it from here, don't worry about it. I'll leave you five stars," he vowed, and climbed out.

The Pike/Pine corridor was already hopping, but it was hopping with a different crew from when he'd been young enough to spend a lot of time there. It used to be all the freaks, geeks, and weirdos; now it was mostly tech bros and their lady equivalents, young and clean-cut and paying a hundred dollars apiece for their T-shirts.

Still a few drag queens. Still some punks and anarchists. The secret goth bar a street or two away was still cranking out industrial music that wafted through the traffic, at least after nine o'clock—or so he'd heard. Still a few gay bars.

It might have been nearly unrecognizable from twenty years ago, but all was not lost.

He actually smiled when he saw Castaways. Steve was sitting out front, shaded by the big golf umbrella. Grady waved at him. Steve saw him, looked startled, and waved back—then ducked inside, letting the door swing shut behind him.

"Uh . . . okay," he mused as he approached. Grady thought

they'd achieved something like a friendly acquaintanceship with the bouncer, but maybe he was mistaken.

He reached the door, and Steve was still missing, so he gave it a little knock.

Leda shoved the door open and stuck her head out. "Wait just a second, would you?"

"What? What the hell's going on in there?"

"Stuff. Things. Shenanigans, you know how it goes. Seriously. Give me . . ." She looked over her shoulder. "Thirty seconds." She disappeared back inside and shut the door.

He groaned and leaned against the wall. What now? Seriously, what ridiculous thing was she up to in there?

The door opened again. Leda stood there, smiling. "Good afternoon. Won't you please come inside?"

Grady frowned. "What are you up to? Because you're obviously up to something."

"You're so cynical. I love it. Get in here." She held the door open and stood aside.

Grady stepped into his worst nightmare. "Oh God," he said, his eyes tracking every banner, every balloon, every streamer, and every bit of Happy Birthday confetti that had been scattered across the floor, across the tables, across the bar. "What have you done?"

Molly popped out from behind the stage curtain. "Surprise! Happy birthday, Dad!"

Speechless and horrified and flattered, he stood there staring. "*You* told them? You spilled the beans. Spilled the tea? Am I using that right?"

She cackled and hopped down off the stage to come give him a giant hug. The speakers started up, and a punk rendition of "Happy Birthday" rang out through the bar. "Leda finally wore me down—what can I say?"

"Wore you down, or paid you off?"

She backed out of the hug and looked up at him with a sneaky grin. "A little of both. Come on! Check it out! Everybody worked really hard."

He let go of her. "You were supposed to go hang out with a friend this afternoon. . . ."

"I *am* hanging out with friends! Jeez, I barely beat you here, come on. That was fast, old man. Where'd you park?"

"I didn't," he confessed as Molly took him by the hand and led him to the bar. "I called a car."

"Whatever works. Hey, Tiffany!"

"Oh no . . ." he said under his breath.

"Hey, Molly!" The bartender swung around to greet them. She'd been arranging the second-shelf bottles behind the bar. "And hey, birthday boy! I've got an official birthday drink for you." She stepped off the short ladder and pointed at the chalk sign that always sat at one end of the bar. Today it read, *A Very Grady Birthday Drink: Whiskey and sour. That's it. That's the drink.*

"Oh, yay!" he changed his tune. "I'll take one of those, thank you!"

"I'll make you a good one, even if it makes me sad that you're so unadventurous with your alcohol palate."

"Sorry to disappoint you, but I'm grateful all the same."

Steve came up behind him and swatted his back. "Sorry 'bout that. Didn't mean to run off on you, but I had very strict orders to let them know when I saw you coming, so. Can't disappoint these folks."

"Absolutely, man." He shook Steve's hand with his right and picked up a drink with his left. "That was slick, and I approve."

Ben swanned into the room wearing pointy boots, a sleek ponytail, and a black velvet duster. He swooped up Grady in a more personal hug-type greeting than might have been expected, but

Grady rolled with it. "Wow, you look great. But isn't that a little warm? In here?"

He waved away such concerns as purely trivial. "Thank you, Detective, but there's more than one kind of comfort. I see you've gotten your official birthday drink. . . ."

"Yes!" He held it up in a semi-toast.

"Thank God you're so boring with your beverages. I was afraid she would come up with something so weird, we'd have to gently tell her no, and then it would be a whole *thing*."

"No, no. It's a good sour. I'm delighted, if boring."

Ben squeezed his upper arm and gave him a wink. "I knew you'd take it in the spirit I intended."

Matt saluted from the sound system, where "Happy Birthday" was spooling down, but apparently there was some sort of birthday playlist on deck; Grady was both impressed and concerned.

Niki rolled in a large cart covered in food trays that were still covered—with steam seeping out at the edges. "Your kid said your preferred comfort food is Mexican with extra sour cream and pico on everything, so we hit up the guys down the street. Hope you haven't eaten yet!"

He tried to say that he hadn't, but his mouth was watering too hard. He swallowed, shook his head with disbelief, and said, "I'm going to absolutely *murder* this. You're amazing—you're all amazing. I can't believe you pulled this together!"

Molly reached around him to poke at a foil container. She picked off the lid, revealing a boatload of queso. "Well, I'm very sneaky. Don't know if you knew that." She popped open a bag of chips and began dunking away.

"I knew that. Now I'm terrified that I didn't know the full extent, though. You know I don't like birthdays . . . I'm not sure why you caved to the pressure. . . ."

When Molly had finished chewing her first cheesy chip, she wiped her mouth with the back of her hand, then grabbed a napkin to swab up in a more formal fashion. "You only don't like birthdays because you never had a good one. You said it yourself."

"I did?"

"You did. Ages ago. Before Mom died, even."

"Your mother understood my dread of becoming old and decrepit," he said with a faint smile.

"You big dork, you just don't like being the center of attention. You'd rather be a gray man," she said with a conspiratorial kick. "You want to be ignored or forgotten. You think it makes you better at your job, but I think it's a coincidence."

Leda leaned around his other side and seized a taquito. She stuffed it into her mouth and bit it in half. Through a mouthful of shredded beef she said, "Your kid is wise. Listen to your kid. The party was her idea; I was just planning to pick up something weird at Archie McPhee and stick a bow on it."

"So you're really the one to blame? Not Leda?" he asked his daughter.

"For making you have a good time? Yes. It's a party full of people, and most of them kind of know one another—or at least they've met—so everyone will have somebody to talk to who isn't you. Get it? You can hang out and have free drinks and eat gooshy hot enchiladas and just accept the fact that people like you and occasionally want to wish you well, okay? But I did say no presents. You never want presents."

"That's my girl."

The door opened a crack, and Sam Wilco's head appeared. "This the right place?" he asked the room at large. Then he answered his own question. "Oh yeah, this is the place." He opened the door all the way and strolled inside with his wife, Angie—a curvy redhead who was a few inches taller than her husband.

She waved merrily, and before Grady could ask, she announced, "We got a sitter!"

Avalon and her ex-husband arrived, and even Jack Garcia showed up—looking a little uncertain about the whole thing, but ready to party down with drinks and other people's food. The place was filling up, but was not full. It was lively but not too loud. It was boozy, but the booze was not unsettling and did not feature kiwi or bananas or anything else fruity and unwelcome in Grady's glass.

It was perfect, and he almost didn't know what to do with himself.

While he exchanged pleasantries with the newcomers, his daughter made him a plate and set him up at a table with her and Leda, and then it was all a little quieter for a while because everyone had a face full of cheese.

When the festivities finally wound down, it was almost dark, and the bar would require cleanup before opening to the public. A sign on the door warned everyone that a private event was in session and Castaways would open at nine, so when eight thirty rolled around, the lights came on and the music came down.

Grady tried to offer his assistance with the party shutdown, but no one was having it.

"Sit your ass down," Matt told him. "Let us do the dirty work. There's not that much of it, anyway—I'm gonna sweep up the confetti and pull down the banner and streamers, and we'll let patrons play with the helium balloons while they wait for Leda to set up for Psychic Psongstress Night."

"Is that happening, too? After this?"

Ben answered from behind the bar, where he was collecting glasses to run through the wash. "It was my one condition! Leda does a show, and we're donating half the profits to charity."

"Which one?" Grady asked.

"The animal rescue group where I adopted Frank." He picked up a heavy tray covered in dirty glasses and vanished into the back.

"Frank?" Grady asked Tiffany, since she was closest. "Ben has a dog? A cat?"

"Cat," she confirmed. "Sometimes he puts Frank in a little rainbow harness and brings him to work. It's exactly as amazing as it sounds. Now, go sit down and let us finish up here. Are you staying for the show?"

"Sure, I guess. Part of it, at least. No one cares that Molly's hanging out . . . ?"

"Nobody cares!" shouted Ben from somewhere unseen. "Call the cops if you don't like it!"

Grady laughed and returned to his table, savoring the mental image of perhaps a white supervillain's cat going to town on Ben's black velvet collection.

Before long, the place looked as normal and birthday-festivities-free as it ever looked, and the small stage was getting prepped for Leda's karaoke fortune cookie routine.

All in all, he'd had worse birthdays. When he said so out loud to Molly, she rolled her eyes with teenage ferocity. "Oh, please. This is the best birthday you've ever had, and you know it."

She had him there.

His belly was full, and he was comfortably buzzed. The lights were low except for the spotlight on the microphone, and the bar began filling up with its usual crowd. Years ago, he'd read the curmudgeonly old adage about life being nasty, brutish, and short, but from his spot near the stage, he couldn't see it. Even with Robin Reddick being put to rest, and Paul being extracted from a tree, and the long-faded tan lines where his wedding ring used to go . . . life was sometimes festive, friendly, and crowded with smiling faces—whether you deserved it or not.

ABOUT THE AUTHOR

Cherie Priest is the author of two dozen books and novellas, including the horror novel *The Toll*, the acclaimed gothic *Maplecroft*, and the award-winning Clockwork Century series, beginning with *Boneshaker*. She has been nominated for the Hugo Award and the Nebula Award, and she won the Locus Award for best horror novel. Her books have been translated into nine languages in eleven countries. She lives in Seattle, Washington, with her husband and a menagerie of exceedingly photogenic pets.